THE ILLUSTRATED MIND OF MIKE REEVES

by
ASA JONES

Asa Jones

Eloquent Books
Durham, Connecticut

Eloquent Books
An imprint of Strategic Book Group
P.O. Box 333
Durham CT 06422
www.strategicbookgroup.com

ISBN-13: 978-1-60693-905-5
ISBN-10: 1-60693-905-X

Book Design: Bruce Salender

Printed in the United States of America

To R

I love you,
thank you for everything.

M

INTRODUCTION

Sarah, a reporter for a small English newspaper, is researching a strange case that began three years ago. A doctor she interviewed then has mysteriously disappeared, re-awakening her interest in the story. He had given his expert opinion at an inquest, surprising some by his suggestive comments regarding supernatural influences. He is an expert in schizophrenia, yet surprisingly he had told the inquest that the voices in the head of a Mr. Michael Reeves may have come from elsewhere. Namely, the spirit world. When pressed to expand, he had point blankly refused, saying that for the inquest, it was enough to say, that these voices were not necessarily a fabrication of the mind. The newspaper's recent investigations into his disappearance have come up with nothing until today, three days after his suspected kidnapping, when Sarah receives a package. The package contains a complete manuscript with an accompanying letter, addressed to her. Both are wrapped together in brown paper and tied with string, typical of the doctor's 1950s style.

She recognises the handwriting immediately. In her opinion, based on previous interviews, the doctor is somebody to trust and respect. She hopes that the respect she had shown him is going to pay off; instinctively she knows she has been selected to read something interesting.

Looking around furtively, she leans sideways; her old brown leather swivel chair creaks as she pulls down the blind. She switches on her brass reading lamp, the light from its green glass shade illuminating her face and desk. After slipping on her spectacles, a serious look spreads over her face.

She reads the letter.

Dear Sarah.

I suppose you have been wondering where I am.

I have been racking my brain trying to think of the best way to tell you. Your questioning all those years ago led me to believe that you are a young woman of great intelligence; you knew I was keeping secrets, didn't you? I confess, I _was_, but not anymore; you are the only person I can think of to tell everything to. There will be no more secrets, I promise.

Your newspaper already knows I love writing. Thanks to you, my short stories have been enjoyed by many. The only way I can think of telling you what I know, is in the guise of a story. It's a tale that must be told, and it must be listened to with respect. I ask that you persevere to the end, and reserve judgement until then. When you have moments of doubt, just remember who it is that is telling you the story, and also remember this: I promise you, Sarah, everything you are about to read, is, to the best of my knowledge, TRUE.

I hoped in time to get this published as a way of sharing my new ideas. I can't get it published now; I don't have the time. By the time you read this, I will have gone to a place you know nothing of (not yet, anyway!)

Perhaps you and Ross may get this published one day. You told me of the trust you have in him as an editor, maybe after reading this, and when you have done what you think best, he might be the one to make it presentable to a publisher?

I specialise in the treatment of Schizophrenia, as you well know. However, this account goes against almost everything I have been taught,

6

and what I now teach students. I wish I had been braver at the inquest and said more about what you are now going to read. I treated Mike Reeves. I grew to like him; he was my most special patient. I first met him after a referral from a counsellor. His wife had been raped quite brutally, and he was as much a victim of the attack as her.

He told the counsellor how the voices comforted him, and advised him, and soon afterwards, he ended up in my office.

He was someone—he <u>is</u> someone—I respect and admire. I feel privileged to call him a friend.

I have pieced this together from newspaper accounts of what people think are unconnected events, and my case notes. I am sorry to sound vague, but most of this story has come from someone who keeps a very special diary, when you get to the last pages you'll understand who! Much of it is first hand from Mike Reeves. He contacted me three days ago, and I will meet him tomorrow. There are things I desperately need to know. So will you, after reading this.

Yours sincerely,

Dr P. Rodgers

Sarah swallowed, her mind shooting back to the office where she sat. She fired glances to both sides, feeling as if she was doing something very bad. She clutched the manuscript to her chest and went to the vending machine for a coffee. Her mouth was as dry as the paper she read from. As calmly as she could, she walked back to her desk, resumed her prior position, and picked up the phone. She dialled zero for the receptionist. "Carrie, I don't care who it is; I am not taking any phone calls for the rest of the day. Unless it is absolutely unavoidable, do not disturb me, okay?"

Hands trembling, she picked up the first page.

PROLOGUE

Monica sat on the edge of the hard, white, uninviting bed and looked slowly around the room. The bars on the high windows blocked her only potential escape. The door had just closed with a bang, and she could hear it clinically locking—not only shutting her in, but keeping her fears at bay.

She knew that she would spend long hours staring at it, awaiting the clinical click again, to unleash who-knew-what upon her. Tears welled up in her eyes as she looked down at her attire: a simple white starched gown, underneath which she was naked and sore. The tears overflowed the rims of her eyes, and she began to weep. "Why has this happened to me?" she sobbed.

Her mind drifted about eighteen months; she couldn't think about anything else. She began to piece the events together.

CHAPTER 1

Matlock wasn't exactly the centre of British commerce or industry; it wasn't the centre of the universe either, but future historians might give it that title. Typical of so many towns dotted in or around the English Pennines, it was made up of old stone and brick buildings living alongside modern architecture, criticised by some, loved by others. It was not a place you would expect to figure in epic tales of how to save time, space, and all else. But, then, future storytellers may say differently.

Travellers would find much to interest and entertain them, including an assortment of pleasing suburbs, historic corners, and access to beautiful, unspoilt countryside. To satisfy their palate and other cravings, both High Street stores and high-class restaurants were available.

Although it was a pleasing place to be in, like most locations in late winter, the town wore a grave expression. The delights of the Christmas season were a distant memory, and the population was collectively getting on with the journey towards spring. This, 1999, was the last year of the century—indeed, the last year of a millennium. People could feel change. The current century began to feel snug, comfy, and warm, like a pair of old slippers. The millennium somehow felt cold, uninviting, and daunting.

Rain and sleet had been falling for almost three days, giving the impression that someone had turned colour off. An overall greyness loomed.

The seemingly endless onslaught of the weather, coupled with failing car batteries, flu epidemics, and so on, were taking their toll. Home and office lights were coming on one by one. Over a cup of coffee, during a break from their work, two men were talking. One was confiding in the other.

"The other night, I had the strangest experience, Eric."

Eric's ears pricked up. Most of this friend's experiences were different, so if this one was classed as the strangest, something good was on its way. "Why, what happened?"

"I was driving home; it was dark and drizzly, the wipers were on, and I saw this man at the side of the road, sitting on his backside with his chin resting on his knees. I drove straight past him." Mike paused, then took a swallow of coffee and a deep breath.

"Mmm, well?" Eric took a bite of his ginger biscuit and began to chew it quickly in anticipation.

"Well, a few hundred yards later, he was there again! He shouldn't have been there; it would have been impossible."

"Bloody hell," Eric said, taking another bite.

"That's only the start," Mike teased.

Eric's head spun. "Why?"

"I slowed down and stopped beside him."

"You didn't?"

"I did, and he got in the car."

"You stupid bugger, what happened?" Eric's eyes bulged like two inflated balloons.

"I asked him where he was going, and he just said he was going to meet someone, someone important, and that I could drop him off anywhere a few miles ahead."

"Didn't the lack of direction make you feel wary?" Eric asked.

"Yeah, but somehow it just seemed all right at the time." He looked back at Eric, paused for a few seconds, and continued.

"The car went cold inside when he got in, and I mean like ice. I think the person he meant to meet was, well…me."

"Then what?" Eric chomped eagerly as crumbs covered his lap.

"We drove on in silence for about two miles, and he said, 'Here, please.' So I pulled up. But he said nothing and didn't move for what seemed at least five minutes until…"

"Fuckin' hell, Mike, until what?" Eric now sat on the edge of his chair.

"He turned to me, real slow, like they do in the movies."

"Yeah, go on," Eric pressed.

"He said…" Mike looked pleadingly into his friend's eyes. "God's honour, Eric, he stared straight at me and asked if…if I believed in the devil."

Eric winced as coffee splashed onto his thigh. He could hardly wait for the next sentence.

"I said, 'Yes, I think so'." Mike swallowed with difficulty. "Then he got out of the car and turned to me, with his hand holding the door." Mike was now sat staring straight ahead, motionless.

"Then?" demanded Eric.

"He, well, it…said…"

The pauses between words were getting longer, and Eric's frustration grew. "What? Oh, fuckin' hell, Mike, what? What did he say?"

"'So you should,' that's what he said, 'so…you…should.'"

"Christ!"

"Exactly. That's who I thought of. Then he just walked away and vanished. I wonder why I was important to him; he must have meant me. I'm sure he wasn't meeting anyone else."

Both sat silent for a few moments, until Mike said, "Keep it quiet, won't you? I don't tell anyone else what I tell you, only my doctor."

"Of course I will; don't I always? Bloody hell, Mike, I'd have shit myself." There wasn't a lot to say just at that moment, so he stared at his friend a while, and then commented, "If you are normal, Mike, I don't want to be!"

was alive, and the spirit felt a sudden, brief feeling of the loss of no longer being part of life. It studied the people in more detail. Some were old, some young, and some in their middle years. A few appeared carefree, mostly the younger ones; but sadly, the rest carried a heavy burden on their shoulders.

Why am I here? the spirit asked itself. Suddenly, something focused its curiosity on two men sitting at two bordering desks. Each had his own individuality stamped on his area: a couple of cartoons depicting sneering observations on life, mugs decorated with slogans and badges of favourite football teams, and pictures of heart-throbs from the stage and screen.

Out of the two, one drew its attention more than the other. *This* man was the reason for being here. It nodded its understanding. Hovering in the rain, each drop lit for a second or two as it passed through the light emitted by the window and through its spectral body, it watched as Mike Reeves slipped into thought. Deep, meditative thought, and not for the first time that day.

Here was an intelligent man at a dangerous age, slipping into the second half of life. The spirit recognised this as a dangerous pastime; life's big questions had begun to drift into this man's mind more and more these last months: *Why am I here?* followed by *What have I done?* and *What must I do with this second half of life?* What, exactly, had Mike Reeves achieved?

The phantom sensed that here was a man who would try to answer these questions more than most, especially the first. It knew all too well that this was a point everyone came to, if they lived that long; for many spirits in waiting over the centuries, it had proved an amusing diversion to watch as they waited. But why was this man so important, so different? And why had his life come to a head so intensely? Why should the spirit sense it enough to come drifting here, drawn by an invisible force half-way across Matlock?

Mike sat pondering. While to every mortal, he looked just the same, he was guided by bright white hands far away; the second move of a complex, strategic game was taking place. The second link in a vast chain of events was almost ready to be forged. If he was to look back in ten years time, and think hard, this would be the moment, he'd remember, this seemingly innocent moment. It was time for a choice, a decision that would alter his life forever.

The office stopped buzzing for one of those brief respites it threw up, usually towards the end of the day. Sound became muffled and far away. Between them, Mike and Eric shut away outside influences.

The choice in Mike's mind was introduced by an intrusion from Eric.

Eric looked over to Mike and smiled at his motionless, expressionless face, staring at the CAD screen. Whatever Mike's eyes were seeing, it was not what was on the screen. He wrongly assumed that Mike was thinking about a recent job advertisement in the company's internal newsletter. "Now, that's a face that says 'should I?' or 'shan't I?' if ever I saw one."

"Mmm? Eh? What?" The penny dropped, and sound flooded in again. "Shouldn't what?" Mike asked.

"Oh, come on, Mike, are you putting in for the job or not?"

"Oh, that." He smiled in recognition.

"Closing date is soon, you know," Eric reminded him.

"Yes, I know. I can't make my mind up."

"Well, me old mate, if this helps, I reckon that you'll be pissed off if anyone else gets it, and you'll end up saying how you could have done the job ten times better. Then you'll end up regretting it, and somehow I'll be to blame for not talking you into it."

Mike sniggered.

"Am I right, or am I right, eh? Ask your doctor next time you go; I bet he'd say a new challenge would do you good."

"You know he's right, don't you?" interrupted a deep voice inside Mike's head. The nagging took over then, and as sudden as a light switch, the spirit understood. This man wasn't making his mind up at all; something else was making it up for him. But how was Mike to know that? This was the only mind voice he knew, the kind that needed him to justify his actions. Without doubt, he wanted the job, and the prestige. The voice had told him so, but he'd also heard of the pressure, the tough decisions, and the stress.

The spirit felt intrusive; the distant hands did not want anyone or anything to witness these events. Something big was starting here, the spirit told itself, and it knew it should eavesdrop no more. Like dissipating exhaust from a car on a cold day, the presence faded away.

CHAPTER 2

The next morning at work, Mike had some photocopying to do. The room was empty, and he set the machine on auto for thirty collated copies of over a hundred masters. He stood looking through the window as he waited, and his attention was drawn to a commotion just outside the door.

Robbie Ercott, a man well liked by everyone, was talking to one of the company directors, who was on one of his outings from "death row"—the employee-created name for the row of high-powered offices that was the pinnacle of ambition for the company's ambitious employees.

"Mr. Taylor," Robert began.

Mike imagined the chewing, the swagger, the hands in the pockets, and worst of all, the arrogant look on the face of the overweight Adolf Hitler look-alike. "Listen! If I say get a job done, I want it facking done, no baggering about. Tell her that if she can't do the fackin' job, we'll get someone who fackin' can!"

"But Mr. Taylor, she's only just come back from a miscarriage, and she lost her mum only a few months before."

"Mr. Ercott," interjected Mr. Taylor, swaying from foot to foot, full of his self-importance, "the same goes for you: if you can't hack the fackin' job, we'll get someone who can, get my drift, laddie? You are too fackin' soft with them."

Laddie? Mike thought, shaking his head. *He's fifty-four.* It went quiet, and he heard the footsteps go in different directions. *If I ever get a job like that, there goes one man I'll try to be the opposite of. I wonder what makes anyone want to be like that.*

The white hands had guided him to the right place at the right time. His mind was made up; he'd put in for the job.

BEEP! BEEP! BEEP!

"Oh, bollocks, it's jammed again."

The mind-nagging continued, re-enforcing the conviction that he would do the job with thought and consideration. The nagging carried on through the application process, rubbing out worries and justifying decisions one by one. It argued its way easily through the short-listing stage, right up to getting an interview. Each argument for easily beat those against, expertly battled by the voice Mike thought he had as a natural inheritance.

Two months later, Mike Reeves found himself in preparation for the interview.

"Interviews! God, do I hate bloody interviews," Mike muttered to his reflection as he shaved. "This is your fault, Sean, you and your bloody ambitions."

"Ambitions my arse! Look who you'll be in charge of, for one thing: Monica, Maddi, and Christine. Look at the fun you could have there; isn't it worth going through an interview to be over them?"

It did sound tempting. *Over them, mmm, that'd be nice,* Mike thought wryly. "Could you imagine that, all them naked at the same time? Strewth, they could keep the winning lottery ticket, that would do me!" he said out loud, probably too loud.

"Yes, and the others, they won't cause you any problem. Think of the image, the status, the name on the door, and the car parking space. What's an interview anyway? Just another stage for us to perform in."

The voice was sitting in a corner of his mind, near a fountain used to heal life's attacks. The air was ionised and produced clear, uncluttered thought, ideal for sound advice.

"And if you really get stuck, you can ask me!" shouted Debbie. "I'll think of something unusual to say."

"Mmm, I bet you will at that," Mike chuckled.

Debbie was the voice's assistant, a female who was always tuned in, and who would offer alternative feminine advice if she thought the time was right. The first voice would often cringe at her suggestions.

"Have you got someone in there with you?" Mike's wife shouted.

"No, dear, just singing," he called back, then stopped shaving to stare at his reflected eyes. "I wish she was," he whispered. "I wish I could meet someone like her." Then he concentrated as he resumed his shave; blood patches wouldn't impress at interviews, he decided. He blew out his right cheek to navigate around a small mole, and his thoughts drifted again. Even the shape of his blown-out cheek reminded him of her, of last night's imaginings. What a bottom! He could almost feel the texture, the fine hair, the goose bumps. He smiled to himself, and winked. His look said, "I had sex last night, and it was cosmic."

But he hadn't. Since his wife's trauma, sex was a mind-only thing. He understood her rejection. But what a mind he had! Not the usual grey type, his was coloured, probably painted by a mad man with one ear. He had a mind with a wonderful world, and wonderful friends, too.

He had been going to a doctor for visits; after his wife's rape, he had needed counselling. As a result of that he had ended up seeing the doctor monthly. Slowly but surely, the doctor thought he was "getting there." Mike had tried to tell the counsellor about the voices he had created in his mind as a way of coping. As a result, the doctor he was now seeing regularly was a specialist in schizophrenia! As time passed, Mike was feeling more and more confident in the doctor, telling him more and more. At his last visit, Mike had been told that his account of his voices were different to any other. This pleased Mike; he wanted his voices to be different, to be unique.

Debbie was the female creation. So beautiful, so sexy, so willing—and she absolutely adored Mike. She stood about five feet, two inches, with a figure to die for. Her eyes penetrated the very soul, and her voice could be whatever he wanted it to be. Her own mind was electric, full of ideas, and bursting at the seams to offer them. Inhibition was not in her vocabulary; if ever the phrase, "I'll try anything once," had been invented for someone, then this was that someone. But the once was negotiable; more likely, she'd try something a thousand, or two thousand times. She was a little imp who flirted with his mind. It had taken years to perfect the art, but now he could touch, smell, taste, and hear her.

Sensual, mouth-watering Debbie; he asked, she did, no problem. She was like a corruption of Marilyn Monroe and Mike's favourite singer from a seventies band.

Sean was his other mind occupant, his mentor, his chief advisor, his comforter, and "the wise one." Mike's best friend, inside or out, epitomised in the image of his screen hero, Sean Connery. He stood six feet, seven inches, with the trademark piercing eyes that said he knew everything. He had the same Scottish accent, with a deep tone that had the ability to soothe, to scold or to advise, and make you feel privileged to receive it. He was an absolute master of body language, although oddly, he had a flaw. His dress sense left much to be desired; yet, somehow, this made him more real. When Mike faced any problem, quick as a finger click, Sean was there.

"ARE YOU COMING OUT TODAY?" Rosie shouted. "Or have I got to pee on the stairs?"

"Sorry, flower, I'll be two ticks." He looked at the tablets as he washed them down the sink. "Sorry, Doc. You'll understand one day, I know you will."

Sarcastic smiles were traded on the landing as they passed. Mike made his way to the bedroom, got dressed in his new interview clothes, looked at himself in the mirror as he held his stomach in, and said, "Not bad."

"Not good, either," said Sean with a smile.

"Bollocks, I'm getting back into my exercise routine again soon, just you wait and see."

He consumed breakfast in silence as he went through probable questions in his mind. Rosie understood the silence and kept quiet herself, until it was almost time to leave. "You'd better get your skates on."

"Oh, dear, is it that time? Yes, I better had." Mike looked at his watch, and the first sign of butterflies went through his stomach. "Oh, shit, Rosie."

"Aw, you'll be all right, love. Just be yourself; if they don't want you, it's their loss!" She smiled at him and patted his crown. "Good luck," she said, kissing his forehead.

"Cheers, love. I'll see you at tea time; I think it'll be an all-day job, but if I get a chance to ring, I will." Their eyes met, held, and said what didn't need to be spoken. He kissed her lips. "Bye, have a nice day."

Poor Rosie, he thought; he could tell by the sudden, slight tensing of her body that even this small contact made her cringe. He could also tell that she detected him knowing, and her eyes looked to the floor. He patted her shoulder reassuringly and walked to the car.

After getting settled in the driving seat, he surveyed the scene before him, a summary of what he had achieved in life. He had a nice wife whom he loved immensely, a pleasant-enough semi on an attractive avenue lined with plane trees, whose delicate shedding of their bark gave an eye-catching, dappled look. Rosie stood waving, and his attention went to her as he waved back. She exuded warmth, but her body language shouted at the top of its voice, "Protect me!"

You deserve better, and I'm going out to get it for us, he thought as he smiled at her. *You deserve better than me, too, really, someone more settled in his ways, someone more normal, with less libido.* He put his thumbs up and backed into the road; an annoyed peep from the horn of a nearby car told him to concentrate on the task at hand.

The journey took about half an hour through busy traffic, accompanied by loud music and Mike's singing, which left much to be desired. He spotted and filled a suitable space in the car park just before a recognised interview rival tried for the same. Smiling, Mike wound down the window and shouted, "Sorry, you can have it tomorrow! I'll have my own space then!"

Sean smiled. He was pleased to see the confidence. "That's it, feel good about yourself, be a man."

Mike took a quick look in the interior mirror, adjusted his tie, and commented to his reflection, "You good-lookin' so-and-so."

"Yes…and with lovely thighs, a pert butt, and just beautiful pecs!" Debbie added.

Sean raised an eyebrow and tutted. "Well, come on then, let's go."

Mike made his way across the car park, through reception, down the corridors, and up the stairs. "Walk tall, look straight, stay cool," Sean guided him.

The wait seemed endless, but once in the interview room, he was on fire. A question, an answer, another question, another answer, further questions and brilliant answers followed. "That's it, knock 'em dead," Sean prompted, and he did.

A relaxed feeling waved through his body, and during the interview, he started to observe things. He was glad Mr. Taylor wasn't on the panel, but Mr. Tigre, the chief executive was. Mike put him lower down the ladder of humanity than anyone else in the firm. He was a flat-nosed, ugly little man, with a poor physique and a wig that covered a skin complaint, badly. He was known to all as *Wiggy*, and the sign of his impending arrival was signified by flapping the hand up and down on top of the head, a trend Mike had started and felt justly pleased about.

After a wait for the result, Mike was called back in. No praise came from Wiggy. He just chewed his lip, nodded, and stood to leave after tapping his papers on the desktop. "The job is yours, Mr. Reeves." He shook his hand. The rest of the panel of six did show humanity. The usual pats on the back and more hand shaking followed.

YES! he thought as he left the office, striding confidently back to his car. He made an announcement to himself. "I'm going to be a good boss, the type I'd have liked, and I'm never going to be like those two!"

At 4:45, the jungle drums had done their job; almost everyone connected with the promotion knew about its results.

Monica looked up from her magazine on culinary delights, swiftly tucking it under her desk as her superior came in. "Mr. Reeves got the job, starts on Monday. Goodnight, Monica. Goodnight, Maddi."

Both smiled like a cobra before it struck. "Goodnight, Christine," they said half-heartedly.

"I bet we're the last ones to know again."

"Oh, without doubt," replied Monica. "You don't think she'd tell us before anyone else, do you?"

"No, of course not. What do you make of that, then?" Maddi enquired.

"Not much. I've never had anything to do with him; you've been here much longer than me. What do you reckon?"

"He's always pleasant enough, and he smiles a lot, which ain't bad for someone who has had so much to put up with."

"Put up with?"

"No, you probably weren't here, but I'd have thought you'd heard about it. His wife got raped about four or five years ago, and they nearly separated."

Monica tutted and shook her head vigorously. "Huh, just what you'd expect from a man; they're all bastards. He should have stuck by her."

"Oh! He did, he did," Maddi assured her. "But she almost went mad, had to be put away for months. She got violent and all sorts. It was really very nasty by all accounts; it was supposed to have been terrible, they used things."

"God, yes, I remember, someone *did* tell me. So that's who it was? The Engineer they called him, the rapist, didn't they?"

"Yep, that's the one. The papers said she needed loads of stitches, psychiatric help, the lot. She was in a mental home for a year, and he was the one who got the brunt of her anger. I think she blamed him for not being there. He'd gone out with what's-his-name, Eric, from Development, and the Engineer broke into the house. They've flitted since, though."

"I should think they had. Mind you, it probably was his fault; he is a man." Monica shuddered.

"Oh, Monica, really!"

"I'll take a lot of convincing before I ever trust another, that's all."

"Well, come on, we'll be on overtime soon. I want to be quick; I'm going to the Elm Tree tonight, a good live band's on. Want to come?"

"No, I'm tired. Thanks, anyway."

Mike drove home with the good news and stopped to book a table on the way. He was eager for Monday. The situation could hardly have been better for him; the previous holder of the post had left much to be desired, new, tough, money-saving managements were on their way in with new ideas and concepts. It was going to be a challenge. Maybe the doctor and Eric were right.

During his last doctor's appointment, he had been told to "work with" the voices for now. So long as he felt he was in control of them, and them not in control of him, it was a good way, albeit a different way, of coping with life's challenges.

CHAPTER 3

The first six months passed by, during which time Mike took great care to project himself both as professional and a gentleman. The workforce could see improvements all round. Although some of the things he did were not popular, people appreciated that it was the company way and not his, and from his superiors' point of view, they were seen as proof of a good choice.

Slowly the team rallied round him, and comments like, "he's thorough," "he's fair," and "he's good," were becoming commonplace. Compassion was shown in the right places, and the opposite for the few time-wasters. The good felt rewarded, whilst the new, the average, and the less confident felt nurtured.

As time passed by, Monica noticed his efforts. She paid attention to the way he dealt with people, to his politeness. Perhaps, just perhaps, here was a man who was different.

She didn't realise just how much notice she was taking, until she was spending one of her regular weekends at her parents' place. Standing at the sink peeling potatoes, she mentioned him again: "Mr. Reeves, at work, is a bit like you, Mum, always asking if I'm all right. He asks everyone, not just me, but the funny thing is, I believe he means it every time!"

"Really, dear. Is there anything else this amazing Mr. Reeves does? His list of good deeds seems to grow by the hour."

"Oh, Mum, don't talk silly. He's just a good boss, that's all."

"It's just nice to hear you speak kindly of a man again, that's all. He does well to reach the standards you set!"

Monica pursed her lips and looked to the sky, then back at the potatoes.

A few miles away, Maddi was walking around the Sunday flea market, as she often did, looking for bargains. One of her passions was collecting ceramic hippopotamuses, or elephants, but nothing had caught her eye. Another passion was lava lamps, and she stood looking at an orange one, when Jim, a casual acquaintance, mentioned that it would go well in her bedroom.

"It's not for me, actually."

"Oh, let me guess, it's for that goody-goody man-hater, the recluse!"

Maddi screwed her eyes and stared at him; he was quickly losing favour. "It's none of your business, anyway. Besides, she's a lot better these days." She smiled knowingly, put the lamp down, and moved to the next stall.

The weekend slipped pleasantly by and a new working week began.

The situation Mike had been waiting for, a chance to seal his approval and reputation, came along. The company was launching a new project—broadband was getting bigger and bigger. The company directors had given Mike the task of leading them into the new horizon it offered. A whole new marketing strategy built on small informative videos via the new website was his idea. He now had to sell it to both his peers and his team. His team numbered about fifty, and he had to give a presentation to them all, as well as a few VIP's.

All were assembled in the presentation room. This was a modern suite, with a sloping set of seats and technological wizardry at the front— it was made to impress visitors, but it was a daunting place for a presenter. Mike was nervous, but his management training was standing in good stead, he knew his subject, and he had rehearsed many times. Monica and Maddi sat in the front row. Both had short skirts on, and his eyes came to rest on their legs longer than he should have allowed. He soon realised he had been spotted and felt his colour rise

Monica and Maddi exchanged knowing glances. Guiltily, he glanced back to his notes, but temptation rose again. Just before he started, he stared at their legs again, and then at their eyes, expecting a rebuke. But the returned gaze from them said nothing except, "we want you to do well."

Encouraged by Sean and Debbie, he did do well, and temptation was removed as the lights dimmed. He did so well that the end brought spontaneous applause, almost unheard of in the company. Again, he blushed, but the team now totally backed him, and believed in him; they wanted to do well with, and for him. Christine had expertly handled the computer presentation, and Mike thanked her accordingly. Without her, he couldn't have done it; her timing was perfect.

She was standing talking to him triumphantly as Maddi and Monica filed past. Monica spoke on their behalf. "Well done, Mr. Reeves. That was very interesting, and we're excited about the prospect."

"Oh, thank you, thank you very much, indeed. Would you wait by the door please? I want to say something." He finished thanking Christine, whose curiosity showed plainly on her face. Then he slowly walked up to the doorway, his arms full of literature. "Er, I'd just like to say sorry; that wasn't very professional of me. Er…staring like that, it won't happen again."

Maddi answered, "Oh, what a shame!"

Monica glared at her and interjected, "Think nothing of it. Your apology is accepted."

Mike said thanks and left, feeling embarrassed. His seal of approval from Monica had been awarded, a high honour indeed.

Christine stood on the ground floor near the reception, waiting for the lift to arrive. Her thoughts were working on career progression. She could see a very helpful rung on the ladder to success within her grasp. The rung's name was Mike Reeves. As she stood thinking about it, *ting!* The lift doors closed. "Blast," she said, "I never saw it come!" She pressed the button again.

Monica and Maddi walked back to the publishing area where they worked. Their superior was based at the end of their suite of offices, and they watched her walk back and go through the door. She didn't return their look.

Christine shut the door and rested her back against it. They didn't bother her at all; she had passed them in the company hierarchy, and her sights were upwards. She looked around her. She had spent her budget well and used the excess to form a bright, modern office. Abstract pictures hung on the walls, lit from above by brass wall lights, and a few plants, some from floor to ceiling, gave a "natural" feel to the room. The teak effect desk, filing cabinets, and computer workstation complemented the surroundings. She liked it, but wanted better.

Three very different women had come into Mike's life. Maddi was tall and long-legged with ash-blond long hair. She possessed a smile that disarmed him. Christine was small, with streaked blond hair, usually dressed in a business suit and always wearing bright-red lipstick. The male office population had voted her "rear of the year," recently. Her confidence impressed him. Monica was dark skinned; she looked almost Asian in appearance. Mike thought she had the figure that was probably a struggle to keep in shape, but it definitely stuck out in the right places. But she gave the impression of a "never-do-wrong," and was most definitely a feminist.

All three had worked together, and were once good friends, but Christine's promotion had "gone to her head" in Monica and Maddi's opinions.

About an hour later, all three went to lunch, although not together. On their way back, Maddi's and Monica's paths crossed Christine's.

Christine followed them with her eyes as they walked back into the main entrance. She glanced at her watch. *Hmm, early for once are they?* she thought. With an assured stride, she followed them.

This timekeeping was a problem. Mr. Rawsen had reported to Mike, in writing, that the two M's were taking too long a lunch break, and also long tea breaks. Mike sat at his desk relaxed, thinking about the problem. *Seems a lot of fuss over nothing, but I suppose I should do something. I bet Rawsen was a right telltale at school.* He sat back with his elbows on the armrests, his fingertips pressed together, and thumbs on his lips. "Well, Sean, how do I play this one?"

"Hmm, this could be a good opportunity. What I would do is…"

"Why don't you spank them both!" Debbie burst in with enthusiasm.

Sean raised an eyebrow and tried to speak, but Mike spoke first. "Good contribution, Debbie, but I think we'll put that on hold." He sniggered.

"Oh, if I can't have your attention then, I'll not bother."

"Sorry, Sean, go ahead."

"Yes, go ahead. Ooh, you are masterful!" Debbie giggled.

Sean ignored the silliness. "Why don't you put the onus on Christine? Remember to delegate every now and then. Send her a memo telling her what a good job she's doing, and how it would be a shame if the two M's let her down at her next appraisal. Tell her you think her work is outstanding, but that they have to tighten up on time-keeping, and that you are looking to her as their superior to keep an eye on things."

"Brilliant! But that superior bit, they'll hate that, won't they?"

"Yes, but it takes you out of the situation. You are just acting on a report, but Christine will know how impressed you are, and in turn, they'll want to impress you. You win all ways round."

"Huh, I couldn't see anything wrong with my idea."

Mike laughed out loud. "Never stop trying to help, Debs. It's lovely, really lovely."

Not quite sure if she had been complimented or not, Debbie shrank into the background of his mind, went to her room, and began to prepare for the night. With a jolt, Mike realised the phone was ringing and dove to answer it.

Christine sat at her desk next morning opening her mail. Her eyes went a little wider as she read.

I think good work should be rewarded. I'd like to point out that the way you run things in your area is a credit to you. Your next appraisal is coming up, and I'm sure you'll get a good report from me. However, just one thing is letting you down, and this is a problem with Monica and Maddi. Mr. Rawsen has reported that they seem to be enjoying privileged lunch times, and extra-long tea breaks. Nip this in the bud now, please. As their superior, I want you to sort it out. Please understand that this memo is really a pat on the back! So don't take it to heart!!
    Thank you
    Mr. M. Reeves.
    Marketing Manager

Right! she thought. *Monica, Maddi, eat this! So, Mr. Reeves*

Later, at a nightclub called The Gateway To Hell, situated in an area of town frequented only on a need-to-go basis, money was changing hands at its usual fast rate. Gaming tables, a disco, and a snooker club were together in one venue. Drugs were changing hands, and prostitutes were plying their trade.

The deep maroon carpet in the foyer had two sets of floor lights. One led to a row of offices and was marked, "No Entry to the Public." Only one office, the last in the row, was a true one, and two bodyguards guarded it. The others doubled as dens of iniquity. The other set of floor lights was marked "Entertainment This Way."

Two vacant heads sat atop powerful bodies that stood on either side of a mahogany-coloured door. The burgundy lower decor and the jade-green upper decor were separated by a matching dado rail. The walls were interspersed with photographs of old horror film scenes, mainly in black and white. No name was written on the door, just "PRIVATE," in big, gold, saloon-style lettering. Not that anyone in his right senses would want to disturb the privacy behind that door.

Behind the door was a man, alone except for his Rottweiler, Sabre. He sat with his face illuminated by the anglepoise lamp, contemplating what was not his first whiskey of the night. A handsome face of sharp angles and chiselled features was spoilt by the right eye, which, although flawed, exaggerated the good looks. The lower lid was pulled down at its outer corner by a small scar, somehow stained dark blue. It was a common enough sight in the area, because many a coal miner wore such coal-stained scars with pride. But he had never been near a mine; his scar looked more like a single tear tattoo, caressed a thousand times by female hands.

In his hand was a favourite possession, a Victorian china-faced doll, stolen from her flat after things broke up. It smelled of her and looked like her, a miniature of the voluptuous body that she struggled to keep in shape, but yet that stuck out in the right places. His Miss Prim, the never-*do*-wrong, who most certainly had with him. The feminist who had turned submissive in his arms and had begged, yes, make no mistake, begged for more.

In his other hand was an eight-inch-long hatpin with a pearl surrounded by diamonds on its blunt end. It, too, was a Victorian memento, which he used to extract information and punish.

Tonight, it was stabbing the doll in its chest, buttocks, and stomach. Each painful prod was timed to repeated questions: "Why did you throw me away? Why discard me? Why reject my love? I was right for you, you bitch. You were right for me. One day, you'll be mine again, whether you like it or not."

"Enough!" he threw the pin, and it stuck in the wall like a dart. He began to bite his thumbnail—well, not so much bite, but to make noises as his teeth slid off his nail and clicked together rapidly. Those who knew him quickly learned that this annoying habit signified anger.

Sabre watched the pin as it stopped vibrating and put his head between his paws as he heard the repetitive click coming

31

from Tony's mouth. He resumed panting in time to the distant music.

The jewel in Tony's ring caught the shade as he reached over to turn the lamp off. Sabre looked up, ears twitching. The expensive gold ring rattled across the lamps rim as he drew his hand away. Slowly, he rotated on his leather office chair to look at the window; the rain was heavy against it. He laid his Monica Doll down gently and stroked it apologetically. Its smiling china face lit by the floodlight outside appeared to say, "It's all right; I understand you."

The Venetian blinds drew black shadow lines of increasing width down his body. As he stared at the falling rain, he thought he saw the shape of a person, but as he screwed his eyes up, it faded away. A rare tear rolled down his cheek.

The same spirit that had observed Mike was staring back, and for a second it thought it had actually been seen; but that was impossible, wasn't it? It saw the tear and shook its head in disbelief; it was indeed privileged to see it, especially as it was the last thing it ever saw of this side. It faded away, the long wait caused by dying out of sequence over. It was glad to leave; the face it was staring at was the last it had seen whilst alive, too, as it had begged for mercy. Tony's face filled it with fear even in death.

The last thing it would remember would be Tony's unblinking eye. The tunnel surrounded it now, thank God; it was on its way, and it felt it had something to tell someone at the tunnel's other end, something to do with the man in the office. It felt sure of it.

Worlds separated by time, laws of physics, and even chaos theories were slowly coming together, and Mike was the unsuspecting link between them.

* * *

Kingdom of Tarol, 1421

Rosa could sense "the coming"; it was time to leave the city and travel across the Lakeland to the Uplands, by the mountain pass to the Western Lodge, and out to the Chimes.

She climbed into her caravan, clicked to her horse, Bess, jarred the reins, and shouted, "Come On!" The wheels came to life, and they set off with pans and cups banging, pebbles crunching against the steel wheel rims. The caravan rocked and rolled along, the whole unit soon taking on the same movement in time to the clip-clop of the hooves, a rumbling, gaily coloured traditional Tarol gypsy caravan.

Stops were kept to a minimum and used for the essential basics of toiletries, food, and axle grease application. She contemplated the scenery, slowly adjusting her mind as she studied the daytime images of the mountains reflected in the lake, and the night-time glowing embers of her campfires.

The days passed.

The journey became a steady ascent. Any travellers or pedlars nodded to her in respect. Her pack of cards was safe in the brass box; she would use them at the crest, the summit of the Western Pass, the home of the Chimes.

After the first tree line in the mountains, the path became steeper and harrowing, a route only for the experienced. The second tree line, mainly of conifers, began to close in. She caught fleeting glimpses of the Western Lodge, especially as the track turned due west in its zigzag route. The overlong white banners with the red-forked edges gracefully sent rolling curves along their length in the wind, which was now a steady, haunting whistle. The pink stone lodge stood proud and glorious, rising in towers and buttresses overhanging precarious drops.

Slowly, Rosa approached the gates that allowed access via the tunnel to the wild lands. The mountains ran in an arc, protecting the land occupied by this graceful, intelligent race. The Western Lodge was one of the protection fortresses, spanning one of the few mountain passes. It was garrisoned by a Baron with his war band and whores. Their only purpose during their one-years posting was to protect the pass, at all costs.

The troops and officers recognized her easily, and the search of the wagon was soon completed. She passed through into the thick woods where very few, even among the brave troops of the Lodge, ventured.

Stories of the inhabitants varied, and it was difficult to choose which you wanted or dared to believe. The final passage to the Chimes would be impossible for most, but not for Rosa; she was allowed to travel here.

It had now been four weeks since her departure from the city. On the crest, Rosa stopped and looked around at the Chimes. Tall, slender trees with blue-green, semi-transparent leaves as hard as glass filled the air with wind-chime like noise. Some had been driven to madness by it. But not people of Rosa's ilk; on the contrary, it was complementary to her craft. If it wasn't the madness which claimed any unwary visitor, then the protecting goblins would.

She brought the caravan around to one of the almost circular clearings of the Chime Woods. After unhitching Bess to roam freely—protected from becoming goblin food by the gypsy mark upon her and protected from the noise by a bandage around her ears—she lit a fire and walked to the clearing's edge. The sun was setting slowly, and the shadows were lengthening as she stood and scanned the magnificent view. Shattered pink, violet, and blue peaks told of the hard frosts of past winters. Vertical rock faces, towered around her, standing as sentinels, guarding Tarol from the rest of the world. Deep fissures, now catching the shadows, created faces looking back at her. A pink sky washing down through orange to purple settled gently on her eyes, a truly beautiful sight that caressed her brain.

Slowly, Rosa walked back to the caravan, stroking the tall grass with her hands, and collected the brass box. Returning to almost the same place, she sat on a large, flat rock, cross-legged. Her eyes darted down to the chasm as an eagle soared past to slowly circle the landscape: it seemed to command the air space. Watching the spectacle, she shuffled the pack, whilst breathing the cool mountain air deep into her lungs. Her posture didn't change until twilight, when she sensed the right moment.

Inserting her long thumbnail into the pack, she cut it three times to reveal what the cards said to her. Each one confirmed what she had suspected for some time. As clear as the air she breathed, the cards spoke inside her head. "The waiting is coming to an end in your lifetime, Rosa. It's time to prepare, and then it will be time to meet the band of the prophecy…the journey is afoot!"

Lifting her gaze from the cards to the darkening sky, she once more observed the landscape. An eagerness to show it to him ran through her body like a wave rushing ahead of the wind. Putting the cards back into the box, she looked at her brown hands and turned the brass lid over to stare into the polished inner surface, smiling at her reflection.

The reflection stared back and nodded knowingly.

CHAPTER 4

Monica was spending another night on her own. The kitchen was an array of herbs and spices, the worktop covered in utensils, as flames licked up from the wok. Soon the treat was finished, and she carried her tray to sit by the window. She'd lit a couple of candles made by herself, scented with her favourite lavender aromatic oil. Puccini's "Vissi d'Arte" from *Tosca, Act II* was playing on the CD player.

From three floors up, she had a good view of Matlock's skyline, the castle standing proudly against the night sky. But her gaze went instead to her reflection. "Oh well, at least I'm safe on my own, in my little nest, eh, Monica? No nasty men to hurt me." She smiled. "Steady on, girl; talking to yourself is the first sign."

She concentrated on the meal, poured a glass of sparkling white wine into her frosted, long-stemmed glass, and began to enjoy the music.

In Mike's house, it was an early night. Rosie was drifting to sleep as Mike sat resting his back against the padded headboard, the bedside lamp illuminating his journal as he wrote. His journal was written in three colours: blue for his own thoughts, black for Sean's, and green for Debbie's. Rosie amused herself with it, saying it was more evidence of his approaching insanity. *Insan-*

ity? He pondered his last few visits to his doctor; he thought that at first, he must have seemed insane to him. But strangely, the more he went, the more he felt that it was doing the doctor more good than him! He felt like he was bringing the doctor the latest, eagerly awaited chapter of a book he was reading. He smiled at the thought and looked down at Rosie, then kissed her goodnight gently.

The feeling of love welled up from his gut, almost bringing a tear to his eye as he sat watching her breathe. Her hand was tucked under her face, the posture reminding him of a small child. He missed not having any children; he'd always wanted them, and he felt he would have been a kind, supportive father. She had wanted them even more. That was another part of her torture—why had that bastard picked her? The memory of the night was unlocked for a few seconds; his body went stiff as the taste of disgust filled the back of his mouth and tongue; his temples hurt, and his eyes stung. With effort, he pushed the memory back. She was safe, and they'd made another nightly step on the long journey of recovery. At least the dreams had stopped. He thought of his doctor and how the visits and simply sharing his life's events with him helped. He was an easy man to talk to, and a good listener. He was a good writer too it seemed to Mike; the notes he scribbled would fill a briefcase. He switched off the light and slid down the covers, clearing his mind in preparation for one of his nightly trips to Debbie.

These were something he had perfected over years of practice. At first it had taken a great deal of concentration, and he had read meditation books to help develop his mind. But now it was as easy as going through a door. He relaxed totally, concentrating on one piece of his body at a time; then he visualised the clouds, pale purple and blue, changing shape and intermittently mixing together. Soon, like stepping-stones, they became solid in places, and he walked on them. Bright yellow stars illuminated the way, and the further from this world he went, the easier it was for him to see the familiar path ahead. Soon he saw the landing platform.

Because of the colours and the size, it was hard to miss. It was suspended by huge chains.

Mike landed on it and felt at ease, at home. Within a few seconds, Debbie and Sean came through the curtains to greet him. *Blue shoes?* thought Mike, glancing at Sean's feet. *Someone will have to tell him one day!*

Debbie took long, slow strides towards him. She was dressed in an emerald-green dress, Chinese in appearance, with the collar high up her neck and the silk showing every hill and valley of her body. She didn't blink once, but stared straight at him as she slowly moved towards him. She put her arms around his neck, locked her fingers together, and purred, "Hello, darling." The perfume was delightful.

Sean, as he often did, looked adoringly at her. He could tell Mike was pleased with her, and that, in turn, pleased him. They all walked through the curtains to the inner balcony. Below them in the inner courtyard, surrounded by stone arches and hanging ivy and wisteria, they could hear the tinkling of the fountain. Going off like spokes from a wheel hub were corridors, all lit by torches in antiquated sconces, fastened to what looked like castle walls. The flickering gave off a comforting feel, as if it were saying, "we like you to be here." The cobblestones were well worn and shiny.

"There's something I want to show you, Mike," Sean said with a hint of seriousness.

Debbie winked, a wink that Mike loved to see—it said everything. She waved with a little piano movement of her fingers, and whispered through shiny red lipstick, "I'll wait for you in my room; would you talk to my body again tonight?"

"Yes," Mike replied. This was one of his favourites. Although he usually decided the entertainment, he liked to be told sometimes, and to be surprised on occasion, too. As she left, he watched her swaying bottom glide down the corridor. His eyes went to Sean then, and together they walked around the balcony. Sometimes he could remember what happened down these corridors, and sometimes not.

They talked as they turned left down one of the corridors. There was no musty smell, no cobwebs, just clean, Cotswold stone and mortar, stained in places by the smoke from the torches, which gave off a slight bitumen smell. A haze gave distant views ahead and behind a blue hue. They reached three new doors, obviously recently constructed in Sean's usual fashion: good, solid oak, set in arched recesses. The doors were marked Monica, Maddi, and Christine. The rooms beyond the doors were bare, except for an exquisitely carved Brazilian mahogany table with its own square, silver candlestick set in the centre. None of the rooms had its own roof; they were similar to the offices at work, rooms within rooms.

Mike could not see the reasoning for the rooms. But as often happened, deep in the recesses of his mind, he learnt just to accept things. Together they entered each room and lit a candle, slowly closed the doors, and left. Alongside these rooms was a set of stairs, which led to a small balcony, running around the rooms' rim. They walked up, and once there, it felt as if they were in one big room with three wells in the floor, each well being one of the rooms below. It was beautiful; all the walls were sparkling white, like crystal dusted with sugar. The light from the wells below reflected all around, reminding Mike of snow that had been frozen by a hard frost; it gave the impression of a million diamonds waiting to be harvested.

In the centre, in a triangle surrounded by the three wells, were three podiums, obviously connected to a room below. Each was about waist height, covered entirely in polished gems. These reminded Mike of the mirrored balls in the old dance halls. The tops were octagonal and had been polished flat so that they looked like mirrors, and resting on each was a jewel. The jewels were multi-faceted and as big as the average decanter stopper, falling just short of obscene, yet firmly into the, "I-want-one" category. He couldn't take his eyes off them.

Slowly, as if about to conduct some deeply religious rite, Sean walked around to the other side of them. He faced Mike, a serious expression upon his face, crowned with a frowned forehead. In a deep, commanding tone, he said, "You're going to have to choose just one of these, very carefully, and it won't be easy. I sense your confusion, and I confess that I don't know the reason myself, as yet."

Mike looked; how could he choose just one? All three were different, but of equal beauty.

"You are at the start of what you should think of as a journey, a voyage of discovery. There will be valleys, and there will be peaks—hopefully some great, lofty peaks, but remember this: if it wasn't for the deepest valley, you would never be able to stand back in awe, and truly appreciate the heights."

If a word was to sum up many of his visits down the corridors, it would be *vague*, and that was how he felt now. What was the significance of what had just happened? What was the significance of the three women?

An immeasurable distance away, connected by an astral thread, sat the white observers; they knew the significance, all possible answers, all possible outcomes, but they couldn't choose for him. For now, they were the only ones who knew the importance. They could guide, but great care had to be taken. Rules of nature and time had to be observed, in ancient, honoured ways. They were pleased with the foundation they had laid, and they nodded in satisfaction.

Mike left the room via the stairs and walked slowly back up the corridor after a backward glance at his now-silent mentor. The image of Sean was still in his vision: a magnificent male, a prime example of the species, standing with his arms akimbo. His head bowed, eyes closed, and dressed in fine robes. Just like a wizard or something, he thought. *Could I have really created something so beautiful?*

"NO!" Sean said emphatically, the noise echoing around the chamber of choice. "You couldn't."

Eagerness took hold of Mike, and the thoughts of what had just happened had already started to fade. He ran up the corridor to the staircase; for Debbie, it was a spiral one in an ivory tower, all carved as if it were an Indian work of art. He ran up two at a time, like a lover who hadn't seen his true love for days. He burst in, panting, and looked around his favourite place in the universe: Debbie's room. And what a room! It was a mixture of art nouveau, and fifties decor, sprinkled with a liberal dash of decadence. A large, circular bed took centre stage, surrounded by shelves of sexual ornaments and items of pleasure. The biggest jukebox ever, with mega bass, now reverberated in his heaving chest.

"Hi," she said, breathing deeply, purposely making her chest rise and fall rhythmically. She was laid on her back, on her bed, with her head at the end opposite the pillows, looking up over her forehead. "Please…talk to my body, like you do, but do it now, straight away. I don't want to wait, not tonight." She snapped her fingers.

At the click, Mike realised he was naked, and smiled. "Eager, eh?" Slowly, he walked towards her, every chiselled muscle enhanced by his sweat, reflecting the purple and pink lights. His manhood swayed from side to side. He also clicked his fingers, and the emerald-green silk dress melted away, like droplets of water on a hot plate. She was now as naked as the day she was created, her smooth, flawless skin also reflecting the coloured light in the most erotic way.

He bent down and started to whisper, and in between some of the words, he kissed her tenderly. "Do you like me to kiss you?"

"Yes."

"Tell me then."

"I like it when you kiss me, Mike."

So passionately and slowly they kissed. His mouth moved in small kissing steps to her erect nipples. "Do you like me to suck these, Debbie? To play with them with my tongue until they tingle? Do you like me to eat your breasts?"

"Mmmm."

"Tell me then." Mike smiled.

"Oh, Mike, I love it when you suck my nipples, when you…oh…when you make them tingle, and when my body shivers. Mmm, yes, that's it, oooh, yes, just…like…that."

He carried on a little longer, until her arched torso started to thrust up and down slowly. Slowly, and in deliberate small circles, he moved his hand down to her groin, tracing lines around her triangle of delight. He saw with satisfaction the next sign; her legs drew up and apart. He moved to the next stage, slowly parting her pussy, knowing exactly where to gently feel and caress. He smiled to himself as he asked, "Do you like me to play with you, Debbie?"

"Yes, yes."

"Tell me so."

"Oh, God!" Her bottom was now bouncing up and down on the purple satin in a frenzy. "I love it when you...ooh...when you...oh, oh, mmm, ohh, keep it there, when you, oh...oooh, yes...YES!"

He flew back into himself as he came in his hand in spurts. He quickly looked over at Rosie, asleep, then at the radio clock. "Bloody hell, an hour...wow." After his breath had steadied and quietened, he went to the bathroom to clean himself. He was glad that Rosie had not been disturbed, because he did not want her to feel hurt. He felt calmness descend on him. He had been satisfied.

At about the same time of night, at The Gateway To Hell, an exotic dancer was asking herself, "Why did I have to meet this bastard?"

He was sitting at his desk, dressed in dark trousers and a black shirt, his left hand stroking the doll's hair, the other holding the pin. As it pointed upwards, the light caught the needle point, and for a second it sparkled like a jewel. "If I say you sleep with him, then you sleep with him. It's quite simple."

"I'm a dancer, not a whore!"

He replied, "If I say you are a whore, then you are. Again, my sweet, it's as simple as that." His voice sounded too calm, she thought. He stood up, thoughtfully picked up the doll, and walked around the glass-topped desk, drawing a finger along its edge. Before he spoke again, he looked at his fingertip, nodding in satisfaction.

Watching nervously, the dancer, barely more than a girl, began to tremble. Dressed in a leopard-skin patterned top, brown hot pants, and knee-length boots, she looked down at herself.

The pierced navel seemed to highlight her provocativeness, and she wished she was better covered.

The atmosphere broke; suddenly his face was an inch from her nose. "Look at my doll. Don't you just love it?"

Thinking most definitely not, she replied, "Yes."

"Don't take your eyes off it." He stood up straight and placed the doll at eye level on the desktop, its eyes staring straight into hers. Clicking his finger, he summoned Sabre, growling and snarling, to his side. The dog drooled, its saliva landing in splats upon the highly polished floor. Taking a step back, the dog sat beside her, filling Tony's place as he moved slowly to her other side. "If you stare at him, he'll rip you apart, and if I command him to, he'll do the same. Understand?"

"Yes." She stared at the doll's eyes; did it just blink? Weren't its eyes wet, like real ones?

"Guard, Sabre!"

The massive dog stopped growling, which seemed worse; all she could hear was its breathing, and she could feel its intense stare penetrating her throat. Goosebumps ran down her spine. The pin moved across her vision, but she dared not follow it. Then the noise of clicking teeth and nail mixed with Sabre's breathing filtered through the air like a mist, and settled on her body. She could smell her own fear.

The voice now sounded higher, cruel, as it asked a rhetorical question: "You like body piercing, do you?" She could smell the faint tang of day-old garlic on his breath. She breathed in sharply as the point of the pin rested on her cheek. "The next time I ask you to sleep with someone, and to perform any sexual act they ask…you'll do it gladly, won't you?"

Only one answer was possible, but a bone-dry mouth stopped her from answering. Her lips felt glued together.

"WON'T YOU?" he almost screamed.

"Y-y-y…yes-s." The reply could have come from a mouse.

"Good girl. Sabre, go to your corner."

His most obedient servant trotted away as if it was a family pet, and she sighed a trembling relief.

43

An acid smile spread across his face; an ice-cold glint lit his unblinking eye as he pushed the pin right through her cheek.

She screamed, and gripped the chair arms. God, the pain! It was unbelievable. She didn't move her eyes from the doll. Did it just smile? Surely it did, no…but it couldn't…could it? The pain hit again, and she burst into tears, as he removed the pin, slowly twisting it. With an exaggerated sucking noise, he licked it clean of her blood. "Leave!"

She did as quickly as possible, her cheek and mind both left with a scar that would be there for the rest of her life.

The worlds linked by Mike's mind took another step towards each other.

* * *

Kingdom of Runa, 651

The shouting and cursing in the inn stopped, except for a heavy, excited panting out of Hilda's range of vision. She stood from her corner table, staring into the eyes of her examiners: tall, tough, rough warriors, male and female. As big and fearsome as they were, they each dropped their gazes in turn as she looked at them. The howling wind could be heard trying to get a grip on the roof and shake it loose, whilst the hailstones tried to pepper it into submission. "Huh," she uttered in disgust as the last gaze hit the sawdust-covered floor. Coughing phlegm from deep in her throat, she spat on the floor and watched as it gathered a small ball of sawdust to it. She put one hand on her rune bag and her other onto her stave, her overlong, warty thumb hanging in the 'V'. Backing away in a mixture of fear and disgust at her stench, the warriors cleared a path for her. One woman, all of six feet, three inches, was still rocking back and forth on the lap of a beast of a warrior, her legs wide apart and full of muscle. Close to orgasm, and then suddenly filled with torment, she stopped as her head spun around; the man gritted his teeth and let forth a muffled cry as he failed to stop his throbbing phallus from filling her in gushes of warm, milky liquid. Then, staring wide-eyed, as if caught committing a cardinal sin, he waited anxiously.

Cackling and waving her arms, she shouted in a curious, tinny tone. "Carry on! Why stop? It's only me! It's only Hilda." Her laughter filled the room. She reached over and grabbed the woman's bottom, giving it a squeeze. "Carry on, my dear."

Possessed and tiger-eyed, the woman began to ride the man like a stallion; the people drew back—they had never seen anything like it. They cheered and jeered as the man showed his discomfort, but she wouldn't, and indeed, couldn't stop. Spurred on by the banging of flagons on tables, and the clapping getting faster, the woman raised one hand and rode the man like a rodeo star, whooping and screaming to her onlookers. The man screamed and begged her to stop, but an orgasm of thunderstorm proportions rattled through her body once, twice, and thrice. She let out a yell and raised both arms in triumph to her fans. The man collapsed, exhausted.

All eyes turned to Hilda as the silence hit the room again. With a look of contempt, she pushed the door open. A blast of hail and wind pierced the warmth of the inn. Sliding her feet through the hail slush, and protected from the biting, sub-zero wind by her roughly sown hides, she looked around the street. Her matted and infested hair blew back in a clump like wire wool; her misshapen face turned towards the mound of fur tied to her wagon, and she whistled. Obediently, the wagon came to her, and she climbed the two stout steps. With a flint in her hands, she reached into the back and sent a shower of sparks into the thick, green, mucus-like liquid, which in turn burst into dancing, flittering flames, issuing a deep, penetrating warmth. "Aaah," she said, rubbing her back as she sat down.

The ball of chestnut fur knew four commands: left, right, move, and stop. To the grunted third command, it moved away.

It was time for the old mage to enter the wastelands, and journey away from her beloved Yggdrasil, away from the sheltering mountains, through the settlements, which, as she had just witnessed, dreaded her rare visits. She had just begun her long trek to the edge of her world again, to climb the pinnacle and receive a prophecy. She sensed that it would soon be the time of his coming, a time of unification of the four worlds, but she needed confirmation. She hated the journey; part of the price to pay for her great, old age, but why should it be so far, and so inhospitable? Could they have found a more desolate place? She often wondered. Her answer was always the same: "Could they? Pigshit!"

No scenery, no up, no down—just a constant whiteout for a hundred leagues. It was enough to destroy the will of a god. The glow from the travelling imitation of an oil lamp kept her from freezing to death, but the total boredom nearly killed her. Four cold, white weeks later, she reached the Pinnacle—a gigantic, natural tower of granite.

She knew that if she touched it, her skin would stay behind on the rock, so she carefully took the rune of communication and placed it in the matching-shaped hole. "Open," she grunted, her mouth dry after four weeks' silence. Four weeks sitting in almost the same position hadn't helped either, and as the door opened to reveal the burning, everlasting torches and the stair-way that seemed to go on forever, she moaned, took a deep breath, and began to climb painfully.

An hour later, gasping for air, she opened the door and walked onto the summit, which was paved with a low wall running around it. Shaking her fist, she shouted with all the strength she could muster: "Why can't you do an old girl any favours, you bastards!" She walked around, looking as if to expect a god to appear over the wall. "Why do I have to climb every time? Eh? Can't you just let me do it at the bottom?" Knowing she would not get a verbal answer, she coughed and spat on the floor, then slowly creaked her way to the wall.

The view from the wall was awesome: the sea crashed in huge waves below; massive whirlpools, big enough to suck a whole ship down to God knew where, protected the wall from any approach. Around the wall's base, in an arc from sea to sea raged the storm, which had lasted since records had begun; flashes of lightning ceaselessly lit the clouds. But at this level, the air was still and cold, a sanctuary from Mother Nature's anger. The only other thing on the plateau was a raised dais in its centre, with a polished, mushroom-like podium of matching granite. She stood staring at it and adjusted her thoughts to the task. Breathing the body-cleansing air deep into her lungs, she felt young again.

In her solitude, she forgave the gods, and thanked them for her gift of life. Then she walked to the stone, lifted its polished lid, took her blood-red bag of runes tenderly in her leathery palms, and reciting an old Nordic prayer, she cast them. Eager, with uneven, bulging eyes, and shaking hands wiping away dripping saliva, she awaited the prophecy. With a clear voice it came, and it was the message she wanted more than any other.

"The waiting is coming to an end in your lifetime, Hilda. It is time to prepare the shield and helm; soon it will be time to join the band of the Prophecy."

She looked up from the casting, tears running down her cheeks, and stared majestically over the Kingdom, eager to show him the Yggdrasil, her tree…when it was time. Looking into the polished dais, she smiled at her reflection and nodded satisfaction.

CHAPTER 5

Maddi was up early as usual, jogging near a lake close to her home. It was a crisp, cold morning. The crispness and the sunshine reflecting upon the lake's ripples hit her senses. The water looked as if it had a million small gold ingots floating on it, and the air felt so precise that Maddi imagined any sudden noise would bring it crashing down in icicles. Taking a deep breath, she exhaled, saying, "Ah, it's good to be alive!" Another eight breaths cleared her lungs; she switched her music back on and resumed her jog to a fallen tree trunk, where she sat down again and switched the music off. This morning was too good to miss; she wanted to appreciate it some more.

Looking back at her footsteps in the frost, then at the sky, a broad smile flooded her face. The air smelt clean and earthy; she could hear water birds calling and the gentle sounds of water on the edge of the lake. The church clock struck seven, sounding clearer than ever before. *Seven? Oh well, duty calls.* She stood up, and with a steady pace ran around the other side of the lake, to a gate, over the road and down a lane to the row of town-houses where she lived.

The first floor was hers, and in the shower a warm glow spread over her body. Things felt good. *Even Monica's a bit more cheerful these days*, she said to herself, stepping out and bending down for the towel.

After breakfast, she drove to pick her friend up on the way to work; it was her turn to be a taxi today. "Hiya, Monica, nice weekend?"

"Yes, lovely. I went over to Mum's, finished my new curtains off, and then Kevin and the kids came yesterday. You?"

"Brill! What I remember of it!" She turned to grin at Monica.

"Keep your eyes on the road!"

"Ooops, I'll tell you at work. I was just thinking earlier how it seems better these days, more organised and whatnot."

"Yes, I was thinking the same as I waited for you. I almost look forward to going!"

But things changed quickly. On arrival at work, they found a message on their desk to see Christine at 9:00 a.m. sharp. It was already 9:10.

The door opened as soon as they knocked, the smell of ground coffee hitting their nostrils. "Right! Late again, I see!" Christine pronounced. "I'm in trouble, and if I'm in trouble because of someone else, then they are in trouble! I've had a stinking memo from Mr. Reeves. You've both been reported, in writing, to him." She used the pause to study their squirms. "You've been reported for *A*, talking too much; *B*, taking too much lunch time; *C,* for having long tea-breaks; and *D,* for generally taking too many liberties! Like coming in when you wish!" She paused. "I'm not having it! I'm not having my career damaged because you two act like silly schoolgirls. He's actually told me that I'm doing an excellent job, and that as your *SUPERIOR*, I've got to sort it out. So, go back to work now; I'll be watching and timing you. Off you go." She opened the door and stood with one hand on her hip, the other on the door handle. They had no time to reply, and in a state of shock, they left, the door banging behind them.

They stamped back to their desks. "The bitch, who does she think she is?" Maddi said in a voice two octaves higher than usual. "I'm going back to clear this up." She made her way to the door, and with her hand on the handle, stared at Monica. "I'm going to tell Madam Lock a few home truths. Superior? Huh, superior *what*?"

Flushed, Monica replied, "Oh, yes, smart move that would be, wouldn't it? We'll both end up with a rollicking off him next. Hmm, just when things were going so well, too. I'll tell you what, let's impress him a bit, and make Madam Muck jealous. The little creep won't know what to do when she has to come and heap praise on us!"

"Okay, but if that doesn't work, I'll scratch her eyes out!"

They both laughed then, which eased the tension. They then made plans to impress.

They didn't have to wait long for their chance. Mr. Reeves did his rounds quite often, and called to see all sections regularly. He tactfully didn't do it so often as to offend his under managers, but enough to keep them on their toes and him "in touch." He knocked on the door and entered. "Good morning, you two. Everything all right?" he enquired.

"Yes, thank you, SIR," Monica said, spinning around on her revolving chair. "We've just been saying, Mr. Reeves, how much better things are in the department, and we are sorry for taking liberties, sir. It won't happen again; Miss Lock's told us off. We don't want to reflect badly on her, and we'll try our very best. Sorry, sir."

He thought how the shadow caught her thigh magnificently, and he felt an erection coming. He covered it with the folder he was carrying. Struggling to get the words out, he said, "Don't call me 'sir'; Mike is fine. And don't worry unduly; I just like to run a tight ship, that's all." He tried to swallow but couldn't.

Maddi added, "Yes, we are sorry. Very sorry." She leaned over the desk to pull down the blind a little, making the short plum skirt ride high.

Stuttering an excuse, Mike left, fumbling at the door handle like an embarrassed schoolboy. "Fucking hell!" he said, resting against their outer wall. Then, slowly he regained control and went back to his office.

"He's just the same as the rest when it comes down to that!" Monica hissed.

"We've got back in his good books, I reckon! Is that the type of 'impress' you meant, then? You flashing your thighs, and me my bottom?" Maddi laughed as she pulled her skirt down to a respectable level.

Monica tutted, and then laughed with her friend. Unusually, it didn't seem to matter that much.

Maddi looked at her friend for few seconds and thought how good it was to see her enjoy frivolity which included man.

Back at his desk, Mike sat in deep thought. *I'd never have thought that of Miss Prim*. The restraints he'd put himself in cracked; temptation took hold and began to tweak at the seams. *I'll find out more about her*.

In the deep corridors of his mind, one of the candles burnt brighter. Sean sat looking at it. "Tut, tut…it's your choice, I suppose."

The strategy for the next few weeks was set: a look on the company personnel programme, then a bit of gossip in the right places. The first drew a blank, but the second produced fruit. The internal mail girl, June, was a good laugh and a brilliant source of gossip. "Hiya, June, how ya doin'?" Mike said cheerfully as she filled his tray. A chat about the weather and her holiday surprised her, but loosened her up. "Tell me, June, what do you know about Monica Hass? She seems quiet lately."

"What's that?" came the interested reply.

"She looks a bit strained. I don't want to overwork anybody. I know you see everyone most days on your rounds." After a little prompting, she soon poured out a story. Gossip was indeed her speciality. "I've heard that she was deeply in love with someone, but after they got together, he turned out to be a right bast—" she started to say then continued with, "oops, sorry, a right swine. He knocked her about a lot and treated her rotten, real dominating like, wouldn't let her do anything without him. A right nasty piece of work, his name was Trev…no, Tony. Yes, that's right, Tony something. And there's more: after the break-up, he took it really bad, he went a bit psycho-like. Not the type of man she thought at all. I bet that's why she's looking bad." After an obviously intrigued silence, she asked, "Did you say she's proper poorly?"

Detecting the change in tone, Mike deflected the curiosity. "Oh, you know me, June. I thought she looked a bit down, that's all, and I've got a lot of work coming her way. I don't want to burden anyone, especially if they are at a low ebb; I'll share it around a bit."

"If all bosses were as nice as you, this place wouldn't be so bad."

"Why, thanks, June, that's nice of you to say so. If ever I want a clerical assistant, you're the one for me!"

He received more news over his next few chats with June. Details on this Tony concerned him. Even allowing for the usual exaggerations, it seemed he was not someone to tangle with. He was well known on the local club scene, with a reputation for drug dealing, protection, and prostitution, all connected with a club he owned. He had no idea how Monica had seen anything in him, but the rumours said he wasn't always like this. When Monica had met him, people said he was okay, but he got mixed up in some weird cult and changed dramatically. Even more worrying was the news that he was approaching Monica at regular intervals, but always being flatly refused any chance of reconciliation. This was making him angry and jealous, so woe betide anyone who came next!

At this news, most men would have backed off, but not Mike; it won his sympathy and made him want to cheer her up. He was a little afraid of the consequences, but why not be a hero? He knew he should not become involved with a coworker, neither did he want to let Rosie down, and had he really enough time to help someone with the emotional baggage she had? But it could be just the thing to win her over—a chance to prove that not all men were bad. Temptation took an even greater hold of his shackles, and began to snatch at them.

Slowly, his visits to the two M's inner sanctum increased; he could hardly resist. Common interests were plentiful, especially in the realm of mystical, mysterious, interesting things, and in particular fortune-telling and divination. This was a topic Mike had studied deeply, encouraged by Sean. However, the subject threw up a disturbing confirmation of what he already knew: Monica told him that she was now very wary of delving too deep into the subject; someone with whom she had had a relationship was into that sort of thing, and it had frightened her badly. She described him as dangerous and frightening, even terrifying.

The threat coming from Tony came a little closer, more dark and ominous; the feeling of an approaching storm filtered through to Sean.

This desire to help a damaged woman justified his slow crumbling to temptation. He wasn't pursuing her, he told himself; he was helping a woman who had just got through a bad time. He was showing her what men were really like, and he would never hurt Rosie.

Seated at his desk, he resumed his thinking position, fingertips and thumbs pressed together. "She's lovely, everything a man could want in a lady friend. It's okay to have a woman friend nowadays; it's almost the new millennium. Are you worried I'm getting too close, Sean? Well, don't. I wouldn't hurt my Rosie, you know that. Anyway, I don't think she's interested in me that way. I mean I could tell, couldn't I? Besides, I'm not that lucky! If I fell in a vat of nipples, I'd come out sucking my thumb!"

Sean laughed heartily. "Very amusing, but be careful. I think that she wants to get even with men, and you might end up being the target in her sights, even if she doesn't realise it herself."

Anger was something Mike rarely showed to Sean, but a raw nerve had been touched. "Oh, Sean, you don't know what you're on about! She's not like that!"

This reaction worried Sean, and he walked to the room of choice. "As I feared, it's getting brighter. There's something about her I don't like."

Debbie walked in. "You're right, I think. Why pick her? He's going to get hurt; she doesn't deserve him. He wants more than friendship, too. Believe me, I know it, even if he doesn't. I wish I was out there!"

It was a day of short fuses. "Well, you're not, you are in here, with me!" He tutted to himself at his curtness. "I'm sorry. I'll try and see that Mike comes to no harm."

Debbie kissed him on the back of the head as she stood behind his seated frame. "Thanks." She then slunk away. *I'll dance for him tonight*, she thought as she walked down the corridor. *PVC...black and shiny I think, and chains, lots of little chains—Punk! I like punk...yes, that's it, spiky hair, the lot, a Debbie special tonight!*

In Gateway to Hell, Tony was playing snooker. The smoke hung heavily in a layer; the shot was a difficult one, and the game depended on it. If he could sink the pink and roll back for the black, he'd win for sure. "Black and pink, huh? She looked good in that." The snooker table disappeared from his vision; instead, he saw Monica dressed in a pink-and-black corset, the light reflecting deeply in her eyes. He chalked his cue and slowly walked around to view the shot from another angle, bit his nail, and spat a bit out. It landed wetly on the table. His opponent's rat-like features grimaced.

"So, your mate Andy says this Mike bloke is impressing her, does he?" The pink shot across the table and rattled down the pocket like a newspaper being snatched from a letterbox.

"Yes, a real smart-arse yuppie type, he reckons. I bet he drives around in his posh car with the fuckin' classiest-ever mobile stuck under his chin!"

"Well, he'll have mobile bollocks if he doesn't watch his step!" Tony replied through grinning teeth, which were locked together in anger and jealousy.

The black rattled each side of the pocket, and sat begging to be buried, right on the edge. A man called Sterling smiled at the predicament.

Sweat dripped off the Rat's nose. "What the fuck do I do now? Dare I win? Dare I, buggery." The white rolled gently across the table; all watching eyes following it in disbelief—surely the fool wasn't going to try and win. It stopped, just touching the black ball. "Bloody hell, I've missed it! I knew I should have hammered it! I was scared of following it down."

Tony bit his nail again. "He'll not compare to me." With a crack like a pistol shot, the black rattled down the pocket, and the white went flying back up the table. "My game." He picked up the money, slung his long, brown leather coat over his shoulder, and walked to his office. Turning back to look at the Rat, he asked "This mate of yours, ask him to get me as much information as he can on everybody closely connected with this Reeves bloke and Monica. Give him a free pass for a night out, and tell him that if he can come up with something I find really useful, he can have his pick of any dancer he likes."

Sabre watched him enter, and as usual was thrown a tit-bit from a green glass jar on top of a filing cabinet. Slavering and grunting, he lapped it up. "Greedy bastard!" Tony laughed, walking over to the safe. "Sabre, door." The hound stood up and obediently walked over to take up guard duty.

Tony switched on the lamp, pressed remote for the blinds to close, and clicked in the numbers of the combination. He opened the safe door and took out an old leather-bound book, about eighteen inches square, with gold protective corners and a matching hinged lock. The inlaid jewels of its front cover revealed the book's importance. He carried it carefully to the table and sat down to turn its pages. Information sank in as easily as water into sand; his capacity for learning occult practices and theory was unprecedented. He poured a whiskey with a trembling hand, took out a notepad from his desk, and began to write.

Monica Doll smiled approvingly, a cold china smile through ruby-red lips. Distant observers, dark, brooding, and ominous, were taking interest through the doll's eyes.

"This Tony Cowley, what do you think?"

"Phenomenal work rate; he's achieved a great deal over the past few years. I like him…a lot."

"Mmm, so do I. I agree with you."

One continued to observe the progress, whilst the other picked up his scythe and honing stone and began to sharpen its blade. After a few strokes, it pulled up the black hood, and through the dark holes that dummied as eyes, it looked up the hill, then walked slowly towards its summit.

The city of Daath loomed up before him, its evening entertainment walking slowly through the gates, chained together. One woman at the back looked almost less than terrified, so raising his blade above his head in bony hands, he glided towards her. With two sweeps, he cut off her head, and then cut through the chain. The head rolled down the hill. Now quaking, the rest of the procession proceeded into the city.

* * *

Empire of the Sun 17/6398

In the third and final land connected to his mind, the Moor stood deep in thought. It was time for one of the rare occasions when he should go over the bridge and through the gates. With meticulous attention to detail, he locked up his curio shop, tidied his desk, closed the office door, and climbed upstairs to the jade room.

Standing on the rush mat, his thoughts went to the time of the coming. He needed to know if his dreams were correct. Would he be the privileged gatekeeper to allow entry to the prophecy? He also thought how nice it would be to be able to talk again.

He wished his journey, and guided by the hands of Chi Lin, the wizard, he drifted through the clouds of pale blue and purple, looking at the bright yellow stars as he passed. Soon the bridge became visible, and he stepped onto it, a gigantic, graceful arch over a land of blue, purple, and white. Blue flamingos flocked in thousands, and pale blue water crashed from immense mountains onto sugar-white sand, to be sucked into oblivion. On the far side of the indigo ocean were higher mountains of royal purple, where even bigger waterfalls crashed into the sea, making huge tidal waves: all never-ending images of time.

His observations ended as he approached the end of the bridge and the heavy wooden gates. He walked up to them and knocked. He could hear voices from the towers on each side. He studied the massive iron hinges, which oozed grease.

The low creak rattled his eardrums as both massive doors swung open, so tall for such a small visitor. The guardians glanced at him through ink-black eyes and certified him clean.

It hit him like a fist in the teeth; no matter how many times he saw it, the shock was the same. Beauty, size, noise, hustle, and bustle. But most of all, the myriad of colour. An artist would have been accused of insanity if he had painted this. Like a mixture of a thousand different cultures, the scene was full of different-shaped temples and gardens. Houses of many styles were spread all over. Paths wound everywhere—too many by far, each lit by Chinese lanterns hanging like glow-worms. Trees were constantly being clipped, and borders tended. Gardeners, the most common caste, were all over the place, constantly maintaining a paradise.

The scented air hit the back of his throat, and an unused voice box could wait no longer. "It's good to be back!" he boomed, and laughed.

He made his way through the maze as if he had never been away, straight to the house of Chi Lin. With an embrace of long friendship, they made their greeting. He stared at the wizard. "It's time, isn't it?"

Smiling at his impatience, the wizard nodded. "The waiting is over, and in your lifetime, Sabad. It's time to prepare. Soon it will be the time of the coming."

Sabad looked to the mirror in the ivory frame behind the wizard, and as he hugged him again, he looked at his reflection and nodded. He was eager to share his homeland with him.

CHAPTER 6

The two people who loved Monica most noted her steady improvement since her break-up with Tony with pleasure. At work, Mike's friendship continued, and when Maddi encouraged someone, things tended to move swiftly. The use of makeup and the shortening of hemlines increased, whilst the incessant fault-picking of men decreased. On her weekend visits to her mother's, the chat about Mike was noted time after time. But caution was also shown; this was a fragile repair, and Tony was never far from their thoughts.

It was only a few weeks until Christine's appraisal. Mike had found he enjoyed appraisals. It gave him a chance to praise someone or bring them into line, to team bond, to ensure aim at a common goal—and a way to know what made people tick. Despite the distractions, Mike took his job seriously, and now that he was not considered new anymore, his own appraisal by his senior manager had taken place. He felt smug; he had been told he was seen as a good choice, and that improvements in almost every area had been noted.

Christmas and a new millennium were also on their way. At the company's holiday get-together, no partners were allowed; it was a company bonding policy. Mike was looking forward to this year's more than ever before. He was tempted to display his skill in magic tricks to his new friends. Since he had been a young child, he had been fascinated by magic in all its forms. In his teenage years and early twenties, he had used his skill to great advantage with the fairer sex. It was, in his opinion, the ideal way to impress and satisfy the natural curiosity of women; they couldn't resist it. Sean encouraged this pursuit, too.

To see if he still had the knack, he rehearsed in his bedroom.

The low glow from the headboard lights gave him a suitable stage effect as he stood in front of the wardrobe mirror. *Try the simple ones first, Mike*, he told himself. *Only four or five as well; you've got to keep 'em wanting more. Nothing is worse than a boring magician!*

The tricks came flooding back, and within an hour, even the more difficult ones were feeling easier. He stood still then, and stared into the mirror. His mind went back to past years, and he imagined he was talking to a beautiful woman he had just met. *Ah-ha! It's all coming back; remember the eye contact; stare them out and make them blush a little.*

He looked at the imaginary blonde. "Tell me, Marilyn, have you ever made love to a magician?" He chuckled as he saw the false shock in her eyes.

"No, I haven't, why?"

"Oh, nothing…but they do say it's a *magic* experience!"

A laugh came from the mirror.

"I know some very good tricks with my hands; would you like me to show you?"

"I bet you do, you cheeky devil! No, I wouldn't—go away!"

"Just let me show you one trick, and if you don't like it, I promise I'll go and inflict myself on someone else. Please?"

"Oh, all right, then, if you must make a fool of yourself in front of someone, it may as well be me!"

Rosie stood outside the bedroom door, a smile on her slightly worried face. *I remember that*, she thought fondly. *I wonder who he's doing this for; hmm, I'll not ask.* She went downstairs thinking hard. He'd changed a bit lately, especially since his new job, and she'd noted a happiness that had been missing for a while. She felt glad, really; it eased her guilt. But this rehearsal worried her. Although she didn't want to touch him—or for him to touch her—she definitely didn't want anyone else to do it. Suspicion floated into her mind, almost unnoticed.

"Funny how it all comes flooding back; bloody amazing, in fact." As the bedroom disappeared into the image of a nightclub, he carried on.

"I could show you how to do one of these tricks...for a price, such as...a kiss." He was now talking to an enthralled, imaginary Marilyn, who had watched the display all agog. "In fact, I could show you how to do them all, but then we would be back full circle, wouldn't we?"

Marilyn looked bemused.

"What I mean is, that we would be back to the first question. Have you ever made love to a magician?"

This made him laugh. The vision vanished, and he was back in front of the mirror looking at his reflection. "You old dog, you, I believe you've still got the Reeves touch!"

He considered what might happen as he sat on the edge of the bed. Since he had got this job, he hadn't used his "gifts" as much. He could, now. The worries of learning a new job had gone, and he was back to himself more-or-less. He decided to go downstairs and find out what life had in store for him.

As he passed through the lounge, he smiled at Rosie. She was watching television. "What have you been doing up there?"

"Oh, a few exercises; I thought I was getting a paunch."

"Oh, I see...right. There's a cuppa in the pot if you want one; I thought I'd just mash one before I went to bed." She stared at his back as he went into the kitchen.

"I'm going to stop up a bit; I'll be in the study."

Rosie knew what this meant, and she left him to it.

In the background of his mind as he picked up the cup and milk jug, Debbie sat painting a picture: a surreal fantasy of a unicorn in a forest of tall trees, the light and shadows fascinating. She loved to imagine different scenes in different conditions, like twilight, dawn, snow, rain, and setting sun. She studied the angles of the light passing through the leaf canopy and was concentrating on what colour and length of shadow would be cast. She sat back to look and wiped her paintbrush on her smock, then placed it between her teeth. She felt tired and stretched; it wouldn't be long until her duty time. Her eyes went to the bed. The punk attire was still resting there. *He'll enjoy that*, she thought. She then looked to her long wardrobe, and the array of costumes hanging in a row: nurse, French maid, secretary, sixth-form schoolgirl, saloon whore...the list was endless. She rubbed her hands and looked excited. What would tonight bring? She thought about starting a shadow, but went to bathe instead. She was eager, as usual.

Mike walked into the study sipping his tea, then sat by the CD player to pick his music. "Mmm, Allegri's 'Miserere', or Gregorian Chants?" It was usually the first, and tonight was no different. He liked it because it seemed to be a tribute to the imagined glens and towering mountains he would soon be flying over in his mind; he classed it as "just right." Another thing that had to be "just right" was the lighting: a low pink glow in the corner of the room. He switched it on and sat to drink his cup of tea and settle his mind before starting.

He liked and studied the mysterious, often passing on what he had learnt to Eric, who was always interested, but too scared to try. He had learnt about divination, and over the years, his fascination with and practice of the arts had increased. Although recently they had gone through a necessary lull, Sean sensed it was now time to resume the path and continue Mike's journey of spiritual development.

Mike's interest was first fuelled after reading about how Chinese government, and generals in their armed forces, made the country's most important decisions by casting sticks and the like. To visualise a country running on such chance captivated him, and as he studied more, he realised it wasn't such a bad idea after all. And based on these theories of chance, he now considered this to be much more than his main hobby; it was a way of life. He had been to development classes and read as many books as he could on the subject. He had created his own combination of styles, to produce the "Mike Reeves Method of

Divination." His imagination made it seem real—too real, sometimes. He'd recently discussed this with his doctor, in another visit of Mike talking and him writing.

His refreshment and mind tuning complete, he decided to begin. He slowly pulled out his chair from the desk and opened his drawer to get out his "tranklements."

First, he placed his green leather writing rest in the centre of the desk. This was a purchase from an antique shop, during an outing with Rosie to Chesterfield, a market town close by. It was a slightly sloping frame of mahogany, with green leather inlaid in its upper surface, used to give good posture and encourage neat writing in Victorian times. Mike kept hand written accounts of every session, and this addition to his equipment seemed to match the seriousness it deserved. He rested his special paper on top. This unbleached thick-textured paper looked ancient and ideally suited to his writing. He imagined it must be very similar to what scribes used in days gone by. His bag of runes, Raider Waite Tarot cards, and special Chinese coins were all positioned in their usual, exact places, along with his accompanying books and favourite fountain pen. To finish, he placed a sandalwood-scented candle into his silver-plated candlestick and lit it. His mystic-patterned silk cloth was smoothed out from left to right. This dark blue cloth with gold stars and zodiac symbols gave what Mike described as "a perfect background to divination." Everything had a place and had to be in it. The CD was set on repeat to his preferred tune.

Seriousness was the key to his success; nothing annoyed him more than people taking this too lightly. Often when he had done readings for Eric and other friends, he had told them in no uncertain terms: "If you approach this as a party game, you'll end up with party game answers; if your mind is cloudy, you will get cloudy answers, so approach it correctly!"

He imagined three distinct places, each being ideally suited for three different kinds of divination.

As he used the tarot, he thought of an old street resembling something from fifteenth-century Florence. He seemed suddenly to be there, an experience almost as real as Sean and Debbie. It was a festival day, and the place was exceptionally busy, with crowds gathering and pushing to the road's edge to get a better look at the procession going past. Men in bright doublets threw large flags into the air, fire-eaters blew jets of flame out of their mouths, and jugglers also played with fire, as burning torches left smoke trails above the watching multitude. Men on stilts strode about, almost, but never quite, overbalancing.

Pushed by the moving crowd, he was ushered into a court-yard full of rich courtiers, showing more refinement than the peasant crowds. He left them all and took a familiar route to a street where an old inn stood on the corner. Entering, he looked around quickly, always a little frightened that she might not be there, but he was never disappointed. A gypsy sat in the corner.

Her name was Rosa. She was as brown faced as the inside of a stained cup, her teeth as white and straight as a row of war graves. The corner she sat in was dimly lit, the light from the fire highlighting her gold earrings. To match was a reflecting row of what looked like miniature horse brasses, hanging from the edge of her headscarf. The tarot cards would be set before her, at the side of an old, polished brass box, and usually read in a Celtic Cross Spread.

So, with the memories of countless journeys to these places coming to the front of his "third eye," he let his mind blend to the music. Serenaded by the plainsong, he fell into the mist of his dreams. Before he knew it, this world was gone; he arrived at the first place of divination. He was sat opposite Rosa.

She was attractive, and looked well into her fifties, but seemed to have become more alluring with age. The cut of her dress was low, and her cleavage deep; and although gravity and age had taken effect, her breasts were still proud. She noticed him looking and enjoyed it, but she pulled her black shawl tighter to show her modesty. The irises in her eyes were almost as black as her pupils; the bright crimson headscarf contrasted against them, whilst highlighting the matching nails.

He stared at the tarot pack. He'd love to hold them, but like all card readers of this world and others, she didn't allow it without good reason. They were well used; all the original white had turned buff with age, especially where her thumbs had rubbed over the years. On closer inspection, he caught odd glimpses of the pictures as she handled them lovingly, all hand painted and cracked with the passing of time; they must have cost a great deal. She stopped caressing them and placed the pack on her lap as she rolled out the green baize cloth, then rested them upon it, face down.

The thumbnail on her right hand was very long, and she used it deftly to separate the pack into the major and minor arcana. Mike thought of how the old word *arcana*, meaning mystery, or secret, sounded absolutely right; it was one of those words which suited its meaning perfectly. He smiled at how faultlessly she split the pack into its two separate parts. She was so skilled that she never looked down, but stared back, smiling at his wonderment.

The major arcana, Mike had learnt, were the trump cards, graded into different stages of initiation. Twenty-two in all, the Wheel of Fortune was significantly at their centre. It represented the turning point of life, the mid-life crisis, the stage at which man peaks, and at which the decline begins. And how cruelly the pack knew this.

The minor arcana consisted of fifty-six cards, divided into four suits, each having ten pip cards and four court cards. The suits were wands, swords, cups, and pentacles, each corresponding with the four astrological elements of fire, air, water, and earth. The court cards were generally thought to represent particular people.

With a dramatic sweep of her hand, Rosa spread the major arcana into a perfectly even arc, telling Mike to point to one, the card that would tell her about him, as he was right now. She looked deep into his eyes and examined his emotional level. Her hand moved to the selected card and turned it over. The Magician—a powerful card. She picked it up and inserted it back into the pack as she shuffled, held his gaze, and placed the cards into the palms of his hands. He shuddered with excitement.

"Shuffle them, and pick out just three. Things have changed, and today it's going to be a three-card spread."

64

Why have things changed? She looks as though she knows something; I feel different here, too, Mike thought.

The three cards were picked to show the past, the present, and the future. One by one, she turned them over.

"Six of Wands, reversed: this means that you must not be afraid of the outcome you seek. You could be your own worst enemy; why fear defeat?

"Mmmm...King of Wands, a chivalrous, passionate warrior, with great leadership qualities: you'll be successful at what you embark on...Oh! Good advice is on its way from someone who knows best; take it!"

Slowly, she turned over the last card. "The Lovers. Uh-oh, watch out. The joys of youth will return, and harmony will come eventually, but possibly—no, more like certainly—after conflict!"

Like a table trickster, she produced the Magician card again, almost out of thin air, and placed it between his hands, putting her own hands on each side of his. This concerned him; he felt her emotions for an instant. She was worried for him, but he knew better than to ask a tarot reader for what was not being disclosed. She gave him an unspoken blessing before she let go of his hands; then he stood and kissed her fully, and without rush, on the lips. He bade her farewell with reluctance, knowing the inhospitable place around the corner.

She touched her lips, then followed him with her gaze.

After a reading here, he would drift over mountains and glens of what looked like Scotland, and over the seas to Scandinavian-style lands, like the Vikings' lands of old.

He would invariably land next to the World Tree, the Yggdrasil, where Odin had found the runes blowing in the wind. A short walk away would be the village. The stench of pig shit would be overpowering, and more often than not, snow, rain, or most commonly, hail, would be lashing down. Water would be running off the low, pole-supported roofs in torrents. Mud would be everywhere, mixed with what he dare not think what. Dogs would snarl and snap, snagging at ropes barely strong enough to hold them. The coldness would seep into his bones; thus, the inn would beckon him with warmth and the smell of food.

Upon entering, the loud laughter and general noise would hush; eyes would look to him, and then to the opposite corner, to where an old, deformed woman sat next to a roaring fire. She would be almost invisible to all but him, sitting in the dark shadows. No one remembered her enter, because she made them forget. Her name was Hilda, and she was a rune caster of the highest order.

WHOOOOSH! The wind had taken him as soon as he had stepped out of the door to Rosa's Inn. The sky darkened, and the usual view rushed past as the rain peppered his skin and turn to ice. The tree beckoned, out of reach, the Yggdrasil. Oh, what a majestic tree, widespread, powerful, and wise. The Tree of Odin, where he spied the runes. Tonight, the wind rushing through its branches turned into a voice. It recited a version of the speech of the High One, from the Old Norse, *The Poetic Edda*, from around 1200 AD.

I know I hung on that windswept tree,
Swung there for nine long nights,
Wounded by my own blade, bloodied for Odin,
Myself an offering...to...myself:
Bound to the tree, that no man knows!
To the tree that no man knows where the roots of it run.
None gave me bread,
None gave me drink.
Down to the deepest depths I peered...until,
Until...I spied THE RUNES!!
With a roaring cry, I seized them up,
Then dizzy and fainting, I fell.
Well-being I won...and wisdom, too.
Mike Reeves, consider this...
From a word to a word I was led to a word,
From it to a deed, to another deed!

What's happening to me? Mike wondered; he could see the words as well as hear them. Never had things been so real. *Why did I stop my progress? This is brilliant! I want more!*

Sean sat in his mind, staring through his eyes, writing down everything he saw and heard. This was the biggest leap yet.

The storm was raging as usual; flashes of lightning lit the tree's wet, shiny bark. The branches were like a thousand arms reaching out into the night sky; the wind whistled angrily—*why had it been made to give one of its secrets away to this mortal?*

The village was before him, and he tried to walk, his feet sticking on one step, then slipping on another. The hail felt like acupuncture on his cheeks. Slowly, he made his way to the stout, oak door of the inn.

He entered. Feeling bold and ready, he walked to the serving table for a wooden tankard of ale. The strange brew had the ability to warm him, so he gulped half of it down; as often happened here, his manners left him. He belched loud and long, turned around, and looked defiantly at everyone and everything.

Wiping the beer from his chin with the back of his hand, he looked at the walls, which were decorated with armour and weapons; runic symbols were carved into the spear shafts, engraved into the blades, and painted onto the shields. As he gulped what remained of the ale, he noticed that even the tankard had runes cut into its inside base. Asleep by the fire were two Great Danes; both were aroused not by noise, but by the hush that settled over the room. They growled.

Comments from the occupants of the Inn entered his mind.

"The visitor is here again."

"Who is he?"

"Look at his strange dress."

"Some say he's the one of the prophecy, and he'll come with an army one day!"

Although Mike had heard the comments before, today they seemed clearer. He could tell the men were afraid of him, almost in awe of him, whilst the ladies stared at him with lust in their eyes. All the men were huge and skilled in war craft. They wore sweaty, acrid bearskins almost doubling their size, and he knew logic said he should be the one afraid of them. But each one lowered his eyes as Mike stared around at them and began to walk to what looked like an empty table. He was going to talk to himself again.

"Dangerous and mad," someone muttered. "That's what he is: dangerous and mad!"

That was the last comment he heard as he sat down before Hilda. *She's lost a tooth since I last saw her*, Mike observed, staring straight into her face. Her gaze was just as steady and determined.

"It's like seeing you for the first time," she said. "It's going to be different from now on! Heh heh! Hee hee!" She took his hands in hers; the feel of warts and calluses made him shudder, and the cold, rough texture of her skin felt as if it drew the warmth from his body like a corpse would, given the chance. "Just a single rune tonight, not the usual cast—it has to be, I've been told so!"

He didn't give her the pleasure of asking, although he was dying to know who had said so.

She began to speak in a fluid voice, the voice of a young woman. For brief seconds, she looked like Debbie and then faded back to herself.

What's happening now? he asked himself, as again the difference hit him. Never had a reading been so alive!

She recited the invocation that was written on the rune stone, at Vasterby, Uppland, in Sweden:

The work of Asmund Karasun, AD 1050
God within me, God without,
How shall I ever be in doubt?
There is no place where I may go
And not there see God's face, not know
I am God's vision, and God's ears.
So through the harvest of my years
I am the Sower and the Sown,
God's self unfolding...
...and God's Own.

She cackled and threw a rune onto the table. It was the rune called Berkana—known as a "growth" or "a leading-to rune." A rune which signifies a step from one stage of understanding to a higher place. Hilda said out loud what the rune was saying to her. "This stage of your learning will blossom, and ripen in a way you cannot comprehend. Dispense with resistance…and flourish."

He finished talking to himself at the table. As he stood to leave, people stared at him. The door banged shut behind him, and coldness shot through his body like heroin; his stomach lurched as he stared at the vanishing rooftops below.

Sean continued to write rapidly; even with his skills and knowledge of the arts, he was only just keeping up with the events.

From there, he would be transported to a place that looked how he imagined Shanghai would have looked eight hundred years ago. The noise on the seedy, brothel-infested streets always shocked him. Chickens squawked as they swung from their wicker basket prisons, shedding feathers as they awaited their fate. People would be bantering and arguing over trivial items, pushing and shoving against him, and standing back as they looked with fear at his strange Western face. Although it was surely a different route he took every time, he always ended up at the same place: a small, Chinese curio shop in a side street. He'd enter without knocking and be greeted by the most fearsome Moor he'd ever see, as black as coal and with lips like glowing embers. His name was Sabad. He never spoke, but by a movement of the arms, he would show Mike to the rear of the shop, and into a small room. The room frightened Mike because of the overwhelming sense that he was balanced on the edge of the world. As he stared between the gaps of the racks and the countless items hung on hooks, he could see no substance, just void, and everything felt not quite solid.

Pushing through the bric-a-brac, the Chinaman would come, dressed in patterned robes that showed his high rank of office. Here he experienced his favourite form of divination, the oldest known to mankind: I Ching, dealt by its supreme master, the wizard magician, Chi Lin.

After leaving Hilda tonight, the mountains glided past Mike as he flew to the Orient. Here, too, it felt more real than ever before. The Easterners didn't just look with curiosity; they seemed to look threateningly at him as he pushed through the marketplace. He was glad to reach the door, where he was shown through to the back room without delay by the Moor. The feeling of being on an unguarded parapet washed through his senses. He looked down at the table and saw the hands resting there, the coins held gently in the palms. Following the robes up the arms with his eyes, he reached the face of Chi Lin, who smiled and nodded a greeting, then invited Mike to take the coins.

Years ago, as he had begun his quest for spiritual enlightenment, he had discovered I Ching, the oldest form of fortune telling on the planet, the art of consulting "The Oracle." As he took the coins from the almost-feminine hands, he cast his mind back to how he had found them.

He had read that he needed to get three Chinese coins, all identical. He was at the local open-air market with Rosie, and he had found a stall he had never seen before—or since. A dealer in military curios and medals had an old "Oxo" tin full of about a thousand coins, buttons, and badges, resting at the edge of the stall. After asking if he could look, he saw a Chinese coin on the top, and after searching through, he found that there were three…all the same. *Another sign,* he thought at the time, that he was on the right path.

After purchasing the coins for a ridiculous fee, he washed them and made them his own by holding them between his hands during a deep, hour-long meditation. He never let anyone touch them, only Chi Lin.

He cast the coins to make the upper and lower trigrams, to build up a hexagram, to use in the I Ching's quaint and often bizarre language. As usual, it suggested various levels of reality, diametrically opposed to Western thinking, to Mike. The I Ching bore little resemblance to the world he lived in, but its naturalistic, intuitive approach, coupled with its extraordinary perceptions, were complementary to his logical thought. It was based on change and synchronicity, a study of apparently unconnected events, either revealed by straws or coins, each cast to produce a line in an image. Based on young and old, yin and yang, the coins produced, as if by magic, a new hexagram: the outcome of the situation or question.

He stared at Chi Lin. "Well?"

Chi Lin spoke thoughtfully. "Things look good, actually. The judgment, the image, and the outcome favour you. The onus is on *Ch'ien*: modesty. Be careful that this new stage of your life does not bring contempt from others; that's the main warning. Remember that politeness and modesty generate success, and maintain a man once he is wealthy or has position. Modesty also reaches great heights and wears down the highest peaks. The coins point to things being well, and they imply that help and good fortune are at hand. But listen very carefully to the whole message: it's telling you that you will have conflict, trouble, a challenge. The rewards will be great, but not necessarily what you expect. I'd like to tell you more, but remember that what you are doing is not for yourself—it's for many, many others."

"What are you hiding from me?"

"I can't say. It's not that I won't, it's that I...*cannot!*" He studied Mike, then attempted a reassuring smile.

At the closing stages, Sean drifted into his thoughts almost unseen. Something worried him. It was Mikes' choice, but Sean still felt that Mike's feelings for Monica were not right for his progress in the arts. He wanted to broaden Mike's horizons a little. Mike's sudden leap in development also meant it could be time to try something he had been holding back up until now, something which, until today, he thought Mike's mind not capable of sustaining. Sean would use the power of suggestive thought. He knew he was almost breaking the rules here; any decisions should really be Mike's—but was it so different from how they worked together all the time, anyway?

Perhaps Maddi or Christine could be useful in my development, thought Mike. *I wonder if they dabble? I wonder if I could find out, or if Debbie or Sean could find out for me. What was that article I read, now…astral travel? Mmm, I'll ask Sean.*

With a broad grin, Sean sat back in his chair, then started thinking about the night's events.

Slowly the images faded, and Mike cleared things away, yawning. *God! Is that the time? Have I been away that long? Wow! It was brilliant tonight; I didn't realise how much I'd been missing it. I think the break has done me good; it's never, ever been that realistic.* He walked through the lounge, still transfixed by what had happened and what he'd been told, and discovered that Rosie had gone to bed. He locked the door and started to climb the stairs, images of the night flying around his head. *Have I locked up?* he wondered, then went back to check. *Huh, Rosie must have done it.*

Debbie laughed. "He's losing it!" She was dressed in her PVC again; Mike had enjoyed it so much, she thought she'd do a repeat performance for him. She bumped into Sean on the balcony, and together they walked to meet Mike on the platform.

Brushing his teeth, Mike spoke to his reflection again: "Dentist check up soon, always just before Christmas." Quietly, he walked to his bed and slid between the sheets.

Rosie grunted irritably, "Yes, tomorrow, can't you see I'm busy? I've got to. . " Her voice trailed off as she fell back to sleep.

Mike grinned. He was glad to hear a normal mutter from a disturbed sleep. Not so long ago, he would have had to comfort her after she woke screaming from another nightmare. *Relax*, he told himself. *Forget all that and the rest. For now, wind down.* He drifted into the limbo between tiredness and sleep, to await the clouds. The stepping-stones formed, and as he walked, it became brighter. He landed on the platform.

Debbie walked towards him, wearing her black PVC, thigh-length boots with matching mini-skirt and jacket, which was hanging open to reveal her breasts. Tiny shiny silver chains hung from her nipples, which jingled as she moved. Her hair was spiked. "Hiya, big boy. How ya doin'?"

"A lot better already, thanks." Mike beamed.

His face turned to Sean, and his eyes followed a few seconds later. "Nice to see you, Sean. I need a word; I've had an idea. A pretty good one, I think."

Sean smiled knowingly. "Really? Let's go to my room, then."

Debbie gave the usual wave, and left for her room. Sean and Mike walked slowly down the corridors, past the ivory tower. He could smell a trace of Debbie's perfume, and he thought of her as they walked in silence: *I love her.*

Debbie sat looking into her mirror. The bulbs around its edge lit up her reflected face against a jet-black background. She paused and looked into her own eyes. "So do I, my love. I love you, too."

They arrived at Sean's door, at which Sean produced a massive key hanging from a rope around his waist, which made his attire resemble a monk's habit. The material was soft and gave him the impression of gliding down the corridors rather than walking. Only the kicking action of his knees against the front gave his walking movement away.

"Bloody hell, Sean, I could clear snow with that!"

Sean laughed a hearty laugh, which Mike liked to hear, and walked into the room like Quasimodo, pretending the key was a massive weight.

Mike often visualised Sean in this room, performing the magical experiments he'd told him about. The room was perfectly circular, its light emanating from unbleached candles held in one magnificent stand to their left. One third of the room was covered in artefacts resting on polished wooden shelves—items of magic, science, and mystery, all well tended and used often. Brass shone warmly and bubbles rose in glass, oddly shaped containers, giving the room the sound of an aquarium. The smell was fresh: clumps of herbs hung on the dark beams, clearing the sinuses, and making the room seem invigorating.

Another third of the room was full from top to bottom with books, the bindings polished with use. Some were jewelled, and others had what looked like gold hinges. The majority looked very old, and extremely valuable.

The final third was covered with a midnight blue curtain, which covered a hidden door. "Don't go asking what's behind there again," Sean said tantalisingly. "It's my secret, you know that, and I don't have many from you."

"I won't." Mike smiled. "I've tried too many times already."

The comfy, well-worn furniture looked medieval, even ancient. There were scientific looking instruments, magical curios, charts, half-open, teasing drawers everywhere. All sorts of interesting, touchable things rested on tables and chests of drawers. "And don't even think about touching that!" Sean instructed, as Mike's finger moved curiously to a huge crystal ball on a stand. "Now, tell me, what's your idea?"

"I've been reading an article about astral projection. Could Debbie or you do it?"

"Yes, probably."

"Would my mind be capable?"

"With a little training, I would say it quite capable, yes."

"Could it put thoughts into people's minds, or find out what they are thinking?"

Things were slowly going a different route than Sean had planned. "I suppose so, yes. Why?"

"I'd like Debbie to 'fly' to Monica's mind and pry a little!"

"Most unethical, most unethical indeed! You can't just go around playing with other people's minds!"

"Yes, I know, and I admit that at first, the idea was to put sexy thoughts in her mind!"

"In that case, NO!"

"No, hold on. What I thought then was, I'd like her to trust me, to like me more. I think my actions are doing that, but tonight's trip was wonderful, as you know, and somehow...I don't know where the thought came from, but I think she is the key to a lock. I think she's important to my development. Don't ask me how I know; the thought just came, as if, like...someone planted it there."

The white observers allowed themselves a rue smile over Sean's predicament. He had pushed the boundaries, and he was now reaping the rewards.

"Leave things to me," Sean said, contemplating various outcomes.

Mike could sense that Sean's attention had drifted, so he made his excuses and left.

This was not what Sean had expected at all; he had hoped to steer Mike *away* from Monica, not straight towards her! But he knew very well that he'd started it, so he'd have to continue. His mind went back over the centuries to when he was learning his crafts. He remembered the all-knowing teachers dressed in white, who had often told him about the consequences of not thinking everything through.

The white observers agreed. They'd said he'd never learn!

Mike ran down the corridor, then up the stairs two at a time. He knocked on the door, then entered.

Debbie stood looking away from him. "Hiya…Mike." She smiled sexily and pressed B7 on the jukebox. "Sit down and watch this!"

Mike sat down at the end of the bed, breathing deeply from the running and his mounting excitement. *I'm glad she's got them on again*, he thought. Already an erection big enough to spin a dinner plate on was swelling his jeans.

She began to dance.

It was the dance of a slave girl to a warrior, of a podium dancer in a New York nightclub…a dance of sex.

"Wow!" was all that Mike could utter in response. She moved her hands up and down her oiled, shiny body, starting with her thighs and running up her tummy, soon cupping her breasts, making them look like they were in goblets. In this position, she sensually moved towards him, offering the cups, full of flesh, to his lips. She moved to the beat as Mike licked her nipples, the small cold chains running over his tongue and his head moving like windscreen wipers from one breast to the other. The taste was one of warmth, of sex, of answered lust. She danced backwards, then towards him again, teasing him in titillating moments of pleasure, interspersed with time for him to look at and appreciate the beauty of her body.

At times like this, Mike showed how he could be more appreciative than even she realised. Each delicate crease in her flesh was carefully noted and adored. The flashes of what was to come made his heart pound; he began to feel the tension in the sinews of his neck start to disappear. The sensation that the base of his skull was attached to his shoulders with taut rubber bands started to ease, as if the bands were melting away. His eyes became ultra-seeing; the light on her fine body hair appealed to his senses.

The smell of woman filled his nostrils; the texture, similar to a grapefruit segment, began to fill his mouth and remind him of a clitoris's touch on his tongue. At moments of extreme desire like this, he would have sacrificed his life for the promised orgasm and the feeling of woman flesh against him. This was the only woman flesh he had access to, and he loved it.

The sight of her breasts brought his concentration to a new height. "Oh, God, Debbie...I love the way your breasts move, oh, they are so...so...ohh!" They continued to move in a way only Debbie could achieve. "Christ, Debs, thank you for this gift you give me."

Debbie loved comments like this. She backed away again, like a cat playing with its prey. He was totally at her mercy.

She didn't want to torment any longer, so she started to give him his reward. His eyes were obviously starting to sting with sweat and a lack of blinks, and other parts of his body needed attention, too. She turned around, looked over her shoulder naughtily, and bent over: the skirt drew up halfway over her bottom, and no knickers were there to hide anything. She stretched her legs wide and straight, bent over at just the right angle, and began to thrust in time to the steadily quickening music.

Mike stroked her bottom and between her legs. She clicked her fingers, and her skirt disappeared; she was going to click again, but he said no, she had to keep the boots on. As he stood and moved over to the chair, specially designed for making love, his legs barely supported him, trembling behind the knees.

Slowly, deliciously lubricated, she mounted his erect manhood, and began to kiss his neck and caress his body with her hands.

Mike touched and kissed everything he could reach, as together they galloped to ecstasy, their orgasms mutually timed to perfection, like the eruption of a volcano and the roll of an earthquake in perfect sequence.

Mike flew back to his bedroom, calling out, "Oh, Debbie, Debbie, Debbie, Debbie." Semen flew high up his chest in spurts.

Rosie was in a deep, undisturbed sleep again. Mike mentally thanked the doctor for her continuing prescriptions.

The Gateway To Hell was wide awake, but without its master. He was at home in Chesterfield, in his luxury flat, sitting in darkness and looking at the moon through open French doors on his balcony. Vivaldi's "Four Seasons" played in the background, and frost was already gathering on the metal railings around the balcony edge.

Monica Doll stood at his feet, and through her eyes, the dark observers were studying his deeds. "This Monica needs removing from his mind, to allow him to develop properly."

The skeletal face rattled a reply: "I suppose she does, but let's leave him."

Their attention was diverted as the *kak-kak* of a magpie made them look to their right. It landed on the rails, its wings flapping to keep balance, and its claws scouring the frost to get a grip.

Tony didn't flinch at its arrival; he had expected it. Soon, another landed, then a third. Monica Doll's eyes blinked.

He threw bread and fresh meat down, to gain their confidence. Sabre growled.

"Shh."

Instantly, the hound trotted back to its corner, still unsure if the magpies were a threat or not.

Throughout history, magpies had been seen as birds of omen. As a child, Tony had been told to salute a single bird, to ward off evil. He had also been taught to see a pair as a good sign. But to see three, and at night, would have been seen as "a happening" by soothsayers. But to see all three bow down to a man and serve him would have signified a man of great magical standing. And all three magpies did just that.

Monica Doll's eyes watched with increasing interest as they hopped to him, submissively allowing him to stroke their necks. The old book had paid dividends; each bird ate a pellet he had prepared from its pages. He uttered three words, also learnt from the tome, to each of them, and then to the moon.

Their plumage took on a highlighted appearance, their dark feathers glowing iridescently as their white mirrored the moon's brightness.

Two were given simple instructions to observe Monica and Mike, and they flew back to their icy perch to await their leader.

The biggest of the three, and leader of the group remained on Tony's lap, put its head to one side, and stared at him. The moon reflected perfectly in the centre of its ink-black eye. He picked it up, gently held it in his hands, and drew it towards his face. Softly, he blew onto its beak. "Go to Christine; make sure she gets this." A perfect little green glass globe encased in a silver cage was secured to its leg. "Peck through this to free it."

Made by Fabergé for a famous poisoner, the little orb was an expensive trinket. All the silver was delicately engraved, and poking out from within the glass centre was a circle of needle-like protuberances.

Stroking the carrier, he stood and walked over to the balcony rails. He threw the bird into the air, and the other two alighted their icy perch. All three went in different directions of purpose-ful flight. The biggest, silhouetted against the moon, slowly di-minished in size to a dot, which turned left and vanished.

The observers nodded to each other satisfactorily. No words were spoken; the only sound was the steady scrape of honing stone on steel, from the one dressed in deepest black.

Tony walked back and bent down to pick up Monica Doll, cradling her in his arms. He sat down and whistled to Sabre, who trotted over to enjoy a stroking hand. With his other hand, he tweaked the doll's hair and twisted it into small ringlets around his fingers, breathing deeply and slowly, listening to the music. He smiled at the thought of the Rat's friend, Andy, getting his reward; the girl with the pierced cheek would be performing for him right now. This Christine was going to be a useful tool.

He fell asleep.

* * *

Kingdom of Tarol, 1423

The caravan was decorated predominantly in red, inside and out. The interior was lit with twelve candles, all burning steadily, free from draughts in the expertly constructed wagon. Rosa sat with one leg tucked elegantly under her bottom, bent over a circular table next to her cupboards and beneath her bed, which was lofted under the ceiling. The candlelight flatteringly lit her face as she busied herself with her calligraphy.

She was warm and cosy. Outside, the wind was blowing in gusts, making Bess whinny. Imagining her mare strutting and stomping, she thought about the extra currycombing that would be required to groom and straighten in the morning. The horse was restless, tired of being idle. Rosa understood this, but she needed to complete her task first; then it would be time to go to the Chimes again, to find out how much time she had. That would make Bess happy.

Creaking back into her wicker chair, she surveyed the pile of parchment with pride. Decorative glass paperweights held her latest work at its four corners. The artwork was done now; all she needed to add were the names of the woods, rivers, hamlets, and passes.

Over the centuries, she had travelled more than any other citizen of Tarol. He would need her knowledge, and that made her feel good. She wanted to please him.

Please him…her eyes looked around her caravan, then rested on the bed. Oh, yes, she definitely wanted to please him.

Her hand gently stroked her stomach and moved down to her warm wetness; she wanted him to please her, too.

CHAPTER 7

Sean felt uncomfortable and resisted looking into Debbie's eyes. He had thought long and hard and could see some merit in Mike's alternative. Things like this didn't happen without reason; he sensed other hands at work, and they knew best. He was way too far away to ask, and he couldn't desert his post even if he wanted to, so he asked Debbie. "Well…. it looks like a new strategy. Mike senses that Monica is important to his development in the arts. If that's so, then we have to find out, and use her. I know more about the grand scheme of things than you two do. I'll let you and Mike know more when I'm allowed; please be patient with him and with me. I feel like I'm walking a tightrope sometimes, and the restraints and laws of time and nature and so on make it feel like I've got to juggle sand, too."

Debbie almost understood, and she nodded. "What new strategy?"

"Well, a stage was reached last night during his reading, I've thought about it a great deal since, and I know he has. I think he might be ready for astral travel, using you as his vehicle."

"Like a bike?" Debbie grinned.

"No!" Sean raised his eyebrow. This was not the time for silly comments.

"Sorry."

"I think we might have to explore her mind, and probably others. You knew the day would come. I hope you remember your training."

Debbie remembered the warnings of danger, too, but had proved to be adept at the task. "Of course. I won't let anyone down."

"I know. The problem now is, how do we initiate it? We can't just go into minds haphazardly."

Mike had often commented that answers often came from unexpected sources, and the answer to this was no different. Mike hadn't lost touch with Eric; he wasn't involved with the happenings, and this made his friendship even more valuable to Mike, like a port in a storm. At work, their paths crossed only occasionally, so a new pattern had arisen in their social lives. A game of pool and a few beers about once a month kept them both up to date with each other's lives. Mike had few real friends, and he saw Eric as trustworthy, and good support when he needed it. He also found him very amusing. Eric often failed to see why he found him so funny, which made Mike smile all the more.

These outings were good for Rosie too. She always went to her best friend's; she usually came back with lots of news and obvious enjoyment on her face.

On their last outing, Mike had told Eric about his revived practice of magic tricks and had treated him to a private performance as a test of his ability. Eric's childlike appreciation, and subsequent pleading to be shown how to do them, was both amusing and a stamp of approval.

Mike also told him about the peep show, at which Eric's eyes had almost dropped out of their sockets. Embellishing slightly, Mike told him that Maddi's knickers had almost been in full view. Tonight, he obviously wanted an update. "Any more peep shows?" he asked. "Tell me all about it if so!"

Eric was an avid Maddi fan, and so often had he asked about her, that now, if he bumped into Mike, he'd ask, "What colour?," and Mike, on passing, would reply, "Red today, Eric!"—

or whatever colour he made up. Eric drooled at a thought.

81

"Wouldn't it be great if *she* rang me up to describe 'em?"

Mike laughed into his beer.

"Bloody hell, Mike, can you imagine that, eh?"

Mike nodded in agreement, and funnily enough, it gave him an idea for another project he was privately working on. He went silent, until Eric disturbed his thoughts once again:

"What were they like last time, then?"

"Oh, white ones, with little purple hearts on, and she must have moved across the chair, because one side had slid over her cheek. It was a lovely sight!"

"Christ...you lucky bastard!"

Mike laughed.

"That's it, laugh at me again." Eric smiled, then took a gulp of his beer. "This'll make you laugh some more; it just shows the difference between my luck and yours. Huh, *you* see Maddi's bare arse, and Monica Man-hater flashes her thighs, and what do I get? I'll tell you. You know that new barrier they are erecting at gate five?"

Mike was laughing quite uncontrollably. "Yes, I've seen it."

"Well, I saw six inches of builders' arse this morning!"

Mike rocked back and forth in mirth. Eric was good therapy. "Hey, steady on, you'll get us thrown out. Look, people are looking at us."

"Oh, let the boring wankers look!"

"No, shh!" Mike could see that Eric might lose control, so he told him about his mind trip, which had the desired sobering effect. He did have to control his urge to laugh, however, because Eric was now eating a packet of crisps, hanging on every word, and still rocking from side to side in a strange manner. Crumbs covered his jumper.

"I think you are bloody marvellous, mate! What, with everything you try and whatnot, and that magshick...I wisht I could do it!"

Mike bit his bottom lip.

"But I'll tell you, one of the bess fuckin' fings you ever shows me, mate...it war that mind-readin' trix you did...bloody marvellous, that were. Tell us how ya did it. Gowon, tellush!"

"Strewth, Eric, how many had you had before I came?"

"Three!"

"I can't tell you. I've told you before, I'm sworn to secrecy about that; an old friend showed me, the one who got me interested in it all those years ago, the chap who was trying to become a stage magician."

"Oh, arr, ah rememberrrimm!"

"Shh, stop talking so loud. Come on, let's go."

Unwittingly, Eric had given Mike an excellent excuse to get Debbie into Monica's mind. They caught a taxi, and Mike walked Eric to his door, by now quite the worse for wear. Louise stood with her arms crossed as the door opened. "Now what have you done to him?"

"Nothing."

"You're a bad influence, Mike Reeves. Goodnight! Come on, you; you should be ashamed of yourself!"

Mike smiled as he walked back to the taxi. Poor Eric!

The man Mike had mentioned was a good friend of his many years ago, but they had lost touch. However, he still remembered what he had shown him. It was eighty percent trickery and observation, but Mike had found that his intuition and insight had given him more out of it than he was told he'd get.

His method was to write down an answer to a question he'd asked them, fold it, and then pass it on to a third party. But the trick was to know the answer to one question by logging a fact previously learnt, such as where something strange had happened. But whatever it was, it had to be obscure, so that they wouldn't realise he knew it, or at least be unsure if they had ever actually told him. So when he asked the first question, he would write down the answer of what he knew instead of the answer to it. He would ask them to say the answer out loud, which would prove to any onlookers that there was no cheating. Then he would ask another question; they would assume he was writing down the answer, when he was actually writing down the answer they had just told him, camouflaged a bit by obscurity. This went on until the person had four remarkable, near-correct answers, which they read out, not giving a thought to whether they

83

matched the order of the questions. It was dressed up by asking them to stare into his eye, as if he was stealing their thoughts.

But this was the strangest thing: he didn't have to pretend so hard. Thoughts actually did come through to him, albeit vague. With his new progress, he was excited by what he might be able to achieve. It had been years since he'd tried it, and he had come so far since; who knew what might happen?

One thing Mike had found to be vital, and this did make it a little tricky. Like the old vampire stories, he had to be invited, no matter how nonchalantly or obscurely, into someone's mind for it to work properly.

Sean had taken this mild telepathy as yet another sign of Mike's capabilities, and he had nurtured it at the time, but now he, too, had stored it out of mind.

So, tired, and a little worse for his night out, he sat downstairs in front of his computer. Rosie had left a note reading, "Gone to bed, don't worry; I have only been on my own a little while, and I feel fine!" He logged on to the Internet, and typed in "astral travel," which led him to the teaching of Nostradamus. Drinking a whiskey, he stared at the screen, engrossed. He learnt how the Neoplatonic philosophies of the early Christian Era referred to Plato's doctrines when they called the dream body *Astrum*, the Latin word for star, and that this body could vacate the human form as it lay, if the mind was capable. It went on to say that Agrippa had confirmed this when he wrote of "vacation of the body," as the spirit was enabled to transcend its bounds by using another astral body.

He then read of the cabala, an ancient magic considered by many to have Jewish origins, which actually managed to use the body whilst awake. Finally, he was linked to a page on UFO's, where he found a reference to astral snooping, and that the USA was conducting experiments in astral spying. He was into the third paragraph when an "illegal entry" note flashed onto the screen and shut it down. He re-entered and tried to find the page again, but it wasn't there. But this was proof; if the world's leading governments were investigating such things, then who knew what was possible? He shut down and went to bed.

Before he saw Debbie, who was dressed as a French maid, he sat with Sean by the fountain. "Brilliant! It's so damn obvious, and so simple, like all good ideas. I must sharpen my thinking a bit; I should sort things out much quicker than this!" Sean thumped himself on the leg. "Well done. I'll rest easier tonight; I'm off to sort out all the details. I knew we'd find a way in! It's an obvious and easy way in, which will arouse little or no suspicion at all. It's just an entertaining trick!"

Mike left for his own entertainment: the maid needed his attention. She'd been very naughty, and had been ordered to the master's room.

With all this planning behind him, he went on his rounds the next day to plant a thought named Debbie in Monica's mind. He walked in after knocking, subconsciously drawing his tummy in after seeing this month's "six pack" on the calendar next to Maddi's desk.

They said their hellos to one another, then fell into a relaxed mode, so different from the early months when he felt on show. He still kept up his professional image as much as possible, but it was good not to be so formal. The conversation went well, and he saw his chance when one of Monica's annoying habits took over. Quite often, during the most interesting conversations, she seemed to "switch off" to stare at someone or something. This made him feel uncomfortable, as if he was boring her. But this time, it was just the right thing. "Cheer up, it might never happen," Mike said to her.

"What won't?"

"What you are thinking about! Don't worry; it'll be okay!"

"You don't know what I'm thinking about."

"Oh, yes I do. Remember the magic we talked about, and telepathy?"

"They're tricks!" Maddi intervened, obviously hoping them to be proved otherwise.

"No, they aren't. It's magic, real magic, I told you!"

"Oh, go on with you, there's no such thing!" Monica snapped.

85

"Isn't there, now? Well, let me read your mind, then. Let me have a little walk round; I bet I can find some really interesting corners."

"Okay, what am I thinking right now? Come into my mind if you can, and walk the little corridors."

The invitation was enthusiastic, straightforward, and open—the best sort.

In you go, Debbie, he thought, seizing his opportunity. He pretended to look shocked. "Oh, Monica, really! I can't repeat that."

Monica and Maddi both laughed, and Monica blushed. Maddi asked just what *had* she been thinking?

Debbie had stood on the platform waiting with Sean, and she melted from his view as Mike sent her. "Yes!" said Sean, taking great, excited strides back to his room, where it would be easier to keep in touch using his paraphernalia. Another leap in development had been taken; the pace of learning was hotting up.

Mike left their room after promising a real demonstration of his mind-reading abilities at a more convenient time. Behind him, Maddi and Monica began a conversation about all the possibilities.

"It must be a trick. Mind you, I've heard he's pretty good at them, actually," commented Monica.

"Yeah, it's got to be. I mean, just imagine if he was telepathic or something! It would be very embarrassing!"

They both laughed again, then started to work. But after a few minutes, Monica spoke again, "Imagine if he could, though!"

Without thinking, Debbie answered, "He can."

"What?"

"Pardon?"

"You just said he could."

"I didn't even open my mouth!"

"Well, somebody did." Monica looked over her shoulder.

Ooops, thought Debbie.

"Well, it definitely wasn't me!" Maddi answered with a curious glance around.

Both of them wiggled their fingers, and said, "Spooky!"

That night in Monica's flat, Debbie watched, learnt what she could, and had a good look around Monica's mind corridors. Monica had showered; steam still came from the bathroom door, and condensation was running down the mirror and tiles. She had put some music on and was drinking wine.

Debbie was surprised to find that Monica was a Mantovani fan; she loved the caress of violin strings on her mind. It was reminiscent of her childhood visits to the cinema with her parents, where this kind of music serenaded viewers until the feature began. It made her feel comfy, warm, and snug, as if she were sitting between her parents, sensing their protection. She had tried to nostalgically, though subconsciously, recreate this feeling through the years. Underneath her black and red negligee, she was naked. The low lights were on, and the glow from the fire gave a cosy, intimate feel to the room. The worries and stress of the outside world felt a million miles away.

The rain was loud on the windows as Monica began settling into sleep. Before she drifted off, she let down her guard and thought about Mike for a moment. He had looked good today— tall, strong, and dependable, all wrapped up in a sexy cable-knit, grey sweater.

Debbie watched as Monica's dreams unfolded. The thoughts of the cold, and the feeling of cosiness swirled to form a picture of Switzerland and a log cabin with a big fire, surrounded by lots of snow. A man, dressed from head to foot in black, knocked at the door. Mike was a cold, lost, handsome, stranger looking for sanctuary on a nasty winter's night. The wind howled, and pine trees shed snow behind him as Monica opened the door and stood looking at him blowing on his hands. He told her of his dire situation in the cold, and apologised for any fear he may have caused. She invited him in. His voice was deep, kind, and reassuring.

"Come in, you poor man. You must be freezing."

He accepted the invitation. As the evening progressed, he told her all about himself, and how kind and beautiful she was. They sat opposite each other at a blue, smoked-glass table with matching candlestick and goblets. In her dream, she was the interior designer of her ambitions, and the room was fabulous beyond compare. He complimented her on her taste—how marvellous she was!

The conversation was intriguing and exciting, unlike she'd had with any other man. Intuitive and gentle, he really knew how to treat a woman. Their eyes never left one another's; she played footsie with him as they shed their shoes. He stood up and beckoned her to the fire, where they stood on the thick, white fur rug. The fire crackled and spit its own romantic tune. They stood silently, stared into one another's eyes, and kissed. He was taller than her; his powerful frame took control of the situation, and their massive shadows entwined on the ceiling.

Debbie shouldn't have, but she couldn't resist. "No, not like that! Take it hard…and rough!"

The silent stranger grabbed her wrists and pulled her to the floor; she was kissed like never before—her body heaved, and her heart pounded with newfound desire. They made love wildly and noisily in front of the roaring fire. Monica awoke to an orgasm from own hands, shattering her body like the vibrations of a jelly when a tube train went by. "Ooooooh! Oh, my God, ahhhh!"

Mmm, not bad, girlie—not for a novice, anyway, thought Debbie in reluctant admiration. *There's hope for you yet!*

Monica sat with sweat running down her cleavage and face. It was one of the best orgasms she had ever had, and the first in ages. She smiled, rested her head on the settee cushion, and slowly went through it all again, so she wouldn't forget.

With his mind half empty, Mike found it difficult to go to sleep, but eventually he did. A dream materialised from a comment Debbie had made months ago.

Mike was in his office. He was giving Monica her review—her standards were at an all-time low. "Well, Monica, I can't think of anything good to say! You've been rude to clients, you upset your colleagues, and your work is poor, very poor. What have you got to say?"

"Dunno."

"Don't you care?"

"No, not really."

"Look, I owe you this much: they are talking of redundancies. This report won't go down well at all, and it's the type of thing they use to score you. You were one of the best when I took this job. But now, well, you are one of the worst."

"They can't do that to me!"

"Oh, yes they can, lady. I hope they don't, I really do. But can you see an alternative? It's like having a naughty schoolgirl on my hands!"

"I was once, but my teacher sorted me out." She took a step towards him.

Mike looked into her eyes and saw lust. He gulped. "How?"

She walked slowly round his desk and stood at the side, her charcoal dress hugging her hips and caressing her thighs as she moved. It appeared to flare out a little an inch or so up from its hem, which exaggerated her curves. "He spanked me...."

Mike did the same, on her bare bottom, her knickers down to her ankles. With his right hand raised, he awoke. "Bloody hell, where did that come from?"

"What?" asked Rosie, waking up scared.

"Eh? Oh, it's okay. I've been dreaming; I'll get a drink."

"Okay, love. Are you all right?"

"Yes, don't worry. I'm okay."

Mike stared at his reflection and grinned. "Now *that's* what I call an appraisal! I'll have to tell the doctor about that, let him enjoy the analysis." He went back to bed after washing the glass. As he lay awaiting slumber, he thought of his visits to his doctor. He was now a friend. He could and did share everything; if ever the visits had to end, he'd miss him, and Mike thought, *He'd miss me too I reckon!*

Awakening the next morning, he sniffled, and his throat felt scratchy. Mind access was difficult and needed both planning and timing, but return was easy. So long as you were not detected, it was just like letting go of one end of a taut rubber band. Suddenly, he felt his mind was full again. "Hiya!" Debbie called. "I'm back"

"Oh, hello."

Rosie stared at him. "Don't you mean good morning?" She smiled. "Or have you been dreaming again?"

"Too much cheese, I reckon! I'm getting up, anyway, before the alarm goes off. It's ten past seven."

Now wasn't the time to ask what Debs had found out for him. He went to work and did his rounds earlier than usual. He was eager to see his two favourite team members.

"How are you two today?"

"Okay, thanks," came the combined reply. "How are you?"

They all smiled at the way they had both spoken together. "I've got the sniffles, and I feel a bit chilled, to be honest. When I woke up, I felt as if I'd been out in the snow all night. I was frozen—still am a bit."

"What?" asked Monica, startled.

"What's the matter with you?" Maddi asked. "He only said he's got a cold. Monica, you look like you've got ants in your knickers!"

Monica blushed. "If you must know, nosy…my bottom feels sore, as if someone's kicked me!"

It was Mike's turn to show surprise. "What?"

"What's up with you two today? Have you both gone deaf?"

"It's my cold, I think." He coughed. "I'll leave; I don't want to pass it on."

When he was gone, Monica shared her secret in graphic detail with Maddi.

Maddi was thrilled for her.

"I've never had a dream like it," Monica continued. "It was so real, I could almost touch and smell!"

"Lucky you!"

"And when he said that about the snow…well, you can imagine, I nearly died!"

"Well, remember our conversation about him being a bit odd? You know, telepathic and whatnot?" Instantly, Maddi realised she had said the wrong thing. Monica's face darkened, and Maddi knew she was thinking of Tony.

"Well, not with me he's not," snapped Monica. "I'll cut him dead tomorrow, just you wait." Her guard came up as a portcullis comes down—quickly and with a bang. "I knew it; he'll be just the ruddy same in the end!" She began to work, obviously upset.

Maddi understood and regretted her comment. She decided that silence was the best tack, and she began work, too.

As she looked up over her screen, she let out a yell. "Oh, my God…it's there again!"

For about the fourth time that week, a magpie flew away from their window ledge. "We'll have to get something done about those; I don't like the evil-looking things."

Mike stood in the corridor, slightly dazed, commenting to himself, "A sore bottom, eh? Bloody hell! "

"Who has?" said June, plodding past, grinning. *I bet he's got piles, poor sod*, she thought as she carried on.

Back in the mind fortress, Debbie and Sean were deep in discussion. Debbie was giving her account. "Something wasn't right in that mind. I don't know about helping; it looked as if it would harm him, to me."

"Why? And be exact."

"Well, at first I hoped—uselessly of course—that there might be another keeper or two. There wasn't, but it felt as if someone had been there, I could sense it. It wasn't private; something had been before me. Her mind felt like a burgled drawer. You know what I mean, don't you? All disturbed and left untidy."

"Go on."

"Her mind is very organised, and I should say it was very pretty at one time—everything is in little ceramic cottages, all with their doors labelled up like ours. But some…well, they were damaged. No, not so much damaged as vandalised, if you get my drift. I think some of the damage was done by her, to cottages like *love* and *trust* and *faith*—they were boarded up as if in a great anger. But other places, and gardens, and lanes, they were broken, as if a gang of hooligans had gone on the rampage!"

"Hmm, this is interesting, and worrying. You've done an excellent job, Debbie. Well done, exceptionally well done."

Debbie left to let Sean think. She was tired and exhilarated at the same time. She felt good, too; praise from Sean was always nice.

Christine was at home, taking a lieu day from the extra flexitime she had worked. She was hanging out her washing when she heard a little tinkle behind her. She looked to the ground and saw what looked like a rolled up piece of silver paper. Had someone just thrown it at her? She glanced all around but saw nobody—just a magpie on the rooftop, so she saluted. She bent down to examine the object. "That's not silver paper; it looks like a little egg. Oh my, it's beautiful." She picked it up, then immediately dropped it. "Ouch!" She squealed, as the needles went through her skin

The magpie flew away.

She went to wash her finger and put the trinket away at the back of a drawer in the kitchen, already forgetting where it had come from.

That same day after work, Mike was driving home, singing along to the radio. A huge magpie dipped as it flew alongside and looked at him. It was flying incredibly fast. He was sure it was staring at him. He looked back at it, the same intense stare that Eric knew so well. Losing its courage instantly, the bird changed direction. Mike smiled in satisfaction. He'd never really liked magpies; they seemed evil to him.

Two black, cold, shadowy beings were discussing him. "This Mike, he's strong."

"Yes, he is, and good, too."

"Yes, but don't forget his weakness."

"Sex?"

"Sex, yes. It's as simple as that; he should have learnt to control it, to rise above the sex chakra, but it's obvious he hasn't. It's his Achilles' heel, and Tony knows it. If he uses Christine wisely, she could be the key to Mike's downfall. Tony could get her to tempt Mike into failure."

"You're right, he'll not resist much; sex is moving towards him like sharks around a bleeding man. It's coming from all sides. What a way to go—he should feel privileged!"

The other grinned and sharpened his blade.

That night, as Rosie fell into her slumber, Mike sat in bed writing his multi-coloured diary. In a way, all that had happened had helped tune his mind to her needs. He always wanted Rosie to go to sleep first after her ordeal; the thought of her lying awake whilst he slept upset him, so in the early days, he forced himself to lay awake thinking, developing what he had learnt from his books and classes.

He wrote about his guilt, his frustrations, his thoughts and temptations, and slowly he began to contemplate the intricacy of his own mind, and its keepers. There must have been a long list of criteria and rules to it all. He was glad of his independence from them, and at the same time, glad of their residence. He could never imagine life without them. *Do they know what I'm thinking right now?* he wondered. *Is it me thinking, or them?* A man could go mad working it all out.

* * *

Kingdom of Runa, 653

Hilda's eyes widened as another shower of sparks, resulting from another blast of the bellows, spiralled into the fabricated chimney. The blacksmith was huge, even by Runaric standards, and he knew his craft better than any other. Both shield and helm were materialising beneath his efforts, each week's work rewarded by the flaxen-haired beauty by his side.

She cackled as she mixed his next hallucinogenic drink in the wooden goblet, she enjoyed the role of the "flaxen haired beauty" it created, and eagerly looked forward to his next re-ward. She knew that all the women in the kingdom would love to handle his manhood. The rumours of him being hung like a sled-hammer shaft were true, but alas he possessed no finesse and was only capable of a steady, rhythmic stroke, like his hammer blows.

The carbon content of the metal had to be perfect: the eutectic temperatures for normalising and annealing were to be exact, but soon the absolutely critical temperature of hardening would be needed, and this skill was kept a secret of the blacksmith guild. Soon clouds of steam from the brine would hiss into the air, spitting angrily, followed by the tempering to blue and purple in the whale oil, where foul-smelling flames would lick the rim of the flue.

Then her task would really begin: the careful engraving by diamond, to two exact depths, either to reveal gold or red, in the form of the Runic symbols of the spiritual warrior.

He looked at her again, grinning between the blows as he paused to drink the energy-giving liquid she told him would hone his senses and skills. A grin revealed paper-white teeth in his scorched, leathery face. Sweat ran down his muscles, following the prominent lines of his veins like small carts following a track, until the sweat fell into the forge and became an acrid vapour in the coal's hot gasses.

She would have to make her journey again soon, but she pushed the thought to the back of her mind as she looked over to her hide-covered bed, lit by the orange glow. She then looked at the refracted grain of the smooth wooden goblet, as the liquid swayed inside. The rhythm made her think of her impending reward. The blacksmith thought the hungry look above those magnificent, upturned breasts was for him, and he beat harder and harder to impress her. Hilda knew better; the look wasn't for him! It was in anticipation of the prophesied one.

CHAPTER 8

Since her threat of bringing him down a peg or two, Monica's and Mike's paths hardly crossed. He felt a little rejected, but work was particularly busy right now, which lessened the impact.

Temptation soon raised its head again, in the form of an ambitious blonde one Saturday morning. He was in Bakewell, another small town in the Peak District. He had been to the library and was pleased with the two books he now had under his arm: one on the history of Chinese magic, and another on board/role-playing games creation, another little pastime of his. His route back to the car park took him by the market. He was looking at a stall selling postcards, wondering if he could add any to his collection of Victorian and Edwardian "glamour" photographs. A voice broke his concentration.

"Hello, there."

He turned towards the voice and saw Christine at the next stall. She stood with an old dress held up in front of her.

"Hiya," Mike greeted her. Gesturing to the dress, he added, "It'll suit you."

He quickly closed the album of semi-naked Victorian maids.

"Not like this it won't! But you wait until I'm done with it. It's a hobby of mine; I get old, good quality clothes, alter a few things, then tart 'em up with new buttons and some embroidery, and just like you…hey, presto! I do a bit of magic on them. You can get some really good labels, and once they are cleaned up, you've got something worth close to a hundred pounds sometimes!"

"How fascinating. If I was a woman, I think I'd like to do that. I'm impressed, Christine; you're very clever."

"Oh, not really. It all stems from when I was a student and couldn't afford many clothes, just another case of invention being born from necessity! It's just carried on from there. It is very interesting, though, you end up reading books on styles from different periods and all sorts of things. I love to watch old films, and I study all their clothes. Some of the old American gowns from the twenties, oh boy, I'd kill for them." She was very animated and obviously enjoyed talking about the subject. "What are you up to?"

"Oh, just picking up some reading." Mike held the books up.

She looked at the titles and frowned. "Oh, how interesting. I'll ask you again: what are you up to?"

It was chilly and had begun to drizzle. Christine rubbed her hands together. "Brrr, I'm going for a coffee. Want to join me?"

He accepted the invitation. She did look radiant this morning: the chill had bought out a rosy glow in her face, which enhanced her pale grey eyes. Together, they walked through the narrow, cobbled streets of the old part of town.

The coffee shop Christine selected was delightful, renovated from an old post office. They got the upstairs window seat, overlooking the busy walkway below. Mike ordered homemade scones and jam and pulled out Christine's seat. They had hardly stopped talking; she was very easy to get on with. Christine pointed to the book on game development. "What are you doing? Improving your strategy at chess or backgammon?"

"Ha! No improvement needed, thank you."

"What, then?"

"Well it's…er, it's…" Mike blushed a little.

"Oh God, spit it out!"

"What, the scone? Can't do that, it's much too nice!"

"Now, don't go changing the subject. I'm intrigued!"

"Well, I'm inventing a game, on and off. I've been doing it for ages, and someone said something to me the other day that rekindled my interest."

The dark observers were waiting for this, and knew it was Tony at work.

Christine was genuinely enthralled; she'd never met a game creator before. What an interesting man—he was into so many things!

Mike let her draw information from him bit by bit. He let her work out that the game was a sexy one, and that he felt embarrassed to say too much just then. "I'd love to talk longer Christine, this has been one of the most delightful chats over a coffee I have ever had. Unfortunately, I have to visit a sick relative this afternoon and I ought to get moving." He smiled a warm friendly smile and held her gaze a while.

She felt his attraction and thought that with a little work, this stepping-stone to promotion could be a very pleasant one. "If you do finish the game as soon as you said you might, and you want to try it out, ask me. I'd love to play; I like fun and games!"

Mike was speechless for a few seconds. He wanted to play, too, and with her would be more than acceptable, gathering his composure he replied to her request, tantalisingly, "Now be careful Christine; I might very well take you up on that offer!"

The dark observers leered; the honing stopped briefly. Sneering, the sharpener said, "We were right: I think he's just taken his first step towards his downfall—another lamb sacrificially slaughtered for sex!"

Christine watched through the window as Mike walked away. She'd changed since the long-forgotten prick on her finger. She knew that what had just happened was going to be good for her. How lucky that they should meet by chance like that. This man was going to be more than a step towards promotion, her intuition told her; and that old book she'd found in that stall the other day, about positive thinking and how to succeed, that had been lucky, too. *Isn't life amazing sometimes?* she mused.

Everything seems to come at once, almost as if some unseen hands place things in front of you!

The voice in her head answered, "Yes, dear."

A week later, after much work on the game, Mike was at his desk writing a memo. The busy work period had subsided, and Christine's review was coming up in a few minutes. He was ready for her. A knock sounded on the door. "Come in."

"Hello, Mr. Reeves."

"Hello, Miss Lock. How are you today?"

"Okay, thanks."

"Let's sit over here, shall we?" He directed her with a wave of his hand to two black leather seats, arranged next to the floor-to-ceiling windows, with the vertical blinds half open. A small, circular coffee table with matching chrome legs separated them. "No formalities, eh? Let's relax and get the work out of the way; then we can have a chat. There's no bad news; all the feedback has been very positive. I don't want to make you big-headed, but you are really good at your job, do you know that?"

"Well, I like to think so. I try hard. Thank you, Mike."

"No need for thanks. I like to praise where appropriate, and you deserve it. Well done!

"So, treat this as an official pat on the back. Your work rate and effort have been noticed, and not just by me, so all I want to do is to get it in writing. As for your next targets, I'm sure we'll come up with something achievable."

She smiled warmly and crossed her legs. "Thank you, Mike. I'm flattered."

Mike smiled his friendliest smile. "Coffee?"

"Mmm, please. I was quite nervous about this, you know, but not now…I'm enjoying myself. I like pats on the…er, well, anywhere really, but the back is fine!" She laughed, and crossed her legs again.

Mike swallowed, and staring down as he wrote, he diverted his stare to her legs; she couldn't see where he was looking with his head bowed. He wrote and asked the necessary questions.

The interview went well, and Christine lapped his thickly spread praise up like a hungry puppy. As he sealed up the final envelope for the personnel file, he gulped, took a deep breath, and offered her a different envelope. He said, "You are in no rush, are you? Er…read this."

"No, I'm in no rush at all. Huh, I'd stop here all day if I could."

"Oh, good. Another coffee?"

"Mmm, yes please."

She opened a small brown envelope and read.

Dear Christine,

By now you will have had what I consider to be the best appraisal I've had the privilege of giving—well done! It's nice to have competent, trustworthy staff, especially when they look so good!!

I hope you don't mind my forwardness; a compliment never hurt anyone. Please read this.

Mike.

She looked up and saw he was sat with a bigger envelope. She took it.

Dear Christine,

I have already said how much I value your work, and I've probably said that you deserve lots of praise. But what I really want to say is that I find you warm, intelligent, and—please don't be angry about my directness—sexy!

If at this stage you are angry at my directness and lack of professionalism, please don't smack me too hard!!

If you recall our conversation over coffee, you offered to try my game. Well, it's finished. Would you be my guinea pig, then?

If not, and you only said this in jest, please accept my deepest apologies. I will forget this and continue with a purely professional relationship. But if you accept, then open the envelope you now see before you on the table.

Mike Reeves.

Please don't smack me too hard! thought Tony. *Smack you? Somebody ought to knock your teeth down your throat, you smart-arsed, jumped-up managerial fuckin' shit-faced bastard.* In his flat, he stood up from the ball he was gazing into and threw a glass he'd been drinking out of against the wall. *How can Monica be attracted to this pillock? He talks like a fuckin' woman.*

Mike slid another envelope gingerly towards her.

Christine crossed her legs again and slid down the chair an inch or two to make her beige skirt rise up, smiled, raised her eyebrows, and took the envelope off the table. She put her little finger into one edge and ripped it open slowly.

Hell's bells, she's going for it! Mike felt his blood pressure rise in anticipation. On the outside, he looked calm and in control, whilst inwardly he thought, *Yes, yes, yessss!*

A candle glowed like a firework for a few seconds, and then began to burn slow and bright.

Two black, satisfied observers smiled, then turned to each other. "Round one to Temptation, I think. Do you agree?" one said.

"Oh, most definitely, yes. I knew our champion would come for an early knockout; he's almost won already, I think."

"We'll see," said the first, and if his skull still had hair, he would have tested the blade's sharpness with it. Instead he steadily began to hone; he was sure it was a little blunt somewhere: those necks had a terrible habit of taking the edge off.

Christine, feeling decidedly moist, began to read excitedly, whilst she, too, showed a calm exterior.

The name of the game is TROPHIES. Use your imagination, and allow for the game being set in a society with low morals, and a high fun level.

In the game, pretend "Mr. X" (me!), is tall, dark, and handsome: quite sexy, and not too old!

Mr. X is an advertising man in an international clothing company, specialising in ladies' attire, especially lingerie. He has recently been involved in the launch of a high-quality, high-cut brand of silk knickers with matching sets of lingerie. His TV adverts have won numerous awards, with a cult male following, leading to him being "head hunted" by other advertising companies.

Miss Lock, his private secretary, has been an invaluable help to him. She is extremely curvaceous, beautiful, and sexy. She adores him, but hasn't the courage to say so.

In an attempt to keep him happy, and to encourage him to stay at the company, they are both chosen as "International Employees of the Year." As a reward, they have been chosen to spearhead the "New European Launch," an exciting new line based on exotic places. They must go on a business trip to visit them all.

Although the NEL will involve some work attending seminars and conferences, much time will be allowed for shopping and sightseeing, interspersed with stops at luxury hotels. Single rooms have been booked, along with many tickets for trips/outings. Travel will be by many modes, such as train, plane, and horse and carriage...all expenses paid, of course.

After their award ceremony at the London Hilton, both sit discussing their future trip, how well they have done, and how well they have been rewarded. The other guests have almost all gone; it is early in the morning, and they've drunk many glasses of wine. The corner they sit in is now a secluded haven; neither wants to leave the other, and the night is deliciously going on and on. The conversation somehow winds its way to the products, and Mr. X asks a question he's been dying to ask for months: "Do you wear them?"

"Ahhh, now then! That's for me to know, and you to find out!"

"Okay, then I accept your challenge. I will find out."

She looks suspiciously into his eyes. "How?"

"Err...well, if I get to glimpse your underwear, by any means I can muster, within reason, of course, then at night, in my hotel room, you have to ring me and describe them in the greatest detail."

"Oooh, Mr. X...I'm shocked!"

"Ah, my dear, that's only the start."

"Mmmm? Tell me more."

*"If I get them to reveal your bottom in some way—by creat-*ing a little private accident or whatever, then you have to ring *me and tell me how you put them on, or take them off, and an-*swer three questions I ask, about anything. If you don't answer truly, you pay a forfeit."

Liberated by the wine, and set free from the chains of teth-ered desire, she accepts eagerly. The trip is going to prove a most interesting one, she hopes. "Go on, then, I think I can handle that. But how do I win? What if you don't succeed by the end of the trip?"

"Oh...er...yes, well, er...I know. You don't have to ring, but instead I'll take you out to lunch, and buy you a pair, or another item of your choice."

"Go on then; the game's on, as they say!"

"Thank God for wine, eh?" he laughs.

"I'll drink to that!" she replies.

Accompanying this little story was a set of rules, game-play scenarios, and charts to fill in, allowing so many words a move. All made up on a graphics package on his home computer, it was quite wonderful, and looked extremely professional. He had sat watching Christine read and change position, captivated by concentrated interest. He felt a spellbinding fascination. An in-tense, beautiful feeling, which he could almost taste, centred be-tween his shoulder blades. He had felt this many times in life, his first memory of it being when he watched a cobbler mend his shoes as a child.

Life's journey had moved into another lane, guilt had taken a back seat, the driver's name was Temptation, and the accelerator was slowly being increased.

"Well?"

"It's an interesting idea...ahem. Er, would you expect me to play for the same prizes? Er, Mr. Ree-Mike?"

"Always call me Mike, Christine, except when we are on show. Yes, I'd like to. I'd like to very much, actually." He crossed his legs to hide a growing physical embarrassment.

Christine enjoyed the powerful moment of making him wait. She crossed her legs yet again, pulled the hem of her skirt down, smoothed the material over her thighs, straightened her back, and took a deep breath. "What was it she said? Er…game on!"

She smiled, then added, "It looks a little complicated at first glance, like most new games and things do. I'll read it carefully and get back to you. How do we make the moves, and how often? And…where?"

"Already sorted," Mike said. "Once a week, or sooner, but no longer or a penalty is paid. You use all the sheets I've made, and pop them in the internal mail."

"A bit risky!"

"Yeah! Good, isn't it?"

"Yes, it makes it more exciting!" Without blinking, she used one of the most powerful weapons in her armoury: a steady, lusty gaze. "What are you thinking, Mike?"

Mike coughed. "Er…ahem. Er…I'm thinking…er." His voice came out embarrassingly high.

"What? Don't be shy now. You've started all this!"

Deeper in tone, his response still found difficulty. "I'm, er…"

"You're wondering how far I'll go, and what I'm wearing under here." She pointed to her breasts and traced lines down her body to her thighs. "Aren't you?"

Gulp. "Yes…yes, I am."

"What would you say if I said I didn't wear knickers?"

"Wow!"

"What if I said, no knickers, just basque, and suspenders, all red."

"Wow…wow?"

She laughed, and picked up all the sheets and envelopes.

"Aren't you? No, I mean, are you? No, hold on, I mean…er, bloody hell, I don't know what I mean!"

"Like the game, Mike…you'll have to find out, won't you?"

Oh shit, what have I started? She's a vamp! flashed across his mind as he stood, stupefied.

She reached across and held his tie, straightened it, and then slowly pulled him towards her, kissing him. A beautiful, soft, tender, lasting…kiss. "I know what you are thinking better than you do!"

"Do you?"

"Yes, do you mind?" came the seductive reply.

"No, not at all."

"Can I read your dirty little mind whenever I please, then?" she said between kisses.

"Yes, feel free, any time you like!"

A long way away, behind thick, closed curtains, sat Tony, alone except for Sabre. He was looking into the crystal ball cradled in Monica Doll's outstretched arms, drops of perspiration falling from the end of his nose. He could see his chance getting closer and closer; he felt like he was just managing to hold onto something very precious between two outstretched fingers. When Christine had said the last words, Tony's eyes had widened, and spit ran down his chin. "Got you, you stupid, fuckin' imbecile; you walked into my trap like a child. I can come into your mind, now, and just you wait 'til you see what I bring. Ha-ha!"

His sweaty back slapped into the rear of the leather chair as he punched the air in triumph. "You are in for such a shock! Oh yes, Mr. Mike fuckin' Reeves, Mr. smart-arse fuckin' boss man Reeves, this is a Pandora's box you've just opened, like you never thought possible. Ha! You've just written and signed your own death warrant! And me? Ha! ME! Let me tell you who *I* am." His teeth rattled like a machine gun around the edge of his nail. "ME? I'm the executioner, pal! Oh, yes, and I'm very very happy at my work! Nobody, and I mean *NOBODY*, is going to have my Monica." His eyes bulged in fury. Sabre retreated to a safe spot, quivering.

Christine left Mike's office and walked back to hers. "Well, life's full of surprises. One day I bump into Monica's old flame and he asks me for a drink, and the next thing I know, Mike comes on strong. Ain't life peachy!" She strutted down the corridor, her high heels clicking, feeling quite wonderful and decidedly sexy.

Tony stood up and walked over to his workbench in his favourite room, looking around. His little private collection stared back: artefacts, books, various jars and apparatus, all in their correct places, and labelled accordingly. He wiped and replaced the crystal ball in its cradle. Talking to Monica Doll as he carried her, he said, "I'm going to get to Daath, you know, one day, but I've got to squash that bastard first. How shall I do it? What would be a dramatic, most excellent way, hm? What shall I send to his mind?" Anger began to well up inside him as he thought of the contact Mike was having with Monica; tooth and nail clicked again. "Inspiration, Monica, give me inspiration." He placed her before him.

The dark observers looked at each other; he was coming along nicely. Monica Doll's eyes moved towards the bookcase, and her delicate china arm moved slowly, its little pink forefinger pointing to THE book.

He stroked her hair and smiled as he rubbed her bottom. "The book? Okay, dear, I'll try again."

Slowly, he walked over to his library, his finger drumming against random books as he did so. Where had it hidden itself this time? The green volume beckoned him to its position, at groin height on the third shelf. His finger stopped drumming and rested upon it. A small convulsion went up his arm, and he stood to stare at it a few seconds before he withdrew it. Then he struggled back to his lectern, something he had done many times, but to no avail; up to now, the book's secrets remained hidden.

He stood looking at it, a hand gripped at each side of the lectern, Monica Doll at its base. He knew not where the words came from, but instead of asking, he demanded: "Give me inspiration! I demand it in the name of Daath, and all the black sorcery it holds."

A mist, pale blue and white like a blind man's eyes, covered the floor and began to lick up in wisps, like cold flames. It moved in a circle around his feet, winding up slowly, coiling upwards over the lectern leg. Like fingers, it crept slowly over his hands and into the book, until it all disappeared from view. Silence descended like a shroud. This was what he had waited for. Nervously, he opened the book to its last pages, which up until now had been blank. His eyes widened, then glowed as if someone was shining a small torch upon them. "I've...I've never...I..." He ran his finger down the index and turned over the pages, as secret upon secret were listed before him, mystery upon mystery beckoning to be solved, riddles and puzzles as old as time itself begging to be answered—all he had to do was look. But...he couldn't, his finger was not his own right now.... It began to slow as it went through the *k's* and *l's* and onto the *m's*, where jerkily it passed the *ma's* and *mb's* and through to the *mi's* where it slowed to a snail's pace, and came to rest on...

MIND WARRIORS—Page 895

The index disappeared.

A blinding flash of blue lit the room like a bolt of lightning from the gods.

For a few seconds, he saw nothing, but when he opened his eyes, he was staring at page 895. An illuminated manuscript, so beautiful it earned his reverence, met his gaze. He was the first person to see this since the devil knew when, and like silverfish running for cover from a bright light, black lines like sperm slithered across the page to form words.

From his research, Tony knew that the greatest warlocks, wizards, and sorcerers of the black arts had written the words aeons ago. They had left this plane to inhabit Daath, waiting for people like him to be guided to the book and unlock its words.

A voice as old as the gods spoke to him from within his brain, silky smooth. "You have the inspiration you asked for, and if you proceed as you have done, it will be offered freely. But beware of failure; it is not tolerated. Have faith, go with your feelings. We have been watching you for many, many cycles. Get quill and parchment and write what you see here. When you eventually get to Daath, take something your most hated enemy desires and needs more than anything. This will be your entrance key, a gift for death to use as it desires."

Frightened that when he returned it may be gone, Tony ran to his bureau and came back with his bottle of black calligraphic ink, a quill, and a sheet of his special parchment–made by himself from young, female skin, and specially dried in sickeningly sweet-smelling magic herbs. He unrolled it and weighed it down with child's-skull paperweights. He began to write, quickly.

* * *

Kingdom of the Sun, 17-6401

Like some mad creation on a canvas, the world continued its meticulous, colourful life.

Clipping his Bonsai tree number sixty-nine to the shape it demanded, Chi Lin thought once more of his major task. He stood back and looked at his work, turned the bowl around through 360 degrees, and nodded satisfaction as he placed the secateurs on the marble worktop. He had thought about the next stages long enough. It was time for an answer to one of the many questions.

He straightened his silk purple gown and smoothed out the yellow dragons that showed his high rank. He spun to face the door and clapped three times. It echoed.

The geishas entered in short, quick steps, hands clasped before them and heads bowed. All five formed a line in front of him, not daring to raise their heads. This was their last test; they had been concentrating on their chosen word. None of their feet were bound now—it had been outlawed years ago, but their movement in magic temples had to be as if they were; etiquette demanded it to be so.

The tops of their shiny, smooth black heads seemed like jet against the pastel-shaded walls, decorated with birds of paradise and flowers. Chi Lin waited for a few seconds, and then spoke. "You are each allowed only one word."

Like a black wave in a sea of lacquered hair, they nodded in turn from left to right.

"Say the name of a bird, each in turn." As he spoke, he let a folded piece of paper drop on the floor before them. They all took a sharp breath at its sight. This simple piece of paper held their future, or failure. Whoever got it right would have the other four as slaves until her death.

They watched his feet.

He clicked his heels as if in response to a military command, so quick they hardly saw his feet move. It echoed. "Begin!"

"Stork."

"Cormorant."

"Shag."

"Eagle."

"Peacock."

Another echoed click of his heels vibrated around the room. All eyes went to the paper.

It crackled.

It rocked back and forth.

It gently unfolded, once, twice, thrice…to reveal a word, a single word: Peacock.

Four distraught, despondent geishas ran from the room, screaming and wailing. Failure after so much work was devastating. One proud girl of sixteen, a virgin now named Peacock, slowly raised her head to stare into the eyes of Chi Lin. A broad grin lit her face—a beautiful, pure white-powdered face with emerald-green eyes—; she stared at him like a pumpkin on Halloween.

He bowed.

She bowed, turned, and left to go to the rooms of learning. Her new life had begun.

Chi Lin resumed his clipping; the wind chimes played a merry tune.

Peacock looked around her luxurious room and lit some candles. She slid the door shut and searched for the book she wanted, curious, and excited. She found the rose-pink book on a pile of what must have been seven hundred others. They must have known she'd want this one first. She sat cross-legged and wide eyed as she looked eagerly at the illustrations—so many ways to lose her chastity, so many positions, so many games! She fell to her back as she saw picture after picture. "This one, I think, no…this one." She put the book down and looked at the ceiling. Surprised, she saw it was one huge mirror. She lifted her robe to reveal her nakedness, and as she watched herself masturbate, she smiled. The reflection smiled back and said, "It won't be too long; he'll be on his way, when you are ready!"

CHAPTER 9

Maddi was in bed, flat on her back with a pencil and notepad, writing. She did it to relax. At the side of her bed was a cardboard filing box, all neatly sorted into categories, ranging from poetry to observations on life. She let the notepad rest on her tummy, put the pencil between her teeth, and let her mind wander. It came to rest on Monica and Mike. *What is she playing at?* she wondered. *I think all he wants is a friend to confide in, but all she seems to see is someone wanting his evil way with her. No matter what I say, it makes no difference. You've got a lot to answer for, Tony. You've spoilt a beautiful person, one who I'm going to help mend.*

She rolled onto one side restlessly, then onto the other, then returned to her back. She dropped the pencil and paper into the box and continued to sort things out in her mind as she watched the breeze from the open bedroom window make the frills around the lilac light shade do a sort of Mexican wave. *Andrew's not the same, not as interesting as I thought and always asking those questions; neither was Jim. I wonder how curious Mike is about me? Now there is a stimulating man.*

He was still basically the same old Mike the spirit had observed all those months ago: a loyal husband, who would stick by his injured wife come what may. His career ambitions were for her, really. He had built strong foundations for the rest of

110

their life, with a good salary and secure, prestigious job. He was still giving it everything, but now that all his systems were in place and ticking over, he had the time for his diversions. His hobbies, especially the spiritual, fulfilled his personal ambitions more and more, taking him away from the stresses and strains of modern living, whilst Eric still popped up at regular intervals for amusing detours from the norm. Sean was guiding him for what he knew would be an exciting future, revealed bit by bit to ensure steady progression and to keep his interest paramount. Debbie fulfilled his deepest-rooted needs as much as she could, a role Sean recognised as absolutely crucial, the foundations upon which everything else was built. He knew that if this area was okay, then the rest would run smoothly.

But the delicate balance of this existence, like the balance of chemicals and functioning organs of the human body, had begun to crack. Similar to the first undetectable cracks of metal fatigue, they were unseen, almost invisible. But like a cancer growing in the body, the unrest caused by the interference of Tony and the dark side was beginning to spread. This strong, dependable man had succumbed to temptation, and like a drug addict who shields the truth from himself, he was becoming more and more drawn into his new habit.

The dark side attacked like the sea against human-built defences, unrepentant and unceasing, probing and deepening the cracks. The weapons of Monica and Christine were as powerful as an atom bomb, but more subtle than any invisible gas. If they could get his job to crumble, along with his marriage, then his skills in the arts, the real target, would crash. The arteries feeding his onward progression, which they feared more than anything, would cease, and his interest would diminish, as failure upon failure would ensue. One of the few obstacles in Tony's way would be destroyed. Still, they tried to interfere as little as possible. They needed to see Tony succeed by himself.

But the white hands still played their part, undetected by any device of Daath. Seeds had been sown which would grow into towering plants; they looked from afar, and rested safe in the knowledge that their choice was excellent. Patience was called for, that was all. They were willing for these challenges to take place: a stronger will would result; a warrior would rise, all in good time.

Monica's mind was in a turmoil. One day it wanted to give him a go, another day it demanded, *Who does he think he is?* But why did these thoughts of Tony keep coming into her mind? Was it her, or was it him? She knew his power, and she was terrified of it; he must never be allowed back into her life. But why did she keep having these thoughts of how nice he used to be? Why did she keep wondering if he could have changed?

Another ambitious mind was also confused. Tony was dangerous, and he was once Monica's. Both thoughts elated her. In some way, she thought she was being used by him, probably to make the stuck-up snob jealous, and that was okay by her. The thought of playing with fire was inviting, and he was much kinder than she had said he was. And Mike, now that was a surprise! Or was it? She'd had an idea he liked her before her interview, and she was flattered. She got the rules out again and read them through. Each time the play was more obvious; this could be quite a sensuous little game he'd made up. She read his little story again, too, and laughed as she reached its conclusion. "Hmmm, a knickers and bottom man, is he? Makes a change from boobs and legs."

The game had been meticulously thought out and prepared, with details of every venue, each with its own curious details, tantalisingly giving clues to the adventure ahead—spiral staircases, boat trips, mirrored ballrooms. Most intriguing. There were even details about what styles she should wear for each occasion—usually short-skirted suits and the like. Evidently, he'd loaded a few dice. But the weather variations, why put them down? Even humidity was in there somewhere. *Some trap, no doubt,* she thought. *Huh, he's put some work into it, like he does in his job; I don't know how he finds the time.*

Then another thought hit her: money. If she was to be his guinea pig, and this game took off, she ought to have some royalties. *Hmm, no less than thirty percent here, my girl.* Then her mind saw an image, and she laughed out loud. *I can just imag-*

ine what he'll be doing if I lose, and I have to describe my knickers over the phone!

Mike was writing in his diary, feeling decidedly smug. Two women in his life! Three, counting Rosie. He felt the need to justify his actions to himself, and he wrote them down: *I've been a saint, a stalwart. I've stood by her and done my duty; she deserves it, too. This is a bit like a safety valve, a release. I could do a lot worse, like go to a prostitute. But I've resisted temptation where other men would have failed. I need something; it's not too much too ask. After all, what is it? Flirting with one and a sexy little game with another, they're only friends, it's a modern world, what harm can come from it? In fact, it's probably causing little harm and doing a lot of good—it's keeping me on the straight and narrow. This keeps my basic needs attended to—like Debbie!—and helps me go through life being a good man. Actually, I deserve a pat on the back. And if this game gets mass-produced, I could end up helping thousands, and saving countless marriages by stopping men from straying.*

Dark observers scoffed at his attempt to justify. "That's it, keep digging your little hole. Soon it'll be big enough to fall in!"

So as usual, the world spun on its axis through the cosmos, like life blundering on regardless of what was ahead. People's paths joined and left each other; actions of one unwittingly affected others; millions of stories started and ended, hopes and aspirations being granted or dashed. Fate was even now decreeing that some lives were to become forever tangled, more complicated, more happy or sad.

Mike stopped writing, turned off the light, and rested his head on his arm to look at Rosie. She was breathing slowly and steadily. He covered her shoulder with the duvet, kissed her gently on the head, and settled down for his trip. He had a slightly different idea tonight, and he hoped Debbie would be happy with it. The platform loomed out of the mist, and the welcome glow of the torches lit it. He felt happy. No sooner had his feet touched it than the curtains parted to reveal Debbie, dressed in

pale lilac underwear. Sean stood behind, looking over her adoringly.

"Hello, you two."

"Hello."

"Hiya."

"Debbie, you look beautiful, as always—and don't take any
offence whatsoever—but would you do something for me?"

"Yes, of course. What?"

"Go and put your emerald-green dress on, the silk one with
the Chinese-style collar I like so much. Tonight, I'd just like to
sit on the balcony with you, and talk as we watch the clouds
swirl."

"What, no...action?"

"No, not tonight." He saw the little colour she had drain
from her face. "Aww, don't look like that, sweetheart. You haven't disappointed me or anything—just the opposite, in fact. I
want you to understand that it's you I love, not the sex, *you*, and
I don't want you to feel taken for granted. I want you to understand that it's a universe more than sex."

"Oh, I see. Er, thanks...thanks a lot." She ran towards him
and kissed him on the cheek, and then, like a will o' the wisp,
she left. But as she ran away, tears filled her eyes. What he had
just said to her was exactly what she had wanted to hear.

Sean loomed out of the background, and Mike turned to face
him. "Oh, dear Sean, sometimes..."

"I know, you don't have to say it; if she was out there, etc.,
etc."

"Yes."

"I don't think I could build a room big enough to house the
candle, or a table strong enough to hold the jewel!" He smiled
comfortingly at Mike. "Don't worry, she feels exactly the
same—in fact, worse if anything. These tours of duty for us
aren't as easy as they may appear to you, you know."

"I guess not." He thought about the jewels.

They walked to the room of choice, and before he knew it,
he stood, seemingly dazed, staring at them. Again, their beauty
stunned him: one attracted but seemed detached; one felt as if it

moved towards him, beckoning him to pick it up; whilst another revealed its prior unseen beauty, very appealingly.

Sean studied him, followed the direction of his stare, and smiled.

"Why have I got to choose one?"

Sean was pleased with his lack of recollection of previous visits. "You've asked me that before, actually, and again, I have to tell you that although things are clearer, I don't yet fully understand myself. But I'll tell you when I need to, all in good time."

"Mmm, okay." His thoughts began to sharpen as he walked back down the corridor. "Where have I? What...? " Then his thought focused on Debbie. "Oh, yes, of course." And before he knew it, he was on the balcony at a candlelit table for two, in the warm evening air. Summer stars were in the sky, overlooking a swirling mist of purple, blue, and yellow.

Their eyes met and held.

"Hello, sweetheart. You look radiant, stunning, and very, very beautiful."

If it was possible for Debbie to look coy, she did right at that moment. A feeling rose from the pits of their stomachs, from the bottom of their hearts, and an aching yearning struck in the middle of their backs. Nothing else mattered; that moment was everything—a moment of intense pleasure and love. Their eyes held, and silence drifted over them like a downy blanket.

"God, you are perfect, Debbie." The candles lit her face and highlighted the depth of her eyes: each flicker caught and enhanced a different facet of her beauty. He stared and sank into her adoring look.

"Thank you, Mike; you say lovely things to me. I know it's not just the sex. I've known it for a long time."

Intimacy allowed Mike to say things he had never said before, and time allowed conversations of normal life to take place. Places they had been, things they had done, music, art, and even musings on the very meaning of life. A myriad of emotions were set free to gallop along the plains of love; time passed quickly, and enjoyment was at a pinnacle, whilst the world's strongest emotion sank into an uncharted ocean, discovering new depths at every turn. "This is absolutely perfect, Debbie. Things can't get much better than this; it's just a shame I can't stay here."

"I know." She looked at him in the way Juliet must have looked at Romeo, and asked him to kiss her, which he did.

Sean was watching from behind the curtain; another vast step was taking place. If this was a controlled goodbye instead of the usual ejaculated launch back to his world, then this was a quantum leap in his development. Fists clenched in anticipation, he secretly watched as they said farewell and Mike walked off the balcony to his world and body.

It was hardly worth going back to sleep as he lay staring at the ceiling upon his re-occupancy of his body. So, feeling relaxed, he got up and made some tea, to which a grateful Rosie awoke. They had breakfast and talked a while, and Mike left for work. He settled in his office, read a few documents, and began to daydream of Debbie. A knock on the door disturbed him. "Come in."

"Good morning, Mr. Reeves."

"Hello, Debbie."

"Who?"

"Mmm? Oh, sorry, miles away...hello, June. What have I got today?"

With a raised eyebrow and curious look, June left him to his imaginings and a load of mail, many of which looked like circulars from various media companies. He opened some of it and felt irritated; most of it was nothing but a waste of paper. He stretched, and as the morning seemed to be a quiet one, he went on his rounds a little earlier than usual. After calls at his usual outlets, he saved the best visit until last, subsequently breezing into Monica and Maddi's room. "Hello, you two. How is everything? Okay?"

"Hiya," came the cheerful response from Maddi, but nothing came from Monica's direction—not even a casual look around.

He stared over in Maddi's direction. With a furrowed brow and pursed lips, his expression asked the silent question of what was up. The silent reply was a look to the ceiling and a slightly discernible shrug of the shoulders.

"Monica, can we have a chat, please? Er…in private." Mike ushered her to the door. Without a look in his direction or any comment, she stood and went into the corridor.

Mike broke the silence. "We haven't fallen out, have we?"

"No, that would be impossible, wouldn't it?"

His hopes were raised slightly by the toneless response. "Oh, and why would it?"

"I'd have thought it was obvious, Mr. Reeves. Before you can fall out, you have to be friends, don't you?" At which she turned around and walked back through the office door, which shut with a slam.

He was stunned; what had he done? Why the sudden change? He knew enough about the female mind, he thought, to realise that to pursue the matter would no doubt lead to disaster. He slowly walked back to his office, pondering what had just occurred.

With a sigh, he slumped dejectedly—or more like reject-edly—into his chair. He picked up the few envelopes he had left and opened the next one. As his finger ripped it open, he spun in a full circle in his chair, continuing to wonder, *Mmm, what have I done?* The letter was rubbish, and he spun around once more to throw it into the copper-coloured waste paper basket. *Ting*—a direct hit. He opened the next, slowly pushing himself around in another circle by crossing his feet one over the other. *I'm sure I was getting the right messages; I know I was. Why act like that all of a sudden?* The second missile hit the rim temptingly, then ran around it before dropping in with a metallic *thud*. A thought went through his mind, saying one of those things he hated: a little challenge he knew he'd have to accept, like not standing on any cracked stepping stones as a child, with the imagined result being dire if he did. This time it was, *If you get the next piece of paper in, things will go well; if it misses…watch out.*

Suddenly, the waste paper basket looked decidedly small and far away. He screwed the envelope up in his hand and spun around like he had done a thousand times before to throw it into the air. As if in slow motion, he watched it arc through the air as it rotated on itself. Gracefully it began its downward descent, hitting the rim. It bounced high, rotating over and over to hit the other side, and bounced up again. He swallowed hard, trans-fixed.

"Yesss! You beauty!!"

Uncannily correct as usual, the waste-paper-basket predic-tion came true, almost instantly. He opened the next letter in the pile. He always opened the letters in order, a little ritual he had; it didn't seem right to open them in any other order. It was an internal envelope, and he recognised the writing as Christine's. His eyes almost popped out, as he saw a picture of a lady dressed in lingerie, probably cut from a home shopping cata-logue. Written in big, red letters around the edge were the words, "I'm waiting and ready for the first move, SEXY!"

Yabadabadoo!! he said to himself. He already had plans whirling around his head, so he wrote down the first move. Feel-ing very daring, he walked down to the staff pigeonholes and popped it into the one marked *L.*

At the end of the day, he left work to go for his doctor's ap-pointment; it was like going to see Eric for a pint or two, some-thing to look forward to. This was reflected in the face of the doctor as he arrived. "Hello Mike, come in, I've already got the kettle on, my note book is waiting, and my pen has a new ink refill in it! Sit down, tell me what's happened since your last visit. The voices, how are they keeping? Sorry, silly of me, I mean, the voices, are they still there?"

"Of course they are."

"Yes," nodded the doctor in agreement. "Of course they are."

The latest news was offered and recorded by the doctor.

A few days passed, and he kept a tactful distance from Monica and Maddi's office, hoping that whatever caused the hiccup would go away. Christmas decorations were everywhere now, and the Yuletide cheerfulness had begun to take over. The company Christmas party beckoned. When it arrived, he was into the sixth game move, with Christine proving an adept adversary. As he had hoped, the game was proving to be interesting and naughty. A few little wrinkles were being ironed out as the gameplay was tested, but he thought he might just have a "seller" on his hands.

With Senior Management's permission, everyone left at lunch. The party was held at a high-class country venue, with a very well known local band and disco. A light dusting of snow and a crispness to the air added to the seasonal feeling. Christmas was almost here, a feeling of well-being and benevolence circulated.

Boom, boom, boom. The base echoed around his chest as he danced with a group. The party was packed, and the meal had been excellent. After everyone got over his or her nerves, the dance floor was nicely crowded. He saw Monica and smiled. She returned it with her own small smile.

He saw Christine go past a couple of times, but in her red, sparkling dress, she was in great demand. She did wink at him, saying that her next move was in the post and he'd like it. Merry Christmas!!"

He laughed. Tonight was a night for general frivolity, not one-to-one encounters, so he kept dancing—quite well, too, as one or two nearby ladies commented.

A touch on the shoulder and a shouted, "Hiya!" made him stop and turn around.

"Hello, Maddi. Having a good time?"

"Mmm, not bad, thanks."

"What?"

"NOT BAD, THANKS!"

Mike nodded, thinking, *Christ she looks lovely tonight. I wish Andy wasn't around.* He said, loudly, into her nearest ear, "You dance well, Maddi; I saw you earlier. Did you used to be a professional dancer of some kind, or have you had lots of lessons?"

"NO, I DIDN'T! AND I NEVER HAVE BUT THANKS!"

Mike leaned over again. "Do you like this modern dance music?"

"YES, VERY MUCH. I WISH WE HAD IT WHEN I WAS YOUNGER! I LOVED ALL THE NEW ROMANTIC STUFF BUT THIS IS MUCH BETTER TO DANCE TO I THINK."

"When you were hungry?"

"NEVER MIND!"

The meal, the drinks, and the happy, relaxed atmosphere broke down barriers and encouraged bold conversation, which went on with Maddi shouting and Mike almost at a forty-five-degree angle. "I see you've lashed out on a new dress—or should I say, a new black belt!"

"IT IS A BIT LOW-CUT AND SHORT, ISN'T IT?" Maddi feigned an embarrassed tug on the hemline.

"It's just right, believe me. I wish you'd wear it back-to--front, though!"

Seeing as it had hardly had a back at all, she got his drift and laughed. "CHEEKY!" Then she sniggered as she added, "WITH OR WITHOUT?"

"With or without what?"

"A BRA!"

Mike laughed as he danced; she was funny and so easy to talk to, unlike Monica.

"CAN WE TAKE A BREAK? I DON'T LIKE ALL THIS SHOUTING!"

They walked over to the bar. "Is this better?"

"Yes, thanks. I like the music, but you can't talk around it, can you? And I like talking to you. Would you like a beer or something?"

"Oh, let me." Mike fumbled in his pocket.

"Oh, you are old-fashioned sometimes, Mike. All that finished a few decades ago." She smiled as she opened her purse. Although she hadn't meant to, she could tell she had embarrassed him.

"Okay, I'll have a pint, please—no, a half…bitter."

"There you go again! I can afford it, you know; I probably have more dosh to spare than you. I'll have the same. Over here! Two pints of that, please." She pointed to the beer pump as she shouted to the bar tender.

The obviously smitten barman looked at Maddi obligingly as he walked over to the pump. "Certainly," he said, smiling.

As she leant against the bar and put one foot onto the brass rail, her dress creased up to enhance her curves. *Bloody hell, legs a mile high, she drinks pints, and she's got a body to die for. I think I'm in heaven*, Mike thought.

"Eyyupp!!" A beaming and slightly rocking Eric slapped him on the back. "Havvin' a goood tiyem, then?"

"Yes, thanks Eric, and you?"

"Bloody marvelloush, maytie, just bloody marvellush. I've almost cracked it wi' Katie from finance; she's got tits made by Hovis, mate. I'll tell ya, they rise up in that frock like newly baked bread."

Mike covered his eyes with his hand and shook his head, glancing over at Maddi.

"I think she's ready for buttering and eating, Eric. Look how hungrily she looks at you." Maddi smiled back to him.

"Eeh, tha rayt there, Maddi. Aahm off, see ya." Thinking Maddi couldn't see him, he gave a clenched-fist and raised-forearm sign to Mike as he nodded in her direction. He tried to put his foot on the brass foot rail, but it slid off, his arm sending a bowl of peanuts showering across the bar.

Mike, as usual, found his friend's antics highly amusing, and he laughed as he shook his head. "Sorry about him. He's a lovely man, really—just no self control, that's all."

"Oh, don't worry about that. It's only the beer talking, anyway. I doubt if he could do what he wants to. Here, throw that down your neck; we seem to be behind everyone else."

Mike took a couple of swallows. Now that his flow had been disturbed, he felt a little tongue tied; her beauty and sexuality disturbed him.

Being the experienced woman she was, she spotted the pause and healed it. "Do you know, Mike, I feel a bit sad tonight."

Sympathy cured his momentary lapse. "Awww, why's that, then? You don't deserve to be sad." He looked quite concerned.

"Well, I missed your little magic show earlier, and Janet, Jill, and Theresa were talking in the ladies, and said how good it was."

"Oh, I don't know if I'd call it a show, exactly; it was just a few tricks. Did they really say they were good?"

She smiled to herself as she thought, *Offer to show them to me then, bozo!* "Yes they did say they were good. That's why I'm sad I missed them."

"I'll show you them if you'd like me to."

"Oh, would you? That would be nice. I want the full works, though, no cheap job. They say your patter is as good as your tricks!"

"Who says that?"

"Oh, stop looking for praise! I didn't think you could be so shallow!"

"Shall we go somewhere quieter?"

"Yes, there's a conservatory down there, right on the other side. It's probably out of bounds, but who cares? I've been here before, you see."

On their way, they went past a couple of office juniors who were kissing so strongly that they never even noticed Mike and Maddi walk by. Mike's mind went to Eric and Katie.

They walked into the conservatory, their footsteps seeming extraordinarily loud in the hush. It was quite empty. "Right then, madam: Magic Mike, at your shervice." He cringed slightly as he noticed his slur. He felt carefree and confident—feelings that he could justify with the beer. It was Christmas; he wasn't doing anything wrong, really; everyone gets a kiss at this time of year, and Rosie wouldn't mind. He looked at Maddi's lips: they looked full and soft.

He pointed to a table and pulled a chair out for her.

"Shthankssuu, shir," Maddi replied mockingly.

He smiled and continued, following the lines from his bedroom scenario. "Have you ever made love to a magician, Maddi?"

"No, why?"

"They say it's magic!"

"Ha-ha, very good."

"I've got some tricks to show you; they say I'm quite good with my hands, and I would like to prove it to you."

"Oh, do they, now? I can't wait then, if that's the case."

Christ, he thought, going into his first trick. It was nice and simple, without too much sleight of hand. His hand didn't shake at all. Then he produced a large key, which he made appear to have a mind of its own as it turned over in his palm. The look on Maddi's face made her look like an angelic, fascinated child. He wanted to frame that look. It was the type of look that made him glad he had put the effort into learning magic.

Her intrigue grew with each little deception. "Now, never, ever, play poker with me, Maddi. I'll show you why." He reached into his pocket to produce a pack of cards. He passed them for her to shuffle, which she did. "Now, deal three cards each, to me first." They picked up their hands and moved to the sofa nearby to play.

Maddi sat at one end and Mike at the other. She held the cards in a fan before her, staring over the top of them.

"Would you bet on them?"

"Yes, yes I would." She laid them down before her: three Jacks.

"They wouldn't beat these!" He placed three aces on top of her cards.

"How...God, how? How did you...? Mmm, yes, you're right: I'll not play poker with you, not any kind, I think!"

"I bet you'd like me to show you how I did them."

"Oh yes, please."

"Well, I can't, really. You see, the magician who showed them to me said it's bad luck to show them more than three times, and over the years I've shown them twice. But for you—just for you!—I might, at the right price."

"Oh, yes? And what's the asking price, eh?"

"A kiss, for one." He looked deeply into her eyes, then down to her lips, then slowly back to her eyes. "But if you want more, then we've gone full circle—a magician's circle, I suppose."

"Sorry?" said Maddi, slightly confused and thoroughly captivated.

Well…have you…have you ever made love to a magician?" He looked at her eyes again, wishing for a kiss.

It was granted. "Come here." Sweeping the cards to the floor, she put her arms around him and kissed him. Far from a Christmas peck, this was a full-blooded, passionate kiss. Her touch exploded into his mouth.

Mike's arousal leapt as he felt real female contact—the first in years. She was "merry," and so was he. Reason fell from his mind, along with guilt and honour. Nobody was around; the party could have been on another planet. He moved his hands up and down her back, feeling the curves and folds of her body. He held her tightly and pulled her towards him; her hands mirrored his. He felt her bottom, and she responded by thrusting herself towards him in rhythmic spasms. His arousal grew in his manhood, and it pressed hard against her.

He knew he should stop, for Rosie's sake, but he couldn't. A barrier was broken; he was helplessly out of control, and every encouragement was coming his way, heightened by the danger of being caught in such a public place.

They both took a more comfortable position on the cane sofa, adjusting the cushions as they kissed and whispered to each other, tongues probing. His hand searched up her thigh, high up inside her dress. Her legs opened eagerly at the invitation.

"Oh God, Maddi, I've always wanted you, I've always…"

"Shhh."

A candle in a certain room burst into light, a light so bright that it shone like a beacon. Sean smiled as he observed the flame. He said, "She would be my choice." Then, he frowned disapproval.

Speed increased as Mike undid the buttons down her dress. Like theatre curtains, it drew apart to reveal what the audience wanted. Mike let out an audible gasp as the framed beauty of her body stunned him. "Oh, Maddi, you're perfect." He undid her bra, and the love fruits bobbled into his hands. He guided them to his lips. He enjoyed her torment as she squirmed in anticipation. He took his turn at each nipple, and his hand pulled her knickers up against her crotch. She adjusted quickly and drew her legs up and apart. Her groans of delight were music to his ears.

"What are you waiting for? Fuck me now, please…please."

God! Maddi has just said that to me!! He went to his knees, drew her bottom to the edge of the sofa, and entered her; a lustful groan escaped his lips. Her legs waved in the air, and her bottom bounced up and down, forwards and back.

"Oh, yes, fuck me hard, up to the hilt, yes…oh, go on…yes, oh…oh…oh…oh."

Gentleness was obviously not a requisite, as he gripped her buttocks and squeezed in time to his long, hard, deep thrusts.

Their noise was loud as they taunted discovery with screams and obscenities, slaps and squeals. Groans of excited orgasm filled the air in a mutual crescendo of lovemaking. A burden of massive proportions fell from his shoulders, as if a yoke full of restraint crashed to the floor. "Oh, my God! Maddi, Maddi, Maddi…yesss!"

Both collapsed, covered in sweat and little else. Gasping for air in great gulps, the reality of what they had done in a glass room dawned on them. It was like being on stage for God's sake, and every boss and his mother was around somewhere. But slowly, silence settled on them. Mike's head lay on Maddi's thigh. He watched her stomach pant up and down only inches away form his nose; the smell of her filled him with ecstasy. Their breathing slowly subsided, almost returning to normal. Mike looked at her, and Maddi smiled back in the way only a well-fucked woman can. They dressed, looking at each other and smiling. Hand in hand, they left the room to walk back to the noise of Christmas. They let go of each other, but stayed close as they walked to the bar.

Eric was stood stupefied, staring at them. "'Lo."

"Hello, Eric. I thought you were with Gertie."

"Gertie? Bloodsy shell no, mate, I'd father put me knob in a bag of hungry ratsh. It's Katie—where is she, anywaysss?"

125

He left, and Maddi stared at Mike, who looked back bemused. Both fell onto each other in laughter. They went back into a quieter bar and spent the rest of the night in conversation, about almost everything.

As their conversation continued in a shared blissful state, magic of another kind was developing elsewhere.

The notes from the green book had given Tony plenty to think about, and he had since spent a great deal of time reading about Samurai warriors. He was impressed by their devotion and dedication to duty, up to the point of sacrificing their lives.

From there he had scoured antique shops to find a suitable sword—one with history—in a black scabbard, decorated with mother-of-pearl flowers and dragons, shiningly lacquered.

Before him stood three bell jars, each with a square of green baize cloth at its side. On each cloth were carefully written names: *Hai Su*, *Tsi Sun*, and *Sat Sen*. His skill in art was excellent, and accompanying these were three paintings of Samurai warriors in richly coloured garb. Further visits to antique shops had produced some old jewellery, which he had taken to pieces. At the side of each bell jar rested jet, jade, and onyx.

Monica Doll was close by, and he felt as if calmness and strength oozed from her to him. Sabre sat on his haunches, feeling uneasy; what was he going to witness now?

Tony read eight words from a page in the tome. As he did, each word slid off the page as if it were a ball of quick silver. They landed in a small, ceremonial plate precisely positioned beneath the sloping book. Slowly, he picked the vessel up, knowing from previous pages that any imbalance would mix the words, and his chance would be gone. Not sure how far he had to lift them, he did so deftly until he got just above chest height. Quick as lightning, they changed shape into one beautiful disk, shimmering like polished steel.

Slowly, he rested the plate on the worktop. Digging his nails beneath the disk, he freed it with a *pop*. It slid against gravity into the palm of his left hand. It reminded him of a toy he'd had as a child, a small plastic maze with a ball bearing in it. He remembered how much he had enjoyed the game—as if it were training for this. He studied the disk. It was split into three, with minute gardens in each piece, similar to willow-pattern plates. In the centre of each section was what looked like a pagoda, with a path winding out. Resting at the start of each path was a ball of mercury. He followed each path, all equal in length, and all leading to a central hole.

From somewhere distant, words filtered through the air, resting on his mind and telling him of his task. Before his vision, a pink pot decorated with intertwining branches of an oriental tree appeared on the worktop, half full with a deep orange powder. A voice said, "Once you have started, the balls cannot stop. All three must drop through together to land in the tree vessel, to mix with these ashes of a burnt ceremonial robe...begin."

Suddenly, as if he were one of the balls, he stood in the pink willow landscape. The voice came again: "Use your will to control the other two, and your balance and sight to control this." The dexterity required was immense. The ball's speed increased as plants, rivers, and bridges flew past in a blur on the periphery of his vision. He could sense that the other balls were taking a similar, perfect route. A temple loomed before him, and with a lurch and shudder, his speed decelerated. Cautiously allowing fleeting glimpses from side to side, he noticed rows of what looked like monks. They sat cross-legged along each side of a corridor of immeasurable length. All were clad in orange and pink, hands clasped before them as if in prayer. As he went past, each monk lowered his head.

One stood in the distance, slowly getting closer as Tony drifted in perfect balance and equilibrium towards him. As he got closer, he saw that the standing monk was slightly to the left of the centre of the path, holding an orange robe in an outstretched arm. As he cruised past, it fell on him, a sliding, shimmering silk that felt like a second skin. *Whoosh!* The increase in speed was awesome, of fairground ride proportions; the force nearly parted the skin down the centre of his face as he sped towards the end of the corridor, the archway growing in size rapidly as he reached it. A fissure greeted him, so deep and wide that it made the Grand Canyon look like a mud crack in dry earth.

Clinging to the rock faces were pink and orange trees. He flew out into thin air and fell like a stone. Two other balls fell with him.

He stood again, watching three balls of magic fall from the disc into the perfectly placed receptacle. They exploded into a million pieces with a sharp *bang!*, which finished almost as soon as it had begun, like the crack of some huge whip above his head. The disc in his hand, which was promising to be a magical keepsake, was wrenched from his grip and flew across the room to the tome, where it became fluid and crept carefully back into the fine crack between the pages. His eyes followed in disbelief. He took a deep breath, anticipating what was to come. He was almost there; just one more act—a disgusting one at that—was to follow.

He picked up his newly acquired sword in his right hand, then held out his left. Drawing in a hiss of breath, he raised the sword and pumped his fist. Slowly, the blade grated against the bone as it severed muscle, tendon, and artery. The spurt and splat made his stomach heave. Blood squirted high into the room and across the ceiling; then, as he controlled its flow, it poured like milk from a jug into the powder . His knees buckled, and he groaned as he lay the sword on the bench top. Grimacing, he pushed his other arm onto the upturned blade, and drew it down to repeat the action. Another bright red line decorated the ceiling, and a noise like a man urinating filled the room as more blood poured freely into the mix.

Strangely, he felt no pain; his lurching and heaving were in response to the disgust he felt as he watched his own actions. He could feel the muscles of his eye sockets wanting to rotate his eyeballs up to the top of his head; he rocked from side to side, and again his knees buckled. The blood overflowed and bubbled. The sword was covered in clots and strands of flesh, the scabbard now decorated to match the ceiling. He slowly drew his hands back towards him.

His arms felt like lead as they slapped against his side. Vomit was rising in a meniscus to the back of his throat, but he hadn't the strength left to bark it out. He was dying. The task had been too much. What had he been thinking?

Blood ran freely down each leg as pools formed around his feet. He sensed movement and looked to his left as a cold, wet nose and warm tongue lapped at the wound. As he rocked and his vision blurred again, he caught sight of the orange robe lying beside him. He knew immediately it was provided to save him. It was a healing second skin. "Sabre...Sabre," he whispered. "Sabre...fetch the robe...bring it." He pointed his head towards it, nodding the best he could in its direction.

With his paws sounding like scurrying rats on a tiled floor, Sabre patted over and pulled the gown to his master. He looked up, his head to one side. Tears in his eyes, Sabre howled like a bloodhound. His expression shouted better than a voice: "Master, don't die...I love you!"

Tony bent to his knees. Slipping, he crashed to the floor. The gown touched him, and of its own accord moved to cover him as a mother would cover a sick child. The waistband slid out of the loops like a snake, and coiled around his wrists, the blood stopped, and the wounds healed.

Monica Doll wept as she watched, and the observers stood stupefied. For the first time in eternity, the razor sharp blade fell from the cold, white, bony grip, to land in a clatter on the slimy floor. For someone so young to succeed at this task was utterly amazing; it belied belief. They were shocked and held Tony in high esteem. He was so brave...so very, very brave.

Sabre sensed immediately that all would be well, so he dragged his unconscious master to his bed, leaving a bloody trail along the floor. Tony's eyes opened briefly, and he smiled. "Thank you." He fell back into the deep sleep of recovery as the cuts healed and his cell count rose.

As a reward, Sabre eagerly lapped up his master's blood. Within minutes, it looked as if nothing had happened; the blood seemed to draw into Sabre's mouth in long strands, like thick, velvet curtains. The stains on the ceiling were somehow gone.

The only area left was the table. Sabre looked over to his master to see if he was allowed to jump up. He heard no negative command, so he did, wanting every last drop of this delicious, thick liquid. Finally, Sabre licked the bell jars clean, his tongue coming out as far as possible to reach into every nook and cranny. The dog stopped lapping instantly, as if the glass had suddenly burnt him. He stared and growled.

Three small Samurai Mind Warriors stood at attention in the bell jars, awaiting their master's instructions. The magic had been a total success.

* * *

Kingdom of Tarol, 1426

The maps were now finished, and Rosa sat with the pack of cards in her hands, playing with them as she listened to the chimes play a beautiful serenade. The trees stopped as one. The silence screamed to her, "Draw the card."

She drew one card and turned it over: The Tower.

She gasped in horror; the shock was almost too much. The rest of the pack fell to the caravan floor. She slapped the card down on the table before her and stared at it, her cheeks clasped in her palms. She saw what he had to go through, and she wept bitterly. "I hope he's that strong, God…I hope he's that strong. This trophy that Tony has to take to the dark ones, why did they have to pick it? Why choose such a task as this? Oh, Mike, you poor, poor man."

CHAPTER 10

The taxi dropped Mike off, and he staggered upstairs. Rosie heard him struggle into the bedroom and greeted him with humour in her voice. "Hell, is it Alcoholic Joe?" She smiled sympathetically at the state of him, turning to look at the clock. "Four o'clock; mmm, I take it that it was a good party, then?"

"Ugh? What? Oh, yeah, I think so."

So long as he wasn't sick, she could tolerate his state quite easily, and she began to undress her now-sleeping husband, murmuring, "You're going to regret this in the morning." Although she frowned when she saw the lipstick on his collar, she wasn't surprised.

The alarm clock did a good impression of a hydrogen bomb as it woke him up next morning. "Oh, I'm dead," he muttered as the clock fell to the floor. "Oh, where's my head? Is it joined on?"

Rosie tutted; he looked terrible in the soft headboard light. She followed him with her eyes as he made his way to the bathroom. "You'd better not try to drive in today."

"No, I won't. I'll get dressed, showered, and shaved. Will you order me a taxi, please?"

Picking up the bedside phone, she watched him and thought he was probably going to do what he had said in that exact order. With amused anger, she chided him: "I've no mercy."

"No, dear, I didn't think you would have." He forced his eyes wider open and smiled. "Sorry."

"It's okay."

"Thanks."

Then, about as subtle as a sled hammer in the guts, guilt hit him as the memory came flooding back. Suddenly, he couldn't look at her. He rushed to the bathroom and threw up into the toilet. Wiping his mouth, he stared at his reflection in the mirror. The dishevelled, unshaven face looked like a devil staring back. *You selfish bastard, what have you done to her?* He sat on the toilet with a thump and cried; he'd let her down, all the years of support vanishing in one night.

"You were drunk, Mike, and so was she," Sean tried to comfort him.

"I know, but…"

"What's done is done; keep it secret. Don't hurt her."

"I feel…"

"I know."

He went downstairs, not able to even glance at her. The taxi arrived a few minutes later, and he stood to leave.

"Don't feel bad. It's Christmas, and you got drunk. That's all."

"Thanks, love. G'bye."

Rosie watched him go and began to clear things away. She saw their wedding photograph and went over to it; that was at Christmas, too. She stroked his face with her finger and put it back. "He's a good man. I'm lucky."

During the taxi ride, he vowed that it would never happen again.

An hour later, he was in his office, feeling decidedly nauseous. He heard a knock on the door. "Come in."

Maddi entered, not looking a great deal better than him. Just how much had they drunk?

"I suppose you want to talk about last night, Maddi."

"Yes."

Mike detected the embarrassment. "Look, Maddi, I enjoyed it, but I'm wracked with guilt this morning. I know what you want to say: life's complicated enough without getting involved with your boss. Last night was wonderful, you were amazing, and I'm so flattered that you could even think of…well, you know. Look, I'll never say a word. Honest, it'll be our secret. I know that you'd never have…er, I mean that if you were sober, you'd never…er, well, you know what with my age and…well, you know what I'm trying to say."

Maddi stared at him for a moment, then said, "That's all I can ask, Mike. Thank you." She looked as though she were about to say more, then blurted, "I think that Monica must be mad, if you want to know the truth!"

Mike was taken aback.

Her attitude and manner changed again. More calmly, she said, "Can I ask you something?"

"Fire away!"

"After all we talked about last night, I can't believe I didn't ask you this question. You know your mind reading?"

"Yes?"

"Is that what it is, or is it a trick?" She looked bemused. "Can you really do it? Look in people's minds?"

"Why? Scared I might find a few secrets?"

"Ha, in a way, I suppose. But tell me honestly…can you?"

"I used to think it was a trick myself. But now I believe I can. Why? Would you like me to come into yours?"

"Yes, I would. I think I would find it interesting."

Destiny, in the form of two old, wise men from the white dome, had guided well. From their great distance, it had taken a lot of doing, but the evidence against Tony from the trapped spirit had warranted this rare intervention. The team was coming together, and this simple invitation was more important than anyone could have ever realised at that moment.

After a pause, Mike responded, "I'll arrange it, then, when the time suits us both."

She nodded and left quietly. Like a lot of things that day at work, quietly and slowly was the order.

Later, it reached Mike's ears that Christine hadn't come in. Everyone assumed it was over-exuberance from the night before; a man had rung in about 10:00 to say she was ill.

Actually, Christine wasn't ill at all. She lay awake on her back, staring at the head on the children's pocket watch as it swayed back and forth.

"Tick, tock. What a reassuringly soothing noise, don't you think so?" said the man's voice.

She agreed.

"Think of the sea, the way the waves lap the edge of the shore, and remember the noise of the pebbles and stones as they tumble over each other...you are there. It's hot, work seems a million miles away, and there's nothing to do but relax. Listen to the waves; don't they seem to be telling you to relax? They keep coming, don't they? Relentless, in and out, slowly lapping. Look at the head on the pocket watch: it's getting tired just like you, all that nodding, just like the sea, it can't stop; how tiring it must be. I'm going to count back from ten, and you'll feel your eyes get tired again like they did last night. Remember when I spoke to you then? How relaxed it made you, and how deep you slept. Ten: the waves still lap; nine: a nice, gentle breeze gets up and blows over your body...feel it?; eight: isn't it warm? It's the type of heat which saps your energy; you have no worries, your mind is clear and relaxed; seven: can you hear the rustle of the palm trees?; six: so, so tired. Why don't you drift into that really deep, deep sleep again? You've nothing else to do; five: yes, why don't you sleep; four: go to sleep, a deep, deep sleep; let my voice make your body's decisions; three: a nice, deep sleep; two: a very deep, relaxing sleep; one: there you are, let me look after you." The man's voice had a seductive, smooth sound to it.

She breathed steadily.

"Now, Christine, listen to me very carefully. I am that voice you've been hearing lately, the one you keep talking to, the one who has been helping you. I still want to, and still will, help you, but I'd like a little help, now, too. Please, will you help me?"

"Of course I will."

"Good girl. Tell me what you know about Mike Reeves. What is he like, what does he do, where does he go, and…where does he live?"

Christine told him all she knew; it was a pleasure to help the voice.

"Oh, well done, Christine. I'm very pleased with you." Slowly and assuredly, the voice went on. "You see, he needs help, but he won't ask. He's so proud, but I want to help him. He's a lovely man, and it's Christmas. Don't you want to help him?"

"Yes, yes, I do. I like him, too; he's ever so nice."

"Well, let's help him together then, shall we?"

"Mmm, that'd be cool."

"Oh, good. I like to help people. They've got your Tony all wrong, you know."

"Yes, I know they have. It's not fair."

"It will be our secret; we'll do good without anyone knowing. We'll be secret philanthropists, so don't say a word, not to anyone at all."

"No, don't worry. You can trust me."

Tony looked at her and opened her eyes with his thumbs, then began to stroke her temples. "You'll need this." He stared intensely and pushed the temples hard.

The vision cleared slightly before her, and a dark, ominous shape loomed in the mist.

With an evil, cold, merciless stare, Tony continued. "He's ill, and something needs to kill his illness. Will you carry these to him?"

"Of course I will. I told you, ask me to do anything." Her voice sounded like an elderly woman's, slipping into the senility of childhood: simple, clear, and uncorrupted by life's memories.

"Then receive this." An ancient Samurai Mind Warrior walked from his mind's eyes to hers. "Take care of him; you'll know when it's time to use him."

"No problem."

"Monica wants him, too." The voice turned ice cold and as smooth and hard as marble.

"Yes, I know, the bitch!"

"I can stop her if you want; then he could be all yours."

"Oh, yes, please!"

"Then you must take this, too." Another heavily armed, gloriously decorated Samurai Mind Warrior walked across the delicately arched mind bridge and leapt through the window. "Now, let these thoughts sink deep into your mind. When you get the chance, you must ask him about mind reading; he will respond. When he does, send the first mind warrior to him. It must be the first; you don't want to hurt him, do you?" He watched seriously as the thought descended into her. "And the bitch, you can have all the pleasure of stopping her. All you have to do is wait for her concentration to drift, as if she has gone into a trance." He allowed himself a sly chuckle. "Rest assured of it: she will lapse; she always has done, ever since I—oh, never mind, that was a long time ago. Just believe me. She will lapse, as if her mind is waiting for something it misses." He paused a few seconds, swallowed loudly, and continued. "When she does, offer her a penny for her thoughts, and when she replies, send the second."

"I will, Tony, I will. Thank you; you are so helpful and kind." Her voice continued in the same trusting, elderly tone.

Then, without her knowledge, the third Samurai Mind Warrior strode confidently into her mind in total secrecy. It would wait until it was needed, until Tony brought him out.

Tony pushed his thumbs into her temples and spoke rhythmically and quietly. "Oh, you've been good...you've been very good, darling. When you awake, you'll feel wonderful." He counted from one to ten and then spoke sharply: "Awake!"

She yawned deeply, bringing her arms above her head and thrusting her small, pert bust out. "Oh-oh-ohhh...dearie me, what time is it?"

"As near as damn-makes-no-difference to midday."

"What!"

"Ha, don't worry. I've already rung in, and they said not to worry; they weren't busy. See, so everything is okay. How do you feel?"

"Remarkably good, actually. Getting pissed seems to suit me these days." She stretched and yawned again, then flopped back onto the bed.

"Stay in bed. I'll bring you a cup of tea, and then I might join you. Perhaps we could try to achieve last night's high again."

"Mmmm, yes, please!"

"Stay there, then. I'll look after you."

"Right, I will. I'm honoured."

Tony walked back to the kitchen. His plan was working. He would destroy Mike's mind, and he would knead Monica's back into its correct shape—after he'd played with it to teach it a lesson. She would have to suffer like he had. Revenge would be sweet. He would walk into Daath with his war trophy and present it to Death itself. It would be talked about for centuries.

The day toiled on, and as Mike's head cleared, Sean filed away his secret with Maddi in a room marked, "most pleasant memories."

Monica spent the day quietly. Her mind seemed to be getting cloudier these days. A few times she thought about Mike: Why hadn't she been more patient with him?

Maddi recovered by lunch. She was used to hangovers. As she was leaving, Andy asked her about her mysterious disappearance last night. She told him to mind his own business.

Christine thought a lot about things that day as she drove home from doing some shopping; her mind felt as clear as crystal. Tony, Mike, and Monica kept popping up, one after the other. Tony was dangerous, and bad, too, or so people said. And he was odd, but in a nice way, she thought. He was nowhere near as bad as they said. And God, was he handsome! "I love that little scar thing on his eye, so interesting," she said out loud. "Now sex, wow! It's like making love to a beast!" But as her thoughts briefly touched on relationship, she knew there was no chance. She felt relieved about that. "It'll not last long," she told her eyes in the rear-view mirror.

It'll last only as long as I dictate, thought Tony. *You've a lot of valuable work to do yet, and then—and only then, if I see fit— I might just let you fly free.*

As Christine neared her home, she felt happy. She was in control of her life, and her rival's ex-lover, and maybe even her boss. "Things couldn't be much better," she said, carrying on her conversation with the mirror. "Ha-ha, I'll lose a bit soon, and describe my knickers to him. But which ones? The black and red I think. Hey, pussy, stop twitching!" she laughed.

That night was Maddi's night to herself: no loud music, no man, no arts and crafts, nor a book. Tonight, she went to her group at The Friends Meeting House, a local Quakers' Hall hired out to various associations. She came as often as she could on Buddhist meditation evenings, to cleanse her body and soul. She saw it as a chance to escape from this world. Other women of similar passion and reasons came too, along with a couple of men. Some of her closest friends were there, and the chat after-wards was usually stimulating. It was different from her usual routine, but so refreshing.

The night started as usual with a cup of tea and biscuits, with time to wind down and prepare, to feel at ease in the company. A gentle meditative tune was playing through the sound system, seeming to come from everywhere, and yet nowhere.

A quiet clap of the hands summoned them, telling them to go upstairs. They were very disciplined, and only needed telling once. Large windows, ten feet high and five feet across, gave a wonderful view to the moors overlooking the town.

She couldn't have viewed the sunset from a better vantage point. It was spectacular, filling the whole room with an orange glow. Maddi took her usual spot facing the windows and began her relaxation and deep breathing, using the breaths to focus her mind. She visualised her Chinese chest, opening the drawers to put her thoughts away into categories, shutting out noise and distractions.

Her leader had taught her well. In the bottom right of her mind's eye was a candle with a steady flame; she learned to use this to stop distractions. A car horn distracted her, and the flame pulled to the east; she consciously pulled it back, and her mind regained control easily. A cough from her meditative neighbour pulled the flame west, and again she pulled it back with ease. She let the music—Tibetan chants, with distant drums and the flutter of prayer flags in the breeze—take over. She could hear the noise of steady rain on leaves, probably large ones in a deep forest. Distant thunder rolled through her mind.

And so did the voice of her guide.

"Tonight, my children, I want you to visualise a wood, a beech wood to be precise. Smell the leaf mould…hear the silence. Walk slowly to the centre of the wood, and take note of the shafts of sunlight and insects. Let the light guide you to peace and tranquillity. It is your escape."

She was there.

"Look! There, in the clearing, can you see it? The tower. Walk to it, away from the track, away from all your worries. Walk through the leaves, through the dry, crunching leaves. The tower is bigger than it looked from over there, isn't it? Now knock three times, and wait. You'll be invited to go in, all in good time. You will, believe it. This is a sanctuary."

The music took her, and she knocked.

"When you go in, climb the stairs, and listen to your footsteps: each one taking you further from your troubles and worries, and each one closer to inner peace. When you get to the top, remember what you see, and learn."

The white observers took their chance. "She is the one! Her mind is only a step away from us; let's make the bond…now."

Time passed quickly for the group as usual. With another small clap, they were all back in the room. The leader pointed to Val, a pleasant, attractive woman in her fifties, and she told of what she had seen, heard, and done. So did Betty and Joan. The leader nodded towards Maddi.

"I've never had such a realistic meditation," she said. "I didn't want to come back. I feel I've left somewhere special, and

I think I know that I'll never go back again." Tears formed in her eyes and rested on her eyelids; Joan touched her arm with a supportive smile on her face.

"Go on."

"I got to the top of the stairwell, and a bright yellow light was illuminating the top floor. I could see everything ever so clearly: the inside of the roof tiles, the cobwebs, the woodwork, everything, even the nails. The tower was perfectly round, and sitting on a rush mat were three…well, for want of a better description, three wise men. Opposite them was a friend of mine, whom I know has a troubled mind. All in one action, neither leading another, they all pointed towards her.

"She turned jet-black, and, brrr…I felt the cold radiate from her, as if she was contaminated, or forbidden somehow…I don't know. That part was upsetting. Then, the warmth from the three flooded back. It was lovely, hard to describe; it caressed you, made you feel safe, like in a womb, I imagine. Hours passed as we sat and…well, felt each other, you know…bonded…er, joined. Do you get what I'm saying?

"Then, all in one voice—a voice so benevolent, so omnipresent—they gave me a message. I know it was a message, not a thought. They told me to trust my instincts, that help to a growing problem was closer at hand than I imagined. They said the man who would be my strength, my tower of strength, would not let me down. He's a man of such importance that he would make this vision seem minuscule in comparison. He's a man I must trust instinctively, a man whom I know will be 'the one.'"

"Maddi, you are indeed privileged, as we all are tonight. Tonight, we have been in contact with the Divine, and you, Maddi, have sat with them, at their table. Yes, indeed, you are the fortunate one."

The leader passed on to the next, who declined the invitation by saying, "How can I follow that?" The class closed early, and quietly. They all left, knowing once more that they had made the right choice in coming to such a group.

* * *

Kingdom of Runa, 656

The shield would have suited a King of the greatest heroic stature; it gleamed magnificently in purple and blue. The gold and red runic symbols appeared to stand proud, floating an inch in front of it. She watched as the last leather strap was secured into its concave side.

The helmet matched the shield. Just one final blood-red symbol on the nose guard, and it would be done, ready for collection by him.

She undid the leather drawstring on the bag, put her hand in to feel for the final rune. "Ouch!" As if a wasp had stung her, she withdrew her hand, with a different rune attached. "Why?"

Slowly, dreading the symbol she suspected, she turned it over. It was worse: it was inverted. She knew in an instant who it was for, and what it meant and what he would have to go through. Her heart almost broke as she stared at it. "Why must he go through that? Why have they made the evil one choose such a prize? Oh, Mike, I hope you are strong enough to bear this burden."

CHAPTER 11

The weakness took another firm, icy grip as Mike opened the letter. "Got you!" he shouted, dancing a little jig. The game had reached the stage where the fictitious Mike and Christine were in an old-style compartment on an old steam train, skirting Lake Geneva. Mike had trapped Christine's loose-fitting, elasticised-waist skirt's hem in the door, and forced her by his last move to reach up to the baggage rack for something. In two previous moves, he had given her only one option: to reach up to the rack for her bag. As she did so, her skirt remained almost where it was, to pull over her hips, past her bottom, and then, to fall to the floor, revealing her knickers to the world. The trap had worked, almost too easily.

"Good morning, Christine," Mike said into the office phone. "I've just opened your last move; poor you."

Via the Samurai, the dark observers looked on.

"Hmmm, I suppose I've got to, then."

"Oh, what's that dear? Got to what?"

"Huh, you know well enough, Mr. Smug. Describe my knickers to you."

"Describe what did you say? Sorry, it's a bad line. Could you say it again, please?"

"Knickers!"

"Sorry?"

"Oooh! You heard me, all right! Knickers, my knickers, the ones I'm wearing right now!"

Mike smiled a broad grin. "Oh those, why didn't you say so? Go on, then—oh, and don't hurry."

"Well, I got up this morning and knew I'd lost, so I guessed this would be the day. I thought, which pair would he choose, light blue? No, too cold. Black? Tut tut, too sexy, you wouldn't be able to handle that. So I decided on the red-and-black ones, my favourite."

Christine was now firmly under the control of Tony, and she was far more daring than ever she would have been.

"Yes, the black-and-red ones, dearest. The colours go together so well, especially against my nice, smooth pink thighs and tummy. In fact, because they go so high up at the sides, they really enhance the shape of my bottom. Oh, and they're a thong. Well, I looked over my shoulder into the mirror, and I bent over slightly as I pulled them up, ever so tight. Then...oooh, then, I followed the lacy edge all the way around, and I thought how nice they tucked into my...well, you can guess. You could really see the shape; I was pulling them up so high. I traced the edge with my finger; it surprised me how warm and sensual the material felt, and especially there, you know...*there*; it was damp, too. I sat on the edge of the bed then, imagining you could see through my eyes. I looked at myself in the mirror, and drew my legs up, to examine—oh it was lovely, you'd have liked it. All the dark, curly hairs were poking out, so I stroked them, and put my hand in them, and...and, well, I really mustn't say. Will that do, sir?"

"Do? God yes!!" Mike said with a tremble in his voice. "You should see the steam coming out of my collar—and my trousers! Bye, I must go to the loo now, quick!"

"Oh, Mike you naughty boy, you'll go blind." He could hear the smile in her voice. "How on earth would you have coped if I'd had my crotchless ones on, and continued before you, in the same pose?"

"I'd have thought myself to death."

"You've a dirty mind, Mike Reeves, and I know what it thinks about all the time."

"You'd never cope with it, dear, believe me!"

"I might. Can I try to guess? Can I read your mind? Can I come in for a look at all those naughty little corners?"

"Yup, go ahead! Come in, come in!"

"Mmm, let me see then. Oh, Mr. Reeves, a man in your position, really, tut tut, so naughty of you!"

She was sexily funny. Mike laughed, and took the phone from his ear. As he did, the Samurai, expertly controlled by Tony, gently slipped into his mind.

He landed on the platform and looked around. Quietly, he slid into the courtyard, then stalked the corridors of almost-forgotten memories. He blended into the shadows, and like the expert assassin he was, he moved in almost total silence. He passed a great pit with a huge slab on the top marked *Sekim Seveer*. Tony knew this was Mike's Demon, the reverse of Mike Reeves. Until recently, it had been housed in safety, since his "free" years, before meeting Rosie when guilt had no hold on him. But on party night, it had come out, and was now peering about his memory with two red eyes.

Swiftly the samurai ran down the corridor, found an old room, with the name of one of Mike's first girlfriends at school on the door, and slipped in. He lit a candle, sat down in the corner, and took a few items from the bag on his back. Using mortar and pestle, he ground the ingredients from a tube and sprinkled the dust into the candle flame. An orange burst of light lasting a second or two brought forth an orange cloud of gas, which he breathed in. He blew out the candle and sat in the darkness as he slipped into a trance, awaiting instructions.

Tony allowed himself a premature victory smile.

Mike replaced the handset and grimaced. He put his hand just above his eyebrow, touching a small scar. "Ouch! Bloody hell, I haven't felt a pain there since what's-her-name hit me with her handbag." He rubbed it. "What was her name? Why think of her after all this time?" The pain went as quickly as it came, and a knock sounded on the door.

Maddi walked in, her usual room-warming smile on her face. "Hello, Mike. Can I have a chat?"

"Sure, sit down. What's up?"

"It's Monica."

"Oh."

"Yes, precisely! How do you really feel about her?"

"I would have thought that was obvious. I think she's lovely, but getting to her is like trying to chip away at a block of marble, so cold and hard. Other times, it's like cutting through butter with a warm knife. I thought she was shouting out for a friend, and maybe a bit more, but...well, she's weird, isn't she?"

"To be perfectly honest, Mike, I don't think anything will happen with any man—not for a while, anyway."

"That's fine. I'm not the type to push in where I'm not wanted. But I think we could have been friends. I guess that's just 'old-fashioned me', as you point out often." Mike smiled. "I would think it very nice to be an older man friend to a young lady, the type of chap who comes out of the woodwork now and then to sort out problems and lend a shoulder.

Maddi returned Mike's smile. "Don't get me wrong, Mike. Keep at it; she's getting very staid these days, but your friendship and flattery are giving her a lift most of the time."

"I won't stop trying to be a friend, don't worry."

Mike sensed she was skirting around something. He waited a minute longer.

"I'm sure she likes you—a lot, actually—but she just seems incapable of letting herself go, especially with a man. I think she's ill or something; her mind's all messed up. It's odd."

"What is, Maddi? Tell me all about it."

"Well...her mind is so alert and interesting; that's why I made friends with her in the first place. But more and more, she seems to drift off into deep thought, and forget things, sometimes only seconds after you say them." She took a deep breath. "You know about Tony, don't you?"

"Yes."

"Well." She breathed deeply again, then absent-mindedly sorted the papers on the edge of his desk for a few seconds. "It's

145

got something to do with him. He's a bastard; I wish she'd never met the…oh! He rings her up and sends letters. And do you know, sometimes when we leave work, he just stands there staring at us as we drive past. It gives me the shivers, so I don't know what she feels. *I* feel like driving straight at him, and mowing him down." She paused, and her facial expression became grave. "I'm scared, Mike. I know this will sound silly and over-reactive, but I think you'll understand."

Mike nodded reassuringly.

He saw the trust in her eyes when she looked at him. "He's evil, Mike, and he's doing something. I know this will sound like a line from an old Hammer horror film, but…but I think he's using black magic against her. It wouldn't surprise me if he wanted to kill her! I honestly believe that if he can't have her back, he'll make damn well sure no one else can! I sometimes wonder if he knows about you. Monica has always said he seems to know everything that happens to her and if he's jealous of you, he might even target you in some way. You understand how serious I am about this, don't you? I've lost sleep over it. She's told me some right tales about him; he's into all that black arts stuff, and in a mega-big way, too. Just ask around, Mike. Everyone knows his reputation; half the town is scared of him, and the other half is connected with him."

As she breathed deeply, Mike stared at her heaving bosom as it lifted the grey blouse up and down. The black skirt suited her, too. He knew even before this conversation that he would do anything for her.

"Listen to this, Mike. I have a friend, who has a friend, who works in that club of his, The Gateway To Hell, and she told me that Tony stuck a long hat pin right through a dancer's cheek not long ago, just 'cause she wouldn't sleep with a friend of his!" Maddi stared wide-eyed.

"Why me, Maddi?"

"Because I trust you, Mike, and I know you will take my beliefs seriously because of all you've told me. You seem to know so much more than anyone else."

Already sure of his answer, the white observers waited with bated breath.

"What do you want me to do?"

"I don't know. I'm at my wit's end; he's so clever. You can't accuse him of anything, and if you did, everyone you spoke to would back off and say you were mad. I'm hoping that you'll come up with something. I feel like I'm in black and white, and I've just come to see Humphrey Bogart in one of those old detective movies. I need help, Mike, and she needs help— anything, something, everything, I don't know."

"Shhh, don't get yourself all upset." Maddi's concern showed him exactly what she was: a devoted friend and a wonderful person. He liked what he saw more and more.

"Sorry, but it's such a relief to spill the beans to someone."

"You don't have to be sorry. I'll do what I can. And also remember this: I don't think anything you have said is silly. I believe you."

"Thanks."

"It's all right."

Maddi walked thoughtfully back to her work area, convinced that she had done the best possible thing. "I really like him."

Monica looked up as she entered. "Hell's bells, they do have loos in this country, you know. Where on earth have you been?"

"To Africa, to see the elephants," she replied with a grin.

Monica tutted to herself.

Maddi smiled as she looked at her friend; Monica returned the look with a glance and a smile. Maddi started work again, feeling a little more optimistic.

Only a few minutes later, there was a knock on their door. Without waiting to be invited, Christine barged in, as if hoping to catch them doing something wrong. "Good morning, you two. Everything okay?"

They were taken aback by this sudden interest in their welfare. Maddi answered that things were fine, and the job was going well. Monica just stared at her computer monitor, seemingly oblivious to what was happening. Maddi smiled at Christine and looked to the ceiling.

He was right, thought Christine. "A penny for them, Monica."

"Mmm?"

"I said, a penny for your thoughts."

"Sorry, I was miles away." She grimaced, instantly going pale. "Oh, Christ…oh, oh, bloody hell, there's such a pain in my temple—ugh, I'm going to throw up." She pushed past Christine to run down the corridor, her hand to her mouth.

Maddi sat rock still, not knowing what to say or do for a few seconds.

"Go and see if she's okay," instructed Christine.

Maddi ran after her friend.

Looking around the room with a smug expression, Christine clapped her hands as if dusting chalk powder from them. "Nothing to it." She locked the door on her way out and walked back to her office.

In the toilet, Maddi stood with Monica, trying to cheer her up after watching her wretch. "I know she makes you sick, but that's a bit over the top, isn't it?" She screwed her nose up at the stench. "Well, I hope you feel better without that lot; it's not done me any good, I know that!"

Monica barked like a dog, then violently threw up again. "I'm going home. Will you tell everyone for me?"

"Yes, of course I will." Maddi saw Monica to her car, then went to report the matter to Christine.

Back in his office, Mike had cleared the important work away and decided to spend a while in thought. He took up his thinking position, chin resting in his hands. "What's going on, Sean?"

"Something different, Mike."

"Great help. Tony's got something to do with it. I'm sure we both realise that, but how much, and what? I know one thing: he's on my mind a lot these days."

A few thoughtful seconds passed by. "Consult your oracle tonight," instructed Sean. "Then come to my room. I think it's time to use Debbie's skills again."

Minutes later, there was another knock on the door. Without being invited, Christine entered, slowly closing the door behind her and resting against it. "Hello, Mike."

At once, Mike noticed the change in her usual tone of voice; she sounded seductive, as she had on the phone.

"Did you like my description as much as I enjoyed giving it?"

"Yes, of course I did, I…"

"What?"

"I…oh, nothing. I just…oh, never mind."

"You are infuriating sometimes! Tell me, what?"

"Well I wondered…are you? I mean, did you? Or was it just something you said to get me going?"

"Well, I suppose there's only one way to prove it to you." She remained resting against the door, slowly reaching down to the hem of her skirt and pulling it up. "I didn't say anything about the rest, though—didn't know if you'd be able to handle it!"

To his delight, he saw stockings with a fancy, pale-cream lace top, which gave a lovely rosy hue to her thighs. "Wow!" he gasped.

"Come here."

As if summoned by an irresistible force, he stood and walked towards her. "We'll have to be careful." He reached past her and locked the door.

Christine put her arms around him and kissed him on each cheek and the tip of his nose. Then she smiled, tilted her head to one side, and closed her eyes.

They kissed.

Mike slowly and firmly caressed her back and shoulders. She mirrored his actions, their breaths drawing deeper and deeper. He pulled himself away. "We can't, not here."

"Why?"

"Why? Well, we just can't!"

"Switch your 'engaged' light on; you won't be disturbed."

Mike flicked the three-coloured switch next to the door lock, and they kissed again. He felt guilt rise and subside. *What am I*

149

doing? The question remained unanswered as he pulled her skirt up and stroked her bottom. *This is wrong; what about Rosie?* he thought as his hand pulled out her blouse, all the way around her waistline. *Oh, Rosie, forgive me...I can't stop. I'm so weak, I just can't.* Christine offered no resistance to his actions; instead, encouragement exuded from her. Again, like a mirror, she reflected his actions by pulling out his shirt and holding his broad, firm back in her arms.

Guilt disappeared like a small puddle in the summer sun, just as it had done with Maddi.

Her blouse floated gently to the floor, soon to be covered by his shirt and tie, then crowned with a cream bra. Her nipples danced across the hairs of his well-toned chest. The embrace continued, kiss upon kiss, interspersed with gasps of fondled pleasure.

Her hand went to his belt. As five years of self-control melted away, he couldn't blame the drink this time. Tenseness lifted from his shoulders like leaves falling from an autumn tree.

His hand unzipped and unbuttoned her skirt. It fell to the floor, and she daintily stepped out, kicking their shoes away in four different directions.

She manoeuvred the jib crane of his manhood out of his boxers and pushed them down. The gentle touch of her hand on his throbbing flesh made it jump, the pleasure running through his body like an electric shock.

"Mmmm."

"Mmmm."

The knickers described to him were pulled down, smoothly at first, until they fell to her ankles. Again, like a wood sprite stepping out of a pond, she daintily stepped from them, naked apart from the stockings.

With one hand on each cheek of her rear, they walked backwards to the desk. She arched over it as he kissed her erect nipples. "Oh, Christine."

"Oh, Mike."

He felt as if he wanted to cry from the relief of knowing that a woman, another real woman, wanted him.

She pushed herself up on to the edge of the desk as he sunk to his knees, kissing her body in stages as he did so. She raised each leg and put her feet on his back as he began to drink her love juices; her ankles crossed as she pulled the hair on the back of his head, making his face press against her. As his head lapped, she urged him on. "Oh, Mike, eat me, eat me!"

Surprised by the speed of her approaching orgasm and nodding as fast as he could, he licked until she came; her hairs crinkled against his face; he smelled her womanness and could hear that she enjoyed the moment. "Oh, God, yes. Oh, God...mmm, yes, yes...ooh, oooh...yes!" She collapsed backwards onto the desk; pencils scattered around her.

He stood and turned her around; she followed his lead willingly. Entry from behind was easy; the love lubricant was overflowing from its delicate vessel. Again she urged him.

"Oh, Mike, take me...oh, sir, fuck me, fuck me, Mr. Reeves. Oooh...yes, that's it—hard and from behind, yes, yes." She was on her tiptoes, her bottom pushed against him.

His dominance rose to a peak, and he showed little tenderness; he could sense the submissive woman oozing from every pore on her body, wanting to be taken with no mercy. It was a game of master and slave, lord and serving wench, gentleman and tart. "Take this!" Mike was almost shouting as he held her hips and thrust deep, penetrating strokes into her. The sound of buttock slapping against belly filled the office.

"Yes, that's it, sir. You show me...oooh, I deserve this. Oh, God, it's what I want, isn't it? Yes, oh yes!"

Thrust after thrust after thrust, he gave her what she begged for. He thought he was never going to ejaculate; sweat dripped from his chin, and his hair beat against his forehead. It was what he wanted, it was what she was shouting for, and he was going to disappoint no one. Eventually he came, and when he did, he could have put out a tower block fire. Spurts of hot semen seemed endless, the shudders shaking his very soul. Christine's second, tumultuous orgasm tightened around him, squeezing and draining every last drop.

He collapsed to the floor, feeling like he'd run a marathon. "Oh, God, Christine, was I too rough? I'm...I...I—"

"Shh, don't even think of apologising. That was just what I wanted; all us girls want it rough sometimes, and boy! Were you r-rough!"

She, too, collapsed to the floor, and rolled to lay her head on his chest as they gasped together. The telephone rang.

His face turned from full red to ashen in seconds as his arteries almost collapsed in shock. "Oh no!" For almost the first time in his life, he had no idea what to do.

Christine coughed, and calmly took control of the situation. "Hello, Mr. Reeves' office." She smiled broadly at Mike before she answered the enquirer's question. "No, I've just *come* here. He asked me to give him some *back-up*; he's only *just finished* and left. I think he said he badly needed to *chase up some arrears*." The emphasis on the words was subtle, but Mike had to cover his mouth to stop himself laughing. At each word, Christine rolled her eyes. "Yes, don't worry; I'll leave a message...yep, okay, ta-ra!"

They dressed and kissed. "Oh, Mr. Reeves, what on earth will I have to do next time I lose, eh?"

"I'll think of something," he answered, hopping around as he pulled a sock on.

"Mmm, I bet you will!" She straightened his tie, and wiped off some lipstick. She wrote the message the caller had asked to, just in case the evidence was needed, and after kissing him twice more, she left.

He walked around his desk straightening the telephone and restoring items to their rightful places. Then he collapsed into his chair, feeling hungry, satisfied, and thirsty.

Sean's voice came into his mind. "Well? Are you happy? That's two out of three."

Like a chastised schoolboy, he sat guiltily at his desk. He resumed his thinking position instantly and replied, "Here I am, wanting to befriend Monica, and all I do is screw her best friend and her worst enemy!" He felt distaste, and fear. "God, if she found out, she'd be the type to sing. She'd show no mercy. I bet she'd report me and the lot, hell's bells! I'd be outta here quicker than a bullet from a gun; my life would be ruined. Oh, shit, and then Rosie would find out and probably divorce me. Oh, fucking hell, everything would collapse. My life would end."

"Exactly," the dark observers said together.

Sean subsided back into his subconscious.

Mike sat with his hands holding his chin. From the dizzy height of euphoria, he had sunk to the depths of despair. The white-knuckle ride of emotions, coupled with his recent physical exertion, drained his strength. If someone asked him to stand, right then, he wouldn't have been able to.

Christine sat at her desk feeling the exact opposite. Her whole body was warm, satisfied, and most certainly alive. Her senses were fizzing. The voice in her head spoke. "I told you, didn't I?"

"Yes, you did. Thanks."

Monica was at home, perspiration running off her forehead in rivulets. She had visited the doctor and been diagnosed a virus. Her strict orders were to, "Rest, drink plenty of fluids, and keep warm." Maddi had stopped to see her on her way home. In the kitchen, washing a cup under the running tap, she spoke to herself. "This is more than a virus."

* * *

Kingdom of the Sun, 17-6404

Peacock was grooming her pubic hair; the pattern of the peacock's tail was coming along nicely. She thought he'd love it, especially in peacock blue.

She wanted him to stroke it, to smell it, to study it, and praise her. She wanted to please him entirely.

Chi Lin walked in under a dark cloud. She didn't change her position; nor did his demeanour change as he placed the bowl of tea between her legs, next to her pussy, on top of the pubic clippings. To her surprise, he picked some up, sprinkled them in the tea, and told her to drink it. She was to leave a little residue in the bottom, to swish around three times clockwise, then turn it over in the same place.

She did so without hesitation. Turning the divining bowl upside down, she sensed something was wrong.

Chi Lin studied the cast, shook his head sadly, and looked at her. "Turn to the chapter on comfort, in volume twelve; he's going to need it." His head sagged as if someone had tied a heavy weight to it, and he pushed himself up with a sigh. As he walked away, Peacock could just hear him ask a one-syllable question: "Why?"

CHAPTER 12

Mike stood drying dinner pots with Bill. "How's work?"

"Fine, thanks, Mike." He screwed up the tea towel to reach the bottom of a wine glass. "You?"

"Pretty good, thanks." Guilt had lifted a little; coupled with the fact that nobody looked like they had found out, he felt secure with his secrets.

Bill had been introduced tonight as the partner of Linda, a good friend of Rosie's, with whom she shared many coffee mornings and fitness classes. Over the past few months, Rosie and Linda had become close, having been introduced by a common friend, Karen.

The men walked back into the lounge. Feeling pleased with themselves for having done the pots, they poured four brandies.

"Actually, Mike, me and Linda have got you and her hubby here to ask you something," said Rosie. "It's an idea we've been toying with for a while now."

"Ha, there you go, Bill. I knew it, didn't you?"

"Yeah, these women have devious minds!"

"Go on then, dear. Lay it on us."

Rosie grinned at Linda, who took up the request. "Well, we'd like a break, in London. We've been saying how it's our capital city, and neither of us has really seen much of it. And we share so many interests, we'd just like to share some time going around art galleries and whatnot, and perhaps see a couple of shows. So…well, we mentioned it to the group, and it sort of took off! They want us to arrange a girls' long weekend, perhaps about half a dozen or so going. What do you think?" She smiled through her teeth, as if expecting a refusal.

"I wouldn't mind going as well, really. But no, I've no problem with it. Hell's bell's, if anyone deserves a break, you do, Rosie." He jumped at the chance to ease his conscience a little, and an idea hit him instantly. "Why don't you visit what's-her-name? The one with the two Dalmatians, whose husband is in the wheelchair. She's always asking you to, and she says to bring a friend. It must be ages since you've seen her; you could go to London with your pals, and then you two go there and stop a little longer, it's really close." He then thought of Bill. "Oops, sorry; do you mind?"

Hardly able to say anything else, he shook his head. "No, not at all. I've a few days due, and I could go fishing with Ian. Want to join us, Mike?"

"No, I'm not into fishing, but thanks. I might like to try it one day, but I'd be as happy as Larry with a few days to myself."

So that was it, and plans were begun. Rosie looked excited, which pleased Mike. He watched Linda and her start to make a list, and he looked through a brochure they had just pulled from under the settee cushions.

The night wore on, and eventually goodbyes were said, with a promise to return the invitation soon. After they were gone, Mike turned to his wife. "I like them, Rosie. I'll look forward to going back to their place. Bill's quite a laugh, what us blokes call a right diamond geezer!" He shut the door and gave her a hug, but instantly he knew he had made an error.

"Get off!"

Mike winced; the tone was like sharp ice. "I'm sorry." He turned to go to the kitchen.

"Mike?"

He smiled to make it look as though he wasn't hurt by the rejection. "What, love?"

"I want to tell you something."

He braced himself, unsure of what was coming. "It doesn't matter; I should have thought. I just forgot for a few seconds. Don't be mad, I'm...I won't do it again. I don't know what I was—"

She smiled warmly. "No, listen. I know men have needs, and I know I don't fulfil yours, and you never moan, bless you. I looked at you tonight; you had them captivated. Linda thinks I'm so lucky, that you are drop-dead gorgeous, and I think you're sexy too, but, oh...even after all the counselling, I just can't stand...I just...oh, if it wasn't for that bastard I'd—"

"Shh, it's okay. I understand, you know that. I love you, with a capital *L*. Don't forget, I still see my doctor regularly too. He helps me to cope, which makes it better for us both."

She surprised him then. "Don't be too bad, will you?" She paused and looked into his eyes. "I know, you know."

"What do you mean, you know?"

"Shhh." She put a finger to his lips. "Don't tell me anything, ever."

She looked sad, and guilty. "Goodnight, Mike."

He watched her climb the stairs. "Goodnight." He stood for a few seconds more. "I'm going to have a brandy. Sleep tight."

"Yeah, don't let the bedbugs bite."

Mike sat down with a thud. "That's how we always used to say it. Five years, five fucking years; where's it gone to?"

He sat there for over an hour, contemplating what she had said. He also wrote an e-mail to his doctor. This had been a new development two visits ago, and was a regular thing now. He could write anything, and always the doctor understood. Last time he had said that Mike's voices were unlike anything he had ever come across. This made him think of his instructions from Sean.

He felt melancholy, but ready to consult the oracle. He placed all the usual tranklements in the usual places, and the air became thick with the scent of sandalwood. After the night's alcohol, he felt more than a little heady, as tarot and runes told him what he already knew, but with more emphasis on conflict. It wasn't often he asked direct questions about people, but as he began the I Ching, he did just that. "Oh, wise one, tell me: is Tony the cause of Monica's trouble?"

The chant ran through his mind and preceded the news. The symbol of fire, *Li*, spoke the answer. "The trigram *Li*…brightness, fire, clinging repeatedly, makes this hexagram. The doubling of these qualities can simply mean a fiery, short temper. But it is more likely to mean an explosive or unstable situation. Clinging is an attribute of fire: it clings to what it feeds, whilst it radiates its glow everywhere. It could simply refer to an energetic businessman, but in this case, it refers to an assertive male lover who demands loud affections as a cover for his own dependence. This is a jealous lover with hate in his heart. This fire has to be controlled; allowed to burn out of control, it will consume all in its path."

Mike needed no more clarification. "It's him."

With this in his mind, he did his usual rounds of the house to ensure Rosie's safety, then went to bed. He drifted. He landed. He was greeted. "Hi, Debbie. Hiya, Sean." A smile swept his face as he studied his mentor; training shoes just didn't suit the image. Why was that? Was it a deliberate attempt to show that he was his own being, with his own decisions? Independent of Mike? As usual, he didn't ask.

"Hello," said Sean.

"Hi," smiled Debbie.

Debbie had known for some time that things were going to change, and Sean's serious face confirmed her belief.

"Can we all talk together, about the situation with the two M's and Christine?"

Both nodded, and together they walked to Sean's room in silence, then sat around the table. Debbie began to play with a small pyramid of some rare stone; Sean raised an eyebrow and coughed. Instantly, she stopped and paid attention.

Sean cleared his throat and looked towards Mike. "Begin."

"I'm absolutely sure that Tony is doing something sinister."

The Samurai slowly crept to the outside of the door and listened.

"I'm not sure what, but I do know it's affecting Monica. He's on my mind a lot, and somehow I can sense him, all the time, as if I know him…it's almost as if he's hovering over my shoulder."

"How?" Sean asked in a serious tone. "Explain exactly."

"I can't put it any clearer than what I just have done!"

"We cannot be too careful, then. Follow me!"

Debbie and Mike stood up, looked at each other, and followed him to his most secret door, behind the midnight-blue curtain. She slipped her hand into his as they watched Sean unlock it with one of the keys around his waist. He sensed Debbie's nervousness. He, too, realised at that moment that things were never to be the same again.

The door swung open with a long, low creak. At last, his curiosity was answered. They stood in another beautiful room, which was both stark and imposing. An altar stood at one end, draped with a decorated cloth showing what looked like a story. It reminded Mike of the Bayeux Tapestry, lots of figures from some unknown history to Mike, recorded tumultuous events. At each side were green candles in resplendent holders, with flames longer than any candle flames he had seen before; the light from them was bright and clean. On the highly polished floor was a magic circle, and an adjacent triangle. The wall behind the altar was full of drawers, from edge to edge and top to bottom. It felt as though they had entered a cathedral. Their footsteps echoed, and a hush fell upon them. The door slowly swung back, without a creak, and clicked shut.

Sean took over, staring into Mike's eyes. "What is said in here is secret—even from you, Mike, as you will see. Anything we say will be safe. I'll let you think about it only when the time is right, understand?"

Mike nodded.

Debbie enquired, "What's happening? What's all this in aid of?"

Sean could feel her resistance to change, and he sensed that she was hanging on to her normality by the last disappearing threads. "You know cabalism, the cabala? Call it what you may, but I'm a Grand Master of it. It's all part of the Purpose."

"What purp—"

Sean smiled. "It's what you've been looking for all your life, Mike. Magic! Pure, absolute, one-hundred-percent magic. Real magic. If Tony is on a quest through the cabala, then he's looking for power. It's a power that people of your world have sought for thousands of generations. The cabala could make him an adversary of the highest order. I sense through you, Mike, that he is on such a quest. I'm glad you have told me what you have." He ushered them into the circle, safely past the triangle. "We are safe here—no ifs, no buts, *we are safe here*. Hold hands!"

They did as instructed; this was not the type of voice you disobeyed.

"No living person, or any other, can penetrate into this spot." Sean breathed out slowly. "Let's begin."

"Bastard!" the Samurai exclaimed, retreating to his room to send what message he could.

In the circle, they thought out a plan. Like all good plans, it wasn't rigid, or planned too far ahead; there was room for adjustments to suit whatever developments arose. The main points were to get Mike to secure Maddi's help, at any cost. He needed to share the secrets of his mind. Sean felt that this was imperative; if Monica was to be attacked or used, then a channel she trusted would be the only way in. They needed information on Tony, and to strike whilst suspicions were low, while his guard was only halfway up. Somehow, they would have to get access into wherever Tony lived. There, they'd find evidence in abundance, if this was indeed his chosen path. Debbie would no doubt have to go on a little holiday into Monica's mind, via Maddi's.

"Why via Maddi?" enquired Debbie.

"Mike isn't as close as he was, and after what has just happened, I think Maddi will be the only person able to get close enough for the jump," replied Sean. He added that it would be a good idea to see inside Christine's mind, too—either to eliminate her from suspicion, or to get her to join their efforts. Sean would set up diversions, and if at all possible, he might have a chance to see inside Tony's mind.

It was a weird night inside his head, and soon it was time to go back to his body. Sean made the plans safe by encapsulating them in three blue, hovering balls to remain in his room, floating within the circle, protected. Mike said his farewells, and kissed Debbie; the salty taste on his lips made him notice the tears on her cheeks.

The next morning, Mike sent for Maddi. When he heard her knock, he beckoned her in. "Don't look so worried. Come in, and sit down."

She looked at him curiously, and he wondered, *How the hell am I going to explain all this?* He smiled and played with a pen in his hands.

"Well?"

"Let's have a cuppa. Tea or coffee?"

"Coffee, black, no sugar. Thanks."

He passed her a steaming hot coffee, the cup shaking slightly in the saucer as he reached towards her. "Er, remember you said that you wanted me to do something about Monica?"

"Ye-es."

"Well, I've something to tell you. I think you might just imagine I'm mad, but here goes." He went silent as he stared at her; she looked stunning as usual. He wondered why he had bothered looking at Monica before her, not for the first time.

Slowly, a certain jewel in a particular room began to glow. Taking a deep breath, and putting the phone on divert, he began. An hour and a half passed by, and coffee was consumed at an alarming rate. For such a surreal situation, the explanation came out well.

Maddi listened intensely, and when he was finished, she said, "Well, I believe you to be honest, and I don't think any other explanation would fit!"

To tell someone so much and have it believed so easily was nothing short of amazing; it was further evidence to Mike of what a fabulous person Maddi was. When lunchtime crept up, Mike asked if she'd share it with him. They went to the staff refectory and sat together in a quiet corner, continuing the discussion. Then they went back to his office.

They sat side by side in the chrome-and-leather executive chairs near the window. "When will Debbie come, then? Will I feel anything? And couldn't she just go straight from you to Monica?"

"No, her guard will be up. Like I said, it has to be someone she trusts—not a man! You won't feel a thing, I think! How does right now sound?"

"Oh, well, I see, er...go on, then. What do I do?" She sat as if she were in the dentist's chair, waiting for a root canal treatment, and had just been told there was no anaesthetic.

Mike smiled. "Don't worry, she's delightful. I'll miss her no end."

He had told her almost everything, including what he and Debbie did; trust had to be built on honesty. She waited and smiled back at him. "Go on, then. I'm ready." She relaxed as much as she could and closed her eyes.

"You had to believe me this much, Maddi, or she wouldn't be able to come. Thank you." He coughed and concentrated. "Can I read your mind, Maddi? Can Debbie come in?"

"Yes."

And that was all there was to it. As welcome as the flowers in spring, and as gentle as a summer's breeze, she stepped through Maddi's window and skipped into her mind. "Hiya, Maddi. How ya doin'?"

"Oooh."

Debbie giggled. "You'll get used to me; I just hope he gets me back as soon as possible. I can't manage without his dick, to be truthful."

Maddi laughed, and with her head to one side, she put her fingertips to her forehead.

"She's in, then?"

"Yes, she's in, Mike."

"Nice place, Maddi, a bit like Mike's. Bloody hell, are you a hypochondriac or what? What are all these pills for on the shelves?"

Maddi started to speak and cut herself short. Instead, she directed her thoughts towards Debbie. *Well, it's to deal with life, really. Read the labels; it's my way of coping sometimes.*

Fascinated by the show, Mike stared at her expressions; he could only guess at what was being said.

"Oh, I see now," Debbie commented. Then she smiled broadly; the ones on the top shelf looked as entertaining as anything on the top shelf in a book or magazine store. "I think I might borrow a few of these fantasies; there's always room for a few more!"

After an hour or so, Maddi left the room with her new thoughts.

Mike felt empty-headed. "I'm still here," Sean said in an attempt to raise Mike's spirits.

"Yes, Sean, I know."

"She'll be back. Don't worry."

"Yes, Sean, I know."

He wasn't raising Mike's spirits very high, so he walked back to his secret domain. Opening one of the thought balls in the circle, he gave an instruction. "Give her a while, and let her settle. Plan your wife's trip, and plan the burglary of Tony's place."

Sean left his room and locked the door with an echoing *clunk*, then went to sit by the fountain. He missed Debbie, too, and he wanted to think. He turned down a little-used corridor and began a long stroll down one of memory's lanes. Arms behind his back, he took long, slow strides, staring at the cobbles. After a few turns, he stopped dead in his tracks. He saw a portion of a footprint—just the slightest outside edge—looking back at him from the dust. It was too big for Debbie, and it

163

couldn't be his; he hadn't been this way in years. He wrinkled his forehead with worry.

How could he have been so stupid? How could he have underestimated how far Tony had progressed, so as not to take precautions against such a threat? He turned, running back the way he had come. His robes flapped behind him, slapping the air; his expression changed with each step from that of a thinker to that of a killer. He burst back into his room, every candle in his candelabra flickering almost to the point of blowing out. He strode to the fire. Hanging above it, on two gold brackets, was his sword. He took it and strapped the long scabbard to his back using two of the three red cords hanging next to it. The other piece he tied around his head, to hold his hair.

Despite everything, his rate of breath remained unchanged. He turned to the door and began a systematic sweep of the whole mind fortress. The balcony, the fountain, the pit of despair—all were safe. It was the old labyrinths of distant thoughts where the threat lay, and intuition led him to where he felt he should commence. Each step brought more stealth, strength, and courage; the hunter's instincts were paramount, and honed to a keen edge.

The Samurai sensed the coming onslaught. He stood and blew out the candle, packed his few belongings, and left the room. He set off down the route he had come, asking himself how he'd been discovered.

The movement of the Samurai travelled to Sean like an electric charge down copper wire. He drew his sword, and held it at the ready. Like two trains on the same track, they were heading towards each other. "Mike! Sit down, now! Stop what you are doing."

Mike, who had just thought of his early girlfriend again, sat down at his desk, taking up his thinking position.

For the first time in his short existence, the Samurai felt fear.

Mike's mind had seen some of what Sean was capable of. But no longer was there just a wise old mentor strolling around his mind fixing troubles or advising future actions. There was much more to caring for special mind than that! Here was the

Sean of his homeland, his true form, which Mike had never seen. All the mind warrior training of that far distant place took over. Sean's lifeblood turned to pure confidence, surging through his veins. He asked himself in a growing, yet controlled, fury, *Who is in my place? Who is in my MIND CASTLE?*

The Samurai stopped, his own breath and heartbeat deafening in the still corridors. He swallowed hard, his eyes moving in all directions. He didn't hear a sound, but at the edge of his vision, the slightest movement caught his attention...too late.

With the speed of a cobra, Sean spun, uttering a battle cry that would have driven a banshee away. The sword took one long, quietly whistling sweep. With a sickening slowing of pace, a squelching thud saw the Samurai's head fly off and hit the wall. An obscene splatter followed, as a high-pressure flow of blood washed the stonework.

His body still stood in shock with no head on its shoulders as the hands lost their grip on the unused sword. It clattered to the floor, sparks rising from its virgin edge.

Sean kicked the body over, took two strides towards it, and rammed the point of his sword into its chest. With the speed and skill of a war surgeon, he cut out the heart. Holding and squeezing it in his hand, the blood ran from between his fingers as he stared at the corpse. His intense gaze made the body burst into flame; the putrid smell of burning fresh flesh filled the corridor, as did the sound of spitting, sizzling fat.

He removed a sacred cloth from his pocket, wiping the blade before he re-sheathed it. He picked the head up by its hair, and rapidly went back to his room.

Mike felt as if some unknown burden had been lifted from his shoulders, but he suspected it was only making way for a future heavy load. He knew that this was not the time to ask anything, so sat there a while longer, hardly daring to move. He'd know when to, soon enough. Whatever was happening in his subconscious kingdom demanded steadiness, and no disturbance, of that he was sure.

Sean slammed the door, dropping the head onto the table, its face still wearing an expression of surprise, terror, and shock. Its mouth was still in the throes of screaming, "No-oo!"

He pulled a polished brass dish off a shelf and threw it onto the table with a noise like a reverberating gong. It was soon accompanied by a sliding *squelch*, as the heart slithered around its rim after being thrown in. Picking up the head and staring into its face, he squeezed it between his palms. The skull sent out sharp *cracks* as it split like splintering timber. The eyes popped out like champagne corks, and after a couple of circuits around the plate, they landed on red blood like two roulette balls. The tongue slithered out, as if in one last attempt at an utterance. Sean tore the ears off and threw them into the obnoxious raw stew.

The head was discarded, and after two nauseating bounces, it landed on the fire.

Anger consumed Sean; it was time to begin the war. Picking up the brass plate in slippery, blood-ridden fingers, he spoke to its contents as they merged into a jelly. "Tony, hear, see, and feel…THIS!" He let go of the dish. It fell with a tumultuous crash onto the table, instantly bursting into flame, shooting upwards like the discharge from a jet engine, and scorching an area on the ceiling over two yards in diameter. He stared into the glowing red ashes, smiled, and took a deep breath.

Miles away, Tony dropped to his knees, his mind filled with a stench that would make a cesspit smell like a rose, and an image of Sean's face distorting in and out of focus. It magnified, then shrank away, and finally rushed headlong towards him. His face thrust right up to the edge of Tony's mind's eye, saying in a powerful tone, "I HAVE POWER YOU CAN ONLY DREAM OF!"

"Who the fuck?" spluttered Tony. The image in his head disappeared as soon as it had come. Filled with nauseous pain, he threw up violently. With the remains of half-digested food hanging from his chin, he threw back a reply. "That was you, wasn't it? Mike fucking Reeves."

As surely as a rock hitting the ground when dropped, the paths of Tony, Sean, Mike, Debbie, Maddi, Christine, and Monica all took a jolt towards each other.

That night, Maddi was ironing, Walkman in her ears, swaying in time to the music. She had been asked to carry on as normally as possible, gently getting used to Debbie being there. Soon the day's toils would be done. "Christ, Maddi, are you always so bloody conscientious? Get fed up, for once."

Maddi yawned, stretched, and looked at the ironing she had done. Then she looked at what was left, walked over to the electrical switch, which the iron was plugged in to, and with a smile, clicked it up. The iron began to click as it cooled. Her mind was beautifully constructed, and probably soon to be on the waiting list for rent. It had, however, no keepers as of yet, and was usually controlled in a strong, single-minded way. Tonight it was different.

She showered.

She powdered the delicate places.

She made a hot, milky drink, and with Debbie drifting in and out of her mind, she went to bed anticipating something. She sat up against the headboard, took a sip of the drink, blew the steam away, and snuggled down in optimistic expectation.

"Go to sleep, Maddi. I'll meet you in your dreams."

"Okay," she answered, finishing off the mug.

She dreamt as never before: the clouds looked so real, the strange yellow light beckoned her, and the mist was so translucently inviting. Maddi touched the clouds with her feet. She was floating, almost, as she looked around, drinking in the panorama. Looking down slowly and dreamily, she saw the hand slip into hers, and looked up into deep, warm, soothing emerald-green eyes. She squeezed the hand and smiled. The hand gripped back affectionately, and the face lit up with a smile like an angel. "Come with me."

Within minutes, the platform loomed and Maddi stared at it in wonderment. Like the touch of a feather, they landed. Led by Debbie, they strolled hand in hand through the curtain, past an astonished Sean.

Maddi stared at him wide-eyed.

He stared back with a raised eyebrow, then opened his mouth to speak.

Debbie said, "Shh!" His mouth closed again; this was not in the plan.

Like two wood elves, they made their way silently past the fountain in the courtyard, then onto the ivory staircase. "This way. Up here is where I call my home."

Maddi stared up. Everything was just wonderful here, so...so *Mike*. She could sense him, even in the stones. The place felt strong, dependable, warm, soothing, and kind.

Before she knew it, the door closed, and she was sitting on the huge, circular bed. "What's your taste in music, Maddi?"

Still bouncing up and down softly on the comfortable bed, she had no idea what to say. "Oh, anything, absolutely any-thing!"

"Okie-dokie. How's about...er...mmm, yes, I know: opera, *Madame Butterfly*, I think!" She pressed a couple of buttons on the jukebox, and the music filled the room; it was as if they were in a speaker. Picking up a small bowl with grapes in it, Debbie plopped down on her tummy besides Maddi. "Want one?"

Maddi took one, noticing how Debbie's bottom looked so cute in her nightdress. Was she wearing that a few seconds ago? *Wow, it's not very thick, you can see everything*, she thought. She concentrated on the music. "I wouldn't have you down for culture, Debbie."

"Neither did I!!" laughed Debbie, wiping a grape seed from her chin. Never had a woman seemed so alluring to Maddi.

They both shared the humour as Maddi relaxed onto her back, threw a grape into the air, and caught it in her mouth. "Bet you can't do that!"

So Debbie threw two grapes into the air, caught them in her teeth, and bit them in half. Wiping her chin with the back of her hand, she popped the other two halves into Maddi's mouth. "God, aren't I a show off!"

Like best friends, they talked about love, risks, escapades, and men throughout the night. Debbie took Maddi like a piece of modelling clay and played with her, and Maddi held nothing back. She wasn't at all surprised when Debbie asked, "Have you ever done it with a woman?"

"Yes, of course I have, at school, actually, with a friend of mine. It was nice, really, sort of innocently sexy and daring. It ended up being one of the best orgasms I can remember."

The reason for the visit back home became apparent when Mike found himself dreaming. He was in a movie theatre, all done up in the gold decadence of the fifties. The light dimmed, the curtains opened, and the screen lit up to reveal Debbie's room. The camera zoomed in on the bed.

Debbie looked up to the screen. She smiled, then winked. Mike stared open-mouthed. The cinema was warm, he was naked, he was alone, and it wasn't an ice cream in his hand.

Debbie clicked her fingers, and Maddi's nightdress disappeared. The show began. "Oh God, Debbie, I've got to see her in the morning."

CHAPTER 13

The next morning, Mike rang for Maddi. A few minutes later, she came through the door. "Look at his eyes, Maddi," urged Debbie. "Look well if he was watching!"

Maddi blushed, and Mike picked it up straight away. "You look a little flushed; are you okay? Doesn't Debbie suit you?"

"Yes, I'm all right, thank you."

"She's wonderful to have around, don't you think?"

"Yes, she is."

"Oh, thank you, sweetie."

Don't mention it. Maddi returned the thought as if Debbie had always been there. She would miss her when she'd gone.

Mike sat down and invited Maddi to do the same. "Tell me, when do you think you'll be at Monica's next?"

Debbie couldn't help but give a little shiver of jealousy, which Maddi faintly picked up. Without any detectable pause in thought or speech, Maddi replied that she would be going that night and might sleep over.

"That would be perfect. Debbie, can you hear me? Or does Maddi have to relay thought?"

"Tell him not to talk like a fool; haven't I always responded to other people's speech in an instant? Sean, too. Go on, tell him."

170

"She says to just speak."

"Right." acknowledged Mike.

"Coward!" accused Debbie.

"*He is my boss.*"

"You know what you have to do, don't you, Debbie?" prompted Mike.

"Tell the bozo, YES! I'm not stupid; I'm to go into Monica's mind and have a look around, to see how far things have gone."

Maddi relayed the message.

"You missed bozo out."

Maddi laughed, and Mike nodded, understanding perfectly well what was going on. "Well done. What about Christine?"

"Huh, tell him that him and Sean are the brains of the outfit. Tell them to work out how to get access."

Again, Maddi relayed the message.

"Smarty-pants; tell her we'll use the game."

Debbie grimaced, and Sean shook his head as Mike thought, *Oh no, she didn't know about the game!*

"Oh? And what game is this, then?" enquired Maddi.

Mike explained, making it sound as if it was part of a previous plan, leaving out the details of how he was winning, and of the reward he had received.

This gave rise to one of Maddi's famous "looks": her back went straight, her eyes narrowed, her head turned slightly, and she slowly drew in her breath—angry, but absolutely captivating. She said nothing.

Mike told them that something had happened in his head last night, but he knew nothing yet; the thought wouldn't materialise, and he was sure Sean wanted it that way.

Debbie was intrigued. With only Sean there, what could have happened? She wished she had stopped to ask if everything was okay when they'd passed him the night before.

All of this would have to wait until the next meeting.

Sean was busy making his preparations, reviewing books and magic instruments, revising and practising his knowledge.

Tony was annoyed by the lack of information from Mike, but the Samurai in Monica's head had sent back the information that Maddi was coming to see her tonight. So he, too, was making plans. Information, information, information: that was what all successful plans depend on. Tony's first priority was to build up a dossier and use it wisely.

Mike decided he should go on a little reconnoitre himself, to Tony's address. He would just have a look, make notes, and get some information. He left the office at lunchtime. Chesterfield wasn't so far away, and he had some advertising magazine proofs to drop off at the printers anyway.

The area Tony resided in was good to look at, but not so good to live in. As the locals said, "every thug and their mother lives there." The neighbourhood consisted of a maze of narrow streets, and four- or five-story converted cotton mills. Small courtyards were lit with large, domed lights. The surfaces were cobbled, and there were plenty of plant containers. All the wood was stained in green and well maintained. The lampposts and street signs were black and gold. Herringbone fences stained green or dark oak separated parking spaces from garages, hiding wheelie bins and waste-disposal sites. The area used to buzz with the *click, click, click* of the looms, but now the mills had been converted into luxury flats by a businessman of ill repute. This was the first place the town police looked for anything connected to a crime, but they never came alone.

It was raining. Puddles were everywhere, and the air smelt clean, fresh, and earthy. Mike's nerves made him sense more: the huge drops were falling from the lampposts and landing with loud splats and plops. The rain landing atop his head seemed colder than usual, and the spray bouncing off the car roof appeared sharper than normal. The area looked more menacing because of it. Even the car looked forlorn as he walked away and looked over his shoulder. *"Don't leave me here! I value my wheels!"* it seemed to shout.

He had some papers in his hand, to make it look as if he was interested in purchasing some property. He looked around at the balconies, the trees, and the tubs with bushes. He could see the attraction, but without doubt, the message being shouted from the walls to him was, "Don't live here!" The river also seemed to speak: "Stop here, and you'll end up in me! Probably with concrete boots, so piss off whilst you've got the chance." It was Tony's presence. This was his territory and his essence had seeped into the whole fabric of the area, even the bricks seemed to know this visitor was not welcome. Everything shouted stop, rethink, go back, but he carried on.

"Number thirteen; Christ, I should have known." He had found the building where Tony lived, and his name was illuminated on the intercom board. Having learnt his trade from a million scripts on TV, he waited for someone to leave, smiled, and pushed past as if he owned the place. He was in. *I've always wanted to do that*, was the surprisingly calm thought he had. He walked slowly, making mental notes of what was here, and what was there. Possible entry and escape routes were logged. He thought, *It's like playing soldiers as a kid.*

Nothing could have been further from the truth.

Again he noticed his heightened senses. The parquet floor was smooth and highly reflective; the brass light switches and lift call-button surrounds looked like they had been polished for a royal visit. The marble walls had a sheen he'd only seen in expensive advertisements.

He saw the arrow pointing to *Apartments 10 to 20* and followed it. With a sideways glance, he walked past. Number 13 shouted to him off the door. *Is someone knocking?* Mike thought. It was a rhetorical question. *No, it's me fuckin' heart!* It thumped deafeningly, and his swallowing was louder than ever before. His pace quickened, and he followed the corridor to its conclusion: a small balcony overlooking the river.

As if by magic, a possible way in was revealed to him. Although the drop and splash looked frightening, a child could jump across to the next balcony. It was obvious this adjacent balcony was Tony's. He had just walked past the door. He was no architect, but Tony's apartment must view the riverbank. The area on the other side of the river was landscaped and beautiful. As he began to feel satisfied with his lunchtime's work, fear hit him. The hairs on the back of his neck stood up, and instinct shouted in its loudest voice, *Get out*! A shiver stopped on each bone of his spine. He could hear voices and footsteps coming towards him, and knew who it probably was. He decided to act as casual as possible; he walked back looking at the papers in his hand.

Tony was talking to a smaller man as he walked towards Mike. He had blond hair tied back in a ponytail. Sunglasses covered what Mike knew would be ice-cool blue eyes on a cruel, but handsome face atop an Adonis-like body. He had appeared in the press on numerous occasions; identifying him at close quarters was easy. He glided past, oozing self-assurance. This was a man who radiated importance and…evil. The smaller man had a slight build and rat-like features. He wore a light grey suit. What a pair! Mike's eyes followed them over the top of his papers, and the smaller man returned his gaze. The sunglasses kept Mike from being sure where Tony was looking. Mike's papers were shaking; he could feel his colour drain, and he was so scared he wanted to piss on the spot.

The pair stopped. The smaller man was about to say something. Mike dropped the papers and gave way to panic, running as fast as he could. He almost slipped on the polished floor. It felt like one of those dreams where you could run forever and not get tired. Without any pause for breath, he ran all the way to the car and fumbled for his keys, which he dropped only inches from a drain. With shaking hands and stinging sweat blurring his vision, he managed to find them and unlock the door. Before he got in, he looked up. There on a balcony were Tony and "The Rat." Mike couldn't stare back; he got in the car and drove away with a squeal of tyres.

Back at the office, he sat trembling almost uncontrollably. The whiskey bottle rattled against the edge of the glass like a rattlesnake as he poured himself a quick "calmer." "What an evil bastard! I felt as if I was staring at Lucifer himself."

"You should have asked me for help; I just can't weigh you up; if it's something trivial, we have deep and meaningful conversations; yet, here you are at one of the worst moments of your life, and what do you do? Nothing!"

"I know, I know. I felt like I was doing it in secret." He took up his thinking position.

""It's okay; I'd have come in anyway, if it was necessary. Actually, you've done a good thing. He'll feel the net tightening, but at the same time, he will consider you a fool, and he'll almost certainly underestimate you. For now, that's a good thing. But listen: there's much more to all this than you realise; it will soon be the time to explain a lot more, but not now. Listen. Listen very carefully. Don't be disheartened, and don't underestimate yourself. When the time comes, you'll be a lot mightier than today, believe me."

Not convinced, Mike shuddered and drank his whiskey. As the day proceeded, he calmed down, and when he got home, he thought he should ring Rosie and see if she had arrived safely in London. She had, and she might be there for quite a while, which was fortunate to say the least. Had Sean had a hand in this, too? He spent the evening writing an e-mail to his doctor—a very long one, which he knew the doctor would devour with enthusiasm. He had much to tell.

Night came and found Maddi at Monica's. She was feeling well enough to hold a conversation. Maddi's presence reassured her. They sat listening to music with a coffee apiece. Maddi looked around at Monica's decor. Castles and cottages in miniature adorned the shelves and fireplace mantel. Candles of varying colour and size were clustered in groups, and a rich mixture of herbal smells filled the room. Books filled shelf after shelf, ranging from topics such as cooking through to culture and religion. Monica's finicky nature was illustrated in particular by her CD collection, all arranged alphabetically. Maddi yawned tactfully. "You crafty devil; go on ask her now if it's still okay for you to sleep over," prompted Debbie.

"Oh, dearie me, I'm tired. Listen to that rain!" Maddi yawned. "I can see the wipers sending me off to sleep."

Monica smiled. "Stay if you want; I've already said you can, haven't I?"

"I knew you'd say that."

"Yes, you often seem to know what I'm going to say. Shows how close we are, eh? How our minds are in tune."

The time was right; having been there before, there was no barrier, and entry was easy. Debbie settled in to wait for sleep. Maddi and Monica took showers, filled the dishwasher, locked the doors, and turned out the lights. Sleep came easily.

"Right," a determined Debbie said to herself. She stood up and went through the mind's window, sprinkling some blue liquid on the ledge from a bottle Sean had given her. She started her exploration. There seemed more desolation than she remembered, so much vandalism, in Monica's mind. What had happened? Surely, it wasn't this bad the last time she came? How could someone do this to a mind?

Sean's voice came to her suddenly: "*GET OUT.*"

Startled, she looked around as if expecting to see him close by. "What? How?" She looked around as panic started to well up inside her. She ran back to the entrance, and a strange, orange glow filled the mind sky. Not far from the mind gate, she stopped to catch breath. The air seemed thin, as if at high altitude.

"GET OUT NOW!" Sean's voice was full of urgency.

Her breath was loud, too loud. She was bent double, hands on knees. She straightened slowly. Her searching eyes looked through a broken window, straight through a small, one-roomed cottage, and out of a broken back window. The Samurai stood at the gateway to freedom, blocking her only escape.

Debbie knew that any attempt of returned thought contact with Sean would bring the Samurai to her like a homing device. A diversion was needed. She thought of what she had seen here and what could help her. She moved slowly and stealthily to avoid detection. Then, at what she thought was a reasonable distance, she ran. Her aim was to find two cottages: one for friendship, the second a blacksmith's dream workshop. She reached the first with her lungs ready to burst and her temples close to popping. Like most of the cottages near the centre, the damage here was minimal.

She walked into Friendship Cottage, where the biggest cupboard was marked *Maddi*. She opened it and deliberately disturbed it. She put papers out of order, stacked memory boxes in mixed colours, any meticulous order in any pile was altered. Whoever straightened things up around here would have a hell of a job to do. She then ran to the dream workshop. "I want a nightmare, and I want it *now!*"

The rusty, metallic figure of a blacksmith opened its eyes. "Mmm? What you say?" Everything in this brain seemed starved of oxygen; thought transfer was slow. No wonder Monica had to sit and gather thoughts.

"Don't act like the village idiot, just listen and do!" The blacksmith was soon working furiously in dream double-time as Debbie ran away.

Monica began to sweat, then to toss and turn. Dream Monica was hanging onto a ledge, her fingernails starting to peel off. Only a few feet away, Dream Maddi was ironing with her earphones and Walkman on.

Debbie, almost at the point of collapse, ran as close to the window as she could without being seen. How could this Samurai breathe so easily in here?

Dream Monica uttered, "Help me."

Dream Maddi carried on ironing.

"HELP ME!"

Dream Maddi tapped her foot to the music.

Debbie concentrated and sent an astral thought flying to Maddi's mind. "Maddi, can you hear me? You must wake up."

The Samurai drew his blade and stepped towards the cottage.

Dream Monica screamed at the top of her voice: "MADDI, HELP ME, PLEASE HELP ME!!!" Real-life Monica sat up, shouting the same words.

Maddi leapt out of her bed in the guest room, running to her friend.

The Samurai stopped dead in his tracks, then turned.

"Maddi, come closer, hug her." Debbie ran to the window and glanced over her shoulder.

The Samurai screamed his death charge. With the blade above his head, he ran towards her.

Debbie leapt to the window.

Maddi hugged Monica.

Monica uttered, "Bloody hell, that was the most horrible dream ever."

Debbie threw the remainder of the blue liquid at the opening. It began to seep into the cracks immediately. The Samurai stood back. She jumped through the mind window. "Phew, that was close!"

"What?" Maddi asked, not sure who she was talking to. She could hardly remember waking up, or coming to sit by her friend.

"Oh, Maddi, I was falling and you wouldn't help. It was horrible."

"Huh," said Debbie, "*I* was just about to be cut in bloody half, and it wasn't a dream, either!"

"How the hell does he cope with this?" Maddi said in a whisper to herself. Then she immediately turned her attention to Monica. "There, there. It's only a dream, just a dream, that's all. Go back to sleep; it's probably just the tablets the doctor gave you. At least it shows they are in your system doing something."

"Well, I wish they wouldn't," sniffled Monica, just before she slid back to her slumber. She looked ill, and dark under her eyes.

Maddi waited a while for her to settle, then walked back to bed, shaking her head. She sleepily wondered why she was mixed up in all this; life felt delightfully uncomplicated before Mike and Company came on the scene. For a few seconds in Mike's head, a certain jewel lost its sparkle. For a few moments, a room in the same place went duller as a candle flickered. As she lay in bed, Debbie told her tale. Maddi's face bore a serious frown. As she listened, the candle began to glow again, and the jewel shone

The next day, Monica took another turn for the worse, and the doctor doubled her dose. The Samurai awaited further instructions. He couldn't contact Tony until sleep came to his master; he was a lower-level mind warrior, and he had done as much as he could for now. He returned his concentration towards keeping the flow of oxygen stifled.

After the doctor's visit, Maddi sat in thought again, and Debbie came through. "Maddi, get me back to Mike as quick as you can. I've a lot to tell, and something seems to say that time is of the essence right now. Don't you agree?"

"Yes, definitely."

She picked up Monica's phone and rang Mike's number.

"Hello?"

"Hiya, Mike. It's me, Maddi. I've got to come and see you as soon as possible. Debbie needs to come back to you." Although she hated leaving Monica, she told her she had to get over to her mother's because she had promised days ago, and said she'd be back as soon as possible.

Mike could hardly wait to open the door when Maddi's car pulled up outside. "God knows what the neighbours will say when they see her walk up the bloody path!" He greeted her and ushered her inside, where they concentrated on Debbie's return. Back inside Mike's mind, Debbie ran off to share her news with Sean. Maddi and Mike answered each other's questions, sharing thoughts and fears.

Maddi talked incessantly whilst Mike prepared a meal. Both were increasingly concerned about Monica's vulnerability; she seemed wide open to attack. They sat down to the meal and went through things again. They needed Sean.

Sean burst into Mike's thoughts like a gunfighter into a saloon. "Mike, listen. You've got to go to Tony's, tonight. I'll cause diversions until tomorrow. Monica is okay for now; Debbie's taken care of things there, so don't worry about that. You've only got tonight, and you need as much information as possible. We need time together, too, all of us. Book a holiday, be ill, anything, just be at my beck and call for a few days. It's very, very urgent. We need time, and Monica needs protection."

Mike looked to Maddi. "It looks as though there's going to be an epidemic; we'll both ring up work in the morning and say we are ill. Tonight we are going out burgling. I'll tell you more when you get back, but right now, go home and get some clothes in a suitcase, you might have to stay with Monica for a few days. I'll explain more later, I promise, okay? Trust me. Monica is all right; she'll come to no harm."

"Oh dear, I suppose so. I'll see you later, then. Bye." She gave Mike a peck on the cheek and left.

Mike watched her leave. When the car disappeared around the corner, he went back inside quietly.

Sean got straight into planning a diversion for Tony.

Monica slept a disturbed, but safe, sleep. Sean reasoned that attacking her mind, although important, was lower down on Tony's priorities than he might have thought. Tonight, when Tony was asleep, the Samurai would report Debbie's little adventure. Now was the time to pay Tony a mind visit.

CHAPTER 14

"Fuck, fuck, fuck, fuck!! What's happening?"

Tony's incantations were not working fast enough, his thought transfers were not coming out correctly, and idiotic thoughts kept shooting uninvited into his head; the more he tried, the more they came in. Irritably, he shouted commands to the Rat and Stirling who had been instructed to guard the doors to his apartment, and his "workshop" which were the adjoining rooms. He didn't want to be disturbed.

Sean was in his room, surrounded by magical equipment, causing havoc by thought transfer. Locked in on Tony, he was producing mayhem. The route provided by the Samurai's body parts was still fresh enough to use as a transmitter to the mind that sent him. It was a fast-track discovery process, and he was finding out that Tony was good. If he could control his temper, he would be even better. The next priority was to somehow get Tony away from his lair. In a few hours, he would probably break down Sean's attacks and then induce sleep to contact the Monica Samurai. The essence of surprise would be gone, he would know much more about Debbie and him, and he would figure out where they were from. Sean could win the first skirmishes, but then a full war would begin.

Tonight, Mike had no specific instructions except to go, look, and report. Sean knew Mike had enough intelligence to realise what was important and what was superficial. Taking quick breaks from the mind attack, he told Mike as much as he could, with instructions to brief Maddi fully.

Mike answered a knock on the door. "Hiya, Maddi. No problems?"

"No." She looked agitated. "You?"

"I'm ready." He quickly explained what they had to do. "I've sorted us a kit; look at this bloody lot!" He pointed to two haversacks and an array of what he thought would be good "burglary gear." "I couldn't find any striped vests and masks, or bags marked swag, though." He smiled weakly.

A faint smile crossed Maddi's lips.

"Can you think of anything else we might need?"

Together they went through it. "No, it seems good to me— not that I'm an expert, of course." She did wonder about the old walking stick, but felt he might be offended if she said anything. She turned around and rested her bottom on the edge of the table. "What about Tony? How do we know he won't be there?"

"Well, Sean's been busy. He'll be no problem for a few hours."

"Before we start, let me ring Monica up." Maddi offered her friend a few words of comfort and told her she would see her in the morning.

Mike told Maddi how Sean had driven Tony to despair, and how nothing seemed to be going right for him. "I think Sean knows he'll have a special place to go to, and with luck he'll go there to sort his mind out. I hope so; we don't want him in residence!" He then told her of what he thought of as "the start of war." "He's only gone and bloody told him it was *me* who was making the disturbances, and that Tony was a low-level magician who would never attain the heights of greatness I will, and that he would forever remain a magician, whilst I would become a Sorcerer!" Mike had been agog when told this, but Sean had assured him that all was under control.

Sean left Tony's mind.

With a glass bottle matching Debbie's, filled with the same blue liquid, Sean stood outside the window to Monica's mind. Unable to enter, he dangled precariously on the end of a delicate astral thread suspended from the platform. Debbie sat anxiously, legs hanging over the edge, watching the thread disappear like a diver's line into the sea of blue mist.

Like a burning Ku Klux Klan cross, Sean burnt a mind spell into the pathway leading to Monica's mind. The spell would be difficult to break down, but not impossible. Sean then bricked up Monica's mind window, using magic that would keep Tony occupied for weeks if necessary.

Tony needed to get away from his apartment; fresh air would encourage clear thought. He knew exactly where to go.

The Rat and Stirling saw him leave, and assuming their duties were done, they left too. "Nobody could disturb him if he wasn't there to be disturbed." They casually told a man in Sterling's service to keep an eye out for anything suspicious and report it to them.

It was a quiet night and the watchman sat in reception with nothing unusual to report; people passed him to and fro, that's all.

Before his quest in the dark arts had begun, years before he knew he would need such places, he had selected two sites. Whilst at University, he had spent much time rock-climbing in solitude. He didn't want crowds, so he hunted for peaceful locations, far from the popular "edges" of Curbar, Stanage, and Froggatt. Another hobby had been studying antiquities, which included the pursuit of standing stones, stone circles, ancient track ways, and ley lines. Each hobby led him to an area around Ashover, a beautiful village on the edge of the Peak District, and Birchover, a mysterious location surrounded by strange rock formations. Legends of witchcraft and reports of mad priests and cults in the area made him take his very first steps to where he was now. He regarded the area as his spiritual home.

Tony had two special places in the area.

The first was "Rowtor Rocks," near Birchover, a cabalist priest had carved rocks intensively in the 1800s; the area also had strong connections with the Druids. The second, his favourite, was "Highoredish," a rocky escarpment near Ashover. Tony had driven there at speed whilst Sean was bricklaying, and now stood on his favourite wind-sculptured slab of grit stone, deep in thought. The air was clean here; a chilly wind always blew, and disturbance was unlikely. The path laid by Christine's mind warrior to Monica would be hard to follow even from here, but if it could be done anywhere, this was the place.

Sean estimated that Tony would break through around 2:00 a.m.—and knowing Sean, it would be an exact forecast, rather than an estimate—he would feel elated, only to find Monica's window bricked up with a message in runic symbols. The message would offer a direct insult at his intelligence by pointing out how easily he had been drawn into leaving his lair.

Mike didn't know what "the Purpose" was, and his head was in a whirl. Who was using whom? He had so many questions, and so little time. All he could do was concentrate on the job in hand. But when tonight was over, he would demand to be taught some truths.

He and Maddi's journey to the old mills was a quiet one. The phrase "dark satanic mills" took on a whole new meaning for them both when they parked outside them. The buildings loomed up into the night. A bright moon, occasionally blocked by clouds whistling past in the wind, all added to the eerie feel of the place. In the distance could be seen the outline of The Crooked Spire of which Chesterfield was famous.

They both picked up their share of the equipment. As Maddi stood by his side, he looked at her, and the lack of any real plan dawned on him; it would be "suck it and see." For an instant, he thought of asking Sean for some quick advice, but realised immediately that any disturbance to Sean's work could be disastrous.

Their footsteps broke the night's silence like glass breaking as they took deliberate, confidence-building strides. Hand-in-hand, they went to the stairs, where entry was once again easy. Everything seemed to be going their way; Sean had made Tony leave in anger, the patio door leading from his balcony into the apartment was left unlocked, as Mike discovered after his leap from the stairwell's balcony. He went back to the edge and held his arms out for Maddi to jump; the distance between them seemed to magnify before his eyes. She jumped, and he held her safe for a few seconds. Their gazes held, and a candle flame spat and grew brighter.

The pleasant wisp of time soon passed, and they both lit their torches and walked in. Mike opened the door as if he were a master criminal. "FUCK ME!" he yelled as he caught sight of the snarling Rottweiler. This was why the door was left unlocked! The dog lunged towards them in a one-tracked frenzy.

Maddi stood frozen in fear as it singled her out for the first attack. At the edge of sound, she heard a click, and it was immediately followed by a silvery blue, lightning-like blur. The swordstick quickly changed its guise and was thrust into the hound's throat; the force of the dog's charge made the blade sink deeper, wrenching it from Mike's grip. The dog landed in a bloody heap only inches away from Maddi's feet.

For probably half a minute, they both stared at the dead animal, then at each other. Mike broke the silence. "Oh, Maddi, let's go. I've n-never been so b-b-bloody scared in my life!"

"We can't! Think of Monica; we are her chance of surviving this. Think of what Sean's doing right now, just to give us this chance."

"I'm sorry. Christ, in the films it's the man who says what you've just said, isn't it?"

"It's okay."

"How can you be so bloody calm with that thing lying at your feet?"

"Dunno, but I know this: you are no coward. How you acted just then was brilliant; I'd have my throat lying there now if it wasn't for you. And to think I nearly said we didn't need the walking stick!"

"It's funny you know, I only purchased it a few week ago. I'd seen one once on a Sherlock Holmes film. It's called a swordstick; the outside of the stick is a scabbard, really, and you release the blade with a button in a flash. I don't even know why

I went in the shop, and the owner said that a man had only just left after buying a samurai sword! I'm glad he hadn't gone for this!"

"Me too!" said Maddi.

Mike smiled then, his usual self returning. He drolly asked, "Am I your hero?"

Maddi smiled, and theatrically replied, "Oh, God, YES."

Mike smiled back at her humour; she was sounding more like Debbie all the time. "Come on, let's get serious and get the job done. Take this camera and photo anything interesting. Keep checking the images to make sure they are clear." He drew the curtains.

They began a systematic search of what must have been one of the strangest, foulest apartments on earth. At first glance, it was normal enough, and this gave rise to the first discovery. Maddi whispered as loud as she dared, "Mike, look at these." At a dressing table were earrings and other women's things, like perfume, foundation cream, and an eyebrow pencil.

Mike stared quizzically. "Can't be his?"

"No, you plonker, don't you recognise them?" She stared back at him. "Look at the earrings They're Christine's. I'm absolutely sure of it. I've never, ever seen another pair like them. The make up is the same as hers; in fact, everything is. Oh yes, it's hers all right, the bitch. I knew there was something about her; I hate her."

Mike thought of Christine's face, then in his mind turned her around, the image of the unusual ying and yang earrings swinging as he had taken her from behind nearly made him vomit. He found it hard to believe the evidence of her being Tony's accomplice. But it was there before him; a mixture of emotions flew into his head as he tried to remember what he had told her. He felt used. He then realised Maddi was staring at him, awaiting a response. "Well, it's worth coming for that information, isn't it?" he offered.

After about ten minutes of searching, a locked door, at the far end of the apartment was jimmied open, and a Pandora's box was discovered.

The first thing Mike noticed were the shackles and chains hanging from the wall, close to the altar. And on the floor was a magic circle with a triangle to the side, drawn quite exquisitely, and very similar to those in Sean's room. Maddi took photographs as they moved on. Soon they found demonic pictures on the walls, swords, strange symbols, and a family tree. Maddi took more photos. As they examined cabinets and nooks, they found an array of torture implements, mutilation devices, and an album of photographs of real floggings, torture, and sacrifices.

They made notes of book titles and took an inventory of cupboards. In a beautifully carved box, they found a pair of ceremonial daggers made from silver and ivory. Their imagined uses sent a shiver down Mike's spine.

"Oh, Christ, Mike, this gets worse. Look." Maddi beckoned her accomplice over to a display cabinet full of jars containing small body parts. Judging by their size, many were from children, and all were labelled and arranged alphabetically. Mike hoped who they were from and how they were obtained would remain a mystery to them. They were almost too terrified to look any further.

Mike heaved, and as his stomach wrenched, nothing would come up—not even words. Maddi was pale and shaking. In a dry, quaking voice, Mike uttered, "Take pictures, Maddi. We've got to; I think one day the police are going to be very interested in all this."

Maddi clicked the camera.

A clock in the distance chimed two. "How much time do you reckon we've got, Maddi?"

She shrugged.

Mike stared at her and realised she was close to fainting. "Sean said not to stay much after half past two. I've seen enough; shall we go?" At this, Mike felt a great burden of guilt for bringing someone as lovely as Maddi to a place so abhorrent. He felt like he had committed a crime against their friendship.

She perked up a little at the promise of leaving. "Mmm, I need a shower."

"Me too."

As sombre as two mourners at a funeral, they had a last look around. Maddi took a sharp breath and pointed to the ceiling. Hardly daring to look, Mike raised his eyes. "Oh God." Painted on the ceiling in a beautifully crafted way, similar to the grand paintings in the large houses of Europe, was a scene. A road to a massive gateway in the distance was depicted, the name *Daath* inscribed over the gate. On each side of the road were crucified children, and young men impaled on spikes in their death throes. In despair were what must have been their mothers, and looking at the scene was a masturbating effigy of Satan.

Mike snatched the camera, and supporting a failing Maddi, he braved himself to stare through the viewfinder and take the necessary photographs. As if to signify the finale, the memory card informed him that it was full.

Monica Doll stood on the coffee table, the observers watching the desecration through her eyes. They didn't intervene; if Tony was foolish enough to let it happen, so be it. They would see what he would do about it.

Maddi stood and looked at it. "Mike."

"What?"

"That doll, it was Monica's. He got it for her as a present once. He said it looked like her, and she thought so, too. I didn't; it looked frumpy to me. It disappeared after they broke up; he must have stolen it."

Mike was drawn to it. He could see the resemblance to Monica as if it was a portrait. He bent to pick it up.

Mike knew that one should never touch a medium whilst it was in contact with the spirit world, and Monica Doll was the observers' medium. Immediately, he felt an icy chill run up his arm. He dropped the doll, its face landing with a hard *crack* on the coffee table's edge. The right eye was now chipped in the corner, to match her Tony's. It rolled to the centre of the room and looked at the ceiling painting as it laid on its back; then its eyes clicked to the right to stare at them. The observers' view was now a little distorted, but their enemies' faces filled it all, and they stared back.

Maddi thought about crushing the doll's face with her foot, but just as the thought came, it fled. Mike wanted to do the same for a second, but then the thought left him, too.

The china face smiled.

Struggling to keep their nerve and composure, they left. The journey back to Mike's was quiet and slow.

On the outcrop above the village of Ashover stood a solitary figure, his long leather coat flapping in the wind. His arms were outstretched to the sky. He felt powerful; his concentration had grown through the night, and his earlier problems were a distant memory. The same moonlit night observed by Mike and Maddi now framed him as a silhouette. A resonating crackle of static discharge flew between his hands, to produce a massive spark. Tony broke through the barrier as the distant church clock struck two. He could see the window to Monica's mind; it was bricked up. In runic symbols was a message:

DID YOU ENJOY YOUR TASK? YOU LEFT YOUR SANCTUM UNPROTECTED, DIDN'T YOU? YOU ARE A FOOL. GIVE IN NOW. THERE IS NO ENTRY HERE!

Using all the strength he had, he could not make even the slightest inroad to Monica's sleeping mind. What did this mean? What had they done? He stormed down the hill, taking great strides of temper, back to his black Porsche with the licence plate reading *MAG 1C* To the chorus of squealing tyres, he drove away.

When he arrived back at his sanctum, he leapt out of the car and bound up to his flat to find Sabre lying dead in a pool of blood. "Aiiee!" He squealed like a pig in a slaughterhouse. In anger that surpassed any he'd felt before, he offered the challenger a location. "Highoredish, Saint Walpurgis night, you bastard! You fucking, lousy, shit-sucking, mother-buggering bastard! I'm going to make you suffer, Mike Reeves. I'm going to turn you inside out, slowly, whilst you're alive, you *BASTARD*!

Do you hear me? HIGHOREDISH, on Saint Walpurgis night. Be there! My mentors want a gift, and I am going to take great pleasure in taking it from you, Mike fucking Reeves."

He walked around the room; it was defiled. He stood and looked down at Monica Doll, lying on her back, her skirts lifted up as if she had been raped. He began to shake. He picked her up, straightened her hair, smoothed her dress, and kissed her. Stroking her face, he saw the damage. "What's he done to you, my beauty?" He looked down at Sabre's body as he stepped over it to walk to the balcony. Bloody footprints followed him. Holding Monica Doll's face next to his, he stared over the town and made an announcement to the world: "I'm going to avenge you, Sabre, and you, too, my sweetheart." He drew his hand up to his mouth and began to click his teeth and nail. "Yes, my darlings, I'll avenge you." His threat was so intense it materialised, leaving his mouth in a brown, foul-smelling gas.

Mike was in his shower, scrubbing himself like a woman who had been abused. He suddenly felt a wave of fear, and threw his gut's last contents all over his feet. The threat from Tony had just arrived in his mind.

Maddi sat with her second whiskey, trembling. They had hardly spoken a word since their night's work had finished.

Sean burst into Mike's consciousness. "We need to rest, all of us. What a night, eh? Sleep now; all of us need to make plans again. I need your information; it's time for you to learn about me, and the Purpose. We are safe for now, but the war has begun, and battle plans need to be made. But you've done well. We'll be safe for a couple of months. Now, go to bed. In the morning, get your runes, your tarot, and the rest. I'll see you at your table, with Maddi. Goodnight." Mike knew he wouldn't be able to go to sleep straight away, so with glass in hand, he switched on his laptop and e-mailed the doctor. His journal now took second place.

CHAPTER 15

Christine was in a spin; this virus was taking its toll. Mike, Maddi, and Monica were all off. They'd had to bring in temps and make adjustments, but demands were too high and the temps' knowledge of the job too low. She missed Mike and wanted him back soon. She didn't miss the two M's at all, and she harboured hopes that they might never come back. But Mike was different. There was the game, for one thing; they'd just gotten into it, when, *wham!* It had all stopped. The next move was even in the post for him somewhere, and the thought of some other boss opening it and spoiling her career plans made her knees tremble.

She got home and showered, and after a bite of supper, she felt worn out. With a milky drink in her hand, she slipped between the sheets. "Goodnight, Teddy George," she whispered to her cuddly bed companion. She kissed him on the nose, drank up, and turned off the bedside light.

The Samurai awoke as the message to return reached him. Just before deep sleep came, Christine felt a severe pain in her temple as the warrior was ripped from her subconscious. She put it down to the day's stress, rolled over, and soon fell into a deep slumber—something she hadn't done properly for a while now.

Tony was deep into his new tasks. He was possessed by it: books, charts, and all sorts of equipment were everywhere. This made the Rat much busier too, and he, in turn, was delegating tasks to other minions.

Having been wrenched from Christine's mind with no finesse, the Samurai stood in the bell jar on the workbench. Christine had served him well, and Tony could almost be thoughtful to those who were in his favour. So for now, the threat to her mind was removed. As a reward, he sent her a dream of sex and power.

Almost in a trance, Tony sat on the laboratory stool, his head resting on his folded arms on the edge of the workbench. Staring at the bell jar, he was impatient to find out how his study was paying off. In the jar with the figure was a sheet of paper, ripped with complete disregard from an old, valuable book. On it was an illustration of a demonic creature and many strange markings. Tony put his hands around the glass prison and slowly said three cabalistic words. The bell jar began to fill with mist; droplets of water collected inside, and it became difficult to see what was happening.

The Samurai looked at himself and stood awaiting his transformation to a second-level mind warrior, when suddenly the humidity was so overwhelming he could hardly breath. He fell to his knees and began his metamorphic change. Tony continued to stare; something was happening, but the inner surface was now so covered in moisture that he couldn't see.

The sound of a claw on glass made goose bumps appear on his skin. He watched a small hand wipe clear a tiny area to see through. The creature stared at him and blinked, then stood motionless with its head bowed in subjection to its master. Tony carefully lifted the bell jar, quickly turning his head to one side as the stench hit him. He looked down to see a pile of ash and the demonic creature; the Samurai was gone. He'd had another success from the tome. This beast had but one purpose: to sacrifice itself for its master.

He would send it to Christine's head, where it would be held in reserve for the right moment, either to attack full-size, or to get into Mike's mind and go berserk on command. If needed, it could self ignite to either destroy all around or to burn the inside of a mind and leave it an empty shell.

He closed his eyes, and the figure faded.

Christine had just reached the end of her best dream ever. She turned over as her subconscious detected the slight disturbance to her sleep. The creature crept via her mind window to settle in a trance in some distant, unused corner. Its surroundings were like an old-style New York, looking as if it were straight from a Bogart movie. The creature found the largest building in the city, named *Ego Tower*. The top floor was *ambition*, but he wanted somewhere quiet to hide. It got off at the seventy-third floor, *conscience*, which was full of unused, distant memories. It would be safe here; quiet corners were plentiful. It drank from the vessel Tony had given it and collapsed into a trance, awaiting the awakening on Saint Walpurgis night. Christine's mind was in no danger; it was just a carrying case.

Satisfied, the next task in Tony's long list had begun. The Rat saw to his personal protection: bodyguards had been set to protect the flat. They were the stereotyped, bull-necked, bent-nosed type, and their appearance was probably enough of a deterrent for most people. Car journeys, walkabouts, and the like had all been delegated to the Rat to be made safe, and all the gang under the command of Stirling had been issued with the same-network mobile phones, effectively sealing their own network. The Rat was feeling good; he'd done his job well, and a reward would be on its way.

The only way in was by mind, and Tony had that angle covered. "RAT!"

"Yes, Boss?"

"Come here!"

Like a well-drilled officer, he came the instant he was called. "Yessir?"

"You've made your allotted one mistake, do you realise that?"

This wasn't what he expected. "Yes sir, I do." It seemed the break-in to the apartment, and he supposed everything else associated with it, was being laid on his shoulders. If he had thought quickly, he might have shifted the blame to Stirling. But he didn't think quickly.

"Make one more mistake, and the visions I give you will be different: no more children, no more little Arab boys. Do you understand me?"

"Yes, Boss, I understand, Boss, yes, I do."

Slowly walking towards the Rat, Tony added, "No, I mean, do you really, *really* understand?"

An image instantly came to the Rat's mind. A childlike gargoyle jumped from the gutter and came to life. The stone splintered and creaked. The mouth opened to reveal bright, blood-red flesh; its head moved to him and its eyes opened to reveal yellow eyeballs. It grimaced as it forced excrement onto the floor, which instantly burnt. It began to click its teeth; it was hungry again. Its attention turned fully to him, its scratching feet stepping towards him.

"Stop, stop!"

Tony did, staring at the Rat until he averted his eyes and dropped his head. "I have worse nightmares for you, trust me. I want you to leave me food here, at nine, twelve, five, and ten. I want no other disturbances unless absolutely necessary...understand?"

"Yes."

"Now...FUCK OFF

Gratitude did not exist in Tony's vocabulary. The Rat had been a faithful servant for many years. In an upward spiral from petty crime, he was now the foreman: he saw to raising money and providing cover for his master's quest. His reward was ecstasy, and every little perverted act a paedophile could ever dream about in the most graphic, realistic way. But now he had seen the other side, the side of failure, and he didn't like it. He blamed one of the recent recruits, whom he had told flippantly to keep an eye on things the night of Maddi and Mike's visit. He went back to his own office next door, shouting a command to two of his men.

"Bring that shithead here."

Two new recruits dragged in a tattooed skinhead of gargantuan proportions. "You failed me," the Rat said, with all the emotion of ice.

"I didn't know; you never really told me what to do, I did my—"

"Don't try and blame me, you bastard. Have you no fuckin' idea why I've brought you here? Eh? Eh? You try to fuckin' blame me! Strip him naked and tie him to the chair." With all the charm of an S.S. officer, he laughed a high-pitched giggle of amusement.

Wild-eyed and screaming NO, the man was stripped and tied tightly to the chair, his legs wide apart and draped over the armrests, his ankles tied so that hardly any movement was allowed. His knees trembled uncontrollably.

The other two were ordered to bring two boiling kettles. They left them on the floor, plugged into an extension lead. Giggling and rubbing his hands together, the Rat enjoyed the moment of expectation. "Oh, I'm going to enjoy this—hee hee!—but you ain't!"

He instructed the other two to leave, with the task of informing everyone that, "Failure is NOT an option."

The two looked at each other and winced as the screams began behind the closed door.

Tony stopped and listened, too. "Ah, that's better, Mr. Rat." He smiled as he went back to his charts, his books, and his apparatus, allowing himself frequent pauses to listen. "Pain...ha! Ecstasy...surely a marriage made in heav—HA!—HELL!"

He walked over to stare at Monica Doll, who was looking through the window.

In Mike's world, it was time for preparations.

The visit to his mind castle would to be different today: Maddi was coming, too. They had slept well, surprisingly, after their ordeal. Their minds alert, the front room curtains were drawn shut. As Mike prepared, he told Maddi what he was doing, step by step. The runes, I Ching, and tarot were all in position.

Sean and Debbie were busy, too, getting ready for their arrival. Everyone would need talismans for protection against spells.

The table cleared, Debbie sat next to Sean. She felt a little like a child with the teacher sitting next to her. Completely out of the blue, Sean took hold of Debbie's hand, stroking her face with the other. He spoke with long, deliberate pauses. "Debbie...I couldn't survive without you. Mike couldn't, either. Don't ever, *ever* underestimate your role in all this."

Debbie didn't answer, but tears welled up in her eyes.

"Right; let's get on with it." Sean resumed his composure after his brief lapse. "Follow my instructions to the letter. These have to be made by female hands from our side. I know all the formulae, and the symbols, so just do exactly as I say."

She lit the candles first, in the sequence instructed, and then read from a book by Ra, Protector of the Pharaohs. Next, she carefully cut out five squares of purple cloth, using gold scissors. She pinned them deftly—flat and with no creases—to each point of a star. A name was written at each point: Sean was at the top point, Mike at the top left, and then clockwise down to Debbie, Maddi, and finally, Monica. Around each letter in the names were intricate green cobras. They twisted up each stem of a letter and slithered around every curve, each one beautifully copied out of an ancient calligraphy book, urged to perfection by Sean.

Time passed so quickly during construction that they had to remind themselves to eat. Debbie made five wallets, each sown up on three sides, out of the same purple cloth. "Right, Debbie. Now, bring your seat around to my point of the star."

Debbie did as instructed. Looking proudly at her creation, she awaited her next instructions.

"Place your right hand on my name, and hold your left arm straight up with your fist clenched around this statuette. Make sure your index finger is pointing skywards—yes, that's right."

Debbie took hold of it and followed the next precise set of rules, with the added proviso that any mistake at this point would mean they'd have to destroy the whole work and start again.

"Read this slowly and diligently—no mistakes now!"

Out loud, she read an ode to bravery, faith, hope, trust, truth, and love. The cloth was then folded in a secret way and inserted in the pouch. Sean was embroidering a name on the pouches in runic writing, and attaching a leather thong, so that they could be worn around the neck.

This complex and nervy task had to be repeated in the same hand and voice for each name. Upon completion, each in their own embroidered pouch, were dipped them into an orange, crystal-clear liquid mixture by Sean. Then he hung each one on a stand of wrought-twisted iron.

"Whew! Well done, Debbie." He smiled broadly at her and patted her shoulder.

"Thank you." Again her eyes welled up, and a tear ran down her cheek.

Sean's expression changed from that of a teacher to that of a proud loving father as he reached out his hand and wiped it away with his thumb. He sucked the tear off his thumb, then placed his hand back on Debbie's shoulder and gave it a fatherly squeeze. "Go and rest now. Mike and Maddi will be here soon, and we need to be alert, don't we?"

Mike and Maddi ate a quiet meal, as Mike explained everything he could to her.

The years of practice had now begun to pay off—his knowledge surprised him as he imparted it. How far he had come since those early days of self-awareness classes, meditation classes, and attunement and advancement classes. The tarot instruction circles; the study of auras, healing, and runes; the psychic awareness, I Ching, and the like—all fitted together like some massive jigsaw. His old chums along the way all came back to him. So did his tutors, but now he had to lead, not be led.

Each tutor had been amazed at the speed at which Mike picked it up. They had all freely given him, their own special gifts of fully understood, but limited, knowledge of their own special areas. Up until now things just hadn't fully locked together. But now as he spoke to Maddi, it all gelled, all made sense. The truth shouted to him, and now he was ready for the

"Purpose" to be explained: it was time to open the box, shake out the pieces, and start to build the next jigsaw, the one with more pieces than grains of sand on a beach.

It was time: the ancient music was playing; something told him the Gregorian chants were to be saved for something special. Tarot and Rune world saw Maddi for the first time, fleetingly, much to her annoyance. She wanted to see more, but this was not a time for sight seeing. She would see more later, Mike told her, as he almost dragged her along form world to world. Now, hand in hand, they were in the Shanghai streets. Time was passing slowly as the two worlds lined up, and tasks were being completed in unison. As if she was on a fascinating holiday trip, Maddi was taking it all in. She had to be pulled from frequent pauses to look at people, stalls, sellers, magicians, and everything else there was to see. But with a firm grip on her hand, Mike guided her to the curio shop. Maddi stared at him with an incredulous expression that seemed to say, "whatever now?"

The bell rang, and the outside world's noise ended as they came through and shut the door behind them. Maddi stared at collectibles on endless mahogany shelves that were so long they disappeared from her view. She would have died for a browse. They passed through the shop facade and went up the steps. The Moor was alone. Mike realized that he never had heard him speak. He showed them the way with a sweep of his arm and a nod. They followed him up a staircase, down a corridor, and around a corner into another room, decorated in jade-green with purple Chinese lanterns. The Moor beckoned again, this time to a simple rush mat. They both stood in the centre of it staring ahead. A jade-green Buddha necklace hung from the Moor's neck.

Maddi watched, almost drooling, as the Moor stripped down to his loincloth, his oiled body shining. He slowly picked up the massive drumstick, and as if he were at the start of a Rank film, he beat the massive copper gong that hung in a stout oak frame, crowned with ox horns. It was all of eight feet in diameter. The noise filled their heads, as if to test the depths of their trance. The mat moved, and they held each other tight and waved farewell to the Moor. The blue and purple clouds came, the balcony loomed, and Sean and Debbie stood in welcome.

Sean was wearing bright, Turkish slippers decorated in gold. Mike smiled, and Maddi made no comment.

The team of four made their way to Sean's room. Again, Maddi's eyes darted everywhere. The thought balls were still hovering in a corner. Mike, Maddi, and Debbie filled three comfy chairs, turning their eyes in nervous anticipation towards Sean. "We are here for what will be the most momentous meeting of our lives. I am to tell you of the protection we have for you, and about…the Purpose. Debbie will tell us about Monica's mind, and you two to will tell us what you've learnt about Tony. I will begin."

The white observers allowed themselves a satisfied a smile; at last, they were together.

Sean paced with one hand on his chin and the other behind his back, beginning an obviously rehearsed speech. "THE PURPOSE!!" he opened dramatically, raising his right eyebrow, right hand, and forefinger. "Mike, you invited the Purpose to yourself all those years ago when you began your quest for wisdom, and began to invent you mind keepers. Huh, invent indeed! It was like placing an advert in our world, so to speak. My daughter, Debbie, and I applied, and we got the job."

"Your daughter! And you let me come and…"

"Shhh! Not now." Sean looked at Mike, smiled, and carried on.

Mike stared, dumbstruck.

"Concentrate!" Sean sat cross-legged at the front of the makeshift classroom, and continued. "Let me give you a little history lesson. Since time now forgotten, man has not been able to cross the curtain to our side—known to you as 'the other side', or the 'spirit world'. There are secrets I cannot reveal yet, especially those concerning your life after death. I'm simply not allowed to impart that knowledge. I can tell you that there is only one way for you to find out, though, and strangely enough, there are never many volunteers. Probably it has something to do with it being a one-way street you have to go down for the answer!"

The small audience laughed.

"Your instincts have served us well for century after century. Understand that although we don't control, we can observe, and even influence on the odd occasion. You usually see these intrusions as something dramatic, what do you call it when we have to move something? Ah yes, poltergeist! You often record them as bizarre happenings; this helps you to keep your fear of the unknown. You humans have many qualities, but two of them frighten us more than any other, and the more we observe, the more convinced we are that we must forever be kept separate. These qualities are destruction and dictatorship. If someone could find a way into our world unnoticed, which could be done by the cabala, we are sure that, no matter what their initial intentions, the power they'd have after such a journey would be too much for them to control. Dictatorship would prove an irresistible temptation, and they would sink to the depths of evil and cause chaos. The fact that they even use the cabala in this way illustrates that they are on a power trip."

Mike tutted.

"Believe me, they would! I know I shouldn't categorically say so; indeed, people like you, Mike, would probably be safe, and even an asset. But then again, I don't think you would want to complete the whole journey. The kind who would reason that breaking through would be acceptable are the ones who scare the shit out of us!"

Mike nodded as Maddi and Debbie looked at him to study his reaction.

"Yes, I know that you want to delve, to explore the depths of magic, and I see nothing wrong in a healthy curiosity. But some people's curiosity is not healthy! Consider that in your dimension, you have reached the so-called 'Age of Enlightenment', the 'Age of Aquarius', the '*New Age*'. It is a time of freedom and discovery. The old anchors have gone, and you are no longer frightened to explore—not all of you, anyway, and especially those like you, Mike. People are meditating, using the tarot, and studying auras, but they are only scratching the surface with a soft, blunt pin. But look at someone like Adolf Hitler! *He* wanted us to help him! Can you imagine? He thought he was meant to contact a like species, that he was destined to be with us, that he had been born on the wrong side of the curtain. He wanted to rule two worlds, and to bring back emissaries like Genghis Khan to rule with him! Why do you think he wanted to kill the Jews and the Gypsies, eh? Because they had possession of the cabala, and understood its use. We did intervene, then…"

The room went silent.

Sean continued slowly. "Make…no…mistake. Tony has the potential to be worse than Hitler, if he learns the power and use of the cabala!" Sean looked at each in turn and held their gaze until they looked away. "Given the chance, he would rule two worlds as a malevolent dictator. Suffering would be the norm, and to succeed, you would have to be devoid of compassion and every other noble feeling. It isn't worth contemplating the chaos he would create. All would be collared slaves!

"Imagine the curtain I talk of as being a physical entity, with a powerful light behind it on your side. From our side, we can see small holes appearing, made by other 'Tonies.' The shaft of light shining through each is a terror of unspeakable proportions, and we are using people like you to patch them up." Sean wore a tragic mask as he added, "Yes, I'm afraid to say this is only one of a few like situations, and the signs are they will increase if we don't set an example." The mask grew more serious as he added, "We have to stop people like him from breaking through, for our good and yours. You see, what we've done is observe people— the good ones, like you—using the magic. We observe your progress; it's easy to pick up, especially now that your people are developing their minds—like I said before—with meditation, tarot, and—" He paused. "The cabala. All we have to do is look for a structured mind and wait for it to 'invent' keepers; it's the logical step to keep everything in order. In fact, you, Maddi, have all the makings, if you would just put your mind to the task! And when the time is right, we arrive…remember, Mike?"

"Huh, do I!"

"You are our weapons on your side, oh yes! You are not alone! The chances of you meeting are almost zero, but do you remember the colour game you used to play Mike? Uptown during lunches? That was your subconscious, the decent fellow he is, trying to find you a comrade!"

Maddi looked at Mike for an explanation.

Mike reluctantly gave it. "Oh, I used to walk around looking at people's eyes. I've always said I saw most other people as grey—no offence to them—and I don't want to sound as though I think I'm a cut above them, but...oh, there are so many boring pillocks out there, you know? They get up, go to work, go home, have cocoa, go to bed, get up, etc., etc. So I used to go out looking for people who weren't like that. Silly, wasn't it?"

"No," said Maddi.

"NO," agreed Debbie.

"No, Mike, you just felt alone, that's all." Sean looked at him sympathetically. "The sad bit is, your chances would have been almost zero. Your world is an amazingly huge big place." Getting back to the main topic before he lost his drift, Sean took on a more urgent tone again. *"The Purpose is to keep our worlds apart but in touch—and to protect the curtain, at all costs."*

Mike sensed that something was about to happen.

"Mike, I ask you this: will you make a decision to move on, to move up a grade, from where you are in your development? It's a giant step, the first one on the cabala, which most never even see! You will never be able—or indeed, want to—go back. The rewards will be great, out of your dreams. Will you help us, Mike? Will you and your compatriot here, Maddi, engage in war to defeat Tony?"

"Yes, I will," Mike replied without a moment's hesitation. He turned to Maddi, as did all the others.

"Of course I will, and not just for Monica, either."

Mike gave her a smile and squeezed her hand. Debbie felt a slight chill of bitterness cross her heart.

"Good. Very, very, good." Sean walked over to pick up the talismans. "Wear these." He handed them around, passing an extra one to Maddi. "For Monica," he told her. Then, he said a powerful prayer and told them how Debbie had made the talismans.

Sean took a drink from a vessel and turned to Debbie. "Your turn to take the floor, Debbie. Tell us all about Monica's mind. I feel that her mind is the gateway to battle, and our entrance to victory!"

In a manner of confident ease, Debbie recounted all the details of damage, and of how Monica's mind was now protected by Sean's brickwork of spells. She also told them about the Samurai Mind Warriors.

This brought Sean back to centre stage, as he described why Mike had had to sit so suddenly the other day.

Sean asked Mike and Maddi to fill in the missing details and tell them what they had found. So Mike took his turn, with interjections from Maddi, and they related the other night's adventure. Debbie looked longingly at Mike, and at Maddi, too, as she thought, *I wish I were out there.*

Then Mike produced the evidence; digital photographs, lists, and sketches filled the table. Sean pounced on the treasure trove; their knowledge was increasing by the second!

Mike noticed Debbie's stare and thought of his previous visits. They seemed so far away since they had got into the thick of things. Would this be one of the things he couldn't go back to? He sincerely hoped not. He winked, and she winked back. Visits like this were most enthralling, but nowhere near as entertaining. Surely soon, when there was a lull, things might take on a more normal slant. But with Maddi so close, things were not so easy somehow. Also, now that he knew Debbie was Sean's daughter, how could he allow such things to happen? No sooner do answers to problems come than infinitely more difficult questions take their place.

Sean broke in. "Now it's time to unravel this little bag of mysteries. No doubt you have oodles of questions for me, so fire away!"

Maddi's confidence in her new company was growing; she admired Sean and found him sexy. He came across as an all-knowing pillar of strength. Mike was a bag of surprises that had only just been opened. How had he managed to survive a mind like this? She confounded herself with thoughts of, *we are here, he's here, and yet, we are all sitting out there, aren't we?* And although it felt strange to admit it, she felt love for Debbie—not lesbian, not sisterly, just a pure, simple, uncomplicated love. And although she knew Debbie liked her, she could feel and understand her jealousy. Maddi wanted to calm the waters and put Debbie's fears at ease. She smiled at Debbie, and Debbie smiled back. "I need a break," said Maddi. "The concentration level is too high for me; I'm not used to it like you three. Can I leave the room a while? Then I'll come back and continue."

"Yeah," Mike said, "no problem. Let me and Sean put this stuff in some kind of order whilst we have a drink. Then, when you come back, we can go through it all more logically." He looked to Debbie.

Debbie jumped up. "Come on, Maddi, let's leave these two to play a while. I'll show you around the place." So together, they went on a tour, arm in arm.

They arrived at a stone bench next to the healing fountain. The air was well ionised by the spray and cleansed the mind. "You want to tell me something, don't you, Maddi? Is it that you've fallen in love with Mike, and as you see to his needs, you'll take him from me?" Tears filled her eyes and overflowed to wash lines down her cheeks.

"No it's not that."

"What, then?"

"Mike loves you more than anything; any fool on earth could see that. He has feelings for me, too; I can see that as plain as the nose on his face. But he's a man who can fall in love easily, and love more than one at different levels at the same time."

"Oh."

"Silly, aren't you?" Maddi said reassuringly, as she held Debbie's hand between hers and stroked it. "I should say he will never love anyone like he loves you, not even remotely. His mind has moved on to another level, and he's got to adjust. He's surprised and worried by what's expected of him, but he needs you, Debbie, really needs you, most of all. Every great man needs a woman to treat him as a child sometimes, and you do that."

"What, treat him like a child?"

"Mmmm, pamper to his every whim!"

"Oh, I see-ee."

"Happy now?"

"Yes, very." Debbie beamed and took Maddi's hand. "Come on, let's go back."

Mike could see that something had happened, and judging by Sean's grin and downward glance, he thought Sean knew exactly what. *Well, I'm not giving them the satisfaction of asking*, he thought. So he walked around the table and beckoned his classmates to join him at their places.

"Right, on with the instruction." Sean started to circle the table. He touched the photographs of all the books and things in Tony's lair. Looking at the assembled group of scholars, he put one hand on his chin and the other arm behind his back. Nodding towards the table, he began. "Let me tell you something of the cabala before we discuss this little lot." He strode to the blackboard and wrote *cabala* on it.

As they looked at the word, it took on the sinister shape of a snake, and slithered to a new form. The word *cabala* became *qabala*. Then it resumed its original written appearance. "It's a Hebrew word for knowledge," Sean told them as he spun around. "It's a method for accessing powers, wisdom, and understanding beyond belief. A way of accessing powers beyond the self, a method of projecting your body to a higher existence, a way of getting closer to the source of all life."

He walked to the table and put both hands on the edge. "Did you know that God was supposed to have whispered the secret of the cabala to Moses at Mount Sinai?"

They all shook their heads.

"Well, he did." Sean strode back to the blackboard and wrote three more words: *SEFER YETZIRAH* and *ZOHAR*. "Do you have any idea what these are?"

"I've seen them, yes. There were two old books with that written on them at Tony's place," replied Mike.

"Correct!" Sean pointed at Mike. "Those are two of the rarest, most valuable and sought after books in existence. They are *The Book of Creation*, and *The Book of Splendour*." He stopped and stood with his arms akimbo. "I'm going to take those books from him; he's not worthy." Sean glowered jealously, then continued again, "Much is written in the Enochian language."

"Enochian?" enquired Mike.

"Yes, yes." Sean tutted. "Enochian. You know, the Elizabethan astrologer John Dee managed to contact the spirit world, and one of our kind foolishly gave it to him. Alistair Cowley—surely you know him, the most notorious magician of the twentieth century?—he used the language to create spells." Sean looked incredulously at their blank expressions. "Surely, you know him?"

Silence reigned.

"Words like *Ecu, Zodocore, Lad, Goho*, etc....no?"

Sean strode to the blackboard again. With overdone movements of his hand, he wrote the word *Stem-ham-forash*. He turned around and looked at them in stunned disbelief.

Mike felt himself blush, Maddi wriggled uncomfortably, and Debbie sat stock-still; she had seen this look before.

Sean started to raise his voice. "Surely you know." Silence filled the air again. "Look at God's name, which cannot be spoken!" He wrote, *YHUH*.

Again his sight was greeted with stunned silence.

"Yod-He-Hau-He, as JEHOVAH!"

Still silence.

With his eyes bulging Sean said, "Tetragrammaton!" Look."
He wrote

y = 10
yh = 15
yhv = 21
yhvh = 26
---72 Stemhamrorash, a 72-syllable word used to separate the Red Sea, a spell all made up from...

Mike shook his head again, Maddi stared down, and Debbie began to giggle.

"What do they teach you in your world? *Nothing?*" He wrote the word *spells* across the board diagonally through everything else, double underlined it, and added the most magnificent full stop the world has ever seen. At that point, to Debbie's utmost amusement, the chalk broke. Sean winced as his fingernail bent backwards. "I remember the days when elementary lessons in your world told children of such things, the use of and importance of plants like mandrake and white bryony."

Mike couldn't help but think, *Is that supposed to impress us?*

Sean looked for a response but got none. He sucked his finger. "This is probably the most important thing ever, and all you do is sit there like a class of gormless, dumbstruck, bloody…toads!"

Mike hardly dared to look; Maddi blushed, and Debbie guffawed behind her hand.

But Sean was right, of course. This was a vitally important moment in their lives, but the stress they were under needed an outlet.

Mike could see that Sean was angry and hurt. "Look Sean," he said, "you seem to have all the knowledge. Let us just ask questions, and you answer. I really don't think we've time to catch up on our collective shortcomings on the history of magic, and to be frank, we are getting nowhere just now. I can see us all becoming bogged down and disheartened, as interesting as it is. Personally, when all this is over, I'd love to learn." He looked at Sean's face and could see it registering. He looked over at Debbie, raised an eyebrow, and frowned. She composed herself, feeling a little silly at her loss of control.

Maddi looked at Sean. "Actually, when you think about it, you are a little like Van Helsing in the Dracula story, and they only needed one with all the knowledge. Couldn't we do the same? Just advise us, instruct us, order us if you must, but just tell us what to do, and when. When further explanation is needed, we can ask, because we know you'll have the answers, being so clever and knowledgeable. It will be like having a walking, talking encyclopaedia of magic with us." She could almost see Sean swell with importance, and as he turned around and walked a few steps to consider, she winked at Mike. He winked back and gave her a thumbs-up sign.

"Huh, I just thought that a bit of learning—real learning, mind—might benefit you all a bit, that's all."

"Yes, as Mike said, at the right time in the correct atmosphere, we would all agree. But we are a team, and as such, I'm sure you can see the wisdom of team decisions. I know you can, anyway, because already I think you are the wisest person I've ever met."

Debbie caught her eye, and put her fingers in her mouth as if to vomit.

Sean felt quite the best he'd felt in years, and he couldn't help thinking how wonderful Maddi was. "Mmm, well, I see the sense in what you say. And yes, we are a team, so...ask away, disciples, ask away!" At which he flung his arms around in mock subjection.

Mike whispered to Maddi, "Well done, that was brilliant!" He asked the first question: "What's astral projection, as this book shows?"

"It's what you do with us, but you do it naturally, whilst Tony's learning, or has just learnt. It's a bit like the U.S. experiments on astral snooping; you recall the TV programme?"

"Oh yes, so I do."

His now-favourite pupil asked the next question, as she picked up another photograph. "What's this book, *The Ancient History of the Cabala and Alchemy?* It looks very old."

"It is. It's a well known and much sought after collection of occult writings by Hebrew mystics over many centuries." Sean was enjoying his role again. "You know your hero, Mike? The I Ching man, Jung? The Swiss psychologist, when did he die now...1961?"

Mike nodded enthusiastically.

"Well, he used this book to base his theories of coincidence on. How Tony got it, I'll never know. You've got to hand it to him: no matter how he got these things, as a collector, he is first class. He has impeccable taste and is very discerning."

"Not so much praise, please. I'd guess he shows them little respect."

"Indeed no! Jung said that magic depends on the principle that all things in the entire universe are bound by a fine network of relationships that continually interact." Sean stared at Mike and nodded approval as he concluded. "Good man, that Jung."

Debbie felt the need to say something. "Who's this one?" She held up a photograph of a Hungarian countess.

"That's Elizabeth Battery, one of Tony's heroines, I think. She used to bathe in peasant girls' blood, with the idea that it helped her with black magic."

"Oh," said Debbie, distastefully putting the photo down. She whispered to Maddi, "Trust me to ask a really intelligent question, eh?"

Maddi smiled and picked up two photographs in which she did recognize the figures: Franz Anton Mesmer and Eliphus Levi.

Sean walked around to stand closely behind her; she could feel his warm, steady breath on her neck and found it pleasant. "Yes, Levi thought that Mesmer, the founder of modern hypnotism, had rediscovered the secret science of nature. Probably via the cabala, I should say that Tony is an expert on hypnotism."

"What's this tree thing?" enquired Mike.

"Aha! Now we are getting there." Sean cleaned the board. "Allow me just a little instruction. Levi was an astute fellow, you know. He related the major arcana cards of the tarot to 22 letters of the Hebrew alphabet. See how you've been trained without knowing? You understand more than you think you do, Mike Reeves."

Sean began to draw on the board. "And these letters are directly related to the Tree of Life—the *Sefiroth*—which in turn were expanded by the 'Order of Golden Dawn', a Magical Society that flourished in the 1890s. This tree is the structure of the cabala! Like a tree, but upside down, the roots show nine por-tions, all numbered…see?"

They studied the diagram and Sean's accompanying ex-planatory sketches on the board: the symbol of the female geni-tals; the *Kethr*, four faces and four crowns, the first incantation to *Hohkmah*, Wisdom, to 3, Dinah; witchcraft, sorcery, and un-derstanding, all the way to number nine, *Malkuth*, the elephant of creativity.

"All these are called *sefirahs*."

Mike stood up and walked over to Sean. "We're getting too complicated again, Sean. You clearly understand it all, and I clearly don't. We'll wait until we need it, eh?" Mike sat down with a dejected thump.

Maddi saw and sympathised with his frustration. " There's so much to learn, so much alternative thought to master."

Debbie then asked the crucial question. "What do cabalists use all this for?"

"What?" asked Sean.

"I just asked what cabalists use all this for, sorry!"

"No, don't be sorry. It's the best question so far—well asked! They use the tree to lead their mind beyond ambiguities, to profound truth and insights."

"How?"

"Yes, how?" added Mike, realising the importance of the question, and considering a new fact. Even on the 'other side', only certain people had this knowledge.

"Magic is power of the mind, Mike," Sean said, as if this ex-plained all. "Cabalists journey through *Selfiroth* to learn it. How far Tony has gone, I don't know; nor do I know, for that matter, how far he will go. But I have an idea where he wants to get to and why, and I'll sit on that a while. But I know the way, and when you've mastered the art of staying where you want to be—that's here!—we might be able to go, if we have to! I should say that one day, you and I will embark on a journey, but let's leave that for now. We have time on our side." Sean continued, "They start by projecting themselves as an image in front of them-selves, and then go through life watching. This is the first stage.

After that, they learn to focus on the image and actually function through it—any harm comes to the image, not to them. Then comes the ascent—a very long and arduous one to their final destination."

"Which is?" Maddi asked.

"They take an incredible journey on the astral plane, which is another dimension of the world, using their astral body. They go through space and objects to the gateway of Yesod, the sphere of the moon, the link…the link between earth and the rest of the universe!"

Mike tutted at his lack of comprehension; some of it sounded logical and easy, but as soon as he stopped concentrating on a particular point, the whole lot got tangled in confusion and indecipherable knowledge.

"I know it's hard for you, Mike, but you've learnt a lot already. You'll be surprised at how it will all come; the tarot will come into its own, especially path twenty-two, the path of Saturn, equivalent to the Two of Wands. It will come, believe me."

"Say what you like; I've a lot to learn, and right now I have serious doubts about whether I'm capable. I think that you think too highly of me, I really do."

"You'll cope, like I said, believe me!" Sean put his arm around Mike's shoulder. "I know the way, and the method. I need a body—an educated, brave, willing body like yours to do it. I know I've made the right choice, I know it!" Sean then looked gravely at Maddi. "And you, too. Your astral body will one day embark with ours; I feel it coming, but I will try to avert it if I can. I'll tell you all in good time. Does it at least start to make sense to you both?"

"Just," Maddi and Mike said simultaneously.

"It will come. Go back and rest now; I know you will, but try not to worry too much. My daughter is a powerful ally to have. We'll sort out and do as much as we can. Have faith, but remember we need you just as much as you need us."

Mike had meant to ask about Sean and Debbie's relationship as father and daughter, but he was confused, tired, and ready to go. In two pairs, they slowly walked back to the departure platform and said fond farewells for now. They waved and walked onto the blue and purple stepping-stone clouds, returning to their bodies for a deep sleep.

Tony was at his second favourite place; it would have been his first if it hadn't been soiled by the mad vicar of Rowtor. This was somebody he hoped to bump into on his journey, and ask the significance of the stone carvings near the village of Birchover. In the late 1800s, he was one of the first Englishmen to learn of the Cabala. It drew him from Christianity to insanity. Some say he ended his days in a lunatic asylum, but nobody knows for sure. It was a strange place behind The Druid's Inn and above a tiny church that contains references to witchcraft. Inside the church is a board, describing the events during an evil time in English history—the hunts of the Witchfinder general. He walked up the winding narrow path from the car park, carrying the heavy yacht-varnished box—which he had made and decorated himself—with a spade strapped to the top.

Around the bend at the top, he approached the small opening. He pushed the box inside with his feet, then scrambled in behind. His eyes adjusted to the half-light slowly. The imitation-Saxon lectern twisting its way to the roof caught his eye. He recollected how he had come across a tramp the last time he was here. He would never come across him again, and that was a fact. The passage led to another small opening and onto a ledge. He dragged and pushed the box out. The treetops below exaggerated the fall. This was the drop where witches had supposedly been thrown in bizarre judgements centuries ago. He looked over to Mock Beggars Hall and The Hermit's Cave. Close by he could just make out the standing stones. To his left was Trumpet Cave. He whispered down the borehole, and the echo came back: "Hello, Tony." He laughed at himself.

Just below him, he could just make out the village. The press coverage all those years ago had shamed the inhabitants. He recalled his youth, and thought of the girl in the coven, whom he had pushed naked and drugged over the edge. *It was her own fault*, he justified.

Taking the spade and ramming it into the sandy earth, he dug a hole big enough to take the box, then lowered it in. He read the inscription on the shiny brass plate for the last time: *Here lies Sabre, my best and most loyal companion.*

Throwing dirt onto its top, he passed on Monica Doll's love, and finished the funeral. He stamped the earth flat and put the spade over his shoulder. Whistling, he made his way back to the car park and back to his tasks.

CHAPTER 16

Sean sat in his room alone. Things were being prepared as well as possible. He carefully thought through what had happened, and what he thought was going to happen. After their visit, he knew that Maddi and Mike would be in a deep, undisturbable slumber; mental stress was often more tiring than physical labour. "They'll need all their strength," he thought aloud, as he went to his private room to study the thought balls. It was time to open number two and send it.

Mike awoke to find Maddi nestled under his arm, her head snuggled into the hairs of his chest. It was two in the afternoon. Gently, he lifted the covers to two naked bodies. He could remember leaving Sean and Debbie, he could remember getting in bed as Maddi showered. He couldn't remember anything after that; he must have fallen asleep and she must have climbed in for comfort...naked! She stirred. Her eyes opened and blinked at him, one eye getting a little stuck, and the expression filled him with desire. He smiled at her and said, "You have some lovely expressions."

"Oh, thanks. Morning...oh, dearie me."

"It's afternoon, actually."

"It never is!" She drew her leg up over him and snuggled down again. "No rush to get up though, is there?"

"No, none at all. It's nice to relax and forget it all for a while." He stretched and pushed his body against hers.

"Mmm, something to take our minds off things would be just right. Any suggestions?"

Grinning cheekily, he looked down at her. "You're a saucy cat!"

"Phwarr! You don't half get me going when you look down at me like that. I feel all protected, by a big, strong man."

"Well, don't feel too protected; this big, strong man wants to break your defences down, not protect you!"

"Oh, all right then, if you must."

She sounded very like Debbie again as she said that, thought Mike. He moved down to a comfier kissing position and stroked her bottom.

They made love with very little noise or words as each explored the other's body. They pushed the covers away, delighting in soft, supple curves and toned muscle. They felt no inhibitions, no worries, and no guilt—just passion and full-blooded enjoyment.

Eventually, out of breath and perspiring, they resumed their positions. Mike looked at Maddi as he stroked her forehead with the back of his fingers. "Maddi, I think…"

"Shh, if you are going to say anything like I think you are going to, it's all over. This is good, but I don't want a heavy-duty relationship with all its brakes and weights pulling us down. I've been in this position many, many times. I'm not ashamed of it; if the knowledge of this hurts you in any way, then that's your problem. Don't try and get deep with me. I'm not that sort, okay?"

A candle and a jewel both faded simultaneously, but the illumination was taken over by the light from Debbie's face as she looked on. She whispered, "Thanks, Maddi."

"I'm sorry, I thought…"

"Shh!" Maddi smiled at him. "It's not a problem if you don't make it one! Don't apologise; there's no need. I'm happy, I'll share. I want good friends, good sex, and good times, that's all.

You supply all my needs right now. I'm happy, things are good, and I hope it lasts a long time. Okay?"

Mike nodded. He was glad she had voiced her thoughts. He decided to keep the intimacy with Christine secret. His battle with the deceit, and guilt about Rosie were pushed away. Bigger battles beckoned.

Her expression changed. "Good, that's that sorted then. I'm going to shower and get dressed now."

"Thanks, Maddi."

"And thank you, too."

He lay listening to the shower running, and he thought about what she had just said. He shuffled towards the edge of the bed, sat up, and ruffled his hair, then looked at himself in the mirror. "You lucky bastard!"

"Yes, you are!" piped up Sean. "Get up soon. I've got work for you to do!"

Mike quoted a line from one of his favourite films. "Okay, Boss, shaking it here, Boss!"

The afternoon passed with a few mundane tasks, and eventually saw Maddi making a ham salad for tea whilst Mike sat in his thinking position in his room. "Okay, Sean, fire away."

Sean's voice came as Mike shut all else out. Mike could see that a day would come eventually when he was more alive with Sean than he was in the real world.

""I need information, Mike. The preparations are going well, but I need a physical examination of the lie of the land where Tony thinks he rules. I want you to go to Ashover, stop overnight, look around, go to Highoredish, search for a base camp—ideally, it would be some consecrated ground—but the Ashover churchyard would be too obvious. I've a gut feeling that the balance of magic will throw something up for us. We, or should I say you, have got to find it, go and explore, and buy a couple of good-scale Ordnance Survey maps."

"Now that's the kind of instruction I like, Sean. Consider it done!" Mike loved the country and a ramble at any time.

Maddi and Mike had tea, washed the pots, made phone calls, and booked a room at The Crispin, an inn in the village. Both had hiking gear, and Maddi decided she would fetch hers.

"Shall I check on Monica?" suggested Maddi before she left. "Do you think it would be a good idea if I told her things, and bought her here?"

Mike agreed and soon after, waved her off.

He wrote to the doctor, saying he might be quiet for a while. It was the last e-mail he sent, and it would be quite a long time before he would see him again.

The Rat sat watching Monica's flat, waiting for a chance to snatch her. He dared not fail; the consequences were unthinkable. He was scared, living as a surfer on the edge of an adrenaline wave. He directed his accomplices to watch the main entrance and the rear entrance to the block. The closeness of the main buildings for the emergency services just around the corner made him feel uneasy. The constant to and fro of police cars made him feel nervous; he liked as much distance between them and him as possible.

Trying to impress, Steve, another assistant to the Rat, dared to offer a suggestion. "Why don't we just go and snatch her?"

"Because, dickhead, we don't want to highlight what we're doing, do we? Tony said no drama and no police. She has to disappear quietly, no fuss. That was a load of bollocks, and when I want the contents of what's between your ears, I'll ask for it." He didn't even look back at him as he said it; the superior qualities of his mind couldn't even conceive of treating people lower on the ladder with any decency. He ruled by distant aloofness and the fear factor in the knowledge that Tony would take his side in any argument.

Time passed uneventfully until Maddi arrived. The Rat pulled out a photograph. "It's her mate, Maddi." He rang Steve. "Her friend Maddi is here: long hair, nice legs, black, shiny PVC coat tied at the waist—have a good look. She's your reward if you do well today. We may as well take her for a little bonus. But just watch for now. Wait for my command."

"Okay, Boss. Nothing else?"

"No, this is what we've been waiting for. We'll just wait for her, her mate, or both to come back out, let them see your guns, tell 'em to be quiet, and frog-march them to me. They'll be too scared to do anything."

"Okay," Steve replied, and watched her walk closer, her heels clicking on the pavement. She passed him, and he looked at her face.

Maddi returned the stare as she passed by. She knew instinctively this horrid looking man was going to say something when she had gone by. Although she felt intimidated, she was determined not to show it.

"Nice ass," Steve commented.

"Thank you…matches your face."

"Fuck you, bitch."

"Huh, in your dreams, dog!"

Despite her calm appearance, she was shaking inside as she pressed the intercom button.

"Hello?"

"Hiya, it's me."

"Come on up."

Maddi did, and after knocking on the door went in and gave Monica a hug. "How are you?"

"Not bad."

"Is everything okay?"

"No, not really. There's a man outside who keeps looking up here. He's sitting in his car. I've seen him before; I reckon I've seen him looking at me in other places. I feel like I'm being stalked."

Maddi went to the window and peeped through the blinds. The Rat instantly looked up and stared at her. She quickly drew back. "Monica, you trust me, don't you?"

"Yes, you know I do."

"Well, will you do as I ask, without question? I'll explain all later, I promise."

"Well, yes, I suppose so. You're very mysterious today, Maddi!"

"More like deadly serious, I'm afraid. I'm sorry for the cloak-and-dagger stuff, but like I said, I will explain. Now pack some things, enough for a week or so, at least, and hurry. Anything you forget, you can buy or borrow."

Monica heard the urgency in Maddi's voice and did exactly as she was told.

As they packed, Maddi picked up a serving spoon off the draining board and gently prised open the blinds to take a peep. "He's on the phone."

"Maybe he's the police looking for someone else?"

"Definitely not! And he's definitely looking up here."

They finished gathering belongings together. "Right, that'll do. Now, do you have any condoms?"

"*Condoms?*"

"Yes."

"Yes, I do. How many? I only have a few and I bet they are out of date!"

"All you have. Do you have any nail varnish remover?"

"Yes, you want that too?"

"Yes, and mousse, and tissues, lots of tissues, and matches…get me some matches."

"Of course, anything you want."

Maddi went to the kitchen and picked up the pedal bin, depositing the contents on the floor. Monica stood staring, the requested supplies in her arms. "Ugh! What are you doing?"

Maddi didn't answer; she put the tissues in the bin and dowsed them in nail varnish remover. "Sorry, I want some newspaper as well, and a great big plate or tray. Hurry." She sprayed mousse over the contents

"Yes, ma'am." Monica went for a few old newspapers and returned. "You have to tell me what's going on, what are you doing Maddi?"

Maddi ignored her plea for information, and spoke louder. "Right, roll them up as if making kindling."

"*What?*"

219

"Oh, shit, just roll the bloody things up like this." Maddi could feel the edge of panic not far away. "Stop asking questions. Trust me, please!"

She laid the newspapers criss-cross over the rest, then sprayed it all with more mousse. She rolled the condoms out to their full extent and laid them on the top. Maddi opened her own bag and removed more condoms; she did the same with these.

She looked around quickly. "Where's the fire escape?"

"Down the end of the corridor—why, what are you going to do?"

"You'll see. Put this cushion up your frock and try to look pregnant."

"Bloody hell, what's going on?"

"DO IT, MONICA! Just chuffin' do it, and stop asking me things all the time...oh, I'm sorry, forgive me—but please, later, eh?"

They picked everything up and went out to the corridor. Maddi scared Monica even more by the way she constantly looked around for assailants, or whatever she was looking for. "Where's the pay phone?"

Monica evened the score a little. "Just there at the end of your nose, look!"

"Hm..." She dialled 999. "Fire, please...Rutland Flats...I dunno, but there's a lot of smoke; I'm getting out now." She let the phone drop. She strode to where the smoke detector was, put the bin underneath, and threw a single match into the homemade smoke bomb. *WHOOSH*—a burst of flame almost took her eyebrows off, and instantly the smoke from the burning, lubricated rubber started to billow. She put the tray on top to stop the sprinklers from doing their job, leaving a hole at each corner where black putrid smoke spiralled out. Maddi coughed.

The sirens blasted as the smoke rose to the detectors. The corridor filled with smoke, looking like a film set. "Fire! Fire! Everybody out, Fire!"

People came like wood lice running from an upturned stone. They rushed past everywhere; the scene was a complete success. "Right, now follow me, and hold on!"

The smoke from two dozen condoms was staggering. With a bag or two each, it was time for amateur dramatics. "Help! Help! My friend's having a baby; we were just going to the hospital...it's starting to come. Oh God, what can we do? Help! Help!"

Monica picked up the script like a seasoned pro. "Ohhh, here comes another...oh hell, I'm frightened. Help me!"

They could almost hear the bugles as two young men came rushing to their assistance, snatching the bags off them and ushering them through the crowds. "Get out the way, she's havin' a baby! Move, go on, move. Let us through!"

People rushed everywhere; the building was emptying fast, sirens were wailing, and screams filled the air. The fire engine sirens were getting closer, and the apartment security staff were ushering people into fire command points. "Sorry, mate, you'll have to let us through to the cars. She's havin' a baby now, look!" said one of the helping men.

"Oh, bollocks, bollocks, bollocks!" exclaimed a security guard. "That's all I fuckin' need, some woman having a kid."

"Well, do something! She'll drop it here if you don't!" shouted the man.

Monica groaned and cried, "It'll die, my baby, it'll die!"

"Don't overdo it!" Maddi whispered. She stared at the security man. "Well? Shit-for-brains, are you going to let us get to my car, or are you going to deliver it?"

The flustered security man was in a panic; the fire engines were there, and the police and ambulances were screeching to a halt. "I've got this lot...and you, and you...oh, bloody fuckin' hell, all right then, MOVE, MOVE OUT OF THE WAY! She's goin' to have a baby, get her to the car!"

A young police officer took the reins. "I'll see to it, ladies, follow me. MAKE WAY, PLEASE, LET US THROUGH!" Turning to Monica, he asked, "How urgent are things? Do you need an ambulance? Is it imminent?"

"No it's okay," said Maddi. "I'm a midwife. If we can get her to hospital within the next half hour, she'll be fine. I just need to get to my car. It's the purple one over there—oh, thank you, officer, thank you so much." Having made his day, or even his year, they waved and drove away.

By now, there were so many people and onlookers that the chance of the Rat, or his accomplices doing anything was gone. They stood still, staring in disbelief and silence as the terror of what had happened began to dawn on them. They had been out-witted! The women had got away!

Laughing despite the situation, Maddi sped away. Monica pulled out the cushion. "Ooooh, a do-it-yourself caesarean!"

"Oh God, that's horrible!"

They looked at each other and laughed again as they spoke about what had just happened. They felt exhilarated, but the se-riousness of the situation took over, and they sat quieter. "Where are we going, anyway?"

"Ashover."

"Ashover?"

"Yes."

"Why?"

"Let us get there, let me gather my thoughts, and I'll tell you everything. I promise."

They pulled into a pub car park en route. Maddi looked into her friend's questioning eyes. She deserved an explanation. "Let me ring Mike first." She got out of the car for a better signal on her phone, leaving a bewildered Monica holding the cushion baby.

Why Mike, I wonder? Monica thought as her eyes followed Maddi around the car park.

Maddi stood tapping her foot impatiently. "Pick up the phone, bozo!" A few more rings, and he did.

"Hello, 633405—"

"Hiya, it's me." In addition to a run-down of what had hap-pened, Maddi advised Mike to lock up the house and go straight to Ashover. Surely the inn wouldn't be booked up at this time of the year; they could book an extra room, she'd meet him in the car park next to the church this evening at six.

Mike followed his instructions, although he was worried. With a preoccupied mind, he finished packing and locked the house. He did a final look round, making sure he wasn't being watched. Then he got into his car and left.

About five miles from his house, he stopped on a country lane lay-by, switched off his engine, and resumed his thinking position. "Well?"

"Don't worry yourself too much; sometimes actions like this decide the chain of future events for us. The trick is to think of as many possibilities as possible, and have a plan. When you think about it, what has happened isn't too bad. I was worried about Monica, and I know you are. But now, although we have an entrapped spy in our midst—the Samurai—we know where it is, and where she is. I wasn't happy about leaving her on her own, you know, not with that in her mind, so now we can protect her. It'll not hear what we don't want it to, anyway, not with the mind wall in place. I should think Maddi is telling her all the details now, and who better? You must keep close together though, and clear up loose ends. Get on your mobile and tell Rosie that there's a crisis at work, and you might not be able to be reached, because of meetings and things, so you'll phone her. I'm sure Maddi can come up with some complaint and get another week off; what about you?"

"Me? Huh, I'm owed loads of leave; they'll just have to bloody manage. Christ, they owe me; I've kept that place going. I'll ring and say I've got a family crisis, and need a couple weeks off. Compassionate leave."

"Right. Well, make sure the two M's do something similar; we don't want suspicious families and friends spoiling things. Oh, and your cars, I'm sure Tony and Co. will know them, so when you get there, try parking them up somewhere and hiring one between you. I'll see you tonight; good luck—the pace is picking up again, isn't it?"

Mike put his cover into practice and rang work to explain the sudden death of his mother--who had actually passed away seven years earlier—and told Rosie of a leaking roof which had destroyed all his important work, which he now had to redo. On route to Ashover, he docked his car and by plastic, he picked up another for a couple of weeks. The new car loaded up, he went

to the arranged meeting place to wait for Maddi. Her bright purple Cabriolet with a white top stood out like a beacon as he
drove into the car park. He was half an hour early, so he parked
up and went in to see if he could find them. They were sitting in
the bar, deep in conversation. "Hello, you two. How are you?"

They both replied that they felt quite positive, considering
the present situation.

"We've booked in for a week but said we may stay longer;
we're in a double room and you've got a single."

"Oh, lovely, thanks."

Monica laughed and added. "And you are a Mr. Sith—we
thought we'd leave the 'm' out to make it look better!"

"What she means is," laughed Maddi, "that my hand was
shaking so much, and we were both so scared, I wrote it wrong!"

Mike looked at Monica; she was lovely, but the events had
really taken their toll. She was pale, and dark under the eyes, and
she had lost weight. It was concern he felt now, not the overwhelming attraction he had first felt. In a distant memory room,
a candle spat and faded, whilst a certain Scottish mind keeper
allowed himself a faint smile and a rub of the hands.

Mike then looked at Maddi. "Maddi, that car of yours, it's
got to go; it's like writing, 'we are here' on the front of the pub!"

"I know."

"I'll see to that; there must be something, or someone,
around here who'll store it, or whatever." He walked to the bar,
and after a couple of question-and-answer sessions with various
bar staff, he was directed to a man called Dave. He was a
friendly, but rather harsh-looking man, with a big nose. Sitting
in a corner with a border collie at his feet, a pint in front of him,
and a pipe spreading a layer of smoke across the room, he
looked very much a "local."

"Good evening. I understand you own a few outbuildings?"

"Correct."

"Erm, I don't expect you to understand, or to agree with our
lack of scruples, but that lady's husband—"Mike pointed to
Maddi. "—wouldn't want to see her here with me, and her car's
a little, what shall we say…obvious?"

"The purple soft top?"

"Yes, could you store it?"

"It'll cost."

"How much?"

"Thirty a day, no less. It's not negotiable."

"Bloody hell, pal, do you own a yacht?"

"You don't have to use me, do you?"

"Okay, fair enough."

"When?"

"Now?"

"Let me sup up, and I'll be with you. I'll see you at my Land Rover; it's just outside the door."

Mike took Maddi's keys. "You carry on telling Monica all about things Maddi; I'll be back as soon as I can. And when I am back, I'm going to study the menu; it smells lovely, doesn't it?"

"Mmm, it does. I've a few details to fill in with you, too, so we'll all have a cosy meal and a good talk tonight then, shall we?" Maddi replied with a smile and a disarming stare.

"Wouldn't miss it for the world. See you." He kissed her on the cheek and went outside to find Dave waiting for him. He received instructions to follow him in Maddi's car.

"Will I be all right for a lift back, then?"

"Yes."

Mike thought that it would probably be hard work getting a conversation going with this man, and he wasn't wrong. They left to lose Maddi's car.

Back in the bar, Maddi told Monica as much as she could, stopping to clarify whole sections as Monica incredulously asked about various points of the unbelievable tale she was listening to. It was evening when Mike, looking jaded and irritable, came back.

The atmosphere of the inn did help to soothe him, though. It had come alive as evening approached, the lamps, beams, reflecting brass, and low wall lights all in carefully picked positions. to achieve a tasteful "old world" effect.

Mike studied the menu at length, and both Maddi and Monica were amused when with boyish pride he ordered a steak, well done.

"What's up? There's nothing wrong with having a steak."

Monica smiled at him. "I know. You just carry on."

Bemused, Mike looked around. "Nice, isn't it?"

The two M's laughed again, and Mike blushed. "What's wrong with saying that?" he asked in an injured tone.

They replied that nothing was wrong. After a glance and a smile, they changed the subject. The adventure seemed to have lifted Monica's spirits.

Throughout the evening, they continued to discuss recent events in detail.

Dave was in his farmhouse, his wife in bed. The crinkled piece of paper the Rat had given him with the list of cars and registrations on also had the number to ring in case a situation like this arose. He dialled it and waited for the Rat's voice.

"Hello."

"Who am I speaking to?"

"Stirling."

"Who?"

"Stirling."

"Stirling who?"

"Just Stirling. Who are you, and what do you want?"

"I'm Dave from Ashover. I'm Ratter's 'eye' for this part of the world. I was given this number to ring if I had any information."

"And do you have?"

"Yes, I've been asked to hide one of the cars on the list by a bloke called Mike Sith."

"Sith? Thanks. We'll contact you."

"Hey, what about me money?"

"It'll come; and if you want to keep your hands to spend it with, keep quiet about this." Stirling put the phone down as Dave was talking. He had heard about the Rat's little failure, even before Tony had. He was well liked by the team Tony had working for him. This was a major opportunity to fulfil his ambitions. He sat down and began to plan.

CHAPTER 17

Tony was almost ready for the practical preparations of the on-coming war; research and development were near enough done, the appointed time was close at hand, and the battle plans were coming to a close. It was bound to succeed, especially with Christine—and soon Monica—in his possession.

A nervous knock sounded on the door.

"Come in!" Tony swung round on his studded leather swivel chair, expecting to see a despondent hostage held before him.

The Rat walked in alone, hardly daring to lift his head to the gaze. The expression on Tony's face changed from expected delight to angry, horror-filled curiosity. "Where the fuck is she?"

The Rat shook; he felt an uncontrollable urge and urinated on the floor, his trousers changing colour down his legs to reveal it, a puddle appearing beneath where he stood. "There was a fire, it was j-j-just bad l-l-luck; her mate came an-and…"

"Are you trying to tell me you've failed, you shit-snivelling little man?"

"No, not really; nobody could have done better, Boss, I…I…"

Tony took a step towards him. "I told you." Another slow step followed. Tony's eyes rolled up to become completely white.

His prey fell to his knees, crying.

"SHH!" Tony hissed. The command to be quiet had immediate effect.

The Rat's mouth shut so hard and fast that Tony could almost hear his teeth break. He saw the terror, the true terror on the Rat's face. He began to rock and tried to speak, but all that came was a stifled hum, mucus bubbling from his nostrils. His eyes widened as he looked at his hands; the flesh slowly began to take the form of an uncooked crumpet. Holes appeared upon them, then began to spread up his arms. His clothes fell away, and his penis developed the same hole-ridden appearance. Running around in a tight, frenzied circle, he saw earwigs; his penis itched terribly as a worm crawled out, and he couldn't even scream, his teeth and now his lips felt as if they had been glued together.

Tony's eyeballs became visible again as he looked coldly at the Rat. He clicked his fingers.

The Rat recovered instantly, then looked pleadingly to Tony for mercy. Surely his punishment was over.

Tony stared at him.

The Rat's next and final vision came to him. Looking around, he discovered he was naked, his hands tied behind his back and his ankles roped together. About twenty angry women were shouting for release and baying for his blood. In their eyes, could be seen one thing: a desire for revenge. These were the mothers and sisters of every little child he had used in his reward time; they were the kin of the children of his dreams. They had scissors—big, wallpaper scissors—and nutcrackers, and hot, branding irons. They didn't have an ounce of guilt, remorse, or mercy between them. He felt his urge; he smiled at them. He didn't want to, but he couldn't stop: he grew a huge erection. He waved it and taunted them, laughing as he hopped away from them.

"The bastard's enjoying it! He's insulting us to the last. Free us now! Please!"

The safety line drawn in the dirt looked reachable—only twenty or so hops, and he'd be there. Tony had given him a target, a sanctuary to aim for, a fighting chance. The Rat had known that he would. He knew his past good work would save him, freedom beckoned. Tony stood behind the line and waved, "come on." The shout went up, and the women charged, screaming insults and threats.

He hopped for his life. Tony raised his hand, and the Rat fell.

"We've got him!" An extremely large, puffing and panting woman shouted above the rest. "That prick is my trophy." A horrible smile spread across her face as she clicked the scissors. The group left an alleyway for her and began to surround him.

Tony watched a rolling, writhing Rat die before his eyes.

Tony's version of justice had been served.

About an hour later, the mess had been cleared away, and the same room found Tony talking to Stirling. "Well done, Stirling; what you say impresses me. You'll find me a good master. Go now, and show me what you are made of—and don't fail me."

"I won't."

"Good; I feel your confidence. Go and get her."

"What about the Rat?"

"Who?"

Stirling smiled. "Say no more; I understand."

"Good; I think we are going to get on. I'll allow you two mistakes in my service I can be benevolent."

"Thank you, Master. I accept. But two will be more than ample. I simply don't fail—ever."

"Excellent. I'm going on a trip. When I return, I want to see her."

"Consider it done, Master." Stirling spoke in his most grovelling voice. He was a proud man, and to most others he was a dominant male, full of confidence. But he was on the first steps of a cabalistic journey, and one of the first lessons was that of subjecting oneself to higher beings. Like animal packs in the wild, he knew his place; he could manage to be like this for Tony for as long as it took. It would be worth it, one day.

"I can see I've made a good choice. Goodbye."

For the two M's, Debbie, Sean, and Mike, the joining of Tony and Stirling was a bad moment. They would be a much more formidable partnership than the Rat and Tony had been. Stirling knew much of the cabala, was eager to learn and ambitious, and he had great hopes.

Tony closed the door of his Porsche and made the engine roar. "Power…yes, my black beauty, I'll have power like yours, too…one day." He roared off.

He had been busy getting the grid references just right. He needed to construct a huge pentacle with its epicentre hovering above Highoredish. At the allotted time, an incantation would bring forth lightning to mark the ground. Each point of the massive pentacle had to be the same height above sea level, so that it would hover parallel. Each point had to be marked with a star marker, each constructed with care, each with its head above ground and its body buried.

Lately, much of his time had been spent assembling these. Now, they rested on the seat next to him, packed away in a specially constructed oak box with purple felt lining and shiny brass fittings. The star markers were glass bottles, intricately painted in beautiful, translucent colours. In a seaside craft shop, they would have fetched a good price and probably sold out quickly. But the outside belied their interior, which consisted of the small body parts from his collection. Each point of the star would correspond with the outer points of a human body: the head, the hands, and the feet. The centre of the star would be the genitalia—female genitalia. This would be the final piece, and it had to come from someone special, at the right time, in the exact correct way.

If Maddi and Mike had known how the body parts they'd seen in Tony's flat were to be used, they would have smashed the containers and burnt the pieces. That would have held things up for years

True cabalists would have been mortified by the catastrophic way in which Tony was heading straight for the abyss. Cabalists feared and dreaded Daath, the city of evil and the home of demons shown on the Tree of Life.

But to Tony, this was the place to attain power of a magnitude hitherto unseen in the world—in fact, in any world. The night of Mike's defeat would be the start of a rocket journey, an accelerated trip through the Tree of Life. The breakthrough to the other side would bring Tony vast rewards, and eventually a position of exultation in Daath.

The bottles, each labelled in Hebrew, jingled along as he drove, Monica Doll resting at their side. The delightful scenery of a country lane rushed past—such a pretty path for such a dire purpose. The village cottages watched him pass, as a million cars had before him. Soon, he reached the first allotted place: a well-known viewing spot, an unassuming seat next to a lay by near Shirland. The hillside overlooked a beautiful valley, and the discontinued route of the old railway could be seen winding its way in and out of a reservoir. As it often was, late in the evening, the viewpoint was deserted.

Tony felt reverence for the occasion and behaved very precisely. He sat and watched the sun go down, lighting the sky as if it were a massive blacksmith's forge in full blast with all shades of red, orange, and purple flame. As the bottom edge of the sun hit the ridge, he stood up. With his arms outstretched, he incanted his first spell, then dug a small hole and buried the first star marker, its tip just above the earth. He finished with another chant, looked around, smiled, nodded, and went back to the car. "One down, four to go." The door slammed, the beast roared, and he sped away to location number two.

Dusk turned to twilight as the short journey bought him clockwise around the pentacle to the Fabrick, another outcrop of rock. As the sky changed from purple to indigo to black, he did the same as before. The second star marker was in position.

South Wingfield Manor, an old, ruined hall, marked the south-eastern point. As if on cue, an owl uttered its cry. Tony nodded in satisfaction; things were going well, and signs like that were the approval of magic. He had taken photos and measurements in the guise of an amateur historian, and he knew the exact place for spot number three. He scaled the insecure fencing and walked silently across the dark field, unnoticed by all except the owl. He scaled the lower window—now just a weatherworn opening—and climbed the spiral stairway up to the fourth window, forcing his torso through. With his chubb hammer, he gave the spike one heavy blow to sink it into the old mortar, and with his prepared loop of strong wire, he secured the neck of the bottle to its place. The belly of the bottle sank into the hole perfectly. He chanted again and left. Halfway across the field, he stopped and looked over his shoulder. "Three!"

The chill of the night reached his bones, and it was time to return to his car for coffee and rum. He sat with his clipboard, ticking off what he had done. This was exciting, the culmination of long, hard work. Clewitt, Harrison, and Brightmore, a local firm of surveyors, had produced the paper he was ticking things off on. They had been quite excited by the fact that they were helping with the plans for the hall's re-opening after many years of repair work; the laser and fireworks show, with classical music in the background, would make for a splendid evening. The money he had donated was welcomed with open arms, and had ensured the event would take place on time. He had almost been heralded as a saviour of the project. "The pillocks," he muttered. "Most people will believe anything, especially when they think it will glorify themselves." He spun the top of the flask tight and put the music from *Lost Boys,* his favourite film, into the car CD system. Singing and rocking back and forth, he drove to his next destination.

This place was a little more difficult. A monument to the local regiment, a bit like a lighthouse, stood on the edge of an old, deep quarry. With a flashing red light warning low flying jets of its position, the tower attracted the gazes of passers-by. So black and camouflaged, Tony scaled the fence and crept across the field. The locked door at its base was no problem. Unseen, he slipped inside, adjusted his haversack, and silently climbed the spiralling stairway to the balcony. This was a nerve-wracking situation: the wind was up, and it whistled an eerie tune through the structure. He climbed out onto the ledge. The drop down into the lake in the quarry looked long, cold, and frightening. He stared down, taking a deep breath. After a couple of attempts—

which unbalanced him and almost pulled him over—he managed to get his grappling iron around the lightning conductor. Reminiscent of a PT instructor going up masts at an Earls Court display, he pulled himself up two-thirds of the way. Carefully, he counted the bricks from the balcony, and struck in a stout metal pin after twenty-three. The bottleneck was attached as before, a small stone removed, and the belly of the bottle buried. Dangling like Quasimodo at the Notre Dame cathedral, he said his incantations.

The course was done in reverse back to his car. Shaking, he spoke to himself. "One more, Tony, one fuckin' more an' that's it, only one more!"

The walk around Masson from the old lead mine was easy. A glance at his Rolex showed that everything was going like clockwork, a masterpiece of synchronicity. The folly looked forlorn as it seemed to look down and enquire his purpose. "I'm here to start my ruling of the universe, Mr. Tower. Is that okay with you? Good, I hoped it might be. If it wasn't you'd be at the top of the list to be destroyed, and I'd use your remains to build an effigy of my prick!" He laughed at his little joke as he climbed. "Ha, there wouldn't be enough stone to do it justice." Grinning, he secured the last bottle. It was close to the slit window, but for anyone to notice, they would have to be floating over the drop down into the valley, or swinging from the cable cars that went close by. Yes, this was the most likely to be seen, but it only had to last a couple of days, so it was almost certain to be okay. The element of risk seemed right to him. *It shouldn't be easy*, he reflected.

He stood at the base of the tower and began to chant a low, repetitive phrase. The bottle started to glow, first emitting a faint jade light. Then, a beam of light shot like a rocket to the next marker.

Thunder cracked as the air was split, disturbing time, motion, nature, and the natural order. A bolt of lightning hit the tower, then charged off to follow the path of the green pentacle. It stopped; the pentacle was too powerful to follow, so the lightning went to the earth. Mother Nature was forced to obey the higher powers at work.

Tony felt good. He shuddered each time a glass was hit, feeling a surge of power inside him. He drove to Highoredish, slammed the car door shut, and ran as fast as he could to his space. Yes! It had worked! The crackling, fizzing noise of pure magic was wonderful, and a visible pentacle hovered in the air, its pencil-thin lines getting more and more solid. The pentacle must have measured twenty feet across, exceeding his expectations. He stared in awe, walking from point to point. He laughed and laughed. "Yes, yes, YESSS!" He held Monica Doll in the air to see.

The pentacle stopped vibrating and became a solid mass of bright magic about eight feet above the ground. Tony drew his Samurai sword and went to each point, swinging the sword in an arc. Each arc brought a flash of permanent, dancing lightning to the ground. All five streaks landed at almost the same spot, only inches from one another. Tony walked over to the spot, the centre of magic...*his* centre of magic.

The night of Saint Walpurgis would see a full cabalistic ceremony. But for now, a preliminary preparation was taking place, and it was a little like preparing the scenery for the main event at a theatre. The circle and standing place had to be identified—along with the adjacent triangle—for the creatures or whatever to appear when summoned. It was now time for his spot to be marked. He held his sword aloft, lightning dancing around his feet. Tony shouted two cabalistic words that were too powerful to be written. It was a thing only the boldest cabalists dared do. As if being beamed up to some interplanetary craft in a science-fiction movie, a beam of bright blue energy came straight down from the centre of the pentacle. It stopped just touching Tony's hair, which rose in the static. His cheeks drew back as if he were travelling at great speed. As a crack of thunder pealed through the air, his whole body turned electric blue.

Slowly, he brought the sword down. Images of the sword's movement were suspended in vision and time, as if a time-lapse photograph of the sweep had been taken. The electric arc smell, similar to geranium leaves, filled his nostrils. When the sword touched the ground, a circle of about twelve feet diameter burnt to bare earth. The lightning from the pentacle took on a more pink hue and danced around the pentacle's edge. Tony opened his cloak and unzipped his trousers, and urinated on the sword. The sword spat and hissed. The smell of burnt urine explained the dreadful smell in the school caretaker's boiler house, from memories long past. The whole sword was tempered as it turned from pale straw to blue to purple. And when the stream of urine hit the ground, a belch of vile steam engulfed him. Mother Earth had been defiled, and on this spot, nothing would ever grow again.

The hovering pentacle disappeared, and he redressed his manhood and turned east to take twenty deliberate strides. Then he stopped and cut three, three-foot lines of an equilibrium triangle. All he had to do was stroke gently with his sword, and a channel two inches deep and an inch wide appeared, whether it cut through soft earth or stone. The indications of the powerful weapon added to his deep satisfaction. On cue, the sun rose to greet him, drawing a line of orange down his face. It was done, and he was ready.

He looked around at the normality of dawn. A rabbit bobbed across his path as if nothing unusual had happened, and he smiled at it. A few jumps later, it landed in the circle. He watched with interest as it lapped up some of the urine. It leapt straight upright about two yards. "Christ!" Tony exclaimed in amusement, watching the rabbit land and run around in a figure eight as if its tail was on fire. He walked up and stared at it. The animal instantly stopped and sat looking at him. It blinked. Tony stared as it blinked again. If animals could smile, this one did. Tony smiled back, and with one sweep of his sword, he cut it in half, muttering, "Fuck you."

Tiredness overcame him like a burden of lead. He walked back to his car to finish the rum and coffee, kissed Monica Doll, and laid her down on a small pillow of dark blue satin. He tucked her in under a matching cover. His mind wandered. "Mmm, I wonder if Stirling has her yet. I'm almost there. Just one more glass bottle for the centre of the circle, with a little something from her...ha-ha-ha, I'll enjoy that...and that'll be it."

The dark observers watched, nodding in satisfaction.

Out of sight of all these events was Mike's little army. Tomorrow, Mike and Maddi were off for a hike to view Highoredish and the surrounding area. But tonight, alone in his hotel bed, Mike wanted his version of normality to return. After saying goodnight to his two friends, he strolled down the dimly lit corridor to his room. As he undressed and washed, he felt Debbie's presence—strongly, instantly, but fleetingly. Quickly he turned around. Disappointment greeted him, but it had felt so real. In his mind castle, Sean stirred quickly as cold whipped through his body. Something was going to happen tonight, and he had an idea what.

Mike looked under the bed and smelt the air. She had been there—only for an instant, but he felt sure of it. He sensed that something was different; was it his urgency? His expectation? He didn't know, and sleep took a long time coming.

But when it did...WOW! She looked ravenous, a woman made for sexual pleasure. She was every man's dream, and she was specially made for him. As he stepped from the clouds onto the balcony, she pouted her lips and moved to him like a jaguar.

"Hello," he said simply.

"Hello...darling."

Mike gulped. "No Sean?"

"He's busy. Come on, I can't wait any longer. I need you, I want sex." She paused. "Ooh, isn't sex a lovely word? COME ON!"

Mike smiled, then laughed at himself for ever imagining a woman like this could exist in the real world, even for a second. *Why should there be?* he mused. *Isn't this the whole reason for imagination?*

Debbie frowned. "What's up?"

"Nothing, believe me, absolutely nothing."

She accepted that, pushed him to one side, and raced up the ivory staircase. "I'll beat you to the top!"

Mike ran up after her, but she beat him easily. Out of breath and giggling, she fell to the bed, and Mike joined her. Side by side, they lay on their backs looking to the ceiling. Debbie turned to him and smiled. "What's your favourite? What shall I do for you tonight?"

"Oh, dear me, so many! Er…I do rather like the massage parlour game, and the French maid, and the naughty secretary, and…"

"Bloody hell, steady on. I'm not that athletic, you know! But I'll tell you what: shall we combine a few? How about a naughty masseur, dressed up as a French maid…with no knickers on!"

"Mmm, tough decision there, Debbie. Let me think…okay, I have thought long enough. Yup, that'll do!"

Debbie laughed, then asked for her directions. "Right, I like this bit. Tell me my part, what I've got to do."

"Well…I'm a visitor to a hotel, and I'm a writer. I've…er, travelled a long way, and I'm stressed out, so I book in for a massage." Mike grinned from ear to ear. "But the porter mistakes my drift, and books me in to a massage parlour close by, and I'm completely unaware."

"Oooh, I think I know the type."

"Right, then you go outside the door, and I'll lay on the bed, naked apart from a towel over me…waiting…okay?"

Debbie saluted. "Yes, sir. One very naughty masseur coming up!"

How could a woman saluting look so damn sexy? Mike lay waiting, and soon there was a knock. "Come in."

Wow! That word gets used a lot these days, Mike thought, *but bloody hell, as soon as I see her; there's only one way to describe my feelings*: WOW!

She came in wearing a French maid's outfit with lots of lace. It was very short, and made all the right parts stick out. A lace headdress with two long tassels hung down the back, and she wore high heels. Her hair was drawn up at the sides and hung straight down her back. Instead of the usual black, the dress was a deep, midnight blue—and boy, did it rustle! She took the long, slow strides of a supermodel towards him. Every step made the dress rustle more. She stopped and stood with a small tray bearing an assortment of massage oils. "Ghood ahfternoon, sihr. My name is Fifi."

"Fifi?"

Debbie frowned at him and raised an eyebrow.

"Sorry. Good afternoon, Fifi. What a lovely name—is it French?"

Debbie couldn't help a little smile as she thought, *Is it French? Of course it's French; why else am I dressed like this?* She regained her composure. "*Oui, Monsieur*, it...er, how you say, it is my Chrrr-is-tian name."

Oh God, she's talking in that accent again. Mike looked at her adoringly. "Oh, how nice."

The supermodel walk continued to the dressing table. About a foot further away than she needed, she stopped. Straight-legged, she put the tray down. Her bare bottom was revealed, and his enjoyment stood up like a chimneystack. She saw the reflection and turned around to point in mock horror. "Oh, sir, what iz ziss before mhy eyes? It frightens me!" She put one finger to her mouth and pointed with her other hand, looking down at it. "Oh, tut tut. Sir, would you rholl ovher please?"

Mike did, putting his head on one side on his folded arms, to look at her...no, to study her. She walked around him, and he turned his head to her new side. "May I just say, sir, what a whonderfhull, strong body yhou have."

"Thank you."

She began to tell him of her technique, about how she pressed harder as she moved her hands towards the heart, about her rolling palms, her thumb pressures. "It has all to doo with ze flow of blhoood."

"Well, I've a big flow of blood in one part. Can you do anything about that?"

"Oh, sir, you are so...how you say...cheeky."

Mike smiled at her acting. It really was quite good, and the accents were out of this world. The German and Irish and Russian were all a joy to hear. She showed off a bit more and explained the rolling-thumb technique in great detail, and about "popping" stress pockets. She asked him if he understood the importance of putting oil on the hands and not on the body, all to do with temperature, and shock. He listened, captivated. The way she almost sang her words sometimes fascinated him. She got a bit tired of the accent, though, and slowly reverted to her normal voice. Mike sensed something coming, but was not sure what.

"Would you like to test it for me? Rub a little on my skin?" She put some oil on his hands and turned around to put the bottle on the floor, again revealing her delightful *derriere*.

Mike's eyes almost popped out of their sockets. "Can I try on this skin?"

"Pardon, sir?"

"Sorry."

She was almost playing the part too well. "I should think so, too, sir." Then she smiled a coy little smile. "But…if you wish to, and promise not to tell anyone, I think I'd rather like it." She blushed like a virgin.

So he massaged her cheeks as she bent over with hands on knees. "Nice?"

"Mmm, thank you, sir, it is…yes, very." She looked guiltily over her shoulder at him, biting her bottom lip as if ashamed at what she'd said.

"I bet you say that to all your clients."

"No, no, I don't, honest. I've never ever done anything so…so bold, so naughty…sir."

Again her tone changed, and so did her demeanour. She actually did look a little embarrassed as she asked, "Mike?"

"Mmmm, what, dear?"

She sat beside him and rubbed his arm; she looked like a goddess, a sex goddess, specially dressed for him. He thought that here was a woman who was going to ask for something extraordinary.

"Have you…"

Interest stood almost as high as his manhood. "Have I what?"

"Have you ever…looked at a woman?"

"What? Of course I have."

"No, I mean when they don't know it."

"What, like a Peeping Tom?"

"Err...mmm...I suppose so, yes. Have you?"

"Well...I have a crafty look at a nice pair of legs getting out of a car, or a short skirt going up the stairs before me, or if the wind blows a dress up I wouldn't look away. But I've never just hid and looked. No, honest!"

"Oh."

"Why?"

"Nothing."

"No, go on, tell me. Why?"

"Well...would you like to?"

Mike laughed a little. "If I knew I wouldn't get caught, yes!"

"Oh, you won't get caught."

The penny dropped. "Ah, would I be right in saying you'd like to be watched?"

"Almost."

"Almost?"

"I'd like to be watched, you know, doing naughty things to myself...and..."

"God, this is turning me on more and more. I like you mysterious, and what, for Christ's sake?"

"Tut tut, don't blaspheme. I'd like to get caught, like as if you were my superior, and I thought you were out, an' I got all excited, thinking naughty things, and you came in and caught me...doing it!"

"Can I be your master and you my maid? It seems a shame to waste the gear you've got on."

"Yes, that's fine. You don't mind, do you? I know it's not what you wanted, and I am supposed to be here for you, not me!"

"'Course I don't mind. You've chosen many times before. It sounds brilliant—keep 'em coming!"

Mike hid behind a screen that dummied as a door. Debbie got a feather duster and began to clean, exaggerating the stretching, the twisting, and the reaching. Her waist seemed so tiny.

"Tra-la-la, I'd better do the candlesticks next…oooh, these are big and smooth." She took one and sat on the edge of the bed. She gripped it in the duster and began to polish, slowly. "Oh, I say, they *are* rather big and smooth…I wonder?" She pretended to look about. "He must be out. I wish this were his…" She giggled. "Oh, naughty, Fifi!"

Mike remembered to blink; his eyes felt sore.

"Mmm." She removed the candle from the stick and lay flat on her back, legs apart, exactly in Mike's line of view. She slowly inserted the candle into her. The groan of pleasure was a gem. The strokes began slowly and increased in length, the noise revealing her wetness. She moaned and writhed, and her bottom began to beat the sheets. Her other hand began to rub. Her legs bent at the knees and drew up as far as possible.

He stood up and slowly walked to her side; her eyes were closed. He gave a discreet cough behind his hand, and stood with one hand behind his back, his eyebrow raised.

"Ohhh…ahhh, oooh…oh, oh, ahh…Oh, GOD! Where… how long have…? I…I…"

"It's okay. Don't stop, and don't apologise. I've really enjoyed watching." He took the end of the candle, and moved her other hand to take over the rubbing.

It only took a minute or so. "Oooooh! Aaaaaah, yes, oh my God, yes, yes, yes!" She had one of her best orgasms ever. "Oh, Mike, that was wonderful. I must do you now; you must be bursting." She sat on the end of the bed and took his purple head into her mouth, moving until he came in colossal spurts.

He was still there!

They looked at each other and waited. Nothing happened. They sat down and talked; it was lovely. Mike shook nervously. "Do you think I'll go soon?"

Debbie shrugged.

They both washed and still remained together. This was fantastic, brilliant, cosmic. They had crossed a barrier; they were able to talk and stay, a real relationship at last, with no time barrier looming over them.

For what seemed like an age, they talked and laughed. Eventually, they got into bed side by side to enjoy a deep, post-orgasmic slumber.

Mike awoke the next morning alone in his bed. The hotel room looked shallow and lonely. As his thoughts came flooding back, he smiled to himself. At last he could stay—not indefinitely, fair enough—but he could stay. He felt sure it could be repeated. He remembered how Sean had said things would be different—indeed, they would be even better!

And so, as Tony had reached a new level on a parallel path, so had Mike. Sean had said things would change. Was Debbie coming to him or was he going to her? What was the significance, in real magic terms? If he could learn to wake up with her, would the magical journey Sean spoke of be possible? Could he stop for days, for weeks, for years? What would happen to real earth time if he did?

Sean was pleased; he understood the significance, and he knew the answers. A great magical leap had been taken, a magical chasm of time had been crossed, and the bridge back had been burnt. The biggest obstacle of all—time—had been overcome. Other barriers would start to topple now. "It took a little longer than I had hoped, but it's come in time…just. Well done, Mike. We are almost ready for our journey!"

As their counterparts had done not so long ago, two white observers looked at each other, nodded approval, and smiled.

CHAPTER 18

Mike went downstairs. He was as hungry as a wolf, and a good cholesterol-boosting fry-up was in order. On the way, he knocked on the two M's door and cheerfully shouted, "Are you two up? Ready for brekkie?" He felt on top of the world.

He heard a couple of moans and a bit of shuffling. He repeated the knock, and again shouted, "Are you up?"

"Yes…see you in a bit," was the annoyed reply.

He went down and helped himself to fried eggs, smoked bacon, fried bread, beans, mushrooms, sausage, fried tomatoes, and a couple slices of black pudding—fried, of course. He ate like someone who had been on starvation rations for a month, and he was busy "mopping up" when Maddi and Monica joined him. Maddi raised an eyebrow and twisted her lips in disgust; Monica just shook her head and looked at Maddi. "Men!"

"Oh, are you that hungry? I'll order you a couple. Hey! Can we have a fried man or two over here?"

"Shh, don't be silly," Maddi said in a disapproving tone.

"Sorry," he replied.

They looked at the menu and ordered grapefruit, toast, and a pot of tea.

Mike drank his own tea and passed comment. "Isn't it funny how a cuppa always tastes better after a fry-up? Have you noticed?"

"No."

"No, neither have I."

Again he tried in vain. "You ought to try, get a nice greasy lining on your tummies. It'll set you up for the day, that's what my mum used to say."

"Good old Mum," Maddi said, smiling to her friend. "You seem cheerful. Was she on form, then?"

He coughed and averted their enquiring looks.

As the two M's tea was poured, conversation began again. Maddi announced that Monica was going to stay behind and have a relaxing, trouble-free day to build her up a bit.

Mike agreed quite readily; the prospect of a day with his new favourite "real-world" woman seemed a pleasant one. "I'm going to go and have a look at my map a bit then. See you later, eh?"

"Mmm, okay then." Maddi smiled back. Monica looked happy and a little more like her old self.

As he walked away, another guest looked over his paper at him, and as he walked past said, "Good morning, lovely day."

"Sorry? Oh yes, it is. We're off for a walk. What have you got planned?"

"I've a busy day arranged. I'm here studying my family history, so I'll be spending a day poring over old ecclesiastical records and things." He nodded towards the church. "And I'll probably be rummaging around the graveyard."

"Sounds interesting; it's something I've always fancied doing. Tell you what: I'll meet you in the bar later, and you can tell me how you've gone on." He smiled and added, "Tell me all about the black sheep of your family. Who knows what you might dig up—although hopefully not in the physical sense, eh?" He laughed at his humour and the man smiled back politely. "I'm Mike by the way, Mike Sith." He held out his hand.

Half rising out of his chair, the man took his hand and shook it. "And I'm Liam, Liam…Silver. Pleased to meet you. See you tonight, then. I look forward to it."

Whistling a tune, Mike walked away. Stirling followed him with his eyes and spoke to himself as he drank his coffee. "Yes, I look forward to seeing you, but it won't be tonight. I—*we*—will be long gone." His eyes went to the two women, and over the top of his paper, he studied them.

About an hour later, two intrepid hikers stood in the car park waving to Monica as she looked out of her open bedroom window. The weather was overcast but dry. They set off feeling cheerful. Mike thought back to his childhood; it was moments like these that reminded him of the nice feeling he'd had when starting an Enid Blyton book. All the children were happy, but he knew that adventures were just around the corner. At that point he stopped thinking; the similarities were all too obvious.

The church bell rang.

Mike looked to Maddi. "It's quiet here, almost lonely. I'm sure that nobody knows where we are, and she has her mobile to call us if she needs us. I could sense how uneasy you were at breakfast. Maybe I tried too hard to be cheerful, but I wanted to make her feel all right. She'll be as safe here as anywhere I can think of. But if you want, I'm more than happy to leave you here with her, and go out exploring alone."

"Oh Mike, I'm torn in two, I want to stop here with her, but at the same time I want to help you." She looked around at the peaceful scene of a pretty country village. "I know how important this is. I know what Sean wants us to do."

Mike tapped a finger to his talisman, hanging under his shirt. "We do all have these, they'll protect us. Monica knows not to take it off; it'll make her feel safe."

Maddi smiled, nodding, she had told her friend how important it was, and she did indeed seem very comforted by it.

Monica knew what they were saying. "Go! I'll be fine, honest."

"She does seem cheerful today, doesn't she?"

"Yes, she does. I'm glad. I hope she has a really nice, relaxing day. She deserves one."

Monica looked out of the small, mullioned window, watching them drive away. She ordered coffee and decided to read the morning paper in the conservatory. The gently sloping lawns of the garden were wet, and the borders well tended. As she viewed it, she commented to herself, "A pleasant outlook for a pleasant day."

Stirling waited and watched, almost blending in to the background.

By midday, Mike realised his fitness level was a bit lower than he'd thought, and although watching Maddi's bottom as she climbed up the hill was a wonderful pastime, he had to call a halt. "Bloody hell, Maddi...slow down a bit. I'm dying on my feet here."

"Shall I carry that a while?"

"No, it's all right. Phew...I can manage."

"Chauvinist!"

She carried on, increasing the pace a little as she amused herself listening to the bracken and twigs break behind her; he was keeping up...just. At the top, she turned and sat to admire the view. Mike was about thirty yards behind, red-faced and panting. "Come on, slowcoach, you're like an old man."

A minute or two later, he arrived and threw down the rucksack. "Oh God! My heart's bursting. Why did you go off like that?"

A smug, satisfied grin came back. "So, this is Highoredish, then?"

After a couple of deep breaths, he replied. "Yes, so...the... map says, anyway...phew!"

Maddi looked at him with concern. "You're not going to have a heart attack, are you?"

"'Course I'm not. I am carrying this, you know."

Maddi grinned and looked at the view. "I did offer!"

"Yes, so you did. You can take a turn then, but if someone comes, give it me back!"

"Oh God!" Maddi replied, as she glanced at her phone to see if Monica had sent a text message or anything.

He looked sheepish, then stared away. It was his turn to change the subject. "Looks like someone's been here…look." He pointed to the burnt circle. "A bit big for a campfire, though."

Maddi laughed, much more than he would have expected at a comment like this. He stared at her, his look questioning. He couldn't help but think of all the times he'd tried to be funny, to no avail, and here she was giggling like a schoolgirl at this innocuous little remark.

She calmed down a bit. "Campfire? It's more like the park after bonfire night. You'd be able to see a fire that size for miles." She started to laugh quite uncontrollably again. "I don't think it was a campfire…ha, definitely not!"

They walked around, not sure what they were looking for. Mike kept his distance; he didn't want to start this crazy woman off again. It was quite a large escarpment, and Mike sat looking at different things on the map, trying to line them up with the real thing. He looked over his shoulder as Maddi approached. "What would you say this was?" he asked. "Over there somewhere, about one and a half a miles away." He pointed towards a patchwork of evergreen and deciduous trees down in the valley, off to their right.

Maddi looked at the symbol and at the explanatory key, and said, "It's just what it says, I suppose…some sort of antiquity. Judging by the cross, I would say it's a…" Then the importance hit her, as she looked him straight in the eyes. "It's an old religious site of some sort."

"Could this be what we are looking for, our pitch to fight back?"

"Let's go and have a look; we've seen all there is here, I reckon."

They started to walk towards it; the air was clean and fresh, and it seemed to take their troubles away on the breeze. Maddi looked at her phone again; the signal was very weak here.

Around the same time, Monica decided to have a shower, get changed, then have a light lunch. Stirling unlocked the door with ease and stealthily crept into her room. He could hear her in the shower humming Brahms' "Lullaby." Slowly and silently, he closed the door and sat down, the gun in his hand. He looked towards the shower and back at the gun, screwed on the silencer, then waited.

Monica turned off the shower as she climbed out, rubbing off the excess water. She stood on the scale. "Ah, well, there's a silver lining to every cloud. I've lost nearly a stone." She put a towel around her wet hair and another around her body, then walked to the dressing table. She hadn't felt this relaxed in ages; could the worst be over?

"Stand up."

Monica froze. She did not recognise this deep, gravely voice.

"Stand up!"

She looked in the mirror and saw Stirling's reflection. He held the gun confidently and steadily, pointing at her head. Slowly, her heart beating fast, she stood up.

"Turn around…Monica."

"Who are…?"

"Shut up, turn around, and keep quiet." The tone in his voice was cold, commanding, and devoid of feeling. "I'll use this if need be, believe me."

She believed him.

A feeling of defiance welled up in her as she turned around. She looked straight into his stare, but like a dog that knew instinctively who was the stronger, she immediately looked down at the carpet. In a few seconds, defiance had turned to fear and submission. "What do you…?"

"Monica, I've just told you to shut up. You would be wise to do as I say. Put these on." He threw her some clothes.

With shaking fingers struggling to match button and button-hole, she did as she was told.

"This gun will be under my coat. If you think I won't use it, think again—I will. I'm not bothered if it's a granny, or a baby, or a favourite pet; if the need arises, I will use this gun on whoever or whatever. Do you understand that? It won't be you—I need you alive—but I am sure you do not want the responsibility of a death on your conscience."

"No, I don't want you to hurt anyone or anything."

"Come with me, then, and act as if you want to be with me; don't do anything foolish." He turned towards the bed and shot four bullets into it in a perfect square. Dust and the noise of reverberating bedsprings flew up. "My trademark, for your friends to find!"

They walked easily through the reception area; nobody took the slightest bit of notice. They proceeded through the car park, to the open-top, bottle-green Mercedes. She sat inside as he held the door open like a gentleman. He reached over as if to kiss her, but instead, he deftly slipped a pair of handcuffs over her wrist and secured her to the door handle. It felt a silly thing to think, but of all the fears going through her head, she thought, *I hope we don't crash whilst I'm like this.*

Nodding to an elderly couple as they walked past the hotel entrance, he walked around to the driver's door and got in. He started the engine. "Well done. You'll come to no harm from me if you carry on like this. And if you hadn't deduced it by now, I'm taking you to Tony."

She had deduced as much, but when she heard it confirmed, her heart sank a few inches more. Fears, anxieties, and even curiosity ran through her mind. Surprisingly, as the curiosity grew, she almost wanted to see him, to look at his eyes again, to hear his voice. She had no idea what would happen, and hoped for the promised protection from Maddi and Mike, but as this thought came...*WHAM*! She clutched at her neck and remembered the talisman hanging by the shower. Why had she taken it off, the very thing Maddi had told her never to do until this was all over? As the journey wound its way to the den, she felt naked and scared.

The intrepid explorers of Highoredish had only gone a few yards to pick up the path when they saw the policeman and woman in the patrol car over the stone wall, parked in the lane.

A police officer got out. "Good morning; can I ask what you are doing, please?"

Maddi looked at Mike, then replied, "Well, Sherlock, would you believe me if I said we were out for a walk?"

"Have you camped around here?"

Mike answered, "Not likely; it's a bit cool for us—we're not that hardy! We're stopping in the village, and walking the area."

"You've not seen anyone who looked like they were out all night, then?"

"No."

"We've had reports of a spectacular fireworks display, and you can see where they had a bonfire. Probably students; we've had it before. Could I have your names, please?"

They gave the names matching the hotel register.

"Thank you, sir. Thank you, madam. Have a good day walking."

"We'll try. Goodbye."

Mike took Maddi's hand as they walked away. Maddi looked up at him as she pulled him back a little. "It's Tony, isn't it? He was here last night doing something." She felt sure of it, deep inside. The thought of him being so close was worrying at the least—and what if he had accomplices? What if they were being watched right now? Again, she looked at her phone.

Mike agreed. "Yes, it's him all right. I feel his presence here, too. You can smell him, sense him. Like a cat leaves its scent, it's as if he's made his mark here."

They decided to look at the old church and go back. The jollity of the situation had vanished in an instant. They plotted their course and made their way to a gritstone stile. The path led from the other side of the wall and through the wood they had spotted whilst on the ridge. The path was overgrown and obviously little used. "We could do with a bloody machete to get through this lot," Mike remarked, as the trees and undergrowth got thicker by the yard.

They reached the old church eventually; it was the only thing the path went to. The church was in a dell, sunken on most sides and surrounded by trees. Although isolated, damp, and mossy, it looked a romantic ruin. At some time or another, it had had a few repairs, but now trees and shrubs grew everywhere. Rubble and baulks of timber lay all around, but most of what could fall already had done, so it was relatively safe. No doors were left, and the arched windows had no glass, but as Mike and Maddi explored, they found the church still retained its beauty. Inside, they could see the altar, and they felt as if they should whisper in reverence. The sun had broken through and lit it up. Shadows added to its mysterious air. If they'd had the time to stay, they felt it might have told a hundred tales.

Maddi walked slowly and carefully, running her index finger along the stone. This place suited her somehow. Her thoughts went to times gone by; she imagined love, weddings, and christenings. She thought of hermits and travellers looking for sanctuary. Her eyes moved around slowly. She felt that she wanted to take this moment in, her first sighting of a place she instantly knew to be *the place*—a place that Sean hoped they would find, somewhere that only Sean knew the real importance of. Her thoughts went back to weddings and christenings, and then to funerals. But oddly, no sign of a burial place could be seen. Yet again, she glanced at her phone. Worryingly there was no signal at all; she couldn't ring her friend even if she wanted to.

Mike came up behind her, also feeling sombre and reverent. He moved a stone to one side with his foot, wondering what had led to the church's demise. Then, making Maddi jump a little, he said. "Sad, isn't it, looking at it like this?"

"It is."

"Do you think we've found our place, then? Is this it?"

"Definitely. I'd say it was heaven sent, wouldn't you?"

"Yeah, I suppose it is—literally."

They spent a few more minutes looking around, then returned to the path and made their way back to Ashover. They felt pleasantly tired. Upon entering the hotel, the smell of the evening meals hit them. Mike's mouth watered. "I'm going to the bar for a pint, I'm gagging. Do you want one?"

"No thanks. I'm going to see what Monica's been up to, and I'll tell her the news."

He ordered his pint, studied it in anticipated enjoyment for a couple of seconds, and devoured half of it in a few gulps. He wiped his mouth with the back of his hand and looked at the barmaid, winking. "I was ready for that!" A visual search of the room revealed that the man he was going to see wasn't around, and he wondered how he had gone on and what his own family tree would be like. Lifting the glass to his mouth to "sink" the second half, he stopped as the door burst open and Maddi came in, distressed. The barmaid and a couple of other guests looked over at Maddi, who stood wringing her hands.; she composed herself and beckoned Mike over. Mike's glass hit the table with a thud, and he followed her all the way to Maddi's and Monica's room.

"Look, she's gone!" Monica exclaimed. They soon found the talisman hanging by the shower and the bullet holes. Despair hit, and victory swung further out of reach.

"Oh, Christ, Maddi. They've got her."

Monica was ushered out of the car, up the stairs, and through the flat into Tony's lair. Her eyes darted everywhere, like a scared animal evaluating any possible chance of escape. She found none.

"Hello, dear. How nice to see you; sit down."

She stared at Tony; he was leaner and more aggressive in his stance. She sat down.

"Well done, Stirling. Come and see me later." He dismissed Stirling with a brush of his hand and no eye contact.

Stirling left quietly and closed the door.

Tony stared at Monica. "Tea, coffee?" he asked.

"No thanks."

"Oh, sorry; of course, would you like something stronger?"

"No."

The door opened and Christine walked in. "Hello, Monica darling. I thought you were ill. Tut, tut, has your halo slipped? I don't know…telling porkie pies to your boss, and then swanning off for a little holiday? Oh, that's bad, very bad, don't you think so, Tony sweetheart?" She kissed him on the cheek and put her hand flat on his chest.

Monica stared at Christine. She looked different, pale and gaunt like a creature of the night; she was obviously under some sort of influence. Tony kissed her. "What shall we do with her?" He walked over to Monica with an evil smile and pulled strands of her hair gently through his fingers. "What do you suggest, Christine? What is your will?" He grabbed a handful of Monica's hair and twisted.

Monica let out a sharp squeal, but she was determined not to show fear. She defiantly stared back at Christine.

"Oh, I don't quite know; the mind boggles, doesn't it?" She walked slowly over to Monica, put one finger under her chin, and stared straight into her eyes. "What would you hate, Monica? Would you like to have to beg me for mercy? Shall I have you laid naked across the table and whip you until you do?"

Tony laughed and walked back to his seat.

Christine looked at Tony, and said, "Wouldn't it be good entertainment to watch a few of your more sexually frustrated helpers use her as they'd like? I'm sure she'd like a couple of rough, fat, beer-bellied skinheads smelling of stale beer and cigarettes." She looked at Monica. Tony nodded his approval. "Would you like that, Monicums? Would you like to be made to squeal like a pig as they took you whilst we watched?"

Tony egged Christine on. "What else? Surely you can do better, Christine."

She walked up to Monica and put her face right up to hers. "I know: let me have her as a slave for a few days, naked…on her hands and knees." She giggled. "Yes, I like that. You could tend to my every whim, and any mistake I could punish with a rod, in front of Tony." She took hold of Monica's face and squeezed it so hard the teeth pressed into the inside of her cheeks and made them bleed. Monica lost control and began to cry.

"Oh God, Monica, is that it? Is that your resistance, no fight back, no clever statement, no call for help to your beloved Mike?" As she spoke his name, Christine gave Monica a mighty slap across the face, making her head spin to the side.

Tony stood watching.

Christine continued. "He's a good shag, isn't he? I enjoyed it; it was lovely. Your so-called friend Maddi did, too. She bounced up and down on his dick for ages, and Mike loved it."

Monica regained some composure. "I know all about it."

"Oh, you know? You know, do you?" And she slapped the other cheek just as hard.

Tony intervened. "Enough!" He took hold of Christine's wrist and pulled her away.

"You can have your amusement all in good time. Strip her and shackle her; this job I have for you will keep you happy." He walked over to a table and came back with the final star marker, the most beautiful bottle of all.

Christine showed no mercy as Monica's clothes were pulled off and she was duly shackled to the wall. Christine stood, and as a final gesture of hatred spit into her face, hissing, "I fucking hate you, you bitch. You were never good enough for these two." The effect of Tony's mind had changed her into another person. Whatever Tony had done to her these last days were much more than Monica deemed possible; Christine was an animal.

Tony gave her the bottle and a razor. "Shave all her pubic hair, and fill this with it."

The delight on Christine's face was that of a greedy child given yet another bun. She did her task roughly and took great pleasure in the pain, humiliation, and distress it caused. At every whimper, she laughed; this was a disgusting degradation, a crime against woman. "Let me shave her head. Please, go on, let me, please!"

Tony gave Christine a resounding slap across her face with the back of his hand. You disgust me sometimes. Go!"

Monica lifted her head, the mascara running in torrents down her face. She was hurt, sore, and at her wit's end.

On the night of the Saint Walpurgis ceremony, a magical masterpiece would take place. Tony needed to show his power, and he was going to have his moment— what better gift than this to offer to the demons of the abyss! He was going to use her in a masterful trick to steal something from Mike, and then offer it as a prize to the black observers.

She stared at him; had he no memories, no compassion, no mercy?

Slowly his expression changed. He stroked her face with the back of his hand, still red from the blow he had given Christine. He unlocked the shackles. As if to explain and excuse all, he told her, "That was necessary; it had to be done by a woman's hand. It is decreed so by..." His expression changed back just as quickly. "Never mind."

He undid the chains and gave her a plain white gown. "Put this on."

Her legs were barely strong enough to support her, but they did as she put the gown on. She was led into a white, tiled room with high windows. Was this all part of some psychological torture? Collapsing onto the bed, she sobbed. "Why has this happened to me?" she said, as Tony clinically locked the door of her cell.

Tony's purpose of having Monica here was twofold: one was to help gain the bribe to the gateman of the abyss. But also, Mike would not be able to stand this pitiful sight of Monica. It would hurt him, and at that precise moment, Tony would break Mike himself. What irony! Monica's last sight of the real world, before insanity took over, would be the death of Mike, and Mike's would be that of his beloved Monica being taken away by the guardians of the abyss!

Back at the hotel, a heated debate was going on. "Think, Mike, what do we do?"

He asked Maddi to be quiet and resumed his thinking position; it was difficult due to the stress of the situation, but Sean broke through.

"This is bad, Mike, but if my brickwork holds, we should still have a chance. Let's pray it does, and that Tony doesn't get total control of her. There is something special about her, Mike, something we don't know yet—probably some simple fact we are unaware of, but to Tony, it makes her a prized jewel. Ask

Maddi if she thinks her friend has the resolve to see this present situation through on her own."

Maddi thought she might have. "But it's touch and go," Mike told Sean. "Couldn't we do something?

"No, I don't think so. Tony has put his own brick wall up around his mind, and I don't think I'd break through in time. And his place is like a fortress now. Even if you went, you wouldn't stand a chance of achieving anything."

The pendulum of power swung well out of reach and approached Tony's outstretched arms.

They decided all they could do was prepare as well as possible and wait. Tomorrow would be spent preparing the old church. It felt terrible not to take any action; the momentum of attack had stopped, and waiting was a poor substitute.

Maddi sat on the edge of the bed, swinging Monica's talisman. "She hasn't even got this; I don't think she's going to survive this, Mike, I really don't." Maddi began to cry, and Mike consoled her best he could, but an arm around her shoulder and comforting words seemed so little.

They ordered a light supper and left most of it uneaten. It was a night of fitful sleep, worrying, and dread.

Similarly, Monica's sleep eventually took hold of her. She had delved deep into her soul, and coupled with Sean's brickwork, she was surviving—although every now and then she felt probed. She knew Tony was trying to get through. If only she still had the talisman.

Tony hoped that soon his adversaries would be destroyed, and his journey would begin, his ambitions fulfilled. He poured a whiskey and pondered the small star marker with its pubic contents, the final part of the body in the pentacle, and from a person with her birthday on Halloween. "Perfect," murmured Tony. "You are my key to the door, a door which has kept out a whole history of events. I will be greater than all."

He held the orange cloak in his arms, the one he had received from the monks. The tome had revealed its power to him. It was a gift of high stature, able to transform shapes and change images. He put it on again and slowly transformed into an image of Adonis. "I'll succeed where Hitler failed, where Alistair failed, and Levi. Ha! They will all bow down to me; everyone will know and respect the name of Anthony Cowley, heir apparent to the King of Magic." He held his glass high and stared at it. "To Saint Walpurgis night, the defeat of the five, and the first and greatest step to Daath." He drank from the Italian crystal glass and threw it into the fireplace.

Both armies were almost ready. Tony, Stirling, Christine, and the black side of the cabala were rushing headlong into the first major battle of magic in their war to defeat Mike, Sean, Maddi and Debbie, "Protectors of the Purpose."

In the middle were Monica and a very fragile brick wall.

Tony stood and stared at Monica Doll. "Almost there, sweetheart." He removed the cloak. He looked and felt tired; the bags under his eyes and the stubble on his chin aged him.

CHAPTER 19

The eve of battle dawned. As surely as if they were awakening under the fluttering banners of a war camp, both armies were engrossed in final preparations.

Finally, Mike had been able to fall asleep and receive explicit instructions for what he and Maddi were to do. They were to prepare the church exactly as directed, sleep there to ensure no tampering, and wait for Saint Walpurgis night to approach.

They ate breakfast, hid the damage to the bed as well as possible, and paid their bill. They checked their tent and ancillary equipment. Before leaving the village, extra items were purchased from the well-equipped local stores. This was a well-known area, and soon, as the tourist season approached, stock would be at a premium. Mike had to go to a few stores for before he found a few rolls of red wool or cord. He hadn't asked why it was needed; he trusted his mentor's choice. But all the same, it seemed a peculiar item for what lay ahead

At about eleven in the morning, they set off. As they drove, he reminisced. "I was just thinking about when I got the job, and how I was looking forward to getting to know you. I never thought it would lead to this."

Maddi looked away from the road for a second or two and smiled at him. "No, neither did I. Do you remember the 'well done' card we got you?"

He smiled to himself, and thought briefly how nice life would be if he didn't have to make it complicated by feelings. For a few seconds before answering, he yearned for normality to return to his life. "Yes, I remember the card; it was a thoughtful thing to do."

"Thanks." She smiled warmly at him.

They glanced at each other once more, then kept to their own thoughts for the rest of the drive. When on the other side of a reservoir, they pulled into a large car park, got "kitted up" in their hiking attire, and set off.

Maddi looked back at the car. "Will it be okay overnight?"

"Yeah, no probs. There's loads of night fishing going on around here, and if it gets nicked, so what? It's not ours!"

They took a path toward the church that was different from their last visit. It was a similar day to before, and again, the normality of their actions really hit home. Anybody who saw them would just see two people on a walk.

Mike loved adventure books and always imagined the feeling of setting off on a quest. *But when it's real*, he thought, *you just don't know what's going to happen. You can't just sit back in a comfy chair and think how you have half a book left to read, and how there's another three or four volumes to come. Reality is that life goes on; nobody you pass or talk to has the faintest idea that you might just be saving the world tomorrow night! You have no idea what's to come, you just have to get on with it and wait.*

The path was just as overgrown at this end, and Maddi thought that it seemed as if it had been hidden by nature for years, perhaps just for this purpose. It was nowhere near as easy to find, and without the large-scale map at hand which allowed them to follow the walls and field boundaries, they would probably have been in trouble.

They reached the evergreen section of the wood, and together they felt something different. Entering the silence was like going through some sinister barrier. Their own thoughts suddenly ended, and they returned from their single-minded conversations with a jolt. The threat of the approaching night felt more oppressive, and the silence deepened. With each step, the eerie feeling filled them with more and more unease. If wood sprites existed, they were here—or at least, something was. They felt watched and unwelcome, as if the wood was telling them it didn't like intruders. Like in the fairy tales of childhood, the wood had eyes...great big ones!

The path was steep, and they were tired, but neither wanted to stop, not here. Soon the path became flagged, probably being a part of an old salters' route, or a monks' path, or some pack-horse way. Mike made a mental note to find out one day.

Then suddenly, the noise of birdcall hit them; the trees around them now were oak, beech, sycamore, and birch. Light came through, and the ground became alive with ants. Insects buzzed, butterflies passed, and friendliness oozed from normality. They had gone through the barrier; mother nature had smelt them and given her approval. Primroses abounded, and so did watercress and other water plants as they approached a brook. The babbling noise invited them to sit a while.

Their worries lifted slightly as they sat eating fruit and drinking.

"I wonder what will happen."

Mike shuddered. "I daren't think about it."

Both thought of the unbelievable things they had seen already.

"I expect Sean will tell us what to do."

"Mmm, I suppose he will."

This was about as conversational as they felt. They repacked their bags and resumed the hike in silence. Another hour passed, and before them, they saw an arched window peering through the trees. The shadows of the leaves as they swayed in the breeze caressed it like a lover stroking a beloved's hair. *Yes*, thought Mike, to the trees, *I think you've been looking after this place, just for us.* He turned to look over his shoulder at Maddi. "We're here."

Cynically, Maddi said, "I wish we didn't have to be!"

Mike tried to look at ease, patting her back for reassurance. He gave out the instructions, and he spent most of the early part of day inside the ruin clearing debris. The fallen masonry was heavy and slippery, and soon they both became sweaty and irritable. The flies buzzed incessantly, occasionally landing and taking bites. They dragged beams of half-rotten timber away until the edge near the door was comparatively clean and tidy. They erected the tent with its entrance pointing towards the main door, and they fastened a couple of Tilley Lamps into two makeshift stands. The place almost began to feel comfy.

Their activity had disturbed woodlice, ants, and wasps. So they decided to have lunch on the ridge that ran around the edge of the path, which in turn circumnavigated the ruin.

To suit the mood and fatigue, they ate the meal in silence. Mike stood deep in thought, and Maddi sat in a similar frame of mind; if anyone had passed just then, they would have felt sure an argument had taken place and that neither were prepared to give in.

They spent the rest of the day on various preparations. One of the main tasks was to mark a circle, to exact details, on the flagstones outside the main entrance to the ruined church. Mike chalked symbols at each point of the compass from his memory, which Sean wouldn't allow him to forget. He created a triangle with markings alongside it, pointing east.

"Hope it doesn't rain and wash all this lot off!" Mike said, standing back and admiring his artistry.

"So do I. Let's make a cuppa and listen to the news and weather on the radio; it's almost on the hour. If it says rain, then we can cover the designs with a groundsheet or something."

He agreed, and they took a "tea break." The forecast was for a clear, dry night, although cool, and continuing cool and dry weather the next day. As dusk approached, Mike announced that one more job had to be done before nightfall, so they resumed work.

The final task was to tie the red cord all the way around the periphery of the church, from the circle, and back to the triangle.

The cord had to remain unbroken and had to be laid counter-clockwise, although Mike wasn't sure why.

They laid the cord with some annoyance, because at places bushes had grown very close to the wall and passing it through to each other was tricky. They both muttered various expletives as scratches and pricks rewarded their efforts, especially as darkness approached. This was finished in about three-quarters of an hour.

Earlier in the day, a stockpile of bracken, wood, and cones had been made and spread to allow it to dry as much as possible. The supply would easily see them through the night. Mike was busy laying a firebase of criss-crossed twigs, whilst Maddi was lighting and securing Tilley Lamps. "Hey! Maddi, what's a rood screen?"

"I don't know. What is a rood screen? Something rude, I suppose."

He laughed. "No, I'm being serious. I've read up about that larger church we saw near the car park this morning; there was a leaflet in the pub. It said it had a well-preserved rood screen from a small, ruined church close by. I assume it must be from this one. So I was just thinking that after this was all over, I might go and have a look, just to get an idea of what it looked like in all its former glory."

The mention of life after this raised Maddi's heart; she had stopped thinking of the future beyond the night ahead. "Oh, sorry. It sounds like a nice idea. I might come with you; I think the idea of being close to Jesus after all this would be very, very comforting."

"I agree…do you feel like praying?"

"Yes."

So together they said the Lord's Prayer, and afterwards in silence, they both silently added a few thoughts of their own, particularly for Monica's protection. They looked up, opened their eyes, and stared at each other. Maddi finished the prayer session off out loud by saying, "And thank you, God, for looking after us so far; help us to do right, and give us courage…all of us. Amen."

"Amen."

Maddi smiled at him, and the firelight from the now-roaring fire danced across her face. A loud crackle sent a shower of sparks flying, and her eyes widened.

He reached over and put his hand on her shoulder, patting it reassuringly. "We'll survive. I'm sure Sean has great plans for us, and he'll not let us fail at this stage."

She was grateful for his attempt to cheer her up, and she smiled. The full darkness of night had now crept up almost unnoticed. The firelight sent dancing, exaggerated shadows around the walls, and coupled with little scurryings and moving branches against the walls, their eyes and ears made them glance with dread from time to time. But tiredness eventually took over, and with healthy hues to their cheeks, they fell to sleep like babes in the woods.

Just as quickly, dawn came, and the chill of morning and birdsong jolted Mike back to reality. He made up the fire and stretched. He stood and looked at his accomplice's steady breathing, deciding to wait for her to wake before doing much more. She did soon, and he enjoyed watching her. She noticed him crouched over and looking at her. "Hiya. What time is it?"

"Six o'clock, madam. Shall I run a bath, order breakfast? Fetch a newspaper, perhaps?"

She smiled. "Oh, yes, please, all three! This is much better than the last hotel; I've never had such personal service." She looked around and waved her arm. "And with such a view, too! Look at the *en suite* facilities, and the privacy. Who could ask for more?"

It cheered Mike to see her resilience.

"I've got to pee!" At this, she dashed up and ran through the church. He began to prepare breakfast.

On her return, seriousness took over, and the conversation made its way to the inevitable. "Did you see Sean or Debbie last night?"

"Yes." Mike laughed. "He had odd shoes on!"

Maddi smiled.

264

"They pass their best wishes on. Like us, they are near enough ready. There's not much more to do except pass the time. Tonight at ten, we have to sit in the circle, and Sean said we'll see them in all their glory, whatever that means. I'm looking forward to it...almost."

So the day passed. It was time for reflection, double checking, and waiting.

Tony was doing the same, checking and double-checking his work. Stirling and Christine were impatient for the night to come, so they could witness the spectacle of Tony's power.

Monica was bearing up...just. The brick wall had survived, although it was damaged. Tony felt sure it would topple in the ensuing night.

Sean and Debbie were secure in the knowledge that Mike and Maddi had prepared everything well on the outside, so the whole day was spent in ceremony. Clothes and weapons were blessed, and a small wooden box with a single topaz inlaid in its lid was filled in a precise order, each item blessed and armed by spell as it went in.

As the allotted time drew near, Sean and Debbie dressed for the occasion; colours and styles for such events were given more importance on the other side than here. Sean was nothing short of resplendent in his favourite green habit with gold edging. Upon his feet were brown, knee-high boots, and upon his head a metallic looking red, silk headband, marked with the runic symbols of a mind warrior.

And Debbie didn't disappoint. She could have been a starring role with Odysseus or Jason in a Greek epic. Her hair was drawn up and secured with a headband matching Sean's. She wore a tunic of the purest white with gold edging, and thigh-high, dark brown boots that gave a view of a few inches of thigh, which Mike would appreciate . A blood-red cloak that reached the floor was fastened to the shoulders with gold discs. But the crowning glory were her breastplate and forearm protectors in gold. The markings were magnificent, and her waist was exaggerated by the fit. The way it came to a delicate point just above the groin would stir a eunuch into action!

They stood on the platform and waited, Sean with the box held at waist height, and Debbie holding a shining sword, with the point between her feet.

Mike and Maddi looked at each other. Talismans were hanging in the two furthest corners of the ruin, with two more to come. Otherwise, everything was just as instructed; lamps were lit, and Maddi and Mike nervously stood holding hands inside the circle.

Tony and Stirling stood at Highoredish, and Christine—who was dressed similar to Maddi in a sweatshirt and jeans—held Monica in her white gown. Stirling, dressed in black from head to foot, looked a sinister threat. Tony was garbed similarly to Sean, but in his orange gift from the monks. Once more, he stood like an Adonis, proud and strong.

As all stood in their circles, they heard the distant clock strike ten.

It was time for battle, and the start of the greatest journey imaginable.

CHAPTER 20

Highoredish transformed, it was now a place of immense importance to the whole universe. It was a wonderment never seen
before, a magical place.

Christine stood with the drugged and bewildered Monica in
the triangle. Christine was also in a trance, awaiting instructions.

Stirling lit the five candles, held in their protective glass and
brass holders and placed around the edge of the circle, at each
point of the pentacle. Tony, his sword in one hand and the final
star marker in the other, entered the circle with Monica Doll. He
removed his cloak, turned back into himself, and wrapped it
around the doll. She looked up at him and smiled. Her hair
turned blond for an instant, and then back to almost black.

It began.

He acknowledged each candle with a nod, placed the final
star marker gently into Monica Doll's arms in the centre of the
circle, and stood astride her. The cloak now wrapped around her
and his feet. With the sword in his left hand, he pointed to each
candle speaking the first five words: "*ECA, ZODOCARE, LAD,
GOHO, GAHAD.*"

A loud crackle broke the silence, as if someone had started
arc welding. There was a brilliant blue flash. The pentacle reap-
peared, fresh from the undisturbed star markers. He had pre-

pared well. Each intersection brought lightning, and each struck Tony on the chest, at which he turned an electric blue.

The circle burst into flame around its circumference, and a channel one-foot wide and deep appeared, instantly filling with quicksilver, a near-perfect conductor of magic. Lightning danced around the channel, fizzing and spitting sparks. Now nothing and nobody could cross without his invitation; he was marooned in an island of pure magic, with only his cherished doll for company. The outside world faded from his view as the circle was closed.

It was possible that something undesirable at this stage could have been trapped, an uninvited guest from the plains near the abyss, a creator of nightmares. So to cleanse the inner circle, he performed the ceremony of the cabalistic cross. This was to mark the cross on the body, the forehead, each shoulder, the genitals, and the centre of the chest, with the right hand. At each point, a word of Elthgar was spoken, words that could not be written. The light of Kalthar appeared above his head.

Reader—yes, you—look for these words in books of magic— oh yes! They are real!—and read the warnings. Most definitely read the warnings. But do not—I repeat, do NOT—take the warnings lightly: they are as real as the thumb at the bottom of the page...

Slowly, Tony looked up. He was drinking each moment; his eyes stared at the light, and his face looked cold and clinical. It was all heightened in appearance by his blue colour; his tear scar turned into a diamond, a faultless gem. In one swift action, he thrust his sword into the cloud. Like ectoplasm, the light drained down his arm, slowly filling his whole body as if it were an empty jug. When the meniscus reached his groin, the word *MALLCUTH* rang around Highoredish as if on the wind.

Stirling watched it pass. As the light reached his chest, the word *DIN* galloped around as if wild, thundering horses were possessed by it. Stirling jumped to the side. And when it reached his head, the word *HESED* was screamed to the heavens by voices unseen. Stirling fell to the floor with a look of dread and covered his ears.

As if on a revolving pedestal, Tony slowly rotated. His eyes, now with no visible pupils, never deviated from their forwards stare. He stopped four times to point at each corner of the universe with his sword, steadily coming to rest facing east. A stream of light came from the heavens and danced around the hovering pentacle. He was only a few steps away from the journey—a travelling epic from *Malkuth*, or *earth*, to *Yesod*, the gateway to the astral world. He said the next line for path twenty-two, a wise choice, the path of Saturn as depicted in the tarot by the Two of Wands. *"TORZODU, ODO, KIKALE, QAAA!"*

A wind, chilled by the dead, blew steadily and with no gusts. On it were carried the howls of a million mourning souls.

With great care and concentration, he chanted the third line three times.

"ZODOCARE, OD, ZODAMERAN.
"ZODOCARE, OD, ZODAMERAN.
"ZODOCARE, OD, ZODAMERAN."

Christine disappeared as he shouted. "My first gift, the first demonstration of power!"

The onlooking angels of darkness watched with interest.

Back near Ashover, Maddi and Mike waited in anticipation. Precisely on the tenth peal the church clock's tintinnabulation, two figures appeared before them, almost more real than themselves. Their presence seemed to fill mind, body, spirit, the trees, the church, the circle…everything.

Their auras were visible in the soft pink glow they gave off. Truly, they had arrived in ALL their glory. Nonchalantly Sean nodded and said, "Hello" in greeting. His dress was flawless—even his footwear. At first, they flickered like candle flames, but steadily they solidified. A gentle breeze fluttered their clothing, and as they stood, the gentle flapping of their garments seemed to confirm that no longer were they dream-like bodies of the spectral world, but solid warriors, ready for battle. The light shimmering from the fire, reflected in Debbie's armour.

Debbie smiled regally.

Sean handed the final two talismans to Maddi. "Well done, you two. I can see everything is just so." He looked around approvingly, nodding his satisfaction. "Finish the protection, Maddi: hang these in the final two corners."

She went off without hesitation.

Mike hugged Debbie, feeling her energy run up his arms like an electrical discharge. A wave of positive thoughts swam through his veins, looking for negativity to banish. "You look absolutely fantastic. I'm glad you're on my side."

Smiling, she asked if he was nervous.

"I'll say I am. Aren't you?"

With certainty, she replied, "NO."

His own confidence grew in leaps at the word. He knew she meant it; she was powerful.

Sean walked over to Maddi. "How are you feeling?"

"Terrified."

"Don't be; have faith in me."

Maddi smiled in return as, like Mike, she felt an immeasurable growth in her confidence. Sean led her by the hand back to the circle for final commands. Wave after wave of positive thought ran up her arm, looking to discard negativity.

Sean told them to sit down. As if back in the classroom, Sean began. "Tonight, we need resolve. Tonight, we need courage, and tonight...we need concentration. You can expect to see anything and all else besides." He walked over to the red cord. "This—" He held it between finger and thumb and pulled it up— "is our barrier." He let it drop with a twang. "Such a simple thing, I know. But its colour, and the talismans, make it like an electric fence to the many surreal beings we will encounter, especially with this entwined."

He beckoned Debbie to bring the box, which she did, opening it. She stood before him, holding it out. He took a small pouch, similar to their talismans, and twisted two extending wires around the cord. It instantly glowed yellow-hot, like a filament in a low-voltage laboratory lamp.

Mike smiled as, once again, he witnessed the widening of Maddi's almost-childlike eyes.

Sean continued with his rules, directing them mainly to Mike. "All within here will be relatively safe, but be warned: some things will get through. At least we won't have to bother with all the lesser beings; they are more of a nuisance than anything. You must listen to my commands; these may come in a variety of ways, but you'll know it's me. Act on them as quickly as possible. I will be a sort of overseer, and you will be the troops." He smiled at Maddi and Mike's expressions. "Very important troops, I hasten to add. As I've mentioned before, without you, victory would be impossible. But remember, whatever I say to do…*DO!*"

He walked up to within a few inches of Mike's nose, stood, stared for a moment, and then continued directly at him. "Tonight, my friend, you will grow in stature. We will lose contact from time to time. When this happens, believe in yourself, and act on your instincts, no matter what they are—*no matter what.* You'll be surprised at what you can—and will, do—believe me."

The red cord hummed and slowly began to act like an insect killer as small, invisible probings began to try to peek. The final sixty minutes of waiting ticked by slowly as they all exchanged comforting glances. They waited in silence for thirty minutes.

"Half an hour to go—gather round."

They all followed Sean's command to stand back-to-back holding hands, Mike facing north, Sean to the south, and Debbie and Maddi facing east and west, respectively.

Time began to move again. Sean shouted words of a language unknown to them. "DAHAG, OHOG, DAL ERACODOZ, ACE."

The earth beneath their feet began to tremor, and they felt the reverberations run through their bodies. Subterranean defences were in place.

"AAQ, ELAKIK, ODO, URDOZRUT."

The air above them turned orange, intermingled with purple swirls, and then settled as a one-foot-thick mist above them. Attack from above had been prohibited.

"UNAREMADOZ, DOERACODOZ."

The red cord sizzled like frying bacon. In a blast that surprised north, east, and west, a screen of glowing embers reached from cloud to earth. Attack could happen now by mind only.

"TONY COWLEY! Hear this: learn your place!" Sean took a deep breath, which made Mike think he was going to explode. "LO, OREZIDOZ, APAL, EJODOZ."

They felt the power from Sean's hands burst through them all. Lightning, similar to that on Highoredish, bounced through and around them. Adrenaline rushed through all of them, alertness taking over every sense. Sean became voice, Debbie touch, Maddi sound, and Mike sight. Together, they formed thought and body, becoming one.

Sean boomed again in a voice so powerful that mortar and stone fell from the church walls: "LEIPADAI, SAD, ADAM, LOCON!" Any surrounding vista disappeared; they all saw the same, swirling mist.

If Mike looked right, so did they all.

If Maddi heard a sound, as softly as a needle fall on velvet, they all heard it.

If Debbie felt a butterfly breath, so did the others.

And Sean spoke for all. In a high-pitched voice, he said, "ADAILI." He followed it with, "EHATUOAH" in a low pitch.

Then, in a voice of mixed sex and pitch, another word was uttered, a word Tony had searched for but could not find: "*SALI*," Sean called for the first time.

"*SALI*," he called for the second.

"*SALI*," he called for the final time.

The combined body of four began to change: their muscles grew, their limbs expanded, and their material and garb transformed and grew to suit their new body. They saw from the inside and out, and all around. They felt and heard in an ultrasensitive way; their skin became perceptive. They were *Sali*.

The clock struck twelve.

Through the mist, their view changed to Mike's office, and standing there was Christine. "Mike, help me. Before it all starts, help me. This isn't me; I don't want to do it. Stop him, please…please."

The look of pleading did nothing. *Sali* in the form of Mike stood and stared.

"For pity's sake, Mike, do something. Save me! He's starting, I can feel it. Please, Mike, remember me as I was. Help me! Don't be cruel, don't ignore me. This isn't a trap. I'll be on your side. What have I got to say?"

Mike stared and did nothing.

"Please, you know I'm telling the truth. Would I hurt you?"

Mike stared in pity, and waited.

"You fucking bastard! I hate you, Mike Reeves, I fucking hate you! Do you hear?" she snarled. "You're as hard as granite, and you have a heart of ice, you unfeeling shit!" The skin on her face changed, first going yellow, and then grey. Flesh turned to slime-ridden rock. The figure from the bell jar burst out of her business suit, ripping it to shreds. "Take this!"

With the calmness of an ancient warrior, Mike fell to one knee as Christine uttered the words; surprise and first strike were imperative.

The beast began to turn to one side, but *Sali* rolled over, and with one sweep of Debbie's sword, the right foot was cut from the creature's leg. A yellow jelly oozed forth, and aghast, the creature looked down. Its master had lied: it could be harmed.

There was no time to think of pain or mercy. Before the beast looked up from the injury, Mike struck again and again and again. Both the creature's hands and the other foot now lay separate. It fell with a crash, looked for mercy in its assailant's eyes, and saw none. Instead, it saw the freeze-frame effect of a dying brain's image as the sword decapitated it. As the head was falling, its last second's sight saw the sword rammed into the heart of its now detached torso…and twist.

Tony staggered back as if dealt a blow in the chest.

The onlooking beasts from Daath saw little promise, and nothing new.

In the far-off mind castle, a candle fell, a silver candlestick melted into a deformed shape, a jewel blasted into a million pieces, and a carved Brazilian stand and multi-jewelled podium fell to pieces in perfect timing. A game remained unfinished, for eternity.

Angry and embarrassed, Tony showed how he could overcome setbacks. *"ZODORJE, LAPE, ZODIRADOL!"*

The mist turned into Hades, and an army of grotesque, deformed, slobbering, naked bodies by the thousand walked out through the gates of hell. Some were men, some women and some neither. They ran screaming down the hillside, baying for destruction and blood: Mike's destruction and blood...*Sali's* destruction and blood.

The force of the attack from all sides was alarming. The complete self-disregard and self-sacrifice as some killed the others in the rush was disgusting. The weaker were ripped apart and eaten as they ran.

Mike saw Debbie's sword in his hand, and he began to hack. Heads, arms, legs, and torsos all fell. He climbed the developing mountain of death and dying. Blood and entrails slithered to make an indiscernible mass of flesh. It was difficult to keep upright; the slipperiness of fresh death was frightening. Mike knew he must not fall or sink as he climbed and hacked.

When he could avert his gaze for an odd second, all he saw was a never-decreasing army, pouring filth from the gates of hell. He realised it would never stop; the supply had hardly been touched. They came, they climbed, squashing, kicking their kin's parts.

Some were pregnant, and as the torsos fell, they burst open to reveal triplets of deformed babies, each little lifespan ending as hordes fought each other to eat the tiny plump bodies. The grabbing filth fought for the afterbirth to the death.

Mike vomited, at which the black observers cheered. He couldn't stop to wipe it away; he was covered in his own bile and bathed in the blood and entrails of his assailants. He began to tire.

They began to excrete their foul, undigested meal and threw it at him. The stench made him vomit again, to the laughter of the watching examiners. This was good entertainment; they began to taunt him, to jeer, and to applaud. They delighted in his retching.

The sword began to get heavier, the sweeps slower. The bodies were now a huge mountain, and the vertigo began to come in from all sides. Panic showed its evil little face—as usual, just when he didn't want to see it. Mike was struggling to carry out the instructions from Sean; the speed of the attack was almost too much to control.

Still they came, glee upon their faces. Their hope was high: soon, they could disembowel him and eat his insides before his dying eyes. Detached arms began to grip him, and legs tried to kick and dislodge him. Mike shouted, "Help! Help me!"

At his feet, he saw the box and realised a voice had been shouting, "Open it! Open the damn thing, come on!"

He picked it up with his free hand amidst the melee. He felt his legs being bitten, and cold bony hands getting a grip. The box opened, and the attack stopped instantly. The viewers from above shielded their eyes and stared in disbelief through their finger cracks. A bright, white light burst forth.

The hoard drew back in fear.

An angel appeared, pure, white, and clean. Mike could feel his own body cleansing. The filth fell away, freshness hit his nostrils, and a refreshing wind blew. His taste began to sweeten.

The angel looked at him, as if to say, "You took your time to ask, didn't you?" With little effort, the angel swept his arm before him. Disease spread through the ranks; every one of the beasts out of the gates died, and more perished as the rush failed to realise what was happening. The gateway blocked itself, and the attack stopped. But the carnage was beyond belief as it burnt and turned the sky red.

Mike turned to look at the box. He knew then that it had been offered by Sean as the first devil-beast had attacked. He must be more alert.

The angel had gone.

The clock struck two.

Were dawn and safety really so far away? He panted, desperate to fill his lungs with clean air, and wished for respite. Weariness filled his newly clean body.

Then suddenly, it was as if he was at home, at his table with all his special belongings laid out in the proper order. But things quickly changed: instead of the usual I Ching, runes and tarot, a game board took their place. Similar to chess, lots of pieces resembling people stood waiting to commence. As he studied them, he realised they were alive; he was white, and his opponents were black.

He looked closely and saw that his game rivals were devils, gargoyles, and various beasts from hell and beyond. They scratched the board impatiently, grunting and snivelling. Were they all to charge at once?

His eyes moved to his own pieces. The front row consisted of cherubs, beautiful, gurgling, happy ones. Behind were proud knights and beautiful ladies with feline curves. Some were seated on unknown animals of stunning beauty. They all turned to look at him. Hope was written in their eyes, and total trust. They saluted him and heralded him as a hero. A great, rousing cheer went up, and banners unfurled. "What the fuck am I supposed to do here?" he asked in a whisper.

He soon found out. As a hand reached out to make the first move, his opponents unfurled their banners, and a guttural cheer arose from them, along with taunts and assorted shouts of abuse. Blades were honed and pointed at would-be receivers.

He followed the hand on the game board to the sleeve, up to the body all dressed in orange. Although he suspected what he was going to see, he stared at his opponent's eyes. Tony stared back, grinning maniacally. A beast moved to the centre square, and a gasp of admiration came from above them. "What a bold move—brilliant!" He resisted the temptation to look up.

Full of determination, but with no idea what to do, he picked up a cherub, very gently. It smiled and cooed at him. *Sean told me to use my instinct.* So he did, placing the cherub in front of the beast.

"Ha, what an idiot!" guffawed an onlooker, and mocking laughter rang around his ears.

But worse than that was Tony's cold laughter. "Bad move, Mike."

The cherub screamed pitifully as it was burned alive. A mocking cheer arose from the enemy ranks. Solemnly, his side slipped into realisation and silence.

Three more beasts were lined up to the side and one square behind the original piece. They turned around and defecated on the squares in front of them, pulling buttock cheeks apart, and yelping as what smelt and looked like hot sulphur poured from their rears.

The stench made him grimace. He held his nose, much to the amusement of the onlookers, who were again passing comment.

Come on instinct, do something! Mike told himself. Slowly, he placed three more cherubs one square away from the beasts, in a line of three, to face the beasts. He watched for what would happen. A cloud arose from the excrement, and liquid ran towards the cherubs. Each melted into it in obvious, excruciating pain.

"He hasn't a clue!" Laughs and jeers rose like an operatic performance, and his army looked at him in despair.

"Why are you sacrificing, Master? Attack him, please. We can see no reason to your tactics."

Mike nodded to the inquisitor, a lord on the game board. "I'm doing my best."

"Look, they actually have to tell him what to do!"

Tony acknowledged the comment from his growing army of admirers from Daath. As if it were a gambling table in an old time saloon, a growing audience was pushing to see. Tony pushed a creature with wings to hover just in front of the line now created.

"Ah, I've seen similar in a game of Damien once," commented one of his unseen admirers.

Mike knew his next move was absolutely crucial. His hand felt drawn to a woman of great pride astride a similar-looking, six-legged equine beast to the type Tony had just placed. He

277

slammed it down behind the attackers. Then he turned her around to face their backs. He was starting to get the hang of it—the trick was to be bold and imaginative.

A gasp came from the enemy.

A cheer and waving of banners arose from his army.

Two beams of red light flew from the woman's eyes. The centre beast and two adjacent ones erupted like volcanoes, their heads flying spinning out of sight.

And so the game continued with cheers, gasps, and comments, until only four pieces were left. Mike felt great sadness at the sight and loss of his pieces, but Tony showed no emotion.

Three black pieces were in the centre of the board, and they looked to be control. The early advantage and breakdown of his defences had taken its toll, and although some of his later moves had almost brought admiration from the unseen, he knew this was his last chance. A deep voice came from above: "Your move. Make it or concede."

He didn't know where the idea came from, but he gripped his king between his palms and began to rub as if starting a fire. He didn't know it was possible for hands to move so fast—they were a blur. He threw the piece down to the board, and like a spinning top, it began to circle the black triangle.

Tony sat back with a look of combined horror and disbelief.

The onlookers went silent and faded.

Like the trumpeters around Jericho's walls, the spinning king had effect. Mike even had to shield his own ears. Tony's three pieces began to rock, then vibrate, until they almost reached the same frequency as the king. They blew into dust-sized fragments. He had won the game. Holding the triumphant king in his hand, he sat forward in his chair and stared into Tony's eyes. "Fuck you, asshole."

Ashover church bells chimed four. In another hour and a half, dawn would be here, signalling the end of battle. He felt sick, tired, and short of breath. He gulped air as fast as he could as the mist returned, and he waited.

The wait was short; the pressure resumed.

On Highoredish, Tony stood staring at Monica and Monica Doll. He threw the orange cloak over them, and somehow they merged into one. He coolly recited the last line of his incantation. His display of learning had impressed, and his steady wearing down of what some said was an impenetrable force had bought admiration. This should clinch it. He felt that his new-found confederates were feeling a similar hatred towards Mike; he had sensed their disgust oozing from them at the end of the game.

They could now see before them a way through to the other side. This could be a general for one of their armies. No mortal had ever done so well at these tasks. They knew the combined form of Sali was formidable, and he was just a man. With work and time, they saw what they had been waiting for: a sharp blade to shred the curtain between them. But this white one, who was he? How had they found such a champion?

"*ZODORJE, LAPE, ZODERIDO, OL!*" Tony shouted. "*NOCOL, MADA, DAS, IADAPIEL…*"

Monica disappeared in a puff of purple smoke; the pubic hair in the centre of the pentacle burnt away to leave a pungent odour. The watching creatures sniffed the smell eagerly. "What taste!…How did he find out?…No one has before; truly, this is a very promising man. Mmmm, wonderful…mmm, beautiful and fresh, yes. He has signs of greatness. Oh, look, she's gone. Let's see what happens next."

Mike stood awaiting the next attack, resigned to his task. The mist cleared. It was a beautiful warm summer's day. A clearing in the prettiest wood he'd ever seen emerged before his eyes. The smell of summer was refreshing; he felt strength coming back to him. Why? Surely they wanted to weaken him, to destroy him, not to heal him and make him strong. He looked around and stared between the bushes expectantly, listening intently. "Mmm, why somewhere so beautiful? I think I'd rather have horrid."

An orange cloak drifted like mist towards the red cord and slithered unnoticed beneath it, across the ground to find its prey.

Soon, music came from the distance, and a voice so pure it could have been out of a Disney Classic. Mike vaguely recognised the tune. He saw movement in the trees, and she appeared.

Then a voice as sweet as any he had ever heard spoke to him. "Hello, darling. You've been waiting a long time for me, haven't you? I do want you, you know. I always have; you just never tried hard enough."

The orange cloak found a delicate foot, and gentler than any butterfly's breath, it climbed, and shrouded. Its prey didn't know what had happened.

Mike studied Monica. She had never been this alluring before; her form was exaggerated, her breasts full and upturned. Her bottom was perfectly formed and proud, pushing against the material of her nightdress. The thin white satin was so revealing that Mike could see the dark triangle between her legs, like a small, black cat dancing behind a thin curtain. The smell of woman-sex was overpowering; she dripped it.

But her face and eyes...everything seemed extra. Her eyes were darker and deeper. It was as if Debbie had draped herself over Monica, then covered her in sex. Her lips were moist and full, pouting sensuously at him with every word she uttered. "Take me, Mike, anyway you like. Try me backwards, try me on top. Let's have oral—or why don't you sodomise me? Just do your will...PLEASE!"

Unseen by Mike, the orange mist was now enveloping its prey, entering the mouth.

"Oh, Christ." He felt his erection rise like the oncoming lava in a volcano. His urge was almost uncontrollable already, his weakness exploited to the full.

A thought, shouted in Sean's voice, implored him to resist: penetration would be fatal to *Sali*, to them all. He must resist, he must!

His legs took unstoppable steps towards her.

She lifted her mantle. "Look at these. Nice? Do you want to suckle?"

They bobbled, they wobbled; sex was turned up to full volume as the magnificent breasts shouted to him, "SUCK THESE!"

Involuntary, he took another two steps. "Oh, fuck the bloody voice. I want, I want!"

Debbie was desperately trying to pull the thin orange cloth away from her face to shout. Nobody could see it but her, she had to let go of her grip of the others; she was suffocating.

Slowly, Mike progressed to within two yards of Monica. Her gaze took him into her control.

"Mike, stop!" Sean shouted.

"Fuck off," Monica Doll replied.

She laid back across a rock, scalloped to perfection for the purpose of making love. She drew her legs up and apart. Lubricant ran in torrents down her inner thighs and down into her bottom, inviting entry anywhere he pleased. The smell filled the air as he was drawn in. Slowly, whilst licking her lips, she pulled her sex lips apart. "Now...do it now."

The temptation was irresistible, and all but one of the voices of *Sali* told him to stop—begged him to stop.

His manhood teetered only inches away from Monica's glistening opening, the throbbing pulses of blood making it rise and fall rhythmically. How was he suddenly naked? She began to pant and thrust. "Come on, Mike, fuck me. Please, please, please, do it, do it."

The voices broke through, and his manhood collapsed.

They were shouting, "Stop!"

He used his instinct, which told him this was Tony's evil creation. He drew the glinting sword, stared Monica in the eyes, and, weeping and hoping, he skewered her to the rock, the blade burning its way deep into the stone like Excalibur.

The scream was awful. Her body thrashed for a few seconds, then stopped as an almighty explosion hit him. For a split second, time stopped: the world stopped turning, and magic and nature met full on in the big, bright-orange capital letters of chaos.

Highoredish was enveloped in an ink-black mist as a tornado of unimaginable magnitude whisked Tony and Stirling— laughing, shouting, and jeering—off to who-knew-where.

Sali fell apart, and Sean disappeared from Mike's view, trying to shout something Mike knew to be vitally important—but he couldn't hear it. He saw Maddi stumble in a daze and start to collapse.

Where was Debbie?

The church shuddered, and Mike fell to his knees as himself again.

Maddi flipped backwards and fell awkwardly.

His eyes searched for Debbie.

Hilda, Rosa, Li Chin, and the Moor staggered with the ferocity of the impact of thought waves, knowing that what they had foreseen had just taken place.

Then he heard Tony's voice come swirling back, laughing at him. "LOOK! I have my trophy to show to the abyss; she is here with me. I have stolen the greatest prize you ever had!"

Pulling upwards behind Mike was the orange cloak, smoking and tattered.

Mike turned aghast to look at the stone, shouting "No! NO! NOOOO!"

He saw the breastplate stained with blood and bent cruelly out of shape with the force of the blow. The face of his beloved Debbie laid looking towards him with cold, unmoving eyes. Her body lay limp. He had killed her, not Monica. But how? It was Monica, he knew it was; it couldn't be Debbie, not his Debbie— oh God, please no, it couldn't be his Debbie.

Tony's laughter faded, the noise covered by Mike's sobs as the vision of his life's true love faded before him. Debbie's body was transparent now. For the first time he could remember, his mind was empty: he was alone. His hands clasped his face in uncontrollable grief, and he collapsed onto his knees. Debbie's body lifted from the rock, and faded away.

Tony had her.

He felt forsaken by friends. He had no answers, and he was alone and betrayed. He asked himself why the fuck he had bothered.

He was a destroyed man, a fragile shell of his former self. Rocking and sobbing on his knees, tears dripped from his chin and his heart. His mind was empty.

Hours passed, and Maddi regained consciousness. She saw Mike and walked over to attempt to console him.

Two more hours passed.

He had wanted to die at first, but slowly and cruelly, he realised he had made a sacrifice for mankind. He knew that, for now, at least, he had just saved the dividing curtain.

He took Maddi's hand, stood up, and slowly, silently, they walked away.

In his mind castle, a jewel fell and smashed and a pedestal burnt, to leave only one, now shining like a beacon. The choice had been cast.

A few doors away, a candle died in darkness, and another burst into a bright flame.

Maddi held him and comforted him, even more so when a battered Monica slowly walked towards them. Together, they headed towards what looked like the body of Christine.

There was no feeling in his eyes as he stared at Monica, just emptiness. The empty shell of a woman stared back. He didn't care about her now; nor did he care for the body what lay before them.

Worry spread into his mind like a cancerous tumour. How were they going to explain this? Who would believe them?

The difficult, almost impossible journey back to normality began. But it was a painful trek from what Mike had accepted as normality.

How could he possible live with no voices?

CHAPTER 21

A scribe sat in his room, writing slowly and beautifully in an illuminated text. He was one of many, who, totally devoted to their task, wrote the never-ending *History of the Universe*, day-by-day, and night-by-night. It was a labour of love for the white observers.

Space wasn't at a premium here; shelf after endless shelf of leather-bound, hand-written books disappeared from view in every direction. Robed librarians catalogued each finished one using their time-honoured classification system. Each individual in the entire universe had his own book, starting at birth and finishing with the inevitable. Each book could be brought out and opened in a nanosecond; computers looked like steam engines in comparison. All those involved were in love with this ceaseless task. They were, quite literally, in heaven.

The scribe wrote, *Summary of events 1063.21*:

Michael. F. Reeves of Earth had reached the point in the prophecy revealed to Hilda, Li Chin, and Rosa, in Runa, Empire of the Sun, and Tarol, respectively. Each wept at the time. But like a sword quenched for the last time before polishing, the cutting edge of Mike Reeves had been hardened. It was ready for use, in their worlds and beyond, even beyond the "illustrated mind of Mike Reeves."

Mike himself wouldn't feel this for probably half an earth year, so short to us here, but a terrible barrier for him to scale. He'll survive; he has to. So much depends upon it, even the writing of these books.

The scribe allowed himself a thought. Indeed, I am the luckiest in heaven, to have this book to write. I am so honoured it is me...thank You. He looked back at the page and continued to write.

Sean had been snatched back to his homeland after the blast, to recharge, and prepare for the journey alone, without his daughter. He hoped Mike had heard what he'd shouted, and worried that he probably hadn't. Would Mike survive? Would he understand anything of what had happened at the end? He hoped his learning and training would see him through. He knew Mike was missing Debbie to the point of distraction, but this would give him the drive needed for this special task ahead. So long as he realises she is not dead, just stolen.

She is with Tony now, bonded to him like a shackled slave, but she's safe. Although she is there with him on the journey, she is spirit only. He can see her, he can hear her, but for now he cannot touch her. He'll learn one day that this is because Mike is still alive: he can't take her over until her old host is dead. She knows this, and she also knows that he'll come for her one day, and time isn't as important to her as it is to Mike. She will have the patience required. She is amused as her master tries, as he lusts for her, and his hands pass through her form, as if it is a mist.

He scoffs as he tells her of his earthly victory, and how her beloved is dead from a broken heart. Then he gets annoyed because she laughs right back at him, and his frustration grows as his anger cannot be vented upon her, so Stirling suffers instead.

The dark ones are in a state of elation, and are even now building an elegant place for Tony to train in Daath. They hope he'll eventually lead one of their armies back to the other side for a final, lasting victory over us. They know it will be a long wait, because it is the most hazardous journey in the universe, but they have as much faith in him as we do in Mike Reeves.

In earth time, it is close to October 21, the time of the rejoining, and the start of the chase…

* * *

Mike sat at a table in the pub at Ashover. He went back often these days; it was a good place to escape from the hustle and bustle of the town. For five months now, he had slowly tried to build a foundation for the future. He was off work and on tablets for stress, suspended on full pay since the hierarchy of Wiggy and Mr. Taylor had found out about his affairs with women in his charge and the mysterious death of Christine whilst in his company.

His doctor was now in regular contact with him. He had told him everything; he'd missed him, and the doctor had missed him too. It was good to be able to talk of his lost voices, and his lost love. The doctor assured him that two things he would not lose were his mind, and the doctor's friendship.

He still had not come up with any satisfactory explanation as to what he was doing at Highoredish or how Christine had died. He wasn't suspected of her murder, he hoped, but they knew he was somehow to blame. Investigations continued, and he regularly helped the police with their enquiries as they put it. He didn't know what they believed or suspected. Just the same questions over and over again. To their annoyance, most of the questions were greeted with his stunned silence All he kept saying was the same sentence "I don't know what happened."

The inquest was only a couple of days away, on October 21. His solicitor had almost given up. Why not tell him everything? he was asking all the time. Why wouldn't Mike give him some weapon to fight with?

"Huh, how can I fuckin' explain this lot? If I told the pompous prat the truth, he'd never believe it." He shot down another whiskey and gulped his beer. He stared at the empty glass. "I need to talk to somebody." Tomorrow he'd call his doctor. He liked his doctor; he'd listen.

Monica had all but disappeared; she was mentally ill and convalescing. For now, at least, Rosie had left him. She could not get through to him. She was back on the same tablets as before, and needed rest. She was staying with her best friend, who acted as a barrier between her and Mike.

The landlady cast him another cautious look. She didn't like the look of this unshaven, dishevelled man in her bar. She was thinking of calling her husband if he ordered another drink, and calling the police if he tried to drive. He'd been in a lot lately, and she bet he had something to do with the recent break-in at a friend's house.

Maddi had comforted him and stood by him; she, too, was suspected of many things and dreading the inquest. Eric had stood firm, too. "I'll be there with you, son, count on me," he'd told him. It was good to have friends, but right now the only companions he wanted were solitude and alcohol.

"Bastards!" he said loudly, then sarcastically smiled at the landlady as she looked disapprovingly at him. The last of his whiskey hit the back of his throat with an audible click, and he muttered to himself, "They should be grateful; the whole fuckin' world should be grateful. And what do I end up with? No wife, my career in tatters, and my head as empty as a tramp's wallet." Instead of feeling rewarded for his efforts, he felt cheated, ridiculed, and used.

He'd been back to his mind castle many times, especially in the first months. It was cold and lifeless. Like a lighthouse that had served its purpose, it had been left deserted: weeds grew as it was left alone, attacked by the elements. The ivory tower was the worst; he had cried as he sat on her bed, and stared around at her clothes and belongings, smelling her in every crevice. Sean's room was almost as bad. So, too, were the courtyard and fountain. The rooms of choice held nothing for him, anymore, except unfilled promises.

One good thing was Maddi. Her candle was still burning, and the solitary jewel gleamed like a true lighthouse. He valued her as high as anyone living on the planet; she was a true friend, like Eric. He fumbled for his keys and dropped them, along with his mobile phone. He stood up, and staggered to the phone at the bar. He dialled her number and asked her to come fetch him.

The night wasn't too late, and she agreed. He sat on the bar stool precariously, put his chin in his hands, forlornly looked at the landlady, and said, "You know, love, sometimes life is like a shit sandwich, and the filling never fuckin' changes!" At this, she shouted for her husband who asked him to leave, which he did without much fuss. He sat on the picnic bench outside and waited for his lift home; he'd fetch his car in the morning, or afternoon…whenever. "Oh, Debbie, I wish you were back. I'm going to find life so hard without you." For what seemed the thousandth time since that momentous night, he cried.

* * *

On October 20, the day before the inquest, Maddi and Mike, along with Eric for moral support, felt sure that their run of bad luck was going to come to a head. They were probably going to hear the coroner's verdict that further investigation was required, that the death of Christine was definitely not a natural one, and that Mike was the main suspect, with Maddi his accomplice. They felt sure that they may well soon be detained at Her Majesty's pleasure, and were at Maddi's home discussing possible lies, trying to think of conceivable alibis Eric could supply. Although his wife didn't care for his best friend, she had agreed out of love to support whatever Eric came up with. One ray of hope was the doctor; he had promised the solicitor that he would speak on Mike's behalf.

And that ray of hope was soon to become a bright shaft of sunlight.

Monica. Would she be allowed as a witness in her condition? Maddi thought, *I know her better than any other person alive; she was a wonderful friend, but I always said she'd make an evil enemy. I blame Tony, not her.*

At the same moment, the scribe sat down in his chair, which was well worn to the shape of his buttocks. He opened the book and began to write. As often happened, at exactly the same time, the doctor opened his journal and began to write as well.

THE ILLUSTRATED MIND OF MIKE REEVES

Sean picked up his belongings, and with a huge smile, he said farewell.

Rosa sat at the Chimes with her cards, an expectant look on her face.

Hilda cackled with glee as she looked into the boiling cauldron.

Sabat unlocked the curiosity shop doors, and turned the sign around to "open."

Chi Lin held Peacock's hands, as they stood on the balcony looking at each other with delight, a beautiful sunset behind them.

Debbie stood with her hands on her hips, defiantly staring at Tony.

The dark observers took a step back from the inner surface of Monica Doll's eye, as a crack ran quickly from top to bottom, and ended where it had been chipped.

The dust in Mike's mind fortress rose up on the balcony in a small swirl and made its way to the curtains, which moved in the wind.

The time of inaction was over; the first steps of "The illustrated journey of Mike Reeves" were taking place, the chase for Debbie had begun. Suffer no more, Michael. F. Reeves. Your salvation is coming...NOW!

Sarah closed the book with trembling hands, looked at her cold cup of coffee, then back to the book and said, "Bloody hell, Doctor, who did you say had written this?" With reverence and awe, she laid the book down before her on the desk, and quickly took her hands away from it.

...and so ends Book One.

Lightning Source UK Ltd.
Milton Keynes UK
03 March 2010

150862UK00001B/13/P